FAITH

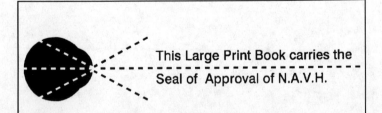

QUAKER BRIDES

WITHDRAWN

FAITH

LYN COTE

THORNDIKE PRESS
A part of Gale, Cengage Learning

GALE
CENGAGE Learning·

Farmington Hills, Mich • San Francisco • New York • Waterville, Maine
Meriden, Conn • Mason, Ohio • Chicago

GALE
CENGAGE Learning®

LIBRARY OF CONGRESS CATALOGING-IN-PUBLICATION DATA

Names: Cote, Lyn, author.
Title: Faith / by Lyn Cote.
Description: Large print edition. | Waterville, Maine : Thorndike Press, 2016. | © 2016 | Series: Quaker brides | Series: Thorndike Press large print Christian historical fiction
Identifiers: LCCN 2016003561 | ISBN 9781410488404 (hardcover) | ISBN 1410488403 (hardcover)
Subjects: LCSH: Large type books. | GSAFD: Love stories. | Christian fiction.
Classification: LCC PS3553.O76378 F35 2016b | DDC 813/.54—dc23
LC record available at http://lccn.loc.gov/2016003561

Published in 2016 by arrangement with Tyndale House Publishers, Inc.

Printed in Mexico
1 2 3 4 5 6 7 20 19 18 17 16

To all those who have lost loved ones who fought for all our freedoms.

PROLOGUE

Cincinnati, Ohio
July 21, 1858
The sound of something shattering woke Faith Cathwell. She sprang from her bed in Frances Henry's house. Scant moonlight defined the shapes of furniture. "Shiloh!" she called as she hurried toward the hall. "Is thee all right?"

Faith flung open her door. Stepped into the narrow passage between the two upstairs bedrooms. "Shiloh —"

A hand clamped over her mouth. From behind, an arm encircled her waist. Tight.

Faith struggled, kicking backward. In vain. She could not break free from the strong arms that kept her silent and trapped.

Close to her ear, a harsh, low voice whispered in the blackness. "You got the other one ready?"

"Yeah. Now we'll take care of this one."

Faith struggled harder. *"Take care of this*

one"? Dear God, help.

A cloth doused with something sickly sweet was pressed to her nose. She tried to turn away, but the man behind kept her pinned to him. *Help us, Lord. Help Shiloh. . . .*

Faith sensed herself losing consciousness. She fought it, but she felt the strength draining from her limbs. *Dear God . . .*

"Faith!" a voice shrilled. "Faith, what's happened?"

Faith lifted her head with effort and blinked her eyes in the morning light. Woozy, she couldn't speak or move.

Shiloh's sister Honoree worked the knot in the cloth that bound Faith's mouth. Finally she snatched it off. "How did this happen?"

Faith gagged, dry-mouthed and nauseated.

Honoree tugged at the ropes that bound Faith's arms and legs to the small dining-room chair. When she managed to pull them away, she caught Faith as she fell forward.

Honoree helped Faith lean back in the chair. Then she ran up the stairs to the bedrooms, calling, sounding hysterical. "Shiloh! Shiloh!"

Faith rubbed her arms, bound for what must have been hours, her hands and fingers tingling with painful pins and needles. She couldn't rise; her legs shook. She began crying, tears seeping, streaking down her face. How had she gotten into this situation? Why?

Honoree raced back down the stairs. Then to the kitchen. Faith heard the door to the garden open and slam.

Honoree returned to Faith. "Who did this?" She dropped to her knees. "Where's Shiloh?"

Sobs welled up from deep within Faith. She could only shake her head. *I don't know. I can't think.*

Honoree ran outside to the street. "Help! Police! Help!"

Faith rocked back and forth, rubbing her arms, powerless. What had happened last night? She tried to recall the memories. Her mind conjured strong, cruel arms and a chemical smell. And the men had said that they "got the other one ready." What had they done with Shiloh?

She stared down at the black mourning dress she wore and whispered, "Patience." The image of her twin, gone forever, flickered in her mind. At a gentle suggestion from her mother, Faith had come to stay with Shiloh. Shiloh worked as a maid for Frances Henry, a family friend's mother-in-law, who was away from home. This visit to Shiloh was an effort to take Faith's mind from her identical twin, buried just weeks ago. Her sweet sister Patience was gone. The other half of her had been sliced from her life. Had Shiloh been ripped away too?

Faith wept harder, slipping to the floor. Shards of icy fear exploded within as her mind failed to resist the conclusion forcing itself on her. She remembered the family stories about Shiloh's mother, kidnapped years ago by slave catchers who intended to sell her back into slavery. Beautiful, freeborn Shiloh . . . kidnapped? *No, no . . .*

CHAPTER 1

On the road toward Jackson, Mississippi, Colonel Devlin Knight glimpsed the gray riders heading straight toward them. "Charge!" Dev shouted. His men spurred their horses forward. The two forces clashed. Gunfire exploded around him.

Dev aimed and fired his pistol till it emptied. The Rebs crowded around him. No time to reload.

He whipped out his saber, slashing any Reb within reach. Black smoke obscured everything. Then, under a unique cockaded hat, a face he recognized appeared through the murky, choking cloud.

Jack?

Dev nearly suffered a saber thrust, but he parried. Threw the Reb from his saddle. Dev plunged forward toward Jack. Was it him?

More troops surged from the rear and the skirmish expanded. Dev lost sight of the face. His saber weighed heavily. He kept his seat, twisting and turning, meeting enemy after enemy. His eyes streamed with tears from the powder. And the gunfire deafened him.

He fell back behind the front. Reloaded his pistol, then plunged again into the fray, the gray Confederate wave regrouping. Dev fought for his life. Had it been Jack? No time. A Reb wheeled his horse and headed straight for Dev.

God, help me.

Darkness was easing in lazily, the western sky toward the Mississippi River blazing brilliant pink and gold. Dev slowed his horse and tried not to make a sound. He wanted no one to see him.

The skirmish had ended not even a half hour ago. After sending his unit back to camp, he was going in the wrong direction — toward the Rebel lines, the enemy lines. The moans of the wounded drew him, led him.

An image from the past: Jack shoving Bellamy, cursing him; Dev stepping between them; the stunning blow . . . He shut out the past. No time.

He began picking his way around dead bodies till he came to where he thought he'd seen Jack fall. And his eyes had not deceived him. There Confederate Captain Jack Carroll lay, staring up at the sky. His horse was nibbling grass nearby.

Jack turned his gaze to Dev. "Come to finish the job, Yankee cousin?"

Only Jack would mock the hand that came to save him. "Yes." Dev swung down from his horse. When he knelt beside Jack, he bit back a gasp. Both Jack's arms were bleeding and one was splintered, the bone poking through the skin.

He whipped off the kerchief around his neck and tied it as a tourniquet around one of Jack's arms, then pulled two handkerchiefs out of his pocket and secured them together for the other arm. "I've come to take you to the surgeons."

"So they can chop off both my arms? No thank you, Dev. I'd rather be dead."

"I don't blame you," Dev admitted. "But I'm taking you with me anyway. A good surgeon might be able to save one arm."

"I don't want your help." Jack cursed him long and low.

"I'd never be able to face your father or my mother if I left you here like this." *Or face myself.*

After shoving Jack's distinctive hat — its side folded up and pinned with a miniature lone star flag — into his jacket, Dev slid one arm under Jack's shoulders, the other under his knees, and rose. Jack struggled, swore, and then passed out.

Just as well. Dev managed to sling him facedown over his saddle before he mounted the horse, grasped the reins, and turned away to head toward the Union lines.

"Stop where you stand," a voice from the trees behind Dev barked.

Dev raised both hands. "I'm taking my cousin with me to get him medical help."

"Your *cousin,* Yankee?"

"Yes, we're from Maryland."

"That man's from Texas."

"Yes, but he was born in Maryland on the Carroll Plantation ten miles from Baltimore."

"So you do know him."

"Yes. Now are you going to shoot me in the back or let me help my cousin?"

"So you'll shoot at him but then return to help him?"

"That sums it up." Dev choked on the irony of it, but he'd faced this over and over, meeting men he'd grown up with and taking aim at them.

An ominous silence hung over the three

14

of them.

"Okay. But God help you if you do him harm."

"God help me in any event." But he doubted God would do any such thing. Dev headed toward his camp, expecting to be shot by a sniper or Rebel straggler at any moment.

He'd fought in the Mexican War nearly twenty years ago, and his goal then had been to serve with honor and survive. He didn't think any man could expect to live through two wars. His lone objective now was to serve and, when the time came, to die with honor. That's what kept him going.

When Dev neared the Union camp, he cut off his cousin's gray military jacket and stuffed it, along with the cockaded hat, under his own jacket. He met the sentry, identified himself. But as he picked his way to his tent, he felt conspicuous, as if he'd be stopped at any moment. Fortunately, more than one skirmish had taken place today, so the camp was busy with care for the injured.

His manservant, Armstrong, stepped out of Dev's tent before he reached it. Armstrong always did this — heard him coming and was ready and waiting for him.

"Help me get him inside," Dev said, glad

of his presence.

"It's Master Jack," Armstrong said in obvious surprise.

"Yes."

Armstrong didn't say another word, just helped carry the unconscious man into their tent. Then he looked at Dev, asking without words what he thought he was doing.

"I will turn him in," Dev assured him, "but first I need to see if at least one of his arms can be saved."

Armstrong gazed at the wounded man, obviously pondering. "The surgeons won't think twice about cutting them both off for sure. But I heard about one of the nurses. They say she better than the doctors. Miss Faith Cathwell."

"A nurse? A woman nurse? Better than the doctors?"

"They say her patients mostly survive. Not all, but enough where some notice the difference."

"And you know this because . . . ?"

Armstrong looked him in the eye. "You know why, sir."

You found out in case I'm wounded. Dev gripped his servant's shoulder. "How can I find Miss Cathwell?"

"She tall with blonde hair. And if what I heard is true, she'll be in the thick of things

16

near the camp hospital."

Dev nodded, turned to go, and then glanced over his shoulder. "Check his pockets in case he still has weapons on him. Keep him here."

"Yes, sir."

His man's response was polite, but underneath it Dev read the unspoken question: *What are you doing harboring an enemy soldier? Even if he is your cousin.*

"Miss Cathwell? Are you Miss Faith Cathwell?"

Just outside the hospital tent, Dev found the woman Armstrong had described and whom three different Sanitary Commission soldiers had directed him to. Surrounded by wounded men lying in neat rows, she was kneeling over a patient, facing away from Dev. She appeared slender and was dressed in dark gray with a modest white cap over her hair, a white bonnet hanging down her back.

At his question, she didn't look up from her place on the ground but continued her work. "Yes, I am Faith Cathwell. What does thee need?"

A Quaker? He recoiled mentally, then paused, watching her care for a corporal.

She'd cut off the soldier's sleeve to expose

17

his wound. She loosened the crude tourniquet above it. Blood oozed out. Rinsing the rag in a basin of water, she swabbed the wound, cleaning away the gunpowder and dried gore.

What possessed a young woman to do such . . . disgusting, unladylike work? Yet her movements were deft and sure and gentle. His tension eased. "Miss Cathwell, I'm Colonel Devlin Knight. I —"

"This isn't the time or place for social calls," barked a doctor standing inside the hospital tent at an operating table.

The man's scathing tone shocked Dev with its rudeness. He straightened up with a snap, ready to put the man in his place.

Miss Cathwell looked up. "Dr. Dyson, is it wise to insult a colonel? He outranks thee." Her tone was pleasant with an edge of wryness. Then she glanced at Dev.

Miss Cathwell's appearance startled him. He'd not expected such a lovely woman to be here doing this lowly work. She had the pale skin of a lady. Her hair was flaxen, and the largest, greenest eyes he'd ever seen dominated her face. Now they considered him with a seriousness that gave him confidence he was doing right in seeking her out.

The colonel leaned close to her ear. "I need help for a wounded soldier. A friend."

She started to respond but paused to gaze at him, assessing. But her hands and nimble fingers continued searching the wounded corporal for, he supposed, any other wounds.

From the corner of his eye, Dev glimpsed Dyson turning away from the patient on the operating table. While the patient was being carried to another tent, Dyson moved between the nurse and Dev. "What do you want, Colonel? I'm the surgeon in this tent."

"My business is with Miss Cathwell," Dev said, straightening and giving full rein to his years of experience in intimidating subordinate officers.

Miss Cathwell rose. "Dr. Dyson, I believe thy next patient is ready for thy . . . attention."

Two Sanitary Commission soldiers lifted the wounded corporal the lady had been nursing. They carried him unconscious across the tent.

The doctor glared at both of them.

Dev did not like the man's attitude, but perhaps the doctor had good reason to disdain Miss Cathwell. Certainly everything he'd heard about Quakers marked them as troublemakers. They'd stoked the fire that had ignited this war.

The disgruntled doctor moved away, muttering epithets.

Turning, Dev found that the lady stood nearly as tall as he, and she was regarding him intently.

"Please, I need to get on with my work," she said for his ears only. "How may I help thee?"

He struggled only a moment with caution, with his guilt. He lowered his voice and asked, "Will you come to my tent?" He motioned and gave her directions. "My wounded friend is there."

Calling Jack a friend was an outright lie, but since Dev had already aided and abetted the enemy by bringing him back here, he felt he had no choice but to continue the deception.

She tilted her head like a bird. "I am only a nurse, not a doctor."

Dev nodded. "Will you come?"

Again she studied him. "Yes, when I am done here. If thy friend is bleeding, keep applying pressure, and please have water warming for me along with any bandages thee can find. However, if thy friend is beyond my skill, thee will have to bring him to the surgeons."

Dev found himself snapping to attention as if leaving a superior officer and could not think why. "Until later, miss," he muttered, nonplussed at his own reaction.

She didn't reply but dropped to her knees by the next soldier and, after giving him a sip of water, began examining his wounds.

Then a snide voice yanked Dev back to his surroundings. "If you want your friend to survive, you would do better to trust me than a woman." The surgeon's words cut the air like a whiplash as Dev strode away.

What am I doing? Asking a woman, a Quakeress, for help?

Faith wished she could completely ignore Dr. Dyson's venom. Like most Army doctors, he hated female nurses in general — but Dyson hated her in particular. Was that why she'd agreed to help the Union colonel with the Southern accent? To flout Flynn Dyson? The colonel contrasted with Dyson not only in demeanor but also appearance. The colonel had a seasoned look about him, deep-set blue eyes with wrinkles around them — no doubt from years of squinting in the sun — and a gleam of silver at his temples. Perhaps he'd even served in the Mexican War as so many officers had done in their twenties.

Across the large tent, Dyson's muttering became louder and more insulting.

Faith focused her mind on the soldier she

was tending.

"Miss . . . would you . . . pray for me?" the soldier asked between small gasps.

She looked down into his young, gunpowdered face then and realized that she'd been thinking of the colonel and only going through the motions of preparing this man for the doctor. More and more she concentrated on wounds alone, not on the faces of the men she tried to help. Did that make it easier to do what she did?

"What is thy name?" she asked.

"Private Browning, miss."

"Thy first name?"

"Jedediah."

She pressed her hand over his and prayed aloud. "Father, Jedediah Browning has been wounded this day, as thee knows. Will thee give him strength to face this trial and bring him safely back to health and his family after this dread war ends? We ask this in the name of Jesus, thy Son. Amen." She patted his hand.

"Thanks. I feel . . . better."

Faith nodded, but she wondered if this man would survive. Death lurked all around them. Were the fortunate ones those who were killed outright?

Faith continued to clean wounds and prepare men for surgery until finally the rows of men ran out. After all, this had been the aftermath not of a full-scale battle, merely a few skirmishes.

She rose and stretched her back, remembering her promise to the colonel. With a sigh, she washed her hands in the last of the basins of clean water, brought over by a Sanitary Commission man, and started off, wiping her hands on her stained and smudged apron.

Honoree, who had been working as usual within Faith's sight, caught up with her. "You are going to help that colonel's friend." More a statement than a question.

Faith nodded, her back aching and hunger gnawing at her.

"It sounds fishy to me. Why didn't he just bring him to the doctors?"

Faith glanced sideways at Honoree, who was a few inches shorter and several shades darker complected than she. Too unsure and tired to respond, Faith merely shrugged. They stopped at their own quarters, a large conical Sibley tent, to pick up Faith's wooden medicine chest.

Before long they glimpsed the colonel pacing outside his tent, like theirs but larger, befitting his rank.

"Colonel?" Faith said, having adopted the use of military titles out of courtesy, though it went against her Quaker ways.

Relief appeared to take the starch from him. "Y'all came." The Southern accent sounded stronger now, probably because of his fatigue and worry.

Faith's nerves prickled a warning.

Honoree sent her a glance that conveyed suspicion.

"This is my friend Miss Honoree Langston." Faith gestured toward her. "She's come to assist me."

With a slight flicker of surprise and a curt nod, the colonel opened the tent flap and waved them inside.

On one of the two cots in the tent, a man lay faceup. His upper body was bare except for a blanket. A tall black man, dressed neatly, stood beside him — no doubt the colonel's personal servant. Again wariness prickled through Faith.

She pushed it aside as she lifted away the blanket and viewed the man and his injuries. He was thin and pale and already burning with fever, his face flushed. Both arms had suffered gunshot wounds. Stained cloths had stopped the bleeding and one arm had obviously been shattered. The other arm appeared to bear a single gunshot wound. She knelt beside him and opened her wooden medicine chest. "Does thee have the hot water I requested?"

"A Quaker?" the wounded man squawked in a thick Southern drawl. "You bring me a blasted Quaker?"

Then Honoree gripped Faith's shoulder. "Look." She pointed toward the man's belt buckle, which read *CSA,* the insignia of the Confederate States of America.

And Faith glimpsed under the cot a crumpled gray felt hat with a cockade of a miniature one-star flag, the Texas flag.

"He's a Reb." Honoree stepped away and folded her arms. "What's a Reb doing here?"

"He's my cousin," the colonel confessed. "I will turn him in as a prisoner of war, but I didn't believe he would get the right attention if I did so before treatment. Please. Without good care he could lose both arms."

Faith sat back on her heels. "Thee is correct, but this is against everything —"

"I know that," the colonel interrupted.

"We help him, and he will just escape and keep on fighting," Honoree said flatly.

Faith felt torn. Honoree was probably right. "He might lose both arms even with careful nursing."

"Then leave me to my fate," the patient snapped. "I didn't ask for any special treatment." He cursed the colonel and her.

Faith withstood the storm of insults, gazing evenly at the man. She'd learned this response from watching her mother face down slave catchers time and again. Wouldn't this man love it if she told him that?

She rose with a sigh. "Colonel, I will help any wounded soldier regardless of which army he serves in, but thee is putting thyself and thy honor at risk with this."

"I know." The colonel moved forward. "Please. I don't have much family left, and when this war is over, I have to face his father. He's *my blood.*" The final two words sounded wrenched from the man.

"My blood." An image of her late twin, Patience, flashed through her mind, followed by Shiloh's image. Patience was lost to her, but Shiloh, long since kidnapped, might still be found. Double grief squeezed her heart. Did this colonel love his cousin as she loved both Patience and Shiloh, or was his conduct just the constraint of family ties?

"I understand, Colonel, but even if I treat him, I can't stay here and care for him as he would need. To save even one of his arms in light of the infection already brewing within him —"

"I can stay," the black manservant spoke up.

"You would help a slave owner?" Honoree accused. "He enslaves our people."

The manservant returned Honoree's direct gaze. "I know, but I can't let a man I knew when he was a child just die before my eyes."

Faith understood this too.

"Thank you, Armstrong," the colonel said with evident relief. "And when I'm not on duty, I will help."

"I am not helping any slaveholder," Honoree vowed. She addressed the wounded soldier. "You are a slaveholder, aren't you?"

"Yes, and you need to be put in your place, girl," he said belligerently.

"I am in my place, in freedom."

"Well, my cousin here, the Union traitor, is no different from me. He's a slaveholder too," the Reb added with audible spite.

Pulling back as if fending off a blow, Honoree turned to Faith, stretching out a hand. "We need to go."

Faith couldn't hide her surprise at this revelation, though it shouldn't have shocked her. Even the Emancipation Proclamation hadn't changed the fact that border states — though still clinging to the Union — remained slave states.

"Please," the colonel implored them, "stay." He looked to his cousin. "Will you promise not to try to escape? Give your word as a gentleman?"

The Confederate grimaced. "All right. I give my word of honor as a gentleman that I will not try to escape. Does that satisfy y'all?"

"And, Miss Cathwell," the colonel continued, taking another step toward her, "I promise that I will turn him in as a prisoner of war as soon as he is strong enough to survive imprisonment. He's my blood."

CHAPTER 2

Faith glanced back and forth between the four near her, conflicted. She inhaled deeply, trying to calm herself. "I cannot leave him untreated, Honoree. Yes, he is the enemy, but we are to love our enemies."

"A man like this —" Honoree jabbed a finger toward the Confederate on the cot — "stole Shiloh from us. For her sake, I will not help any man like that."

The hurt that never left Faith roiled up and almost choked her. Nearly five years had passed since that awful night. She forced the painful memory down. "I understand. Go then in peace, Honoree. I'll return as soon as I can. Perhaps thee can find us some food?"

Chin high, Honoree swept from the tent, her navy-blue skirt billowing behind her.

Faith knelt again beside the cot, on the warm earth. A wave of fatigue rolled over her. "The warmed water, please." She opened the wooden chest beside her and withdrew a packet of herbs, then loosened the bandage nearest her.

Armstrong set a basin of steaming water beside her.

"Fresh bandages? Cloths?" Faith requested.

The man returned with a metal box of rolled bandages and swabs.

"Thank thee." For the next few minutes she concentrated on creating poultices with herbs in muslin pouches, steeped in the hot water. Honoree's mention of Shiloh had cut deep. Yes, they'd come south to nurse the wounded, but chiefly to find Shiloh. And thus far, they'd made no progress in finding her.

The war had let them travel south, but now it forced them to wait yet again. Two armies danced around each other, a deadly pattern, and they were caught in the reel. Neither of them mentioned Shiloh's name often because of the pain it caused both of them. If Faith was near tears, how must Honoree be feeling? Grieving, Faith applied the steaming poultices.

The patient gasped at the heat on the open wounds and surrounding flesh.

"I'm sorry, but I must draw out the infection or thee will lose both arms."

The man did not reply but closed his eyes; his jaw tightened against the pain.

After treating and binding up the shattered arm, Faith shut her own eyes, gathering her waning strength. "I've done all I can do for thee now. The rest is up to God."

The Rebel said nothing in reply.

Head resting on her arm, which was propped on the cot, she spent a few minutes explaining to Armstrong what he needed to do and how often. She rose and staggered, the long, exhausting day catching up with her after many such days.

The colonel caught her before she fell. "I will accompany you to your quarters."

"That's not necessary." But she staggered again.

"I am coming with you." The colonel claimed her hand and drew it through his arm. Lifting the tent flap, he urged her outside into the last of the summer twilight. His man handed him her case.

As he led her, Faith tried to ignore the glances from the soldiers they passed. She did not usually accept any man's particular courtesy if she could help it. As a woman in these unusual circumstances, she must be above reproach. Though the general soldiery treated her with respect, too many in the medical community had until recently deemed nurses women of loose morals. This taint lingered and doctors often spoke of them as nuisances, not as a help.

"I'm afraid I haven't slept well with Rebel forces roaming so near, and there has been one skirmish after another, so we are busy around the clock," she murmured, excusing her weakness.

"I'm sorry I put you in this difficult situation," he said.

"Thee is in a difficult situation." A Southerner from a border state, he clearly wanted to preserve the Union but maintain slavery, an impossible combination. Faith had trouble understanding how one person could hold such opposing views simultaneously. "How is it that thee keeps Armstrong enslaved now that President Lincoln has issued the Emancipation Proclamation?" she challenged him.

"You are very direct, miss."

"I was raised to be so. Does thee have an answer for me?" The hum of voices surrounded them. The comfort of the strong arm supporting her drew her closer against her better sense. Oh, to have someone stronger to lean on for even a brief time.

"I have long promised Armstrong that I will free him on his fortieth birthday, June 9, which is quickly approaching."

"Why wait? Since he is not presently in a border state, he is already free." The proclamation had only freed the slaves in Confederate states, not states like Maryland that had not rebelled. But this colonel's manservant was in a Rebel state now — Mississippi.

Colonel Knight didn't reply.

Was it because he did not want to answer or because his answer would force him to admit his self-deception?

Her own birthday was drawing near, a day that should be happy but never was. Would there ever come a time when she would no longer feel the loss of her twin?

Too tired to ponder this or to press the colonel about Armstrong's freedom, she let herself study his profile. He had a firm chin, a broad brow, and honest eyes. He needed a shave, and she resisted the urge to brush the stubble on his cheek with the back of her hand. Foolish thought.

He wore his fatigues, the everyday uniform of a cavalry soldier, with a short blue jacket and gold braid. She knew that a cavalry company spent much of its time scouting for enemy movement and reporting back, a dangerous duty since it positioned them on the ever-changing front lines. "Will thee have to go back out on reconnaissance tomorrow?"

"Yes, we're pressing on to Vicksburg."

No reply was needed. She'd heard enough in the course of her duties to know General Grant needed to take Vicksburg — the last remaining Rebel-held Mississippi River city — to control that great river and cut the Confederacy in two, west from east. Union forces already occupied New Orleans to the south and St. Louis to the north.

"I understand why thee helped this Southerner, but I still do not trust him," Faith felt forced to point out. Nearly spent, she found herself leaning more heavily against him for support, feeling the buttons on his sleeve through the cotton of hers. "Thy cousin did not even seem grateful for thy help." This had been blatant.

The man laughed without amusement.

"Be watchful of him." Then she sighed as she saw Honoree waiting in front of their tent, holding a cup toward her. Reading this as a peace offering, Faith hurried forward and accepted the hot coffee.

"I got eggs to fry and half a loaf of bread," Honoree said gruffly, urging Faith onto a canvas camp stool.

"Colonel, has thee eaten?" Faith asked.

Honoree stood stiffly, staring the colonel down.

He bowed very correctly. "I will go back to my tent. I'm sure my man has something for me too."

"Honoree is not my maid." Faith narrowed a glance at him. "She is a qualified nurse and she is my friend." *And much more.*

He bowed again and hurried away.

Without speaking, Honoree set some of the bread on prongs to toast and fried the eggs over the small fire. Then she made up a plate for Faith and sat down across from her.

Faith devoured the food, ravenous.

Honoree poured her another cup of coffee from the pot on a trivet near the fire. "You're a better Christian than me."

Faith shook her head. "No. Thy hurt is too deep and caused by men like the one I just nursed."

Honoree wiped away a single tear with the hem of her apron.

"Shiloh is my friend, but she's thy sister." And Faith knew how losing a sister tore up one's peace, never ceased to ache. Her own dear sister was beyond hurt now, but Shiloh was in all probability caught in a life Faith didn't want to contemplate. *God, please help us find her.*

"But I know you love Shiloh like a sister," Honoree said.

Faith reached out and rested a hand on Honoree's sleeve. "We'll find her. I'll never give up trying."

Honoree pulled back, suddenly stern. "Why were you clinging to that colonel's arm like that?"

"Fatigue." It was only part of the truth. This brought to mind Josh, her betrothed until the war took his life, his face vague in her memory. The recollection didn't pain her as much as it once had. Was she merely lonely for another man to lean on? That was a dangerous frailty.

"Finish that coffee," Honoree said, breaking into Faith's thoughts, "and then we best get to sleep. Who knows what will come tomorrow."

Faith nodded, feeling how weak she was with exhaustion. No wonder she'd slipped into this foolish mood. She would sleep tonight — if the dreams, the nightmares over Shiloh didn't wake her.

In his shirtsleeves back inside his tent, Dev sat on a canvas camp stool and ate the simple meal Armstrong had prepared for him. He gazed at his unconscious cousin, letting memories roll over him. Their boyhood in Maryland. The Mexican War. Jack's brother, Bellamy . . . He felt splintered and broken into jagged pieces that could cut and gouge him.

As Armstrong brushed Dev's navy-blue linen jacket before hanging it up for the night, he sang softly, " 'When I lay my burden down, all my troubles will be over, when I lay my burden down.' "

Dev felt all the old burdens weighing down on him. How had it come to this? Bellamy was long dead. Jack lay near death. The country was killing itself, and he and Armstrong were far from home — and likely the next to die. The Quaker's question poked him — *"Why wait? . . . He is already free."*

With both hands Dev scrubbed his face and eyes, burning with fatigue. "Armstrong?"

"Yes, sir?"

"Thank you." He could say no more. He couldn't imagine life without Armstrong, especially now in this fight to the death.

"We'll do the best we can, sir."

Dev nodded, yawning. Then he let Armstrong pull off his boots. "I'll take the first watch. You sleep."

"Sir, you will have duties tomorrow."

Dev gripped Armstrong's shoulder. "I know. I'm tired, but I don't think I'll sleep right away. You rest, and I'll wake you when

I begin to nod off."

Armstrong removed his own boots and moved toward a makeshift pallet on the ground.

"No," Dev said sharply, "you sleep on your cot as usual. He's my cousin. He took my bed, not yours."

"But —"

"Good night, Armstrong."

Armstrong shrugged and lay down on his cot.

Dev sipped his coffee and listened as the camp outside their tent quieted for the night. His cousin lay still without moving. The face of Miss Cathwell came to mind. He saw so little beauty in this dreadful war that he couldn't dismiss hers. A Quakeress, probably an abolitionist, nursing his cousin — what next? And who was this Shiloh the other woman had spoken of? What had happened to her?

Just after dawn Faith approached the camp hospital with Honoree beside her. Last night they'd helped in the surgical tents for the newly wounded. Today they would carry out their regular duties with the recovering patients at the hospital that had been set up in a large, empty cotton warehouse near a destroyed railroad yard. Faith tried not to dread another hot day of bad smells, grue-some sights, hard work, and disrespect — the last of these almost the hardest to take in stride. She and Honoree came prepared for the day, carrying buckets of water over their right arms and cloth sacks of fresh bandages over their left.

Then Faith heard the sound of muffled weeping. She stopped, seeking the source of the lament. She walked around the ware-house, the sound becoming louder with each step.

Behind a shady elm she found a pretty, very young woman with pale-blonde hair, her forehead pressed against the rough bark of the tree.

"What is the matter?" Faith asked softly.

The girl straightened up and began to wipe her tear-washed face with her hands. She turned to leave.

Faith offered the girl a handkerchief. "May I help?"

The young woman couldn't speak for a few moments, so Faith patted her shoulder gently, calming her. She was dressed very simply in a blue cambric dress, not fashion-able but modest. She wore a poke bonnet that had slipped down and hung on her back. "I . . . I thought I could volunteer. You know . . . help around the hospital. My husband is a new recruit."

Faith nodded, sorry to hear another wife had been brought along to the war. "And what was so upsetting?"

"One of the doctors told me he got enough women messin' in his business. He didn't need one more." She hiccuped.

Faith frowned slightly. "Let me guess. This doctor was tall with red hair and —"

"And a rude mouth," Honoree added, coming up behind Faith.

"Yes," she said, eyeing Honoree.

"Thee wishes to help with the wounded?" Faith asked.

Now the girl stared at her. " 'Thee'? Are you a Quaker?"

"Yes, I am a Quaker. Does thee wish to help?"

She nodded, still staring at Faith with an occasional peek at Honoree.

"The man who was rude to thee is Dr. Dyson, but he is not in charge of the hospital. Captain Slattery is the head of the hospital and Dr. Bryant is the head surgeon. Both of them would welcome thy help. Has thee nursed before?"

"Just family."

"What is thy name?"

"Ella — I mean, Mrs. Landon McCullough."

Faith introduced herself and Honoree. "Come with us," she invited, gesturing toward the rear entrance. "We'll help thee begin. We need all the help offered us." Faith put an encouraging smile on her face, though on days like this, that didn't come easy. With each step today, thoughts of the wounded Rebel and of his cousin, the colonel, plagued Faith. That kind of situation made this war all the more distressing. The enemy was not an unknown people but their own kin, brother against brother, father against son.

Ella stayed close to Faith as they entered the hospital. Faith greeted the other nurses on duty and watched for the head surgeon. With Ella as her shadow, she stopped by each patient assigned to her, examined their dressings, and helped them feel as comfortable as possible on their canvas cots.

A few times she discreetly sprinkled an herb onto a wound she was rebandaging. She could tell that the young wife beside her wanted to know what she was doing, but Faith forestalled her questions with a glance that said, *Later.*

The captain of the Sanitary Commission hospital unit — Slattery, a short, thin man in his thirties who always looked sour — entered the warehouse and came straight to

Honoree as if she were a magnet and he iron. "You, girl," he snapped. "Go out by the pump and wash last night's bedpans."

Faith and Honoree froze where they stood.

"Captain, we've discussed this," Faith began in a gentle tone. "Honoree is a trained nurse —"

"She's here, and the work must be done."

"Then I'll —"

He cut her off again. "I decide who does what."

With a fulminating shake of her head, Honoree marched out the far door in resentful obedience.

"Captain," Faith pressed on before he could leave, "another moment. This is Ella McCullough. She has offered to volunteer."

"Fine. I'll expect you to train her." The captain walked away without looking back.

Faith made a face at his back and then composed herself. She must think of some way to keep Honoree from being so disrespected. If only Dr. Bryant were here, she could have appealed to him. The wounded Rebel's similarly sharp reprimand to Honoree rang through her mind: *"You need to be put in your place, girl."* The memory tightened her resolve to obtain for Honoree the respect she deserved.

"He doesn't seem very nice," Ella whispered to Faith.

Sending the girl a glance of agreement, Faith started toward the nearest patient.

Ella kept up with her. "How can that black girl be a trained nurse?"

Faith sighed as she heard the disbelief in the girl's tone. "I attended a school for midwifery in Pennsylvania, and so did Honoree." Though even in that Quaker school, Honoree had been forced to sit at the back of the class alone, separate, as if her black skin were contagious.

"Oh, my," Ella replied, looking shocked.

Faith shook this off, trying to focus on her next patient.

"Hello, miss," he said with a tentative smile.

His brave courtesy caught around her throat. Smiling in return, she gazed down at him, noting his glassy eyes, a sign of fever. She pressed a wrist to his forehead. Faith often wondered what caused fever in the wounded. So much she and even the doctors did not know about disease. "I will put on a fresh bandage."

The man nodded his thanks.

Folding back the sheet, she worked efficiently on his shoulder wound. She felt Ella watching her every move, and though the girl gasped, she didn't turn away. Faith did not look back, letting the girl have some privacy as she confronted the dreadful sight. Finally Faith sprinkled herbs over the wound before securing the new bandage. "I will be coming in later to take down letters. Will thee wish me to write one for thee?"

"Yes, please. To my wife —"

"What did you put on that wound?" Dr. Dyson barked.

She jumped and bumped into Ella. He'd come in so quietly she hadn't noticed him.

"Lemon verbena," Faith replied, keeping her voice even. *Among other herbs.* "It is fragrant, and in this place a pleasant smell might be welcome." She looked at her patient. "Does thee agree?"

"Yes." The man smiled at her. "Reminds me of my home. I recognized the scent but didn't know what it was called. My mother must have used it around the house. Nice."

Faith nodded, then looked sideways. "Good morning, Doctor. I hope thee slept well." *It would be nice if thee got up on the right side of the bed for once.*

Dyson glowered at her. "You're just a nurse, not a doctor."

She let her brows rise. "Of course, and I am trying to nurse my patients." She kept her tone even with only a slight edge to it. She must not let Dyson know how his

44

insults needled her. And the way he maligned her skills.

Ella stayed behind Faith, no doubt trying not to be noticed. Dyson leaned closer to Faith as if trying to intimidate her.

She smiled serenely and went about her work, attempting to ignore him. She moved to the next patient, Ella still trailing her, and began changing the dressing on what was left of his arm.

"Wait!" Dyson barked. "I told that young woman with you to make herself scarce."

"Is there a problem?" The voice of the head surgeon rolled over them.

Faith and Dr. Dyson turned toward him. Dr. Bryant was in his late forties. Compact and bearded, the senior surgeon always presented himself as professional and efficient, unlike Dr. Dyson, who generally looked as though he'd slept in his clothes.

Faith liked the head surgeon. He valued nurses, in contrast to so many of the other doctors.

"No problem, sir," Dr. Dyson replied.

Dr. Bryant stared at him until Dyson finally excused himself and walked away, muttering about a patient.

Then Dr. Bryant faced Faith. "Nurse Cathwell, I wanted to speak to you about our staffing. I think we need more help, and

I think you're the one to spearhead that task. I want the nurses to concentrate on caring for patients, not performing menial chores. With the upcoming assault on Vicksburg . . ." He let his voice trail off, not verbalizing that there would be many more patients to come.

"Of course, Doctor, if thee thinks I am able." She gestured toward Ella. "This young soldier's wife, Ella McCullough, has offered to help at the hospital."

Dr. Bryant bowed. "Ma'am, we thank you. Do you have any experience with nursing?"

"Only when I helped my ma with the young'uns," Ella said with a curtsy. "I just thought I should offer to help in any way I can."

Dr. Bryant considered her. "We will put you to work, then. Why don't you go to the back and help roll the freshly laundered bandages?"

"Yes, sir. Thank you, sir. I think I could do that. Easy."

The head surgeon smiled and motioned for her to move to the rear of the warehouse. Ella whispered her thanks to Faith and headed toward the stack of laundry.

Dr. Bryant stepped closer to Faith. "Nurse Cathwell, back to our need for more hands to help. You seem able to evaluate and deal with black people. I confess I do not understand them." He gave an impatient shake of his head. "But we must use all available hands. Be sure to get hard workers."

The pervasive idea that blacks were shiftless rankled Faith. "I'm certain I can find good workers."

"Laundresses, orderlies, and maids. Several of each." He finished by stating that the pay would be four dollars a month.

Faith felt a wave of relief. Now Honoree wouldn't be relegated to bedpans when she should be nursing. And the nursing staff might be a little more ready to cope with the aftermath of the upcoming battle. Elated at the doctor's decision, Faith finished her rounds, then went outside to seek Honoree.

She found her friend at the pump, muttering to herself in the shade of the overhanging roof. Faith took over pumping so her friend could finish up more quickly. As she worked, Faith explained Dr. Bryant's request. Then they both scrubbed their hands with the soap they carried in little wooden boxes in their apron pockets.

"Are you going to check on that Rebel today?" Honoree asked as they returned the bedpans to the hospital. Evidently she hadn't been able to let go of that situation either.

Faith didn't want to reply. "Thee will not like my answer," she cautioned.

Honoree made a sound of disgust, frowning.

Finally, before returning into the scorching sun, they both drew up their full-brimmed Quaker-style bonnets, which had been hanging down their backs.

With a wave toward Ella, who was still rolling bandages, they set out for the contraband camp. Faith hated that name. *Contraband* was the term for confiscated property. Why did the Union Army still refer to former slaves as property? Weren't they fighting on the side of abolition?

Honoree remained silent as if still wordlessly scolding Faith, who tried to ignore it. Soldiers sat around camp in whatever shade they could find. Even though it was morning, the summerlike heat was wilting Faith's starched collar and cuffs.

Honoree let out a sound of disgust. "That young army wife can't be sixteen yet."

Faith had thought the same. What had forced the young woman to follow her husband into war?

"Miss Cathwell!" Colonel Knight hailed her from behind. "I was just coming to look for you."

She and Honoree turned, her friend

48

stiffening beside her.

"Him again," Honoree muttered, sniffing in disapproval.

A mix of reactions churned in Faith's midsection. The most surprising was the lift at seeing this man again. "We are on our way to the contraband camp if thee wishes to join us."

Coming alongside them, the colonel nodded but said nothing, Honoree's obvious animosity possibly constraining him.

"We are seeking to hire some more hospital staff there," Faith said.

"You, of course," Honoree said to the colonel, her tone belligerent, "think that these escaped slaves should have stayed with their masters."

Ignoring her tart comment without rancor, Dev kept his motive for seeking them out today to himself. "I am sorry that I irritate you, but I have seen the runaways coming to the Union Army for shelter ever since we started out from Tennessee. Are they any better off here in such wretched conditions than with their masters at home?"

Faith laid a restraining hand on Honoree's arm. "I cannot disagree that the conditions in the contraband camp are dreadful. But right now we have an opportunity to find a few we can help. What can I do for thee,

Colonel?"

Honoree's jaw hardened but she said no more.

Dev didn't want to speak in front of her. He chose to bide his time and merely said it could wait.

The Quakeress let this pass.

The three of them continued toward the railroad depot surrounded by the wrecked and upturned rails. Dev hated this wanton waste. "We destroyed their railroad to keep them from using it to move men and supplies."

"This war is their doing," Honoree said bitterly.

"War is destructive beyond any civilian's imagining," Faith murmured, trying to smooth over the tension between the two. "Sometimes I wonder if anything will be left," she whispered.

Or anyone. Dev kept this thought to himself. How had he managed to survive nearly three years of war? And this was the second war for him.

He, Faith, and Honoree neared the contraband area, guarded by Union soldiers. The contraband camp was increasing by the hour, it seemed. Every manner of fleeing slave gathered in the shade of the depot building and sparse trees, fanning themselves with hats and rags. The human suffering he saw etched on the faces that turned to them deepened his own gloom and restlessness. He didn't want to be here.

They approached the sentry.

"Why do they need to be guarded like prisoners?" Honoree asked.

"It's for their protection too," Dev was goaded into saying. "The armies are always moving. And civilians around here don't like runaway slaves."

Honoree looked the other way as if he hadn't spoken.

Fine. He leaned close to Faith's ear, finally coming to the point. "Miss Cathwell, when you're done here, would you have time to come to my tent?"

She nodded, but was it to his request or just to the sentry who was allowing them to pass?

Faith hurried ahead of him and Honoree as if to distance herself from the conflict.

Dev followed her while the black girl turned toward a nearby group of escaped slaves. He overheard Honoree say, "I'm bringing an offer of work, but I'm also looking for someone. Her name is Shiloh Langston. . . ."

Then he couldn't hear any more as he accompanied Faith toward a cluster of women with small children just inside the depot entrance. She introduced herself as a nurse. "I am looking for laundresses. Do any of thee have experience doing large loads of laundry?"

"What you need large loads for, ma'am?" one very thin woman asked.

"The hospital needs more workers. If thee can do the work, it would be a job."

"It a payin' job?"

"Of course."

"You a Quaker?" another woman interrupted.

Faith nodded.

Dev could not help but notice the way the slaves relaxed at the revelation that Faith was a Quaker. These abolitionists were hated throughout the South by virtually everyone but the slaves. How did they even know about Quakers?

"Again, I'm looking for laundry workers," Faith continued. "It is an arduous and demanding job, so I must find strong women."

"I'm strong." A large woman wearing a ragged, soiled dress loomed up beside Faith.

Faith studied her and held out a hand. "Thy name?"

The woman shook Faith's hand with a kind of wonder. "I'm Cassie. I been praying

God would bring me work to do. I hate this lying around and beggin'. I work hard for you."

In short order, Faith hired four women as laundresses and three young women to work in the hospital as maids. Then she moved toward a group of young black men under the overhang of the depot roof.

Dev followed, observing how she treated all with the same respect. *Be not a respecter of persons,* his memory prompted.

"Gentlemen," Faith said, "I need to hire a few men able to lift patients and carry stretchers and just generally help with the heavy work at the hospital."

A few moved toward her. But more looked to Dev. "Sir," one young man said, "some of us want to 'list in the Union Army. How we do that?"

Dev gazed at the hopeful faces, his gut twisting. The idea of blacks becoming soldiers disturbed him at a deep level. But he dismissed his marked reaction. The Union needed every willing recruit. "I will ask the sergeant in charge of enlistment to come and speak to you."

"Thank you, sir." This was repeated several times by many there.

Dev bowed his head slightly in acknowledgment and watched as Faith hired three strapping young men who looked as if they could use a few more good meals. But then, his own belt was tighter as well. At its best, camp food was never anything but filling. But being on the move meant hardtack and coffee instead of regular meals. And some of the canned beef the Army had bought could kill a man.

Faith stopped at the depot entrance and spoke to a few more women, asking about their needs and whether they had families in the North whom they could go to.

Dev tried to hold in his frustration. He needed Faith to come help Jack. Was she deliberately delaying?

Finally the three of them left the contraband camp, an entourage of new employees in tow.

Within a few yards of leaving the sentries behind, Faith turned to Honoree. "Will thee take these people to Dr. Bryant so he can make certain the captain hires them?"

"And you're off to help . . ." Honoree pursed her lips and glared at Dev. "Very well. I'll do what you ask." After leaning closer and whispering something in Faith's ear, she waved to the new hires. "Follow me. We need to get you all on the payroll."

Faith's expression had lit up at Honoree's whispered words. "Thank thee, Honoree, for taking care of this. I will come to thee as soon as I am able." She gripped Honoree's forearm for a moment, their gazes meeting, communicating — what? Then she turned to the group of contraband she'd recruited. "And, friends, I will see thee soon to discuss thy duties and make certain thee are given quarters and new clothing."

There was general approval of her words — grins and thank-yous and curtsies.

"Colonel," she said, turning to him, "lead on."

Dev began to guide her away. "Who is Shiloh Langston?" The unexpected words bubbled up, surprising him. "I sense that your . . . friend's dislike of me has something to do with that woman, whoever she is."

CHAPTER 3

Dev waited for Faith's reply, sensing that he'd brought up something she didn't want to discuss. As she continued to walk beside him in a silence that became heavier with each step, he was more aware of all the soldiers they passed, sitting in the shade, laughing or silent. The smell of sweat and tobacco smoke and worse filled the air. He regretted upsetting her and nearly reached out to touch her shoulder.

Then he watched as she unstoppered the small vial she wore on braided twine around her neck and lifted it to her nose. So near her, he also breathed in the sweet and soothing scent of lavender.

Finally she replied without looking at him. "Shiloh is Honoree's younger sister. Born free, she was kidnapped and sold south three years before the war." She recited this in a way that did not invite him to pursue the topic.

Shock hit him. No wonder the black girl hated slaveholders. "I'm so sorry." The words were totally inadequate to address the seriousness of this evil act. Why couldn't people just obey the laws? Follow orders? And then he recalled that he himself was breaking military law by harboring the enemy in his tent. But for most of their lives Jack had been both family and enemy.

They arrived at his tent and he waved her inside.

"Miss, I am so glad to see you," Armstrong said, sounding worried. "I have been following your instructions, but he's . . ." He gestured toward Jack.

"His fever must be very high," the Quakeress said, hurrying toward the patient. She bent over Jack. "Oh, he is burning up. Does thee have any alcohol here?"

"Whiskey," Dev replied and turned to retrieve the bottle from a small open trunk.

"No medicinal alcohol?" she asked.

"No." Dev handed her the whiskey bottle.

She opened it and drew out a square of cotton from one of her apron pockets. Kneeling beside the cot, she began to swab Jack's red face with the alcohol. She pushed back the sheet and swabbed his bare chest too.

"Has he been able to drink anything?" she

57

asked, not looking up.

"Some coffee early this morning," Armstrong replied, standing over her. "Nothing since."

"We must bring down his fever so he can drink or he'll die — especially in this heat," she said with urgency.

"I'll help," Dev volunteered, moving to the narrow space on the other side of the cot. He drew out his own handkerchief.

"Armstrong," Faith said, "will thee go to the hospital, find my friend Honoree, and discreetly ask her to give thee a bottle of wood alcohol? We need this whiskey for other purposes."

"I didn't kill Bellamy," Jack muttered through lips so dry they stuck together, staring at them with unseeing eyes. "Father!"

The words chilled Dev; the old pain and unreasoning guilt clutched at him. But why would Jack say he hadn't killed Bellamy? Jack had always been hot at hand and undisciplined. Did he regret it or was it just delirium?

The Quakeress rose and poured water into the speckled blue-and-white washbasin. "We'll just use water till Armstrong returns."

They worked together, swabbing down the heated flesh with wet cloths. Then she undid the soiled bandages and applied new poultices to both festering arms. "I must continue to draw out the infection. And bring his fever down."

Taut with worry, Dev concentrated on swabbing his cousin's chest, trying not to react to the fiery inflamed skin on each arm. "Is he suffering from blood poisoning?"

"He's coming close, but the poultices should work . . . if we can keep him alive long enough. If thee sees streaks of red going up his arms toward his heart, we've lost the battle."

That would mean death or, nearly as bad, amputation. What man wanted a helpless life without arms? He wouldn't wish that on the worst man alive. Despair swallowed Dev whole.

They fell silent, Dev grieving over what might come.

Finally Armstrong returned. "I have it." At the Quakeress's instruction, his man poured an inch of the wood alcohol into the empty basin.

Dev and Faith began swabbing with the alcohol, its pungent smell wafting over the tent.

"Armstrong," Faith said, "please mix a glass of water and whiskey with a few drops of laudanum."

He handed it to her.

"Colonel, please lift your cousin's head."

He did so, and she started to dribble the liquid into Jack's mouth. Jack choked at first but then, without opening his eyes, began to swallow.

"Good," she said when he'd drunk most of the glass. She rose. "I must return to my duties in the hospital."

Dev stood too, almost desperate. "Do you have to go?"

She met his gaze with a sad smile. "I must. I will be missed otherwise, and I don't want to be forced to explain where I've been."

He nodded reluctantly, conceding.

"Just continue doing what I've shown thee. Bathe him to bring down the fever. Offer him whiskey-water often. He needs fluid in this heat and in his fever. The laudanum helps him cope with the pain, and the whiskey offers some nourishment. And continue the poultices. No one can do more than this. As long as thee cares for him, I'm not needed."

Yes, you are. But she was right. She must leave or draw unwanted attention. "Thank you," Dev said, trying to load the words with all the gratitude he felt.

She merely nodded and left them.

Now he felt a glimmer of why the slaves felt safe around Quakers. They helped even when it was illegal. Or at least this Quaker-ess did.

Feeling the loss of her presence, Dev dropped to his knees to continue bathing his cousin.

"I've been praying," Armstrong said. "It's all up to God."

Dev didn't bother to reply. Words meant little now.

Faith walked away from the colonel as quickly as her voluminous skirts would let her. She didn't like the attraction she felt to this colonel, nor did she appreciate the questionable situation he'd drawn her into.

And his saying Shiloh's name had felt like someone dashing water in her face. Through the heat of the day she hurried toward her tent, where Honoree was waiting.

She and Honoree chafed daily at the lack of progress they'd made toward their goal. Before the war, the South's hatred of aboli-tionists, Quakers, and free blacks had been virulent and often violent, and had pre-vented not only Faith and Honoree but everyone in their families from coming to seek Shiloh. And now they were at a stand-still once more.

But before Faith had left the contraband camp with the colonel, Honoree had whispered that she had news of Shiloh. This was not the first time they had questioned escaped slaves about Shiloh, a light-skinned woman of color with distinctive green eyes. But it was the first time they'd received any information.

Oh, Lord, where is she? Lead us to her.

Even as she hurried to Honoree to find out the news, she couldn't help wondering who Bellamy was and why the Rebel's father thought he'd killed him. And *had* Jack killed him? Faith wanted to run but forced herself not to draw attention.

Faith saw that Honoree was waiting for her outside their tent, pacing. Faith rushed up to her. "What did thee hear about Shiloh?"

Honoree grabbed her wrists. "A woman said she heard tell of a light-skinned slave with green eyes at a plantation named Annerdale."

"Where's that?"

"Northeast of here in Madison County."

Faith absorbed the report, fighting the excitement of this first lead. "Does thee think this news is credible?"

Honoree released her grip on Faith's wrists. "I don't know. I hope so. Shiloh's green eyes do make her stand out."

Faith pulled Honoree to her and they

rested their heads on each other's shoulders. Faith, Patience, and Shiloh all had the same green eyes. The bond between the families was stronger than friendship. "We will follow up this lead."

Honoree let out a sound of disgust. "As soon as the Army lets us."

"Battles must be fought. Our private quest is unimportant to generals. Thee knows that I, a Quaker abolitionist —"

"And I, a free woman of color, aren't safe in enemy territory, away from the Union Army."

Faith nodded against Honoree's shoulder. "Yes. We might be close, but until Vicksburg falls, we must wait."

They stepped apart then and turned to go back to the hospital, where they were needed. Neither spoke. Faith allowed hope to flicker within. Annerdale Plantation in Madison County. When they finally were able to go there, would they find Shiloh?

Nearly two weeks later in the surrounding predawn gray, Dev and one of his crack companies of close to a hundred saddled up their horses. Jackson, the state capital of Mississippi, had just fallen. Standing beside his mount, he finished adjusting his saddle and turned back to Armstrong. "I have a feeling I may not see you for days. Depending on events, you may have to take Jack to the hospital near here." Jack was still feverish but lucid again and taking nourishment, seeming stronger. "Keep that incriminating belt buckle and hat hidden."

"You want me to continue to pass him off as Union?" Their conversation was buried among the sounds of restless horses and men speaking to their mounts and to each other.

"Don't offer information," Dev said. "But if asked, tell the truth."

Armstrong nodded.

"If anyone challenges you for this, say you are acting upon my orders."

Armstrong grinned. "Yes, sir."

"Good man. I plan to turn him in as a prisoner of war when I return." He nodded once and mounted his horse.

"Just come back in one piece," Armstrong said — his usual farewell.

"I always do," Dev replied in kind, knowing someday he'd break his word. He led his men out to the road they were about to head west on.

Up the road, he paused to take stock of everyone and explain their mission. "We are to range over the roads toward Vicksburg. According to the map, there are three. Keep close in your groups. I will stay upon or very near the southernmost road. Ride back to me with any report of Rebel sightings. Keep your carbines loaded and your heads down."

A few chuckled at his familiar advice, and then they were riding down the road and soon spreading out over the waking country-side.

Dev reflected on the days before, and again the face of the lovely Miss Cathwell lingered. She would probably remain at the hospital near Jackson. He hoped the black girl — the one the Quakeress called a friend — wouldn't give away Jack's secret. But he couldn't do anything more than he had. As his horse moved under him, Dev hoped for a keen eye and ear, to live through another day.

"Wake up!"

Faith swam out of a deep sleep toward Honoree's voice. She blinked in the morn-ing light.

"We got orders to get with the Sanitary Commission wagons. We're on the move again." Honoree and Faith had been deemed young enough to face the rigors of being sent to the front to give first aid to the wounded before they were transported to the hospital. Then Honoree added, "I heard cavalry leaving earlier."

That meant that the colonel might already be in harm's way. Not letting herself dwell on this, Faith threw off the sheet that had covered her and parted the mosquito net around her cot. In a few minutes she had freshened up with a bit of water and soap and was packing her few possessions to be sent with the wagons and selecting some packets of medicinal herbs to take along on her person. She and Honoree ate porridge standing up since all around them their tent and furniture was being folded up and carried away to the wagons. This was good news: any progress toward Vicksburg brought them closer to the time they might venture to Annerdale Plantation.

They finished the meager breakfast and, still sipping their morning coffee, hurried to the large wagons. Some were filled with supplies and others with camp equipment that would be needed after the battle when the wagons would trundle the wounded back to the hospital tents.

Turning, Faith found the young wife from the day before.

"Miss Faith, can I come with you today?"

"Ella McCullough, thee must not come with us. Only a few trained nurses go onto the field."

"But what if my Landon, my husband, is wounded? He'll need me."

Faith glanced around. She had a few minutes to spare before she would climb onto a wagon and be off. "Come over here." She led the girl around to the far side of the nearest wagon, Honoree following. "I know thee is worried, but —"

"He's all I got," Ella said, wringing her hands. "We had to run away from home. They said either Landon joined the local Confederate Tennessee militia or else. Called us Yankees. Threatened us."

Faith realized that trying to stop this flow of words would be impossible. She merely patted the girl on the arm, encouraging her to let it all out.

"I . . . We had to leave everyone behind. All our kin. Now he's going into his first battle. What will I do if anything happens to him? I need to be there to take care of him."

Faith claimed the young woman's hands. "Ella, I understand thy concern, but only a few well-trained nurses such as Honoree and I are allowed to go onto the field to care for the wounded." Faith tried to come up with the words to describe what she and Honoree would no doubt face today. "Ella, it is too much for thee." *Almost too much for me.*

"She is telling you the truth," Honoree added.

Ella looked surprised that Honoree had spoken up.

"Ella McCullough, wait near the hospital tents. If thy husband is wounded, thee can help him there."

One of the wagon masters, an Irishman with thick red curls under his hat, called to them. "Ladies! Time to roll!"

Faith squeezed Ella's hand and hurried off behind Honoree.

The Irishman threw their valises up on a nearly filled wagon, and with his help, they climbed onto the back and sat, resting against the sides.

"If I weren't so tired, I'd walk," Honoree said.

Faith nodded. Riding in the wagons could not be called comfortable. The main army, not just the cavalry companies, was moving forward today, and the knowledge tightened her with dread anticipation. They wouldn't be mobilizing the Sanitary Commission wagons unless this was true.

In spite of these worries, she was still tired enough that if she could, she'd have lain down and slept more. Grant's relentless drive to take Vicksburg was pushing them all to the extreme.

Faith arranged her skirts modestly around herself and hoped that today would not make Ella a young widow.

She thought also of the colonel and his wounded cousin, a family divided. She'd planned on stopping in today to see how the Rebel was faring. But this war waited for no one. And another battle loomed at any time this day or the next.

The Reb she'd nursed must have been part of one of the numerous Confederate raiding parties, headed by notorious raiders such as John Morgan, Nathan Forrest, and Joe Wheeler. Colonel Knight and his men would be out in front of the main Union Army, prowling, searching for raiding parties or the Confederate Army itself under Pemberton. She prayed for the men moving forward, the colonel among them. Much as she tried to push it away, his face refused to fade from her mind.

Midday, Dev leaned close to his saddle, ducking gunfire. He'd divided his men into companies of ten and sent them ranging over the landscape, seeking the enemy. And now he'd spotted some Rebs who looked to be an opposing cavalry, not just a small party of raiders. He didn't have to shout orders. The soldiers with him knew what to do. They scattered in every direction, spreading out, harder to bring down. But unlike the musket he'd wielded in the Mexican War, the rifles he and his men now carried possessed a deadly accuracy.

From his vantage point against his mount's neck, Dev urged the horse toward a copse of trees and mentally evaluated the force they had come upon. How many? Where were they headed? He must carry the news back to headquarters or Grant would be fighting blind. He reached the cover of the trees, hoping there would not be any Rebs waiting there to ambush him. He found none and reloaded, then turned his horse eastward toward headquarters.

After evading a number of pursuers, Dev rode hard with his small squad straight to the headquarters tent. He slid off his horse and saluted the sentry. "Reconnaissance," he said and was waved inside.

He was startled to see General Grant himself inside the tent. That meant this really would be a major thrust forward. "Sir." He saluted.

Grant removed the cigar from his mouth and returned the salute. "What news, Colonel?"

Dev read recognition in the general's gaze.

Their years of training at West Point had overlapped. "We met a large number of the enemy on the road to Champion Hill, sir."

Another of Dev's company entered and saluted Grant. "Sir, we met the enemy on the north side of the road toward Vicksburg." The man saluted Dev. "Sir."

"How far?" Grant asked.

"About five miles east of here," Dev replied, and the other soldier nodded in agreement.

"Then we must move fast to meet the enemy. They must not reach the fortress at Vicksburg. Thank you. Dismissed."

Dev led the member of his company outside. "We'll gather our men together to join the battle." Then he glimpsed the Sanitary Commission wagons that must have moved forward with the main army. The wagons were waiting here in readiness for the upcoming clash. He saw the Quakeress and her black girl talking to one of the drivers. He knew nurses came onto the battlefield to aid the wounded after the fighting. But he didn't want this nurse so near danger. It was not his decision to make, however.

Dev mounted his horse, as did the other cavalryman from the tent. "Men, we're in for it. Let's warn our fellows."

71

The armies clashed on the road to Champion Hill. Rebels poured down the road. Union artillery thundered, thundered. Throwing up earth. Deafening. Billows of smoke rose around Dev. Dismounting, he urged his men forward. He fired his carbine and held his saber in the other hand.

He plunged into the fray. He felt it. He fell.

Faith and Honoree huddled under the wagon. The battle had begun and was raging within a mile or so of their position. Usually the Sanitary Commission wagons didn't get this close to combat, but with two armies trying to find or elude one another, nothing was certain. Battles were unpredictable. Faith found herself praying and trembling with each blast.

Ready to move if necessary, the wagon masters stood at the heads of their teams, soothing the horses. The teams were somewhat accustomed to the sounds of a nearby battle, but the horses still remained restless, uneasy, and Faith felt the same.

At any time the opposing army could envelop the medical contingent, and they could find themselves under direct fire. And Honoree would be in the gravest danger if they were overrun by Rebels who didn't take kindly to free blacks. Yet telling Honoree to stay back in camp never met with success. *Father, keep us safe. And give us victory.*

The ground underneath them shook with cannon fire. Faith felt it shuddering through her. Why was bloodshed required to end slavery? This dreadful war had become the only way slaves would be set free. Faith prayed, and as the battle sounds deafened her, words failed and she depended on the Light of Christ to pray for her.

The battle had moved on — or Faith hoped it had. She and Honoree had filled their apron pockets with bunches of herbs and rolled bandages, and now they hefted several canteens of water over their shoulders and headed toward the wounded men who had been abandoned as the battle had progressed.

Faith silently repeated the Twenty-third Psalm as she met the first casualties. This was surely the valley of the shadow of death.

A soldier in butternut, the homemade gray of the Confederacy, moaned. Faith dropped to her knees and offered the man water.

"Thanks," he muttered.

She quickly assessed his injuries, tied a tourniquet around his arm, and bandaged his forehead. "Thee is still able to move. I'll help thee up."

"What?"

"Thee has suffered the shock of being injured, but I think thee can walk." She helped him rise. "Try a few steps."

He did so, then stood leaning on his rifle. "Which way?"

"I think west." She gestured.

"Thank you, miss. I was . . ."

"Stunned. Thee has lost blood and is weakened."

He stared at her, registering her words. "You a Quaker?"

She turned to the next soldier who showed movement. "Yes, and one of those vile abolitionists."

The Rebel moved away, staggering a little and muttering in disbelief, "A Quaker."

"What good does that do?" Honoree protested. "He'll just go on and kill some of ours."

They'd had this type of exchange many times before. But Faith had an aversion to sending men to prisoner of war camps. "Or be killed himself. It is all in God's hands."

Shaking her head, Honoree moved farther

on, bending or stooping here and there.

Faith tried to keep track of her amid the not-so-distant sounds of gunfire and cannon.

Then more troops — blue and gray, firing at each other — poured up the road and over the open field. Men screamed, bellowed. Gunfire exploded. Faith threw herself facedown among the wounded and dead, her face buried in the wild grass. Grapeshot pelted down all around her. As if caught outside in a violent storm, she squeezed her eyes shut and prayed.

But troops rarely stayed in one place long. Soon the gunfire had moved southward, away from them. Faith rose cautiously, scanning the area, seeking her friend. "Honoree! Honoree!" she called.

She received no reply save the groans and cries of the wounded. Panic fluttered to life. She'd lost Patience and Shiloh. *I can't lose Honoree too.* The urge to run pell-mell nearly overwhelmed her. She stilled herself, swallowing down the panic, and began threading her way through the bodies around her. A few men grabbed her skirts as she passed, and she stopped to minister to them.

"Honoree!" she cried again and again. And finally she found her, lying unconscious. But breathing. Faith dropped to her knees, lifted Honoree's head, and put the canteen to her lips. "Honoree, please wake up. Please."

In the summer twilight of a long day, Dev led his men and their horses to a creek they'd glimpsed through willow trees. His head still ached and he'd jarred his shoulder when he fell from his horse. But he was alive.

Hot and dry, he and his men took their mounts farther downstream to drink. After a time, they drew their horses away from the water before they could drink too much. They secured the horses to the trees.

Then the men found an area upstream for themselves. Some, like Dev, dropped to one knee to scoop the cool water up to their mouths, and others lay down on their bellies to lap up the water. The scene reminded him of the story of Gideon. But Dev surely hadn't been called by God. He was no judge, just a soldier.

The battle had been a maddening dance. Just trying to stay within the Union lines had been tricky. His mind, now free of battle tactics, let his worries surface. Had Armstrong been forced to take Jack to the hospital? Were the Quakeress and her black girl safe?

Soon he and his men had filled their empty canteens and bellies with water. He wet his handkerchief and wiped his gritty face and neck, wishing he could shed his fatigues and float in the cool water. But no. They must get back.

"Let's try to find headquarters and get food and any new orders," Dev said. His men mounted and he led them away, hoping he was taking them in the right direction. He did not want to surprise any Rebel stragglers now that the sun was nearly down.

After they'd traveled a few miles eastward, he heard his name called repeatedly. "Colonel Knight!"

It was the Quakeress.

He turned his horse toward her voice. "Miss Cathwell?"

"Here!"

He directed his men to go on while he headed toward her, picking his way through the carnage left by the battle. Many of the bodies, lying in a haphazard maze, were beyond human help. He glimpsed Sanitary Commission wagons in the near distance, where men on stretchers were being lifted onto wagons like cordwood.

"Thank heaven I saw thee," the Quakeress greeted him with audible relief.

He slipped from his saddle, wondering what she needed.

"I have been busy giving immediate aid to the wounded, but I've stayed here near Honoree." She gestured to her friend, lying motionless nearby among the wounded men. "I think something struck her head when the battle veered around us. I need to get her onto one of the wagons back to the hospital."

He almost asked, *Why have you waited?* Instead he offered, "I can take her to the wagons on my horse."

"Thank thee, but also I need someone to watch over her. I must remain here, nursing. There are still men who need me. But I don't ever let Honoree become separated from me near the enemy or a battle." The last sentence was embellished with fear.

"I don't understand. The wagons will take her back to the hospital tents, won't they?"

"I told thee what happened to Shiloh." She moved toward him. "I'm not losing Honoree."

"You think she might not be safe," he asked, "even among our troops?" Or perhaps she thought the girl wouldn't get good care.

"I can't take that chance, or I would have sent her back already. I hoped she would regain consciousness by now, but she hasn't." The final words were touched by panic. She clutched his sleeve. "Please, will thee take her to the hospital? The wounded men will take precedence. And don't let anyone but Dr. Bryant — he's the head surgeon — treat her."

Dev owed this woman — period. "Very well. I will take her and watch over her. But won't you be coming in soon? It will be dark anytime now."

She pointed toward a lantern at her feet. "There are still wounded who need my help. The wagons will carry the wounded till the horses can no longer walk."

"What about you?" he said as he lifted Honoree and laid her facedown over his saddle. His horse was also nearly spent. He hoped the walk to camp would not be far. He was nearing the end of his strength too.

"When I can no longer work, I will lie down in one of the wagons. Don't worry about me. God will protect me."

He hoped she was right. He turned his horse, and on the eastern horizon, opposite the setting sun, he glimpsed high the smoke from campfires. And he saw one of the hospital wagons heading that way, creaking and groaning under its load. He sucked in air and started off. "Keep safe!" he called over his shoulder.

"Thee too!"

He shook his head. He didn't care what anybody said. A woman did not belong here doing this work, especially not this lovely young lady. Her family was derelict in their duty to keep her from such dreadful scenes. He wished her father were here in front of him. He had *several choice words* he'd voice.

CHAPTER 4

The miles back to camp in the deepening twilight pushed Dev toward the limit of his endurance. All the energy and excitement from the battle had left him. He felt drained, sucked dry, yet he had to get Honoree to the doctors. He owed Faith Cathwell.

To the sound of distant moans and occasional sniper fire, he staggered beside his horse, keeping himself up by holding on to the reins and pommel, and often leaning against the horse as it plodded down the dusty road. He felt himself almost falling face-first. He fought to remain upright.

As he limped along, he often checked Honoree's neck for a pulse. Her heart was beating and she was breathing, but she was deeply unconscious. He spoke her name several times: "Honoree, wake up." But she did not move or even groan.

Finally he saw the Union camp and smelled the campfires where, after a hard day, men were heating coffee and beans over the coals and sitting very still, gazing wordlessly into the flames.

Dev headed toward the camp hospital with its tents and coming and going Sanitary Commission wagons. He tried to close his ears to the sounds of suffering, but he couldn't. Mindful of Faith's request, he remained with Honoree. In the turmoil around the hospital and tents, he stood apart with his horse and tried to pick out a doctor or surgeon.

Finally, in the last light of day, he spoke to one of the men at a Sanitary Commission wagon, who directed him to a particular surgical tent. Dev waited outside till the doctor exited for a brief break between patients. "Dr. Bryant, will you help me, please? Miss Cathwell sent me."

The man looked up, appearing exhausted, his surgical apron bloodstained. "Yes?"

"This is one of your nurses." Dev motioned toward Honoree on the horse. "She was struck unconscious during the battle, and we can't wake her up."

Dr. Bryant came over, pressed his fingers to Honoree's neck, and then turned to Dev. "I have seen this before. I can do nothing. She will either wake or she will not. I think she will wake. But she may suffer some memory loss or confusion."

Someone summoned Dr. Bryant from inside the tent. "I'm needed. Just watch her and pray." The doctor turned away.

Left with nothing to say and on the edge of exhaustion, Dev led his horse to his tent. Armstrong, as usual, was waiting outside for him. "Help me get her down and carry her inside, please."

Armstrong looked surprised but moved to receive Honoree's shoulders and help Dev carry her into the tent.

Dev was about to suggest that they lay Honoree on Armstrong's cot, when he saw that his own cot was empty. He nearly dropped Honoree's ankles. Had his cousin died today? He'd been almost well enough to turn in as a prisoner of war. "What happened? Where's Jack?"

Because Dev had stopped, Armstrong also paused. The manservant looked and sounded strained. "I went to fetch water, and when I returned, he was gone."

A punch to the gut. Shock shuddered through Dev in waves. "He broke his promise? He broke his word?" He couldn't believe it. A gentleman did not go back on his word, no matter what.

"I looked for your cousin, but I couldn't find him in the turmoil with the battle and all. He took a white shirt of yours too."

"I didn't think he was even strong enough yet to join the prisoners of war." Bewildered, Dev couldn't help himself. He glanced around as if Jack were hiding in the corner.

The girl moaned.

"Let's set her down on my cot," Dev urged.

They did so. She lay still. Jack's betrayal goaded Dev into action overriding his exhaustion. "I can't stay. I've got to go find Jack if I can." *And make him sorry for betraying my trust.* But he felt himself staggering with fatigue. Armstrong gripped his arm, holding him up, guiding him to a three-legged stool. Dev sat down, too tired to move.

Deep in the night Faith lifted a soldier's head and dribbled onto his lips the last of the water from the last of her canteens. She tried to speak but her dry throat scratched. Finally she managed to whisper, "It's empty." And so was she.

The man nodded in the waning lantern light and closed his eyes in resignation.

Rising higher on her knees, she glanced around. No one moaned anymore. The wounded had fallen asleep for the night. Or for good.

She tried to see where the Sanitary Commission wagon was, but in the dim moonlight she did not find it. The lantern oil gave out and the light winked off. Utterly depleted, she could not go on. She reached into her pocket and brought out a peppermint drop, unwrapped it, and slipped it onto her tongue. She hadn't eaten since breakfast. A bit of sugar often steadied her.

Her stomach rumbling, she lay down on her back on the already-dew-wet grass and stared up at the starry sky, sleep coming for her wrapped in waves of fatigue. When Vicksburg fell, as it must, then they might be able to continue searching for Shiloh. Her last thought was a prayer for Honoree. And Shiloh, wherever she was.

Dev woke in the very early hours of the new day and realized he was lying on the ground in his tent, a blanket covering him. About to try sitting up, he heard voices nearby. Squinting, he could see the shadow of Armstrong in the low lantern light, moving toward Dev's cot.

"Miss, you're safe," Armstrong said quietly.

Dev saw the black girl raise her hand and touch his servant as if making sure he was substantial, real. "Mr. Armstrong?"

"Just Armstrong, miss. May I offer you some cold coffee and hardtack?"

"If that's what you have, that's what I'll take," she murmured with a touch of humor.

"I wish I had better to give you." He turned to pour the coffee, which splashed against the bottom of the tin mug. "I was worried about you, miss. You've been unconscious for many hours." He helped her sit up on the side of the cot.

"I was not completely unconscious," she admitted, taking the cup and holding it in both hands, which still trembled. "My head hurt, so I couldn't open my eyes. And my mind . . . was scattered like scraps of paper on the wind." She shook her head, moaned, and then pressed a hand to the back of her skull. "Must have been part of an exploding shell that hit me."

"You're lucky it didn't shatter and the shrapnel kill you," Armstrong said, sitting down on a camp stool close to her.

The girl sipped her coffee. "Where's Faith?"

"She is still on the battlefield, I believe."

Dev knew he should make his wakefulness known, but lethargy muzzled him.

The girl rested her head in one hand. "I should be with her."

"You couldn't help being struck unconscious and dazed."

Looking around, the girl suddenly stiffened. "Where's the Reb?"

"He ran off yesterday while I was out."

"The dog," she snapped. "I suspected that's how it would end."

Dev cringed at her comment.

"Mr. Jack was never one to trust," Armstrong said.

Dev held his breath. The judgment was just.

"Then why did the colonel trust him?" the girl asked with asperity in her voice. Her scathing tone cut Dev to the quick.

"My master always hopes for the best, especially from his family."

She started to shake her head again and then stopped, wincing with obvious pain. "After the Emancipation Proclamation, why do you stay a slave?"

"The proclamation came in January. I will be forty on June 9 this year. The colonel has always promised to free me on my fortieth birthday."

"You believe him?" she asked tartly.

"I trust him. And it means something to me. I don't know how to explain it, but I want *him* to free me, to show me that regard."

Dev did not want to hear any more about

his family or himself or Armstrong's upcoming birthday, which would profoundly change their relationship. Forty had seemed so far away at twenty. He forced himself to rise to a sitting position. "You're awake . . . miss. I'm glad."

The girl looked at him in the gray morning light without any welcome in her face.

For some reason her dislike of him sharpened his distress over Jack's betrayal.

"Yes, sir," she said at last as she dipped the hardtack into the coffee. "Now I'm worried about my friend Faith."

Her reference to a white woman as a friend jarred him once again, but then he looked to Armstrong and admitted to himself that his manservant was the nearest thing he had to a best friend. But he'd never said that out loud, nor had Armstrong. One didn't.

The girl proceeded to nibble the edges of the hard bread.

"Miss," Dev continued, "she asked me to bring you back to camp and to keep you safe. She said that when she could no longer nurse, she'd get on one of the wagons."

"I hope she did so. But it's just as likely that she didn't. She might still be out there, but no one would hurt her." Uncertainty touched the final few words.

The three of them stared at each other as if silently communicating concern over the Quakeress. But they could do nothing. Certainly no honorable man, Reb or Yank, would harm a decent woman, a nurse. Then again, not every man was honorable. "I'll go and look for her after breakfast," he promised.

The girl started to rise. "I should go to our tent —"

"No!" Dev blurted out. "I promised to look after you. I know it isn't proper for you to stay here with two men not of your family, but you must. I promised her. Lie back down. I'll bunk on the floor like I've been doing." He held up a hand, forestalling their objections.

Armstrong accepted the empty coffee cup from the girl and helped her recline again. Then he went to his cot and snuffed the lantern light, each of them trying for whatever sleep was left to them. The drums would sound wake-up soon enough.

Wrapping himself in his blanket, Dev lay in the dimness on the hard, still-warm earth, exhausted, embittered by Jack's escape. He attempted to wrestle down the outrage that roiled in his chest. Jack would pay for his treachery, pay for dishonoring his family. Dev would make certain of that.

■ ■ ■ ■

Shiloh was weeping. "Where are you, Faith? I need you." Faith tried to move, but her feet were frozen to the ground. She stretched out her hands, trying to catch hold of Shiloh. . . .

A red glow through her eyelids woke Faith. Dawn. The bad dream ended abruptly and she lay still, absorbing waves of sorrow like cold water washing over her. How long would it take the Union Army to capture Vicksburg so they could finally go to Annerdale Plantation to look for Shiloh?

A loud moan caused her to open her eyes to the dawn's thin light. She sat up and scanned the field around her. Some men had wakened too and were moving and moaning. She looked down at her empty canteens and pockets. She had nothing to offer the soldiers. Her throat and mouth and lips were dry as sand. Her stomach felt caved in for lack of food. Her body ached as if she'd been beaten. She lay back down, unable to move. *Lord, I need thy strength. Send help. I have none to give.*

"Wake up, miss." The Sanitary Commission driver shook her shoulder. "We're back at camp."

She blinked open her eyes in the full morning light. She sat slumped on the high wagon bench where he must have laid her earlier. "Thank thee," she muttered through dry lips.

He helped her down, and though she thought of the wounded in the back of the wagon, she knew she would not be of any help to them until she ate and was strengthened. She stumbled along toward the nearby hospital mess tent. The men working there asked no questions, just helped her sit down and brought her a mug of coffee and a bowl of hot oatmeal. She had to eat a few bites and sip the coffee before she could speak her gratitude.

"Long night?" the man who'd served her asked.

"Yes." She went on eating, though just lifting the spoon exhausted her. The man was soon called away, and persevering in her efforts, she felt the food and coffee lifting her from her stupor. Her spoon finally scraped the bottom of the empty bowl.

"Miss Cathwell?"

She looked up into the blue eyes of Colonel Knight. For one moment she nearly threw her arms around him, seeking his strength. Then the worry she saw in his countenance stiffened inside her like icicles, even in the heat. Had Honoree taken a turn for the worse? "What is wrong?"

Without replying, he held out his hand.

She let him help her rise, his rough hand drawing her near. Resisting the pull toward him, she carried her empty bowl and mug outside, where dishes were being washed. Her mind conjured Honoree's unconscious face as she finally allowed the colonel to lead her away. "What is it, Colonel?" she begged. "Is it Honoree? How is she?"

Dev regretted not telling her right away. He tightened his hold on her small hand. He longed to pull her under his arm, protect her. Instead he released her. "I'm sorry, miss. Your friend is awake. She's at my tent. Come. I'll take you."

The camp around them had come fully alive. A drummer was sounding the daily sick call, which struck Dev as unnecessary. The wounded were still being brought in on wagons, but except in the midst of battle the routine of military life never changed.

"What's wrong with Honoree?" The Quakeress broke into his silent, unhappy musings. "Is she ill?"

"She's recovering." Dev still couldn't speak aloud of his cousin's treachery. His tent was ahead. He waved toward it, silently asking for her patience. Soon he let her precede him and then he followed, dreading the coming revelation. His cousin had shamed his family, shamed him.

The Quakeress ran toward the black girl, who was sitting on the edge of his cot. "Honoree!"

The girl rose and the two women clasped each other close, shedding tears of evident relief.

Dev stood back, moved by the depth of their caring for each other. Armstrong came to stand beside him, and Dev had the urge to reach out and grip his man's shoulder. He resisted the gesture. His man wouldn't leave him and go home to Baltimore after his birthday, would he?

Finally the two women parted. The Quakeress turned to him. "Thank thee. I was so worried. Has she been seen by Dr. Bryant?"

Dev cleared his throat. "I took her to him straightaway. He said he could do nothing, so I brought her here and Armstrong helped me watch over her."

The Quakeress stepped toward them. "Thank thee, Armstrong." She offered him her hand.

Armstrong hesitated and then shook her hand. "I was happy to help, miss. But your friend merely needed rest. She was dazed and confused. Is that not so, Miss Honoree?"

Dev did not miss the warm look that passed between the two. It caught inside him. Had Armstrong found someone to care for? Certainly soon his man would be free, and why shouldn't he marry? Dev looked away, his own bleak, and no doubt brief, future taunting him. *I could die in this push to Vicksburg.* At least Armstrong would survive this war.

"My head still aches," Honoree replied, "but I can think now and I'm not dizzy anymore."

Dev could hold the truth back no longer. "Miss Cathwell, as you can see, my cousin is not here. In the chaos of battle, he has escaped."

Honoree made a loud sound of disgust.

The Quakeress looked suddenly weaker.

Dev moved forward, urging her to sit on the camp stool by his cot. Again the fact that a lovely young woman like this would be here in these harsh and debilitating conditions aggravated him. "You need to go to your tent and recover your strength." *You need to go back to where you belong.*

"Yes, I am fatigued, but I'm sure I'm needed at the hospital." She rested her head in one hand.

"You will go to our tent," Honoree stated firmly, "and sleep for a few hours and then freshen up and eat another meal before I let you go near the surgeons' tents. I'm not going to let you ruin your health. That won't help anyone."

The Quakeress sighed in quiet acquiescence.

"We will come with you and see that you have what you need," Armstrong said, surprising Dev.

"Yes, we will," Dev agreed. "I'm afraid I've been distracted by my cousin's perfidy."

And that was how it came that he and Armstrong escorted the two women to their tent.

As Dev began to leave, the Quakeress stopped him, a gentle hand on his sleeve. "I'm sorry thy cousin broke his word. But I find that the evil one sends a kind of blindness to those who avoid the Light of Christ."

Dev could think of no reply, so he merely nodded. With a sinking sensation, he realized what honor demanded of him, and without delay. "Thank you, miss, for your help."

"Thee kept my friend safe. Thank thee. God bless, Devlin Knight."

Her use of his given name softened his heart, but he steeled himself. He headed

95

toward the headquarters through the camp of many thousands. He must now face the punishment for trusting his untrustworthy cousin.

Soon Dev approached the tent of his immediate superior, Brigadier General Peter Osterhaus, to confess and face his punishment. He could be court-martialed for hiding a Rebel. His stomach churned with bitterness. Before he could speak to the aide outside, Osterhaus stepped out and saw him. "What is it, Knight?"

Dev saluted. "I need to speak to you, sir."

After returning the salute, Osterhaus waved him inside.

Dev entered the weathered tent.

"What is it?" the brigadier general repeated, standing near a table with a map spread out on it.

Dev stiffened himself. "I'm afraid I'm guilty of aiding the enemy."

Osterhaus straightened, looking surprised. "How so?" he asked, his voice mild.

"Earlier this month in a skirmish east of Port Gibson, I met my cousin, who is in the Confederate cavalry, and saw him fall." The memory brought back that awful moment when he'd thought his cousin dead. But it paled in contrast to his cousin's dishonor.

"Afterward I returned and found him, wounded in both arms but alive." Dev was aware that someone had entered the tent behind him.

The brigadier general straightened to attention and saluted. Dev knew he should turn and do the same, but he was desperate to get his confession over and done. He plunged on. "I carried my cousin back to my tent and tended his wounds." Dev decided not to mention Miss Cathwell's involvement. "I intended to turn him over as a prisoner of war as soon as he was well enough. He gave me his word as a gentleman —" Dev's voice caught in his throat — "that he wouldn't try to escape."

"But he broke his word," Osterhaus concluded, nodding at Dev, an indication that he should acknowledge the officer behind him.

"Sad business," the man behind Dev said with evident sympathy.

Recognizing the voice, Dev turned and his chagrin heightened. General Grant had entered with his young son Fred, about thirteen years old, who acted as his orderly. Dev's humiliation was now complete — not only was Grant the highest authority here, but Dev and Grant had a history.

Dev also snapped to attention and saluted.

"I regret trusting him, sir, but I had no idea that he'd —"

"Violate his word," Grant finished for him. He motioned toward the brigadier general. "At ease, Osterhaus."

Unable to speak, shame heating his face, Dev remained at attention, stiff with anger at Jack and at himself. He waited to hear his punishment.

Osterhaus and Grant exchanged glances.

Dev waited, his collar tightening around his neck.

"You had a cousin who served with us in Mexico," Grant said. His son gazed at him, obviously listening carefully.

"Yes. That was Lieutenant Bellamy Carroll. He fell at Monterrey. Jack is his younger brother, who enlisted as a private and came west in the infantry."

Grant nodded, gazing at a point over Dev's left ear as if recalling scenes from the past. "Monterrey," he muttered.

That had been a bloody day Dev would never forget, Bellamy dying in his arms . . .

"Upon your agreement, Osterhaus," General Grant finally said in his quiet way, "I think Knight's losing a month's pay is commensurate with this . . . incident. This war is a civil war. We can't help meeting family and old friends across the field." He gazed toward the brigadier general, who nodded once in agreement.

Dev stood frozen, stunned.

"Colonel, you are dismissed," Grant said in a kind voice.

Racked by relief and guilt, Dev saluted and left. Outside, he paused to catch his breath.

"That was lenient," he heard Osterhaus say within.

"Calvary colonels face death on the front line practically every day. Knight's a good man. We need him."

"You're right. He's a good officer, and we do lose colonels at a more rapid pace than any other officer."

Grant rumbled his agreement. "My point exactly."

Dev walked away then, not wanting to hear any more. Instead of a court-martial, he'd received a slap on the wrist — all because they expected him to be killed sooner rather than later. They weren't wrong. He'd already accepted that he'd die in this war.

Meeting his end was just a matter of time and chance. But before he died, he'd find Jack and make him pay. This was war, but not even in war did a gentleman heap dishonor on his whole family. As it was said,

"Death before dishonor." And Jack had chosen the latter.

CHAPTER 5

On her cot, Faith blinked herself awake to the sound of the drummer, beating the tattoo that would call every soldier to evening roll call. She lay staring at the drab inside of the conical tent, recalling images from the aftermath of yesterday's battle. Pushing these dread reminders away, she realized she must have slept the day away. A dull hunger gnawed at her.

But then the image of the colonel's expression as he confessed his cousin's treachery reared up and dominated her mind. She was an abolitionist, a pacifist, and he was a slaveholder and a soldier. But God had brought him into her life. So what was she going to do about him? She should distance herself from him. Perhaps it was the situation with his cousin's injuries and escape that had drawn her sympathy. The colonel did not deserve this backhanded blow.

Honoree ducked inside, holding a plate

heaped with beans, rice, and corn bread. "I was delayed getting back from supper at the mess tent." She held out the plate. "Sit up and take this. I will go pour you a cup of coffee."

Empty, Faith did as she was told. She began eating, not really tasting the tepid food. Her stomach clamored for her to eat faster, but she knew that would only cause her upset.

Honoree reentered and set a tin cup on the dirt floor beside Faith.

Faith glanced up, drawn from her thoughts about the colonel to her friend's obvious recovery. "Thee is better, then. I'm glad."

"My head aches less than before. I know I should have gone to nurse today, but I put us both on sick call and stayed here with you."

Chewing, Faith merely nodded.

"I'm going to take a walk before bed."

Unwilling to have Honoree out walking alone, Faith tried to stand. "Wait. I'll come with —"

"I have an escort." Honoree smiled a real smile.

Noticing only then that her friend sported a freshly ironed white apron and a red kerchief over her hair, Faith raised an eyebrow.

"Armstrong is here to accompany me."

"Oh."

Honoree chuckled as if amused by Faith's reaction. "I won't be too late. We just wanted some time to talk." With that, her friend left.

Faith heard the tones of Armstrong's deep voice, and then the two moved away, shadows on the tent wall. So Armstrong might be interested in Honoree. Faith continued to force herself to eat the lukewarm plate of almost-tasteless food. Had they even run out of salt? Nonetheless, one must eat, and she needed to restore her strength.

Finishing the chore, she rose and shook out her rumpled dress, then brushed and repinned her disordered hair under a cap. Sighing, she went outside. Her destination was set — certainly not where she ought to go but where she could not help going. What had been the ramifications of his cousin's escape?

The summer twilight gathered around the quieting camp as she walked directly to the colonel's tent. At the entrance she spoke his name. "Colonel Knight."

She waited. Had he been called away to duty? She repeated his name.

The tent flap opened. He gazed out at her. He looked surprised. "Miss Cathwell?" As usual he had the air of a gentleman, with his cultured voice and well-tailored uniform.

"Yes. May we speak?" *Of matters thee probably doesn't want to discuss?*

"A moment." He stepped back inside. Soon he returned with a camp stool in each hand. He set hers down and waved her to it. Then he sat very properly on the other side of the tent opening as if they were in a parlor. "How may I help you, miss?"

Perching on the canvas stool, she tried to come up with a polite topic of conversation. But she couldn't make herself waste words on vapid subjects that meant nothing. "What was thy punishment?"

He looked startled.

"Thee doesn't have to tell me, but I can't help asking —"

"A month's pay." He looked down, ashamed.

She let this settle in her mind. "That was generous."

He said nothing.

She sensed his distress and wished to help. "I will not pry, but . . ."

"Jack and I have never gotten along." He announced this as if he didn't want to but couldn't help himself. Deep hurt lay beneath the words.

She nodded to signify she'd heard him.

Then she recalled something she'd meant to ask him. "Who was Bellamy?"

Again he looked surprised. "Why do you ask that?"

She waved a hand and met his gaze, trying to let him know he could trust her. "When thy cousin was delirious, he mentioned the name." She waited. Either he would answer or he would not.

Caught between wanting to send this prying woman away and wanting to pour out the whole story to her, Dev struggled with himself. But Jack's betrayal of his trust had ripped the scab off the old wound, and her soft voice was so sympathetic.

"We — Jack, Bellamy, and I — grew up in eastern Maryland. My mother and Jack's father were sister and brother, raised on a tobacco plantation. My mother married and moved to the city, to Baltimore, but of course we visited often. Bellamy was the elder brother and Jack the younger, the only two to survive to adulthood."

"I am the youngest of my family," the Quakeress murmured conversationally.

Her nonjudgmental, easy presence invited his confidences. "As Bellamy and I were nearly the same age, we attended West Point together and graduated the same year, just in time for the Mexican War."

"Thee served together, then?" Her gentle voice encouraged him.

"Yes, and at only seventeen Jack enlisted in the infantry and fought too. My uncle was livid — both his sons off to war. He needed an heir for his tobacco plantation." Dev paused. He was sure this Quaker would infer that this meant his uncle owned many slaves. It was the bone of contention between his uncle and his mother, the reason she had moved to the city.

He cleared his throat. "But if Bellamy was off to war, so was Jack. He always competed with his brother." Letting the truth come out began to roll back the weight of the past. He drew in a deep breath.

"What kind of man was Bellamy?"

Dev bent forward, elbows on his knees, remembering Bellamy. He realized that speaking of his lost cousin was something he'd long wanted to do. "He was taller than Jack and more fair-minded." Though what he meant by the last remark, he couldn't have explained.

"I understand. He was not always trying to compete with Jack, but Jack was with him. Is that it?"

She had stated it exactly. A yes was forced out of him. "Bellamy would never have violated his word."

"I couldn't help but notice that thy cousin sported a single star on his hat cockade. What does that signify?"

"It's the symbol of Texas. After the war Jack married a Texas girl, a rancher's daughter, and stayed there."

"But his father needed a son for the plantation," she objected.

Dev couldn't stop his mouth twisting into irony. "I don't understand it either, really. Jack . . . I think Jack always felt his father favored Bellamy." *And me.*

"Brothers, rivals. I don't want to seem sententious, but it sounds like Jacob and Esau."

Dev barked a sad laugh. "I think that sums it up."

"Did Bellamy die in the war in Mexico?"

He sent her a sharp glance.

"Recall," she prompted, "what thy cousin spoke in his delirium. He seemed to be justifying himself to his father that he hadn't killed Bellamy."

Dev tried to think what this might have meant. Unable to, he finally shrugged. "Jack was merely another private in a vast army. He couldn't have killed his brother. He was delirious after all."

"Sometimes our truest feelings come out in dreams or nightmares."

He glanced sideways, now wanting to turn the conversation away from his family and its conflicts. "Do you have nightmares, Miss Cathwell?"

"I am human, Colonel."

Then he recalled her telling him the story of Honoree's sister Shiloh. He nodded and, his tongue loosening, asked, "Are you still trying to discover where your friend who was sold south might have ended up?"

"That is the primary reason Honoree and I came south."

He stared at her. The idea of her actually looking for her friend still flabbergasted him. "Do you really think you'll be able to find her? Two women? In the middle of a war?"

Faith considered him in the waning light. "Neither of us — Honoree nor I — could even contemplate coming south before the war. An abolitionist and a free black? Both of us would have been in danger." She spoke resolutely. "Yet one fact is certain. If I did not come, I would never find Shiloh."

He realized that though she was unlike most other women, in an unexpected way, she was similar in temperament to his genteel but tenacious mother. The sunset was dimming, and he should get her back before dark. "I will accompany you to your tent." He expected an argument, but she merely rose.

He folded the camp stools and set them inside. Then he offered her his arm and they set off.

"Thy family is from Maryland," she commented as they threaded their way through the tents and men. "My mother and Honoree's mother are also from a tobacco plantation there."

"Really." He wondered which plantation, but he was finished with conversation about families for this evening.

Still, he breathed easier. This woman and her conversations had calmed his mind.

"My mother met and married my father in Pennsylvania," she continued. "He's deaf. We communicate with him through finger signs."

He looked at her sharply.

"Just checking to see if thee was listening." She sent him a saucy grin.

He smiled but kept walking in silence.

"I know thee feels indebted to me, and I don't want to impose. But if any opportunity presents itself, would thee get permission to help me pursue a bit of information we've gleaned?"

"About what?"

"Shiloh may be on a plantation called Annerdale, near here."

"What makes you think this is a credible lead?"

"Shiloh is very distinctive in her appearance. She is light-skinned with golden-brown hair and green eyes like mine."

Dev absorbed these details. He wanted to ask many questions about Shiloh, but since the situation and the request were disturbing him, he refrained. He gave the only reply he could. "I am at your disposal, but only if my duties permit. And if we gain permission to go into enemy territory."

"I understand." As they walked around a knot of men, he tucked her a bit closer, protectively. A few glanced at them with inquisitive expressions, but Dev kept her near.

Within steps of the women's tent, they encountered Armstrong and Honoree. His suspicions about their growing attachment must have been correct. He bowed to Faith and nodded to her friend. Armstrong bade the women good night, and the two of them walked in silence back to their tent.

Inside, Armstrong helped Dev undress for bed, a nightly ritual. "You're interested in Honoree?" Dev asked finally.

"I do find her very . . . interesting. It's time I found myself a wife."

And she is free and has family far from here,
Dev added silently.

"Honoree is very eager to seek her sister," Armstrong said.

Dev did not want to discuss this. "So I understand."

Armstrong accepted the snub and they went on with their routine.

Much as Dev hated to admit it, once Armstrong left, he might be completely alone. The thought sucked away the remainder of his energy and he fell onto his cot, hoping for swift sleep and no nightmares. He was human too.

After breakfast the next morning, Faith and Honoree entered the camp hospital tent in time to speak to the night nurses before they left to eat breakfast and then retire to their cots and sleep.

On the way there, Faith had told Honoree about requesting help from the colonel to go to Annerdale. Honoree had not seemed very impressed. Faith sensed she did not like the colonel or trust him.

Faith had no time to think on what the colonel had revealed about his family. After the most recent battle, the camp hospital was so filled with wounded that there was barely room to walk between the cots, and many new patients lay upon the ground with only a blanket between them and the dirt. The crush of duty nearly overwhelmed her.

Unlike most of the nurses, Faith wore few crinolines under her skirt so she could pass more easily between patients. The suffering surrounding her wrenched Faith's heart and she began praying silently, *God, help us. God, help us save some.*

Despair whispered, *No one can save them.* She shoved this out of her mind. Just outside, at one end of the large hospital tent, a Sanitary Commission worker tended a kettle of porridge on a trivet over a small fire. The advance to Vicksburg continued. Along with the other morning nurses, Faith began to feed the wounded who could not feed themselves.

Ella McCullough, the young wife who was becoming a faithful volunteer, entered the hospital and came over to Faith. "May I help again today, Miss Faith?"

"Of course, Ella McCullough. We can always use another pair of helping hands." Faith leaned closer. "After thee finishes feeding the patients, I insist thee eat some too."

The young girl blushed but nodded, not denying that extra food would be welcome.

"I will. Thank you."

Faith watched the young woman receive her first bowl of porridge and begin feeding a patient. The girl should be at home, not forced to elope because she and her husband supported the Union and Tennessee had seceded. Faith surmised that Ella's husband must lack family and land of his own and was forced to bring her into danger with him. She was not alone. Many wives with no other resources had "followed the drum," as it was called. Some even brought children with them to the camp, and no doubt the Confederate Army also had women and children in its midst. Faith closed her eyes a moment praying for all such women.

She drew in a breath, aware of a sense of impending disaster hanging over the hospital. The young Ella looked fretful, and with good reason. Everyone knew the push to Vicksburg would go on — maybe they would even get there today.

Faith tried not to think about all these things. She greeted the next patient, a captain. "Good morning. Let me help thee eat breakfast." She propped up the captain, too weak to help himself, and began feeding him, spoonful by spoonful.

Then in the distance she heard gunfire.

Though it was what she'd been expecting to hear, she nearly upset the bowl she held.

"No rest for the wicked," the captain muttered in the sudden surrounding quiet. Ella glanced in the direction of the gunfire, obviously strained with worry. All around, the nurses, doctors, and even those patients who were moaning with pain became silent, listening intently. Their comrades were facing hot lead.

And Colonel Knight would be at the forefront. Perhaps at this very moment. Suddenly she couldn't breathe, but slowly she forced herself to inhale. "If thee doesn't mind," Faith said, raising her voice so that all could hear, "may I pray?"

Her patient nodded.

She spooned more porridge into his mouth and said aloud, "Heavenly Father, please protect our men and give our leaders wisdom and insight so that they may achieve their ends swiftly and with as little loss of life as possible. Our complete dependence is upon thee, since only thee can bring us victory and an end to this battle and this war. In Christ's name, amen."

*Amen*s echoed around the room. Faith heard Ella's soft one, somewhat belated as if she'd been praying silently. The battle was the Lord's. Faith added inwardly, *Please,*

Lord, protect Colonel Knight. He has an honest heart. She nearly shuddered, thinking that this caring man would be killing other men today. Or might be killed himself. *Oh, Father.*

As Faith continued feeding the hungry, Honoree began singing an old song with her low, rich voice. " 'Hold on. Hold on. Keep your hand on the plow; just hold on.' "

Occasionally the battle sounds competed with Honoree's voice, but it was strong and resonant and lifted Faith's spirits and quieted their patients. Ella finished the last breakfast for a patient and went back to sit and eat her meal alone.

Dr. Dyson entered the hospital and shouted, "Stop that infernal singing, girl!"

Kneeling by a patient on the floor, in the midst of washing his face, Honoree stopped and looked at the doctor.

"You shut up!" several voices rose as one. "Let her sing!" A palpable wave of anger swept through the conscious men, all directed at Dyson.

Dyson looked like he'd been struck.

Eyeing the man, Honoree began singing again. " 'I shall not be moved. When my cross is heavy, I shall not be moved.' "

Faith hid a smile and continued feeding her patient, her heart praying for Colonel

Knight, whom she realized now she'd begun to care for — even though he was killing and wounding men today. A Quakeress caring for a man of war, an abolitionist caring for a slaveholder. Hopeless, foolish beyond measure.

Once again scouting toward Vicksburg, Dev reined in his horse, who snorted and pranced.

Sniper fire.

"Spread out!" he commanded his men. If they didn't, the snipers might start picking them off. Then he heard rapid gunfire. No doubt others of his men were encountering the rear guard of the Confederates, Pemberton's soldiers. On the heels of yesterday's victory, Grant was pressing on to Vicksburg, trying to stop the Rebs from reaching cover in the fortified city.

Dev sent two of his riders back to the main body of the advancing army to give this report. "Forward!" Dev gestured at the company around him.

Soon Dev glimpsed a number of Confederate troops ahead of him positioned behind swampland in front of a river. They'd put bales of cotton ahead of them and before that an abatis — an outdated military defense consisting of mere branches of trees stuck in the ground in a row, with their sharpened tops directed toward the enemy. Even with obstacles in place, this defensive position showed that Pemberton was no one to lead these men. Dev mentally excoriated the Confederate general's lack of strategy. He should have positioned all his men with the river before them, not behind them! No wise general took up such an untenable position. He'd heard that Pemberton had graduated from West Point, no doubt at the bottom of his class.

"Dismount!" Dev slid from the saddle and, along with the rest of his company, handed the reins to several men who were taking their turns remaining in the rear to hold the horses. The US cavalry acted as scouts and as dragoons, which meant fighting mounted or on foot when necessary. "Spread out and join in!"

His men obeyed and he followed suit. The main body of the army was advancing close at their backs. Pemberton must know that. "Fool," Dev cursed under his breath.

The infantry arrived at the cavalry's rear within minutes and Dev's companies blended into their ranks. The artillery rolled into place and began barking hot lead over their heads. The blues swept onward, some sinking waist-deep in the swampy loop left by the meandering river. All under fierce attack took positions wherever they could hunker down. Still their assault on Pemberton's forces was relentless and without mercy. The blues drove the grays back toward the river. Some of the cotton bales, hit by hot grapeshot, caught fire. Dev cursed their general again.

The gray line finally broke. The Reb drum call for retreat came. Gray soldiers poured onto the bridge over the river, but others boarded a steamboat on the river, crowding it dangerously. A bullet seared Dev's cheek; he ducked down. Ahead, the remaining Rebs did their utmost to protect the retreating soldiers.

The blue wave steadily pushed more and more grays onto the bridge or the steamboat to escape across the river. Dev urged his men on. If they could catch the Rebs out here, Vicksburg would fall quickly without defense. The killing could end . . . here.

The man beside Dev screamed and fell. Dev dropped to one knee to help him. Dead. Dev closed his eyes and, crouching, moved forward. They had to stop the Rebs from getting to Vicksburg. If they could halt them now . . .

A shell burst and Dev fell to the ground, covering his head with his arms.

Faith's face flashed in Dev's mind. He shoved it aside. He had to stay alive. That was all he had to do today. Just stay alive. With honor.

When the gunfire finally fell silent, Dr. Bryant harried the wagoneers to set out. At the edge of the usual commotion of gathering supplies for the wounded and getting teams of horses harnessed, Honoree and Faith stood outside a hospital tent, overseeing the loading of fresh bandages and stretchers. Ella was busy filling canteens for the nurses to take with them.

Faith tried to focus on what she was doing, but Colonel Knight's face lingered in her mind. Did he still live? Had they stopped the Rebel retreat?

"You!" Dr. Dyson appeared out of nowhere. "You, girl," he said belligerently to Honoree. "Go with the wagons."

Faith moved with Honoree, heading to their tent to get more supplies for the battlefield wounded.

"Not you, Quaker," he snapped. "Just the girl. You stay here."

Faith turned. "Wherever Honoree goes, I go. Thee knows that."

"You're not in charge here. Now for once do what you're told."

Faith stared at him, taking Honoree's hand. She lowered her voice and leaned close so he could hear above the surrounding voices and noise. "Thee knows that we are volunteer nurses and thee has no real authority over us."

His face flushed.

"Please do not embarrass thyself any further. Now either I go with her or Honoree stays here with me."

Only hours after engagement, Dev watched the Rebs burn the bridge behind them. Flames shot skyward, white smoke boiling high. The sun blazed over them and the fire heated the air in undulating, transparent waves. Ash fell around him. Dev waited as some of his men gathered close.

"McClernand again?" one of them said with disgust.

Dev didn't reply, but he felt the same. Grant had tried to prevent the Rebs from retreating to the fortified city, but the Union's own General McClernand had failed to move quickly enough to stop Pemberton. Now the bridge over Black River was destroyed and the steamboat that had ferried all the live Rebs away also burned, sending flame and smoke skyward. Disgust roiled in Dev's belly. Two incompetent officers, one on each side, had cost lives. Both were equally culpable in today's slaughter. Pemberton should have gotten his troops across the river, then burned the bridge and steamboat to hinder the Union advance. No general worth his salt would back any of his men up against a natural obstruction. How many Rebs lay dead because of that foolish decision?

"Let's regroup and see what casualties we've suffered," Dev said, channeling his ire.

The few men around him nodded, their faces streaked with gunpowder and sweat. They turned and began threading their way through the wounded, picking out fallen comrades. Dev again thought of Faith. He did not like the idea of her facing this carnage. But stopping her was not his responsibility — on the contrary, he deemed it an impossibility.

A hand gripped his trouser leg. "Water."

Dev dropped to his knee, opened his canteen, and helped the soldier drink. He surveyed the man and quickly devised a tourniquet for his leg. "The hospital wagons will come soon." He squeezed the man's shoulder and moved away, still searching for his own men.

The first of the Sanitary Commission

wagons appeared on the eastern horizon. Dev scanned the nurses perched high on the benches. He thought he glimpsed the Quakeress's distinctive bonnet. He hoped he was mistaken and she was back at the hospital.

Then he noticed one of his men lying nearby. Dev hurried to him and helped him sip water from his canteen. He did a cursory survey of the man. He appeared to be suffering from a saber slash that had cut through his scalp. Dev whipped off his neckerchief and tied up the man's wound. "Help's on the way."

The man tried to speak but couldn't.

"Lie still. I'll stay with you till your head clears."

The man closed his eyes and let out a long sigh.

Dev recalled the black girl's dazed condition after the battle at Champion Hill. He scanned the field, spotting others of his men kneeling by comrades, as well as the nurses, now moving through the wounded, pausing with water and giving assistance.

Then Faith appeared beside Dev. Relief flooded him.

Without a word, she ran her hands over his comrade's bandaged wound.

The man opened his eyes and mumbled.

"I don't think he is severely injured. It would be best if thee would help him to rise slowly —" she put out her hand to guide Dev — "in stages. Sitting, then kneeling, and so on. Assist him to the wagons or help him back to camp."

"Our horses are near," Dev said.

Another of his men approached with a horse as if he'd overheard them. "I'll help you get him up, sir."

Dev put an arm around the wounded man and slowly shifted him to a sitting position.

Faith lifted off the dressing Dev had applied to the man's head wound and poured something out of a vial from her pocket. "I'm using this to clean the wound." Then, prodding the skin together, she expertly and tightly bandaged the slash. "That will do for now. He may need stitches, but the more seriously wounded will take precedence."

The man moaned but seemed to be coming back to himself. "My head."

Dev helped him to his knees and then to his feet, supporting him for a moment. Soon he and the other man lifted him to lie across the saddle.

"Your horse is over there, sir," the cavalry-man said, motioning toward a copse of trees where a private remained with the few horses that hadn't yet been claimed.

"See this man back to the camp hospital, Corporal," Dev ordered.

The man saluted and led the laden horse away.

Faith had already moved several feet away from him, kneeling beside a man who was screaming uncontrollably and thrashing. He nearly knocked Faith off her feet.

Dev hurried over to help her. He dropped down across from her and grasped the man's waving arms.

"He is out of his mind with pain," Faith said. She slipped another vial from her pocket and put it to the man's lips. She managed to dribble some of the dark liquid into him. "Laudanum," she murmured.

Within a few minutes he calmed enough for her to examine him. Dev watched as she shut her eyes for a moment as if gathering strength, then reopened them. She looked at Dev and shook her head. She rose and moved away.

The action was so unlike her that Dev didn't follow for a few beats, but then he jumped to his feet and caught up with her.

She leaned toward him. "His wounds were abdominal. I hope the laudanum will send him into unconsciousness so he won't suffer more. There are others I may still be able to help."

Dev absorbed this like a jab to his own midsection. He hadn't realized that this young lady was forced to make these kinds of judgments.

She didn't wait for him but moved on.

He felt compelled to follow her. Someone had to help her.

Several hours passed. Finally Dev and Faith's multiple canteens were empty. She rose and stumbled.

He caught her arm. "We need water too." He glanced toward the river.

"That water will be defiled with blood and worse. Come to the wagon. They have well water in barrels." She led him away.

"I must check on my horse." He turned and strode toward the copse of trees.

Dev told the private there to go back to camp with both their mounts and see to them. Then he hurried to the nearest Sanitary Commission wagon and found Faith and Honoree nearby. Both were filling canteens. The sound of trickling water brought his thirst rushing to the surface.

She turned and took his canteen from him and filled it. "Drink what thee needs."

She paused in her duties and lifted her own canteen to her lips. "We must keep ourselves watered or we will be unable to help others. Thee is staying?"

He swallowed. "Yes."

"Thee sustained no hurt but this?" She touched his cheek.

He winced and reached up to touch where she had. "Must have been grazed. Lucky again."

"I do not believe in luck. I believe in Providence." She wet a handkerchief and dabbed at his cheek.

He knew he should object. It was such a small wound and so many injured soldiers were spread out around them, but her touch was so gentle he could not break away. Then she dabbed some oil on it from another vial in her pocket. "Let us fill the rest of my canteens."

He took them from her and began using the dipper to fill them.

She smiled and turned to the wagoneer. "I need some more bandages, please. And I forgot hardtack."

Soon the two of them were supplied with what they needed. Faith looked to him. "Remember, thee can go back at any time. Thee did thy part already."

He nodded. "I know. Let's begin."

She smiled then, and a warmth that had nothing to do with the Mississippi summer burst inside him.

■ ■ ■ ■

Well into the night, Dev caught Faith's arm again when she stumbled.

"I'm out of everything," she told him.

"Let's go to the wagons, then."

"Yes."

She allowed him to take her arm. Ahead, Dev glimpsed Honoree already slumped in the back of the nearest wagon.

"I'm glad you two are ready to go," the wagoneer greeted them gruffly. "I've got a full load and must leave."

Faith wobbled on the step up to the high wagon bench.

Dev picked her up and lifted her onto the bench. He sat down, still holding her.

"That's a good idea," the driver said. "I'm always afraid she's going to fall off."

Faith shook her head and slipped out of Dev's arms.

The wagon shifted under them as the driver turned it toward camp. In the darkness Dev slipped a protective arm around Faith's waist. He expected her to object, but she made no demur. To be able to help this selfless woman even in this small way gave him a satisfaction he'd never known.

He remembered her request then about

going to a plantation to seek the girl Shiloh. The possibility of finding Honoree's sister was almost nonexistent, like the proverbial needle in a haystack — and in the middle of a war. He shook his head. Women could be so unrealistic.

Yet being close to her, even under these conditions, made him feel something he barely recognized, something tender and protective and for her alone. If only they weren't in the midst of a war, a war he wouldn't survive.

CHAPTER 6

At the break of the next day, Dev and the other cavalry officers gathered to receive orders from Brigadier General Osterhaus at his tent. Grant had the Confederates on the run, and he was determined to halt them before they reached Vicksburg, high on the bluff above the Mississippi River. Today promised to be as hot and uncomfortable as the last. But in the cool of the morning, Dev listened to the orders and then turned to leave the tent and go to his men.

Thoughts of Faith tried to break his concentration. He forced them away. He had to be about his business, and his business was war. Near the horse corral and tents, he gathered his company leaders and issued them their orders about the push to stop the Confederates. After losing so many men and horses in the past two days, their mood appeared very grim, but that was to be expected. Along with them, Dev mounted and headed toward the front, toward the Black River. Somehow they must cross it and catch up with the Rebs.

A sense of urgency tingled through him, and he could sense it in the men around him. If they didn't stop the Rebs before they reached the city, who knew how long Vicksburg could hold out in a state of siege? Sieges were nasty business.

The crack of gunfire. One of his men dropped from the saddle. A bushwhacker was near. Another of his men paused to help their wounded comrade while the rest of their companies spread out in the high grass, leaning low over their horses. Dev focused his attention. *We must get the Rebs.*

In her tent, Faith rose and felt as if she'd been struck by a train. This march to Vicksburg was pushing them all to their limits. Then, unaccountably, a sweet sensation overcame her, the memory of the colonel lifting her in his arms last night.

On her way to the washbowl and pitcher, she stopped and let the memory spread through her. For those few fleeting moments, she'd wanted to nestle deeper into his strength and stay there. But of course she'd resisted and he'd set her on the wagon bench, thereafter only steadying her as they negotiated the bumpy road.

Already dressed for the day, Honoree glanced in through the tent opening. "You just going to stand there all day?" she asked with a tart edge to her voice.

Faith smiled ruefully and moved to the basin of tepid water to freshen up. So many newly wounded needed them, and though Honoree tried to hide behind gruffness how much she cared about their patients, she never deceived Faith. "It was very thoughtful of Armstrong to set up our tent last night," Faith said, changing the subject.

"He is considerate and knows our work keeps us going till dark or after," Honoree agreed. "We need to get to breakfast and to the camp hospital."

Faith heard the urgency in her friend's voice and quickly brushed her hair, braided it, and coiled it under her cap. "Let's be off then." When they left their tent, they found young Ella waiting outside to walk with them on their way to the hospital tent. Faith invited her to join them for breakfast at the mess tent for medical staff, which was bending the rules. But the girl helped them and deserved at least a good breakfast.

For a moment the number of wounded men — thousands in just the past few days — threatened to overwhelm her. She forced herself to reflect on one of her favorite psalms: *"God is my refuge and strength, a very present help in trouble."* She could not survive on her ability alone. *God, fill me with thy enduring power.*

After breakfast, when they reached the hospital tents, Armstrong was waiting outside one of them. "Good morning, ladies."

Honoree tried to hide her beaming smile. And failed. Faith hid her understanding grin, relishing the idea that her friend might have found love in the midst of war. Faith shied away once more from thinking of the colonel. Yet again he would be at the forefront, in danger every moment. Her pulse sped up.

Ella paused just ahead of them at the hospital tent, looking somewhat confused by Armstrong's presence.

"I came to offer my services." Armstrong held up a hand to stop any objection. "The days are long and my duties slim. I'm here to fetch and carry and lift."

"Thank thee." Faith accepted his hand and shook it. "Come."

Ella stopped Faith with a hand on her sleeve. "Miss Faith?"

"What is it, Ella McCullough?"

Armstrong and Honoree proceeded into

the hospital.

Ella waited and then asked right by Faith's ear, "Why did you shake hands with that colored man?"

Faith sighed silently. "I did so because I was grateful for his offer of help."

"But whites don't shake hands with coloreds."

Faith pressed her lips together. "Ella, thee noticed the first time we spoke that I am a Quaker. Many Quakers treat people of color as lesser, but my family never did. Honoree and I grew up together, almost as cousins."

Ella stared at her. "It ain't right. Blacks and whites don't mix. They got their place and we got ours."

Faith decided she would gain nothing with further persuasion. The majority of whites north and south would echo what Ella had just stated. "We need to go in and relieve the night nurses."

Ella nodded and followed Faith inside.

Limp with fatigue, the night nurses could barely relay information about their new patients. Faith and Honoree began their rounds, Ella helping as much as she could.

The army had moved, leaving behind the hospital near Jackson and their patients there. But the new fighting had produced many new patients here. And no end in sight.

Ella managed to draw near to Faith. "Can I ask you — is that black man courtin' Honoree?"

Faith smiled. "I don't know if he is, but I think he might like to."

Ella shook her head. "Maybe that's best. Honoree won't have to worry about him."

Faith understood. Ella had a young husband to worry about, and she . . . she had someone to worry about as well, much as it pained her to admit it. Then she heard gunfire in the distance.

More killing today.

More dying today.

More wounded today.

For a moment she was drowning. She gasped for God. His peace did not come. Or was it there, and she just couldn't receive it? She envisioned the colonel riding toward danger.

God, please help.

When Dev and his company reached the Black River again, the question of how to cross its depth had already been assessed and addressed. The army engineers were busy building a bridge to cross the river on what looked like bales of cotton.

The engineers waved to them, and soon his men had dismounted and were moving through the water with the cotton bales, setting them where told to and then laying sheeting over them. Dev had a hard time believing what he, a cavalry officer, was doing. But cotton was all the engineers had to work with, and he wouldn't order his men to work while he stood by, idly watching.

Bushwhackers kept up the pressure, so they worked hunched over, giving less of a target but with their backs aching. Finally the bridge was completed. Holding their fire-arms and ammunition belts over their heads, Dev and his company chose to swim their horses across. They must get to the other side and root out the snipers or make them flee.

Grant needed the cavalry to be his eyes, needed them to relay information about Pemberton's actions. Grant must halt the enemy. Or they'd suffer a siege in the steamy heat of a Mississippi summer. Dev nearly despaired.

Then he thought of Faith. He saw her again, moving among the wounded to the point of collapse. Quick action could save lives. Determination flooded him. "Spread out! And keep your heads down!"

■ ■ ■ ■

Grant hadn't prevented the Rebs from reaching Vicksburg. The dreaded siege had begun. Now the noise of the daily artillery barrage aimed at the city ceased for the evening meal. The pattern had been set. Three times a day the almost-constant barrage halted for meals.

A numbed Faith, her senses battered, sat in the hospital mess tent on a hard bench and tried to drink yet another cup of wretched coffee. The Union forces surrounding a besieged Vicksburg — what they and no doubt the Confederates had dreaded most.

As usual she sat at the colored table with Honoree and the workers hired from the contraband camp. She refused to observe the degrading separation.

"How long this shellin' gon' last?" asked the large laundress Faith had hired near the Jackson depot.

"As long as it must to break the Rebs in Vicksburg and take control of the Mississippi," Honoree replied.

"The Confederates won't be able to get

any help from the West, then, or any trade through New Orleans," Faith added.

The others at the table nodded solemnly.

In the two days after the Confederates had reached the cover of Vicksburg, General Grant had attempted to rush them, shake them from the city while they were demoralized from their defeat. The onslaught had failed at dreadful cost. Thousands more soldiers had been killed or wounded.

Restless, Faith rose, unable to sit any longer. "I must walk." She gripped Honoree's shoulder and then hurried from the tent, her feet carrying her exactly where she should not go. Her need to see the colonel overcame her good sense. And as she thought she would, she found the colonel tending his own horse in the makeshift corral near the rear of the encampment.

She watched him from outside the fence rigged around the horses. Other cavalrymen were also grooming their horses. She knew she should leave. She was revealing much of what she felt just standing here gazing at his deft movements, listening to his quiet, one-sided conversation with his horse. She leaned the side of her head against a post, unable to pull herself away.

Then he saw her.

The sudden glad recognition in the change

of his expression burned through her like rays from the Mississippi sun. "Miss Cathwell."

"Colonel."

"What do you need, miss?"

She had no answer for him. She needed to speak to him, to be with him. She must not allow this. But she had come anyway.

Then the evening barrage started up again and she couldn't help herself. Tears welled in her eyes. She turned away and began to hurry somewhere, anywhere else.

Within seconds, the colonel caught up with her. He claimed her arm and halted her. He leaned close to her ear and declared, "I will walk with you if you please."

Again she knew she should make her excuses and return to her tent and rest. But she could not. Something within her craved this man's company and she could not refuse him. She nodded, not meeting his gaze.

He offered her his arm, and she slipped a hand into the crook of his elbow. He smelled of leather and horse, a pleasant aroma that reminded her of home. For a moment the scent drew her back to Sharpesburg as a young girl, helping her father groom their horses in the barn, standing close to him, happy in his loving presence. As she clung to the colonel's strong arm, feeling him close, she was able to draw a full breath for the first time that day. And some of her fatigue melted away.

She wanted to broach going to the plantation named Annerdale to see if Shiloh or news of her could be found there. Yet she hesitated, not desiring to spoil this brief respite and the pleasure of their companionable silence.

Dev had no idea why Faith had sought him out, but he was absurdly glad she had. In spite of her presence, his army's failure to keep the Rebs from hunkering down in Vicksburg twisted and moved inside him like the gears of a slow waterwheel. How long would it take for them to root the Confederates out?

He shoved all such thoughts from his mind, forcing himself to merely revel in the presence of this woman who shouldn't be here but who was. From the corner of his eye, he examined the soft contour of her cheek, unhappy to see evidence that she was becoming drawn. No doubt from fatigue. A few wisps of her pale hair had slid out of their pins and tantalized him. He almost felt the soft skin of her nape as he imagined brushing the hair back into place. He held

himself in strict control, merely being grateful that she had sought him out.

They walked to his tent, where he brought
out camp stools and set them at the entrance as before. While inside, he'd also dug
out of his trunk a tin of individually
wrapped hard candies and now offered it to
her. She chose one and sat opposite him.
He tried not to stare at her, though conversation was impossible under the booming
cannons. They would all leave this war deafened.

Finally twilight fell and the artillery
company halted for the night. The sudden
silence hit him in waves. For a few minutes
he could hear nothing. Then the evening
sounds returned, insects humming, voices
nearby, and finally the woman beside him
saying his name.

He looked directly into her eyes. "Miss
Cathwell?"

She sighed. "What a relief."

He nodded. "You appear to be distressed."
Then he realized how ridiculous that obser-
vation was. They were all distressed.

She smiled at him ruefully. "I have a vex-
ing situation. Someone is stealing supplies
from the food stores for our patients."

He shook his head. "Unfortunately that is
a problem in every branch of any army."

She looked away as if uncertain of what she wanted to say now. "And I'm still wanting to follow up on our information about Honoree's sister. Is there any chance we might pursue this now while the army is at a standstill?"

He wished she hadn't brought up this doomed venture. But he must deal with it. "In light of this siege, I will ask about taking leave to accompany you."

"Thank thee." She sighed. Then she voiced the question everyone wanted the answer to. "How long till we breach their defenses and put this dreadful siege to an end?"

"We won't." He wondered why he was telling her the truth. He should be comforting her, softening the dreadful truth for this lady. That's what he'd been taught a gentleman did. But if he proceeded that way with this lady, she would view it as a lack of respect and would react with contempt. He drew up the truth. "The fact is the Rebs will surrender eventually." He pressed his lips together, thinking about the conditions within the city. "Probably due to starvation. They can't get supplies from land or the river. We have them boxed in."

"Why don't they just surrender now?"

"Pride. Perhaps hope that General Johnston will come to their rescue."

"Will he?"

"I doubt it." He inhaled the hot air. "Let's talk of something else."

"Yes." She closed her eyes for a moment before regarding him again. "Often I like to think of my garden." Her tone was hesitant.

"Garden? Here?"

"Not here," she said, teasing. "I have an extensive garden at home, and I like to think of the plants I will have after . . . after this war is over. I have even gathered seeds as we've moved south."

"What kind of garden?" He grasped at this topic, so removed from the business of war. "What kind of seeds?"

The corners of her mouth lifted.

He longed to reach out and run his fingertips over the soft lips. Instead he merely savored the thought. And wondered why, after all his lonely years as a career soldier, this woman had penetrated his defenses.

"I've always been interested in herbs and their uses for healing." She pulled a small cloth bag from her apron pocket and opened it, bringing out a few dried flowers. "This is verbena. A pretty flower and an herb that will help a wound heal with less risk of infection."

He shifted his full attention to her, accepting the dried flower.

"I have over thirty healing herbs in my garden and have collected around ten more as we moved through Tennessee and south to Mississippi." She looked to him. "What does thee collect?"

Her unexpected question delighted him. "Books."

"Ah." Her tone was approving and she smiled again. "What books interest thee?"

"I like the classics: Aristotle, Ovid, the Greek playwrights."

"Does thee read in Latin?"

He nodded. "The dead language is so much more exact than ours."

She chuckled. "I have an older brother who studied at Oberlin College in Ohio. He used to chant Latin declensions as he worked in the kitchen garden with me."

"I was an only child. Do you have a large family?"

"Modest. There remain six of us siblings."

"Remain?"

"Two older siblings died very young before I was born, but . . . I also had a sister, a twin sister. Patience." She bowed her head. "We lost her when she was only nineteen. A fever."

"I'm sorry." True regret enriched his voice.

"She planned to study to be a midwife,

and I was going to help her practice with my skill with healing herbs." Her voice caught on the last word. "When she died, it was like half of me was torn away, and within weeks Shiloh was kidnapped. I think that's why losing Shiloh hurt so deeply. It was like losing Patience all over again. We must find her."

He gingerly patted her hand, then drew back.

She inhaled a deep breath and plainly erased sorrow from her expression. "How many books does thee own? And where are they now?"

Though touched by her bravery in pursuing their conversation, he chuckled. "I brought my ten favorites with me. The rest are at my mother's home in Baltimore."

"I'm glad to hear thee laugh. How many books in all?" she pressed him.

He chuckled again. "I've never counted, but one wall is covered with bookshelves and more are piled around the room. My mother shakes her head but doesn't remonstrate with me."

Faith shut her eyes as if picturing the room. "Is it a small room or large?"

"Average, I suppose."

"How many windows?"

"Two tall ones. The ceiling of the room is

high, and the other walls are wainscoted in oak. I've often thought that I would like to have another wall done in bookshelves, but I haven't asked my mother."

"Thee doesn't have thy own home, then?" She glanced at him.

"No, I've spent most of my life moving here and there according to the army. My mother keeps my old room and the study for my use when I'm home."

"Thee is a nomad?"

This time he laughed — a clean, hearty sound to his own ears. "I suppose so. A Bedouin perhaps?"

She smiled. "I don't see thee in a turban and robe."

"You are the most interesting woman."

She shook her head. "I am merely myself."

Yes, you are. Everything within him wanted to pull her to her feet and wrap his arms around her. He sat very still, willing this to pass. It was merely the situation they were in and her innate bravery that drew him to her. They were not suited for each other, and he would surely remain a bachelor for the rest of his days . . . however few they might be.

In the shelling lull around breakfast, Osterhaus acknowledged Dev's salute. Dev had

145

come to request leave to find out where Annerdale Plantation was and to go there to ask about Shiloh. Though he didn't really want to pursue this lead, he would hate disappointing Miss Faith.

Osterhaus addressed him before he could make his request. "General Grant has decided you are the man for this job."

What job? This didn't sound promising. But it would provide him an excuse to put off asking about the plantation. In this dreadful time of war and disruption, he foresaw disappointment at Annerdale. Slaves were fleeing masters every day. And the girl might never have been there. Better Faith keep her bit of hope for success than have it shattered so soon. "Sir?"

"A number of the contraband have asked to enlist in the army to fight for the Union."

Once again the Emancipation Proclamation, issued early this year, came to the forefront of discussion. It had altered the purpose of the war from merely keeping the Union together to freeing the South's slaves. This would change everything for the South. Did his uncle Kane Carroll home in Maryland realize the potential impact of this shift? How could a plantation survive without free labor?

Then Dev recalled that he had relayed one

of these contraband requests himself. Was that why he had been chosen? "Sir?"

"General Grant has authorized the forming of an African Brigade of around six hundred men. You will be the senior officer in charge of training them. We will let you choose your subordinates to help in this. The recruits will need to be outfitted in uniforms, trained in basic formation marching and military courtesy, and of course taught to shoot straight."

Dev took a moment to digest this. Arming black men? Former slaves? Some part of him reared up in dissent, but he pushed it down. The Union Army needed every man in order to win and put an end to this war. "The general is sure that I am the man for this job?"

"He didn't say why he chose you, but you're the one he wanted to begin this training. He's still deciding who will take permanent command of the brigade."

Dev wondered what Grant's reasoning had been, but it was not for him to ask. "Where are the enlistees?"

"They are assembled at the rear near the quartermaster's tents." Then, abruptly, the after-breakfast shelling started with a blast, and Osterhaus raised his voice. "You can begin today. We want them ready for duty within two weeks at the most."

Dev silently reeled at this. Two weeks to train raw troops. Men who had come straight from slavery. What if they couldn't do it? What if he couldn't?

He was dismissed, so he saluted and left. He first went to his company and chose a few noncommissioned officers for assistants before heading to the quartermaster's tents near the rear of the camp.

As he approached, a sea of black faces turned to him. Those who had been sitting on the ground rose. He paused to decide what to do.

The quartermaster approached him. Leaning close, the man said, "As you can see, I have given them uniforms but I hesitated to issue them firearms yet."

Another disbelieving wave rolled over Dev. This endeavor hit him deeply as wrong. He imagined his uncle's face, and it was aghast. Dev recalled the shock that had vibrated through the slaveholding South when John Brown had tried to steal weapons from the armory at Harpers Ferry, Virginia, to arm slaves for bloody revolt. Dev let the emotion work through him, trying to dissipate it, shake it off. *I am not my uncle.*

Yet he couldn't so easily dismiss a lifetime of living with slavery. He knew that Armstrong would have made an admirable soldier. But thank God he'd never have to be one.

Now Dev had a job to do, this job. He saluted the quartermaster and turned to the recruits. "Men," he bellowed against the shelling behind him, "I am going to assemble you and begin to teach you how to conduct yourself as soldiers."

The recruits, almost as one, straightened and faced him squarely. He read the determination on each face. Because of the noise of the shelling, he and his sergeants moved to collect small groups of recruits to begin the work of teaching them how to salute and showing them marching order. After each man had been instructed, Dev and the sergeants led them farther to the rear, where they would have more room to move.

He ignored his reluctance as best he could. He was a soldier and these were his orders. And slavery would not survive this war. He admitted that but shut his mind to all the ramifications it would unleash.

The head cook of the hospital kitchen, a woman whom Faith had hired at the Jackson contraband camp, hurried inside the hospital tent and came straight to Faith late in the morning. "The thief at it again," the cook, named Mary Lou, spoke into Faith's ear. "We missin' a pan of corn bread, a big sack of beans, and a tub of lard."

Faith finished with her patient and led the cook outside into the heat of the sun. "This is distressing. The warning hasn't worked, then?"

"No, I think it jes might-a warn' our thief to be more careful," Mary Lou said with an ironic twist.

"Well, he might have taken the corn bread for his own appetite, but the other items he must be selling."

"Yes, and food so short round here, who know who he selling to." Mary Lou let an irritated look say, *Probably to Rebs.*

Faith gazed around at the camp. Nearby, in spite of the constant shelling, an infantry sergeant was holding a marching session for new recruits who'd just arrived from the North. The summer heat was wilting Faith's starched collar and cuffs. She wanted to go to Annerdale now. But the war held them captive here. So though she didn't want to deal with this issue, she must because food was scarce.

Till the Union controlled the whole length of the Mississippi, supplies would have a hard time reaching anyone — Union as well as Confederate. Rations had been reduced once already. Fresh irritation gripped her. Some soldier was profiting from selling much-needed supplies, if not to enemy troops, then perhaps to the locals surrounding them. She pitied the people who'd suffered hunger already and would continue to suffer, but the Union Army could barely feed themselves, much less the enemy. And the hospital mess was tasked with feeding the sick and wounded. She wanted to shake the thief, whoever he was.

"What we gon' do?" the cook prompted.

"Set a trap." Faith sent a determined look to the cook.

Both of Mary Lou's eyebrows rose. "What you proposin'?"

Faith pondered this. "I will think of something. And soon." She turned to go back to her patients. "Leave it to me."

The cook nodded and headed toward the large open kitchen nearby. "I will!"

Faith entered the hospital and ran straight into Dr. Dyson's path.

He stared at her, then brushed past her disrespectfully. "So you've finally found a man, a colonel to boot," he muttered. A sudden lapse in the artillery din made his comment audible not only to her but to a few of the patients nearby.

Faith stiffened but did not deign to reply.

She moved forward. As a woman in a field dominated by men, she was an easy target. And plainly Dr. Dyson was one of those sour individuals who were never happy unless someone else was unhappy. She moved Dyson out of her mind and tried to come up with a plan to catch a thief.

At the end of the long, hot day, Dev sat on his cot in his tent, clutching a cup of cold coffee during the supper cease-fire. Armstrong had gone off somewhere. The day of training the African Brigade had been demanding. He hadn't trained a large group of recruits for a long time, not since '61, and with the artillery barrage going full blast, he'd been forced to come up with hand signals instead of shouted orders — which made everything more exhausting.

He sorted through his thoughts, bringing them under his authority. The recruits had been eager to learn and intense in their desire to become soldiers. Part of him had reveled in that and another had despaired. They had run away from their masters and now would very likely die in battle. Which was better — life and slavery or freedom and death? Patrick Henry had declared, "Give me liberty, or give me death." And the new black soldiers appeared to agree.

His barrage-dulled ears identified Armstrong's voice just outside the tent. Dev nearly spoke his name, but he also heard Faith's friend's voice. His man was not alone.

"I will get us camp stools," Armstrong said.

Without thinking, Dev jostled his cup and lay down quickly as though napping. His eyes shut, he heard some movement and then Armstrong's voice as he returned outside. Dev just didn't want to face anyone right now, not even his trusted manservant.

"The colonel is sleeping," Armstrong said. "He has had a difficult and strenuous day training the recruits."

"I was surprised that General Grant allowed the contraband men to enlist," Honoree replied.

"He needs all the men he can get."

"Faith and I were hoping the colonel would have time to take us to that plantation to see about my sister."

"I'm afraid that will be delayed until this duty is done."

The girl sighed long and loudly.

"This war is worse," Armstrong commented. "Much worse than the Mexican War."

"You were there?"

"Yes, with the colonel. Or I should say the captain. That was his rank at the time. I was . . . We both were so much younger then. My fortieth birthday is only weeks away."

The reminder clutched Dev tightly. Another change. Another loss. Where was Jack? Was he still alive?

"I will enlist then," Armstrong said.

Dev stared at the inside of the tent and let shock roll over him. *No.*

"I wish you didn't need to, but I won't try to discourage you," Honoree said. "A freeman makes his own decisions."

"Honoree, you are the only good thing to come out of this wretched war," Armstrong said.

The girl chuckled, but the sound halted abruptly. "I don't like to think of you fighting."

For once, Dev was in complete agreement with her. Until recently he'd thought that after he freed Armstrong, life as he knew it would go on, except he would simply pay Armstrong wages. Now Dev knew that was not to be. What could he do to keep Armstrong safe? And the idea of losing Armstrong . . . one more loss. Unbearable.

CHAPTER 7

At the end of another day of ear-numbing shelling, Faith resisted the urge to seek out the colonel as she left the mess tent. She must overcome this attraction to a man who, while worthy according to his principles, did not embrace hers.

Within moments Honoree had gone off with Armstrong for their daily walk. Faith declined to accompany them in case they ended up at the colonel's tent. She returned alone to her tent and entered but then stood in the middle, coming to grips with her agitation. Or trying to. If Dr. Dyson had noticed her predilection for Colonel Knight's company, others must also. She did not think her reputation had suffered or would suffer, but she could not allow herself to become "entangled" in the midst of a war.

And with a man who owned a slave.

Whenever she recalled that Armstrong

belonged to the colonel, the idea unsettled her afresh. Unable to be still, she began pacing in the confined space. Armstrong didn't appear to be mistreated, so the colonel probably didn't realize that holding him in bondage was wrong, abusive in itself. In any case, was Armstrong really whom she was most concerned for? Thoughts, memories of Shiloh, had plagued her all day. *I want to be free myself — free to find Shiloh.*

She halted and bowed her head, seeking the Lord's peace, the peace that humans could not know without him. She asked for Christ's light, the Inner Light, to glow within her, a light in the darkness, her comfort in the midst of this war.

As much solace as she derived from her moments in the colonel's presence, she must steer clear of him. But he was the only one she could count on to help her go to Annerdale Plantation to seek Shiloh. Frustration consumed her. He was her opposite; he was her friend; he was her thorn in the flesh.

On this, the third day of training, Dev had brought along some other members of his regiment so he could break the African Brigade down into even smaller squads in order to teach them how to load, clean, and fire their Colt sidearms and Springfield rifles.

He still grappled with arming blacks who, until recently, had been slaves. After being born and raised in a slave state, he could barely reconcile this decision with what he'd been taught all his life. Faith's image came to mind. She was frowning at him.

He dismissed this illusion and focused on the job at hand, on the group of African Brigade recruits gathered around one of his sergeants. The unceasing noise of artillery forced the men to huddle close around the sergeant in order to watch and hear his instructions, barely giving him room to maneuver his rifle. Dev watched the intent black faces around him. And when he recalled Armstrong's intention to enlist, he imagined him here, learning how to fight. Caustic dread filled him.

"Men, this is a rifle, not a musket," the sergeant said, holding the weapon loosely in his hands. "Now, muskets have very poor performance. A rifle is so called because of the rifling inside the barrel."

He ran his hand along the underside of the barrel. "Rifling causes the ball to spin." He demonstrated by rotating his index finger. "A spinning ball goes farther and straighter than a musket ball, and with greater destructive accuracy."

Dev tried to keep his focus on the earnest face of each new recruit, not letting his imagination bring Armstrong here. Did these men realize that rifles would also be pointed at them? Could rip into their flesh and snuff out their lives?

"Sir," a tall, thoughtful-looking recruit named Carson asked, "how does riflin' make the ball spin?"

"They etch a spiral inside the barrel and the shot follows it." Again he demonstrated the motion with his index finger. "See?"

"And that always makes the gun shoot better?" Carson asked.

The sergeant nodded. "Yes. In the old muskets the ball shot out and eventually just dropped. The spinning propels it farther. Now we're going to load our rifles with ball and powder."

Dev moved to another group to observe how others were faring. Once again, in his mind he heard Armstrong say he was going to enlist as soon as he was free. Dev felt sicker with each step.

In front of her tent the next evening, Faith gazed at a soldier whose brother she'd nursed earlier this spring, wondering what had brought him here but glad of the distraction. In spite of her wise intention, she'd almost set out to the colonel's tent again. Her longing to see him, to hear his voice, had nearly overcome her better sense.

"You took such good care of Garner." The corporal offered her a water bucket filled with small reddish-purple plums. "I wanted you to have these. I don't know how the tree has survived the cannon fire, but I found it on a hill north of here while on reconnaissance, and it was covered with wild plums. At home they wouldn't have been ripe till fall, but . . ." He shrugged.

"Thank thee. Here, let's empty the plums into my bucket." They made the transfer. "I will find a good use for them," she promised. "Did thy brother reach home safely?"

"Yes, miss. I received that news in my last letter. Our mother is feeding him up and getting him back to normal health. Our family is grateful. They include you in their prayers."

"Please thank them for me."

He bowed his head and left her.

The man's brother had lost a leg. He was one of the few she'd managed to save from infection, and now he was home. Satisfaction swelled within Faith.

She gazed down at the bucket of wild plums, and an idea of what to do about the

159

food thief began to form in her mind. She felt almost vicious contemplating such a thing, but as the siege continued, food stores were becoming tighter and tighter. She considered how much worse it must be inside Vicksburg itself.

The dire situation within the besieged city rose in her, an ache, and she pushed it down. The Confederates could surrender anytime they wanted. She recalled the colonel's cousin, who had broken his word and escaped. The South was fighting to save its way of life, but couldn't they see that day by day, their land and people were being destroyed?

She could not deal with that fact; it was too big for her. She concentrated on how to carry out her plan. She couldn't stop the fighting, but she could stop or try to stop a mean thief who didn't care if their patients were stinted in their rations.

She headed toward the tents of the kitchen staff. Faith trusted the head cook. She was the perfect woman to put this plan into action. In spite of her frustration, Faith admitted she was glad to have something to distract her from thoughts of Colonel Knight, from Annerdale and Shiloh.

The next day Faith arrived early at the mess

tent. The head cook stood in the opening at the rear. She motioned for Faith to come. Faith hurried to her.

"I did what you tol' me and I set one of my he'pers, Dan, to watch and see if it works."

"Excellent. Thank thee."

The cook nodded once and turned back to the cook tent. Soon, inside the mess tent, Faith sat at her usual table and ate breakfast, her stomach knotting. Would her trap work?

"Today," Dev informed the sergeants who had been training the African Brigade recruits, "I'm going to let y'all go back to your normal duties." For some reason he'd let his Maryland drawl become more pronounced today. He commanded himself. This assignment would end today for him as well as them.

Grant had chosen a seasoned officer to command this new brigade long-term. Dev would introduce this officer to the African troops now.

The sergeants saluted and left Dev. The nearly six hundred black soldiers remained, awaiting their new commander. "Captains!" Dev called.

The newly commissioned African officers snapped to attention. He recognized the alteration in these men, now dressed in sharp blue uniforms and standing with ramrod posture. The soldier named Carson who reminded him of Armstrong stood among the brigade captains.

"Your new commanding officer, Lieutenant Colonel Hermann Lieb, will now take charge."

There was an exchange of military courtesies and Dev fell back, giving the new commanding officer the forefront.

Lieb addressed the men. "Today, Captains, you will take your companies through the daily military routine: roll call, rifle practice, and —"

The after-breakfast artillery barrage began, interrupting him. With a wave of his hand, Lieb mouthed, "Proceed!"

The new African captains saluted and headed off, motioning for their smaller companies to follow. As the members of the regiment went through their duties, Dev headed back to his own command. Lieb would do as good a job as anyone could with these raw recruits.

Dev had rarely seen such fervor in any troops. Again the thought of Armstrong enlisting curdled in his midsection. And he couldn't help reflecting that he hadn't seen Faith for days now. Was she avoiding him?

Or was he avoiding her?

Faith turned from freshly bandaging a soldier who'd lost an eye. One of the black orderlies, a teenage boy who'd practically run up to her, was waiting impatiently. "Miss Faith," he said with definite excitement, "I think I spotted who it is."

A combination of excitement and fear whipped up her spine. "Yes?"

"He been to the latrine four times already this mornin'. You won't b'lieve who it is. Come 'n' see."

Faith decided not to press him — to see for herself instead — but she needed one more person to witness this so there would be no doubt about the thief's identity. "Thank thee. Go watch for the culprit. I'll come soon." She swept toward the nearby tent, where Dr. Bryant was painstakingly washing his surgical tools for the day. "Dr. Bryant, I think we've discovered our thief."

He stopped his task and turned to her, drying his hands on a towel. "How?"

"Come." She waved him to follow. "I'll explain so thee can confront the culprit."

Evidently caught by her urgency, he hurried along beside her. "Well?" He spoke next to her ear since the bombardment continued unabated.

163

"The head cook has been reporting to thee that our food supplies were being stolen," she began.

"Yes."

"Well, I set a trap for the thief: a strong purgative mixed in with wild-plum pie."

"What!" Dr. Bryant halted, gawking at her, then caught up with her. "I take it we're headed for the latrine?"

The humor of the situation suddenly burst over her. "Yes. The culprit is now reaping what he has sown."

Dr. Bryant merely shook his head at her. "You stay behind. I'll handle this."

She let the doctor go on ahead and hung back, sheltering behind a nearby tree where she could observe unnoticed.

He quickened his pace and reached the latrine just as the head of the hospital, Captain Slattery, staggered out from behind the stretched canvas barrier.

"A bit under the weather, are we?" Dr. Bryant roared at the man.

He flinched and encompassed his abdomen with both hands. "I'm sick."

"Yes, from the purgative in the wild-plum pie you stole early this morning!" The doctor bellowed so loudly she could hear it between artillery blasts.

Slattery bent double and hurried back

behind the canvas.

Dr. Bryant returned to her. "I'll have the man's tent searched for more evidence and notify headquarters."

She drew out a small bag from one of her apron pockets. "Here's an herbal remedy. I don't want him to become really sick."

He smiled and accepted the pouch, then offered her his hand. "Thank you, Nurse Cathwell. Your intelligence and abilities always amaze me."

Faith felt herself blushing. "I just do what I can, Doctor."

He squeezed her hand. "Leave this to me now."

She curtsied, something she rarely did here, and went back to the tent and her patients. As she reached the rear entrance, Dr. Dyson pushed past her, clutching his abdomen, heading straight for the latrine.

Faith halted, startled to her toes. This she had not foreseen. Were the two men in this together? Or had Dr. Dyson been offered a piece of the stolen pie? Or become ill in some more innocent way? She was glad to leave this situation to Dr. Bryant. And she hoped he'd keep her part in it secret.

After supper and during an early end to the daily barrage, Faith and Honoree walked

165

side by side toward the colonel's tent. Over one arm, Honoree carried a covered woven oak basket. Concealed inside was a gift from the head cook, a wholesome plum pie draped with a starched dishcloth. After giving two slices to Ella for her and her husband to enjoy, Honoree had decided they should share the rest of this rare treat with the colonel and Armstrong. Faith knew she should not have agreed to come along, but here she was. And perhaps she'd have an opportunity to ask the colonel about going to Annerdale. She felt as trapped by this siege as the residents of Vicksburg.

Armstrong, who must have been anticipating Honoree's arrival, came out of the tent. He greeted them, and the colonel stepped outside too.

Having avoided him for several days, Faith experienced some awkwardness, and she saw it reflected in the colonel's posture.

"We have pie," Honoree announced in a discreet but cheerful tone.

Armstrong beamed and quickly waved them inside.

Faith hung back just inside the open flap. It was not quite proper for them to enter a bachelor tent when not engaged in nursing, but she understood the dilemma. They didn't have enough pie for the surrounding soldiers, so propriety would have to bow to this necessity for the sake of discretion. She entered the tent.

Quickly Armstrong produced tin plates and forks, and Honoree served the pie, cutting generous pieces for each of them. She also murmured the story of Faith's plan with the other pie. "And it worked. Slattery will no doubt be court-martialed as soon as he's strong enough to face it."

"In the end I felt sorry for him," Faith said.

"You would," Honoree responded, shaking her head.

"He's laid up in the hospital —"

"And that rude Dr. Dyson is not feeling too good either. We don't know if he knew the pie had been stolen, but either way he probably saw it and demanded a piece. He deserved what he got too." Honoree tried unsuccessfully to hide her smirk. "I'm just being honest, Faith."

Someone cleared his throat outside the open tent flap. "Miss Faith Cathwell?"

Faith turned toward the corporal at the open flap. "I am she."

"I was told you might be here. General Grant asks if you would come to his tent with your herbal medicines."

"Is the general ill?" Faith asked, handing

her plate of half-eaten pie to Honoree.

"No, miss, and you can finish your dessert. But would you please come to the general's tent when you're able? His young son has a problem."

Faith wished the man would be more specific, but she'd met with this before. Men weren't supposed to discuss physical problems or medical needs with a young unmarried woman. The fact that she was a nurse didn't change this ingrained hesitance.

"Has Dr. Bryant been consulted?"

"I'm not sure. I only know that I was ordered to bring you."

That sounded odd. "Very well. I will come soon."

The corporal bowed, saluted the colonel, and departed.

"I wonder what that's all about," Honoree commented.

Dev rose somewhat gladly. His man and Honoree were exchanging glances, which made him feel as if he were intruding on them. And which sharpened his feeling of separation from Faith. He'd missed her the past days.

Why was she avoiding him? He would try to find out tonight, and he had something to give her as well. The paltry offering might heal their rift — if he could persuade her to tell him what had caused her to draw away from him.

Faith rose from the camp stool. "I must go."

Honoree moved as if to rise.

"No, stay and enjoy thy evening. I must fetch my chest," Faith said, moving to leave.

Dev stepped toward the door too. "I will accompany you."

"That isn't necessary."

"No, it isn't, but it is polite and prudent. I'm coming with you."

She gazed at him and said with reluctance, "As thee wishes."

Dev avoided glancing toward Armstrong and Honoree and exited the tent behind Faith. Without speaking, they walked toward her tent to collect her medicine chest. He tried to come up with a topic of conversation, but since she had been avoiding him, he didn't know which topics he should forbear. What had he done to alienate her?

Then he recalled the nature of this woman he was walking beside. He slipped his hand into his inner pocket. "Do you know what this plant is?" He'd picked it during a break in training the African Brigade.

"That's calendula." She smiled at him, accepting the dried golden flower.

"I recalled your garden." He shrugged,

feeling like a school-boy trying to interest the prettiest girl in the neighborhood.

"It's good for digestion and is often mixed with arnica for muscle soreness." She bowed her head, and he thought she would have said more had they not reached her tent.

He waited outside while she went in to get her medicines. When she came out, he appropriated the heavy wooden chest. Carrying it by its bone handle, he led her away.

His gift had not had its desired effect. The conversational well had run dry. He tried again. "I've been busy training the African Brigade."

"I heard that. There was much talk about Grant's authorizing it." And that was all she said.

So she was forcing him to take total responsibility for their conversation. Well, he was a soldier — he did not quit easily. He forged on. "They learned so fast —"

"And that surprised thee."

"I didn't think their former lives predisposed them to soldiery."

She made a muted *hmm* sound. "How many young white men straight from the farm were predisposed to soldiery?"

"Most farm boys have some knowledge of hunting."

"Some," she conceded.

They walked in silence the rest of the way. Dev had been sure picking a wildflower that looked interesting would open her to him again and bring back the communication he longed for. He could not forget the pleasure her unusual conversation brought him. He tasted bitter failure.

At the general's tent, they were admitted. Grant raised one eyebrow at Dev. After his salute was acknowledged and Dev was at ease, he murmured, "I thought it best to accompany the lady since it's getting late."

Then the surgeon Dr. Bryant stepped from the shadows. "Nurse Cathwell, I'm afraid the general's son Fred has contracted dysentery."

Faith concealed her reaction. Dysentery untreated could be fatal. She approached the cot where the boy, barely in his teens, lay curled on his side as though protecting his abdomen. He looked at her sleepily as if he'd been drugged. "How far advanced is the case?" she asked.

Grant replied, "As a longtime soldier, I knew what it was as soon as Fred showed signs of diarrhea. I called in Dr. Bryant immediately."

"Very wise," Faith murmured, wanting to examine the boy but unwilling to overstep.

"Nurse Cathwell, I don't need to tell you

that this young man will need careful nursing. That's why I thought of you. You are my best nurse."

Faith much appreciated his compliment but let it pass without comment. "What has thee done already, Doctor?"

"I've administered castor oil and laudanum."

She nodded. "Thee wants me to stay with the young man?"

"Exactly. The general is going to move out and let you take over the tent. I didn't want to transport Fred to the hospital, where he might contract something else while in a weakened state."

She drew in a long breath. "I concur. And of course I'll stay here with the patient."

"I think the treatment will begin working soon," Dr. Bryant continued, picking up his black medical bag, "but I want him carefully watched, and I know you have herbal remedies that are often effective. Feel free to do what you think will help Fred recover."

His belief in her ability ignited a warm glow within. This man was not afraid of giving a woman credit for her intelligence. So unusual. "I will, Doctor. And I'll call for thee if anything out of the ordinary occurs."

"Thank you, Miss Cathwell," General Grant said, bowing. "It's times like these that I miss his mother even more."

She curtsied in reply.

The general accepted her curtsy with a nod. "I hear it was you who found out who was stealing from the kitchen stores."

"Oh." She let out the sound in surprise.

He chuckled. "Quite an interesting ploy. I only wish someone had brought us some of the untainted plum pie."

"I'll talk to the head cook at the mess tent." She moved to press a hand on the boy's forehead. He already had a fever. "I'm sure she can rustle up something for thee."

Dr. Bryant excused himself, and both he and the general left the tent, the doctor to return to his quarters and the general to his command tent so nothing would disturb his son. Faith busied herself with her medicine chest, drawing out herbs that could soothe the bowel.

She turned to Fred and appeared startled that Dev was still present. "Colonel?" she asked, sounding nettled and evidently wanting to know his reason for remaining.

Dev gathered his courage here in this tent where none other would enter save the general. "What did I do to offend you, Miss Faith? We have barely seen each other over the past week. I look for you, but you are always busy."

She gazed at him. Would she deny the truth?

Fred gave a loud moan. "Ooooh."

Faith stepped closer to his side. "What is it?"

"Who are you?" He clutched his belly. "Where's my fa— ? Ooh. I need to use the . . ." He sent her a painful look.

"I am Faith Cathwell, thy nurse." She turned to Dev. "The chamber pot is beneath his cot. He's weakened. Will thee help him?" Not waiting for his answer, she stepped outside quickly.

Dev moved to assist the boy, and when he could, he helped the boy back onto the cot. "We're finished, Miss Faith," Dev called quietly.

She returned and embarrassed both men by examining the chamber pot. She nodded to herself. "Call the corporal inside, please."

The corporal took care of the needs of sanitation, and when he returned, Faith requested boiling water. Dev stepped outside and helped the corporal get the water boiling over the fire, then carried the kettle in to her.

She opened her medicine chest and began brewing what looked like herbal tea.

Dev hovered in the background, hoping she wouldn't ask him to leave.

Soon he was helping support the boy while she spooned tea into her patient's mouth.

"I'm as weak as a cat," Fred apologized roundabout.

"Thee will be better soon. Dr. Bryant has treated many cases. He gave thee medicine and has asked me to stay and be thy nurse," Faith said in a soothing tone. "Thee must merely do what we tell thee and all will be well."

Dev hoped she was telling the absolute truth, not simply trying to encourage the boy to keep up hope and obey.

"I feel . . . ," the boy stammered.

"Thee can tell me about thy physical sensations," Faith said, continuing to spoon in the tea. "Part of being a nurse is listening to the patient's symptoms and treating them or calling the doctor if needed."

The boy gazed at her, unconvinced.

Inspiration came to Dev. "If you were sick, who would take care of you after the doctor left, your mother or your father?"

"My mother."

"Well, then it shouldn't be hard for you to tell this nurse about your troubles. And lots of soldiers have done so. Isn't that right, Miss Faith?"

He was gratified when she sent him a

quick smile.

"Yes, I have been nursing for many months, Fred. I have cared for hundreds of soldiers, some with what is ailing thee."

Fred nodded. "That tea tastes like hay."

Faith chuckled. "But it will calm thy body inside, and that's what we need so thee doesn't have worse spasms of the bowel."

At the mention of the bowel, Fred flushed, one red dot on each pale cheek.

Finally Fred drank all his tea, lay back down, and fell into an exhausted sleep. Faith curled up in the general's large traveling chair beside Fred's cot.

Dev murmured that he would stay to help her with the boy. She did not object, so he lifted a folded blanket from the top of a trunk, rolled up in it, and lay down nearby. He dozed on and off, waking to help Fred when needed.

Finally, when dawn was breaking, General Grant quietly entered his tent.

Faith rose and Dev scrambled to his feet and saluted.

Grant nodded for him to be at ease. "How did Fred pass the night, miss?"

"Thee was wise to call Dr. Bryant right away," she said. "Thy son will have a few more uncomfortable days, but quick treatment has already slowed and is stopping the debilitating effect of this disease on Fred."

Grant sighed with relief.

"I am going to my tent," Faith continued, "and will send another nurse, Honoree Langston, to take over today. She is my friend and tentmate. She will know what to do while I rest. I will return in the evening to relieve her. Thy son will need constant nursing for the next few days until Dr. Bryant feels he is near recovery."

"My thanks, miss. That is a weight off me."

She curtsied and closed up her medicine chest. "I will leave this if thee will keep it safe till my friend Honoree comes."

"Of course." Grant turned to Dev. "You stayed all night?"

"Miss Faith needed my help so your son would not be so embarrassed," Dev said.

Grant nodded.

Dev decided to take advantage of the situation to perhaps smooth matters between himself and Faith. "General, Miss Faith has discussed something of a personal matter with me that you might be able to help with."

"Oh?" General Grant cocked an eyebrow at him.

"The other nurse's sister, a free woman of color, was kidnapped before the war and sold south. Miss Faith has been inquiring in the contraband camps and has finally gotten word of a woman fitting the description of her friend at a plantation near here in Madison County."

Grant nodded, encouraging him to continue.

"I have just turned over command of the African Brigade and would like permission to take Miss Faith to the plantation — after Fred no longer needs her skills. We know it's a long shot, but . . ." He shrugged.

"I think after Fred recovers, we can let you have a day to do this. But do not accompany Miss Cathwell alone. The surrounding areas are hostile. More than one band of Rebs is raiding and harassing us. Take a company with you."

Faith looked surprised. "Thank thee, General." She then allowed Dev to usher her outside and she accepted his arm this time.

Until they were well away from the general's tent, neither spoke.

Faith broke the silence. "I did not expect thee to ask that of the general."

"It has been on my mind . . . among other concerns." He let this sink in as he walked her through the waking camp.

"I have been avoiding thee," Faith confessed.

"What did I do to offend you?" He was glad the morning barrage had yet to start so they didn't need to raise their voices.

"Nothing." She paused, still walking but looking down pensively. "That unpleasant Dr. Dyson made a remark to me about . . . our friendship."

He gave a brusque hiss of irritation.

"He was the one who was so rude to me at our first meeting. And he is ever thus."

"Then why let him influence you?" *Affect us?*

"I'm sorry I did. I just didn't want to be the subject of gossip."

He considered this, listening to the routine morning camp sounds — men's voices and the sound of coffee bubbling over campfires. "Miss Faith, I understand your sentiment. But I will not dissemble. In this awful siege I find your companionship a comfort, a distraction —"

"I find the same in thy company."

"Then why, in the midst of this war, should we let one sour person or idle gossip deter us? As long as we observe the proprieties, let them talk. We will have nothing to be ashamed of."

"I agree." She beamed at him. "I thank thee again for helping me last night."

"I'm glad I was able to do so." He walked

beside her now, content to merely experience her presence. For however long that
would be possible.

CHAPTER 8

After several minutes by her side, the colonel had to be about his duties, so Faith walked alone the remainder of the way to her tent so she could freshen herself to meet the new day. She woke Honoree and requested that she nurse Fred today. Then Faith brushed out her tangled hair, letting herself enjoy the feeling of peace that had come from her reconciliation with the colonel.

Yet around her nothing had changed. The camp smells she strove to ignore still forced her to sniff the vial of lavender she wore around her neck. The sound of the drummer keeping the thousands of troops in military time and routine still pounded. The Mississippi heat caused perspiration to bead on her forehead and upper lip. And she knew the bombardment of Vicksburg would again blast to life after breakfast.

But nothing could quench her joy.

Honoree sat nearby on a stool, rebraiding her own hair and humming "Swing Low, Sweet Chariot." Faith hummed along, feeling as if she were wrapped in a soft cloud that not even a night spent nursing could pierce.

The lonely days away from the colonel had been put behind them. Did he feel the same way as she did this morning? And he'd done more than give her this wonderful feeling. She remembered she had good news for Honoree too.

The cloud still softening every harsh reality around her, she glanced at her friend. And realized that Honoree looked pleased too. "Why so happy?"

Honoree looked up from bending her head to braid the short hair at her nape and grinned. "Armstrong kissed me for the first time last night."

Faith gasped. "Honoree!"

Honoree chuckled. "I thought it was time."

Faith's cloud expanded. "Thee is serious about him, then?"

"Of course. He'll be free very soon, and after the war, I'm sure we'll have a future together. Armstrong's not the kind of man to lead a girl on." Honoree looked down again, wrestling with the ends of her short hair.

Faith remained silent, letting her friend savor the sweetness of a first kiss, savoring it vicariously herself. She remembered her first kiss shared with the man she'd thought she would marry. In a letter from her mother, she'd learned he had died at Antietam, more than eight months ago. A stitch in her heart. *God, be with his family in their grief.*

This brought to mind the danger Colonel Knight faced each time he led his men on patrol. She shut her eyes, willing away the fact that the war could snatch him from her at any time.

She opened her eyes and looked to her friend. "Honoree, I have good news. When we were at the general's tent, Colonel Knight asked if he could take me to Annerdale. And the general granted the request."

Honoree's head snapped back as if she'd been slapped. "Truly?"

"Yes."

Honoree rose from the camp stool and the two of them embraced. "I hardly even let myself hope anymore," Honoree murmured.

"I know," Faith replied in kind. *Our sweet Shiloh.*

"Sometimes I wish I'd lost her like you lost Patience. I think I could accept her death —"

"No!" Faith jerked away, realizing again no one understood what it felt like to lose half of oneself. How could Honoree even say this? "No." In spite of the humidity hanging in the air, she shivered. "Where there is life, there is hope. I believe that. And Shiloh knows we will never stop looking for her. When this war ends, if I have to search every town in the Confederacy, I will."

Tears welled in Honoree's eyes. She leaned forward and kissed Faith's cheek. "You are my sister too — the sister of my heart. And I will not give up hope either. We will search till we find her."

Faith embraced Honoree again and stepped to a small mirror propped on a trunk. She tucked and pinned the end of her braided coronet and donned one of the white caps she always wore under her bonnet. She then tied her bonnet ribbons loosely around her neck but, because of the burgeoning heat, let the bonnet hang down her back till she went out into the sun.

After she and Honoree had filled her apron pockets with cloth packets of herbs, they set out for the mess tent. Thinking of

Shiloh had muted Faith's elation but hadn't snuffed it completely.

Faith savored every memory of the colonel, and this morning she'd tucked the calendula he'd given her into the special pocket inside her apron. What a tender gesture. A man of war picking wildflowers for her.

Honoree nudged her. "What are you smiling about?"

Faith shook her head, refusing to reply. She realized her heart was facing the firing line of hurt and sorrow. However, better a few tender memories with a fine man than none at all.

Dr. Dyson accosted Faith as she and Honoree stepped into the mess tent. "You're the one behind that tainted pie."

At this the soft cloud around her evaporated like morning dew in the heat of the sun. Faith said nothing, merely stared at him.

"You made me sick," Dr. Dyson accused, "cost me a day of doctoring, and I had to defend myself against the charge of complicity in theft."

"Why do you always pick on Miss Faith?" Honoree fired up, thrusting herself between Faith and Dr. Dyson.

The doctor ignored her. "I'll not forget this."

"Is that a threat?" Honoree demanded.

"What's going on here?"

All three of them swung around to face Dr. Bryant.

Dr. Dyson tried to speak.

But Dr. Bryant's voice overrode him. "Dr. Dyson, just be glad that your claim of innocence was believed, or you would be with Slattery in the stockade, awaiting court-martial. Now let these nurses eat their breakfast. Don't you have enough to keep you busy?"

Red-faced, Dr. Dyson nodded brusquely and stalked away.

Dr. Bryant bowed to them and followed Dyson outside.

Faith and Honoree exchanged telling glances, then moved forward to receive their bowls of corn mush and cups of coffee. Faith was glad she was able to help catch the thief. But Dr. Dyson's animosity still bothered her.

Initially the surgeons, to a man, had resented female nurses, and some had been more than merely rude. But as time had passed, a few like Bryant had come to value them. In any event, the out-and-out rudeness had waned except from those like Dr.

Dyson. Dealing with thousands of wounded at a time, the doctors had realized they needed all the help they could get — even from women. Was there any way she could live more at peace with this sour man?

After breakfast outside his tent, Dev tried to focus on the day — not last evening spent in Miss Faith's company, even if it had just been to help her with a patient. He could not afford to let those sweet moments soften him. With stiff military posture, he strode toward the staging area of the African brigade. Today they were marching to their post, and he wanted to see them off. He'd been told they would merely be guarding a supply depot northwest of here at Milliken's Bend, right on the Mississippi.

Since they'd received so little military training, this duty came as a relief to him. They wouldn't be marching into battle and sure death. But a worry nagged at the back of his mind. What if some Rebels tried to take those precious supplies of food and ammunition the new soldiers would be guarding?

Ahead, he saw the African Brigade standing in ranks at attention, and the sight hit him with a familiar haunting sensation he hated. He couldn't help but think of that term for the common soldier — "cannon fodder." It was a heartless view of their fate, but one inherent in war. A general had to think not of individual lives sacrificed but of the bigger picture of strategy and winning battles and thus ending this war for all.

But that reality was not reassuring when Dev considered Armstrong's individual fate. *I don't want him to be a soldier, a pawn in this deadly game of battles and campaigns.*

Looking ahead, he recognized the African Brigade's new commanding officer, Lieutenant Colonel Lieb. Dev approached the man and they exchanged salutes.

"The general told me you were leaving today for your post," Dev said, opening the conversation.

"Yes," Lieb said with his slight accent. Dev had learned that he'd emigrated from Switzerland and settled in Illinois. For a moment, Dev wanted to ask him if, when leaving his native land, he could have foreseen becoming the commanding officer of an African Brigade in a war between the American states. War did make for strange acquaintances. Would Dev himself ever have thought he'd find such pleasure in, of all things, the company of a Quaker lady, an abolitionist, a female nurse?

"I thank you for your work in training

these men," Lieb said.

Dev replied politely, "I was glad to be involved." He turned to look out over the men. Each face was set with determination and each back was straight with pride. Among the ranks, he glimpsed Carson, who had recently been promoted.

Did they have any idea what they were facing? He recalled his own first battle — the chaos, the panic. His stomach tightened. No words he could say would prepare them, but he wanted them to know he acknowledged their commitment to preserving the Union. But he did not want Armstrong to make the same commitment. How could Dev stop him?

"I'd like to say a few words to the men," Dev requested, "before the morning barrage begins, if I may."

"Of course," Lieb said and stepped back, waving Dev forward.

"Men!" Dev said. "You have done all I asked of you with a determination and eagerness that speaks well of you. It has been an honor to help in your training. I know you will stand and fight." He found he couldn't say more, his throat clogged with emotion. So he finished by saluting them smartly.

The brigade returned his salute, almost as one.

Dev shook hands with Lieb, and then the morning barrage blasted to life behind them. Dev turned away and headed toward his regiment and his duties for the day.

After reporting to Osterhaus's tent for orders, Dev approached his men where they waited after roll call. He gazed at them as he had the African Brigade earlier. He did not like today's orders, but what did that change? Nothing.

"Men, today we join the digging of the breastwork of trenches around Vicksburg."

He saw the dismay on their faces, heard a few groans from the rear. They were cavalrymen. But the breastworks provided the troops with cover and, just like the daily barrages, kept up the pressure on the besieged city. "Form ranks and follow me."

They obeyed, and he led them forward to pick up their shovels. It would be a hot day of hard labor under the unrelenting sun, with the barrage overhead and perilous sniper fire from embattled Vicksburg.

He thought again of walking beside Faith the night before. And reminded himself that she was talking to him now. The tightness in his chest eased.

Dev just had to make sure he didn't get

picked off today by a Reb sniper. Then he could look forward to another evening in her restful yet lively company. Maybe she would have an idea of how to dissuade Armstrong from enlisting. Perhaps she would see matters his way . . . for once.

After cleaning up from a day of digging, Dev stretched his shoulders. He'd helped on and off to encourage his men, and his muscles would no doubt ache tonight. Fortunately none of his men would suffer anything more than that. They'd come close with that failed attempt to breach the city wall. Though tired, he'd still changed clothing from the skin out. He'd been drenched with sweat from a day in the sun.

Now Dev left his tent and wended his way through the crowded camp toward Faith's tent. He already knew what she would think about his hesitation over freeing Armstrong. But she hated war, so in light of that, perhaps Armstrong's intention to enlist would give her sympathy with Dev's view. And he had to talk about this situation with someone. Perhaps she could help him decide how to persuade Armstrong not to do this. Dev presented himself at Faith's tent.

She must have been watching for him

because she was waiting just inside the entrance. "Colonel, was thee near that awful explosion today?"

His men had not been part of setting off a cache of dynamite in a forward tunnel, a plan intended to break into the city. They had, however, been forced to drop their shovels and pick up their rifles after the failed attempt.

"Unfortunately I was nearby," he said. "My ears are still ringing. My men had to help retrieve the soldiers pinned down by sniper fire after the explosion." He offered her his arm. "I've come to escort you to the general's tent if you —"

"Yes, I must go so Honoree can eat supper and get some rest." Faith set her bonnet over her cap and braided hair, tied the bonnet's ribbons, and accepted his offer.

Leading her away, he groped around his mind for a means of introducing the topic foremost in his thoughts. "Some of the new recruits were in the thick of things today. They don't get enough training to suit me." He considered the African Brigade and how little they'd received. God help them if they were attacked. If Armstrong enlisted, that's exactly what would happen to him. The thought sat like a load of lead shot in Dev's belly.

"Why did thee choose to become a soldier?" she asked, surprising him as they approached a surviving copse of pines.

He looked at her askance. He didn't want to discuss himself and his decision to be a soldier. It was Armstrong he worried about. But he swallowed this objection. One of the main reasons he enjoyed this woman's company was her unexpected depths.

"I saw it as my only option," Dev said, choosing his words with care. "My mother left her family's plantation and married a Baltimore businessman." He guided her around a group of men sitting together on the ground, playing cards.

Faith nodded, encouraging him to continue.

"So as a gentleman without land, I could either pursue law or go into business like my father. I had no interest in those vocations. That left the military." He led her forward, wishing they weren't heading toward a night of nursing, wishing instead for a quiet place for just the two of them.

"So thee didn't dream of being a soldier, a colonel? Thee came to it by default."

Her words startled him in a way he hadn't expected. "I suppose that's true."

When he'd secured a place at West Point, he'd known he would become a fighting man, an officer who commanded others, but in this war leading men to their deaths was becoming harder with every battle. He thought of Grant, who threw men into battle with a ferocity that stunned the enemy. Stunned Dev.

"What is thee thinking?" she asked. Someone began playing a harmonica nearby.

No one ever asked him this. He was just given orders, and as expected, he followed them. But at her question, his reflections poured out. "War has changed. The weaponry is so much more accurate now." *More deadly.* He looked into her large green eyes. "Marching into battle in close order is . . ." He paused, not wanting to be overheard criticizing General Grant.

"Is responsible for the high casualties we experience?" Faith finished for him.

He let her precede him through a group of men going in the opposite direction. They were nearing the general's tent.

"Yes," he replied, lowering his voice close to her ear. "Muskets were so inaccurate and only lethal at such a short range that if one were wounded or killed, it was practically by chance." He stopped, not wanting to bore her with details. She was a lady, after all. What lady was interested in weaponry?

Faith brushed away a flurry of gnats in

front of her face. "Dr. Bryant also served in the Mexican War as an army surgeon. He once or twice has mentioned that more accurate rifles mean more wounded and more battle deaths."

They had reached the general's tent. Their confidences were at an end, and he'd still not been able to broach the subject of Armstrong's enlisting.

The general was not there. They greeted Honoree, who spoke to Faith about what she'd done for their patient during the day. Then, with an unhappy glance toward Dev, Honoree left. They entered the tent.

Faith felt Fred's forehead. "Thee is still feverish."

"I'm —" Fred twisted his face — "some better."

"That is all to the good," Faith replied. "I'm sure Dr. Bryant will check on thee tonight before he turns in."

Dev felt unnecessary now, but he couldn't make himself leave.

General Grant entered.

Dev snapped to attention and was put at ease.

"Miss Cathwell," the general said, "Dr. Bryant tells me Fred is making progress."

"Yes, General," Faith said. "He still has a fever and symptoms, but I think thy quick action has saved Fred from the worst of the dysentery."

"Good. Good." Grant drew near to his son and began talking to the boy. Faith led Dev outside to give father and son some privacy.

Outside, Dev tried to induce himself to leave Faith and still found he couldn't. He blurted, "Armstrong intends to enlist."

Faith nodded. "I know. Honoree told me. I didn't know Armstrong had mentioned it to thee."

Dev steered her toward an open area between tents, wishing they could find somewhere to be alone. "He didn't. I overheard him telling Honoree," Dev admitted. "I can't stand by and let him do this. He could be killed." The last sentence forced its way through his lips.

Looking back at the general's tent, Faith considered him. "Just as thee could be killed. Thee chose the military. Armstrong will choose it too. That's what freedom means — making thy own decisions. Didn't thee know that?"

Dev reeled from her calmly spoken words. He wanted Armstrong free, but he wanted him alive, safe.

She drew a small woven palm fan from her apron pocket and began waving it in front of her face to stir the heavy, hot air. "Colonel, why did thee promise to free Armstrong on his fortieth birthday?"

Why had she asked him that? Voices hummed around them. Now and then a word or phrase lifted above the constant buzz. Dev felt torn, affronted by her series of questions. But he wouldn't endanger their detente. Only the truth would satisfy this woman.

"I made that promise when we were both very young," Dev said. "It seemed a fair way to solve the problem presented when my uncle gave him to me as a gift." Dev sucked in the humid evening air. "My mother is not an abolitionist per se, but she left the plantation because she didn't approve of slavery. My uncle inherited the plantation and the slaves. Mother and I never owned slaves."

"Except for Armstrong," she commented, fanning herself. "So thy mother and thy uncle were at odds over slavery?"

"Yes."

"Did thee ever question why thy uncle would give thee a slave as a gift, knowing that thy mother disapproved?"

Dev did not want to follow this line of discussion. He had lost his own father, and Uncle Kane had been good to him. And

197

somehow Jack's rivalry with Dev was tangled up in this complicated family history too.

Faith didn't press him. "What will thee do when Armstrong turns forty?" She continued fanning her face, watching him.

"I'm not sure. I've always given him a Christmas gift that equaled a year's wages so he would have funds saved up for a house or whatever he wanted. I thought that once I freed him, the only change would be paying him monthly."

General Grant took them by surprise when he cleared his throat. "Sorry to intrude. But I must go out again." He gazed at Dev and Faith. "I couldn't help but overhear what you were speaking about. Are you intending to free your manservant, Colonel Knight?"

Dev felt his face heat. "Yes, sir."

Grant nodded. "You know my wife's family was originally from a slave state, Maryland, before moving to Missouri in 1816. In the decade before the war, I managed my father-in-law's plantation, White Haven, and the slaves who worked there. But when I myself was given a slave in 1857, I freed him two years later. What's holding you back?"

This confrontation from an old comrade

who was now his commanding officer embarrassed Dev. "Sir, how could I foresee that his fortieth birthday, the day I promised to free him, would fall in the midst of a war more bloody than I could have imagined?"

"Thee couldn't, of course," Faith chimed in. She looked to the general. "His manservant plans to enlist."

"I see." Grant shook his head slowly at Dev as if comprehending the dilemma. "But we need every man we can get." He turned to Faith. "I must deal with some official correspondence. Miss Cathwell, will you please return to my son? Again, I only wish I could repay your and Honoree's careful nursing. I am in your debt."

"Honoree and I are happy to do what we can, General." Faith took Dev back into the general's tent, where she once more examined her patient, who'd fallen asleep. Dev then ushered her to the camp stools outside.

Dev leaned close to Faith and said, "I don't want Armstrong to throw his life away." A bark of laughter from a nearby tent punctuated his statement.

"I don't want thee to throw *thy* life away either," she said, gazing directly at him. "Thee knows well that I don't believe in war. The incredible waste of lives . . ." She threw a hand up. "I think the whole world must be insane. The South is steadily being destroyed and stripped of its men." Her tone rose, agitated. "The wealth they are trying to protect will not survive this war. What is the point?"

He felt himself breathing quickly as though he'd been running and realized that he must appear as agitated as she. He couldn't argue with anything she'd said. "There should have been a way to settle the issue of slavery without this war." He could think of nothing else to contribute.

"There should have been. The South blames abolitionists like my family, like me, but even if we'd never helped one runaway slave to freedom, a house divided against itself cannot stand. Our president was right — and only quoting Christ."

Dev didn't like where this conversation was going.

Faith began fanning herself once more. "Even if the North had let the South secede without resorting to war, slaves would have continued escaping to the North. The same tensions between slave and free states would have escalated. Don't they realize that the secession would only have led to a continuous border war?"

Everything she said was true. He'd never met a woman as intelligent and forthright.

She left him with nothing to say.

"Tell me more about thy library," she said abruptly, once again startling him. "And what bookshop does thee most love to browse?"

He was grateful for the sudden switching of topics, welcoming the chance to discuss something besides the mayhem all around them. "There's this little bookshop on Saratoga Street in Baltimore."

Yet even as he described this shop and its offerings, he could not escape his thoughts. Armstrong had served him through two wars. He'd seen the cost of combat. And now he enjoyed the prospect of a wife and family. What had possessed him to want to end up in the line of fire?

Realizing he had trailed off, he turned the conversation to Faith. "Now tell me what herbs you would like to add to your garden."

He wished he hadn't overheard Armstrong telling Honoree of his plans. But if wishes were horses, then beggars would ride.

Milliken's Bend, Louisiana
June 7, 1863
To keep track of enemy movements, Dev and a few of his cavalry companies had been sent to rove over the territory north of Vicksburg. Some Rebel troops in addition

to the raiders still remained outside the city, and it was suspected they might make trouble. Since Dev and his men were heading north today, he would get the chance to check on the African Brigade at Milliken's Bend, right on the Louisiana side of the river. They'd been in his thoughts.

General Grant's son had recovered almost completely from his bout with dysentery. Grant had urged Dev not to forget to take Miss Cathwell to that plantation soon. But his regular duties had kept him too busy.

A private galloped toward him. "Rebs ahead, sir!"

Almost simultaneously rapid gunfire sounded in the distance. "Proceed with caution!" Dev ordered. "Fire at will! Spread the word!"

Dev's heart pounded as usual in the face of a skirmish. He checked his carbine for ammunition and loosened his saber. Then he thought of the African Brigade. They were ahead. Had the war found them?

Dev and his men fought their way to Milliken's Bend, hot mile by hot mile. Smoke boiled up over the river. And before he reached the riverside levee, he heard cannon fire from the river itself. Union gunboats had joined the fight.

Before long the smoke began to clear and

he glimpsed the water itself. The Confederate line was falling back, heading south toward Vicksburg. He urged his men forward.

Then he saw that familiar cockaded hat, or thought he did. Jack? The rider turned in his saddle. Saw him, raised a crooked arm, and gave the Rebel cry.

Dev nearly lost his seat on the horse. But the distance and the smoke billowing on the wind intervened. Had it been his cousin?

He leaned forward and soon came upon the remnant of the African Brigade and the white Iowa troops serving with them. They'd been decimated.

"Dismount! Give aid!" Dev followed his own orders and hurried to do what he could. He glanced around and saw a hospital tent nearby. So many had fallen — hundreds. He moved to help lift the wounded and carry them to the hospital tent. At first he didn't realize it, but he was searching for Carson, the soldier who so reminded him of Armstrong.

Finally Dev found him and bound up his wounded leg. He helped him to the hospital tent. Carson still breathed, so Dev returned outside to aid others, disgust galling him. He hadn't wanted to send these men out so ill-trained. But he'd been given no choice.

Grant had dealt with that hard truth too. He needed men to face the enemy, and he couldn't let himself dwell on the loss of lives. Ending the war alone would stop the slaughter — the quicker, the better.

After many hours, all the wounded had been moved and were being treated or waiting to be treated. He gathered his men and began the effort to dig graves for the fallen.

Lieb saw Dev and came to him. "They fought bravely. They were a credit to their race."

Dev nodded, but from what he'd seen, most of them had died today. And it sickened him. What good did freedom do a man if he was dead?

In deep twilight Dev and his men hunkered down near Milliken's Bend for the night, his heart heavy and his back aching. Had it really been Jack with the Rebel forces attacking the African Brigade?

The cockaded hat had certainly been Jack's, and the bent arm was consistent with his injuries. So what if it was Jack? Dev already knew that his cousin had escaped to return to the war — a man without honor. Why should the sight of Jack fighting again surprise him? But his fury at Jack's betrayal still burned.

■ ■ ■ ■

Coming back to camp late the next day, the eve of Armstrong's fortieth birthday, Dev avoided returning to his tent as long as he could. Then he decided he had to face this head-on.

Armstrong was waiting inside for him. Dev looked into his eyes and realized something had changed. It seemed the polite veneer that Armstrong usually masked his true feelings with had been drawn back.

"You're not going to go through with it," Armstrong stated flatly.

Dev stared at Armstrong's hard expression, letting the man's anger roll over him. He didn't waste words asking what Armstrong was talking about. "I overheard you that night when you were taking care of Honoree. You said as soon as you were free, you planned to enlist —"

"Yes, I do plan to enlist." Armstrong cut him off.

"I saw what happened to the African Brigade yesterday." The memory clogged Dev's throat. "They . . . were slaughtered."

"So that's it. You're going to break your word, do to me what Jack did to you."

Dev bridled at the accusation. The two

things were not the same. Couldn't Armstrong understand that Dev only wanted to act in the man's own interest?

"I've been free since January when President Lincoln issued the proclamation." Armstrong's jaw jutted forward. "I could have left then."

Dev knew that, but he hadn't questioned Armstrong's staying with him. He suspected he knew the reason. "Why didn't you?"

"Because I have imagined my fortieth birthday for a long time. You would write out my manumission paper and then offer me your hand to shake, treating me as a freeman. Your equal. But I'm never going to get to shake your hand, am I? Because you are never going to see me as an equal." Armstrong snapped his mouth shut then, glaring at him.

"Why would I want you to be free if all you plan to do is throw that freedom away? I just don't want you to get hurt." *Get killed.* But as Dev watched him, the mask tightened over his face.

"As you wish, sir."

With his cool tone and formal words, Armstrong set himself apart from Dev in a way he'd never done before.

"I'll draw up your manumission papers as soon as the war ends," Dev promised, sounding weak in his own ears.

"That won't be necessary, sir."

And Dev realized Armstrong spoke the simple truth. He'd not thought that far ahead, but now he was forced to. When this war finished, slavery would be at an end. No doubt of that lingered in Dev's mind. He felt foolish. *But I won't be around at the end of the war.*

Fear that Armstrong might suffer the same sad fate prompted Dev to try coming up with words to persuade Armstrong not to enlist, but none came.

Armstrong left the tent.

Clenching his hands, Dev glanced around, struggling with his own turbulent feelings. He turned to go, instinctively seeking Faith. Only she could help him. If she wanted to.

And she stood there, just outside his tent.

He halted abruptly.

"I came to see if thee had returned safely." Yet she stared at him as if she didn't know him.

"You overheard?" He stated the obvious.

"I didn't come to eavesdrop, nor did I want to, but yes, I heard. Thee plans to break thy promise to free Armstrong tomorrow."

At hearing the bald truth, fury roared through Dev. "I saw what happened to the

African Brigade. He'll get himself killed."

She gazed at him and shook her head.

What did her expression signify? Sadness or disappointment or both — he couldn't tell.

He brushed past her, nearly running. He must find Armstrong and persuade him to see sense.

"Colonel Knight!" the Quakeress called after him.

He didn't turn his head or slow his pace, not wanting to hear her. He didn't know where he was headed. This war would kill him. Did it need to kill Armstrong too? Was this war going to leave no one he valued alive?

CHAPTER 9

As Dev and his company rode back into camp, the artillery had already fallen silent, earlier than usual. That felt like an ominous portent.

Today was Armstrong's birthday, and Dev did not relish facing his man after they'd crossed words yesterday. This morning before Dev had left, Armstrong had barely spoken to him. And he hadn't told Dev to come back in one piece as he always had before.

At the horse corral, Dev waved away the private who offered to tend his horse, trying to work out his tension by thoroughly brushing down the animal himself. Finally, unable to delay any longer, he trudged slowly back to his tent to face Armstrong.

When Armstrong did not come out as he always did when he heard Dev approaching, premonition chilled Dev once more. He opened the flap and entered, then stood frozen with one hand holding up the flap.

Except for Armstrong's cot with its bedding neatly folded on top, none of the manservant's belongings remained in the tent. Dev let the tent flap fall.

He's left me. Emotion clogged Dev's throat and threatened to spill out of his eyes. This desertion hit him worse than Jack's. Dev hadn't been overly surprised that his cousin was capable of dishonor, but he'd never even contemplated Armstrong's leaving him without a manumission paper, not even though he legally could.

Armstrong's words from the evening before played in his mind: *"I have imagined my fortieth birthday for a long time. You would write out my manumission paper and then offer me your hand to shake, treating me as a freeman. Your equal."*

For a long time he sat on his cot and gazed around at the half-empty tent, unable to do more than recollect images of Armstrong from their boyhood together, through the war in Mexico, to different military posts, and now in this war. Dev felt as if a part of him had been sliced off without morphine. Finally Dev rose, his hunger spurring him — not just physical hunger but hunger to know where Armstrong had gone and to see the only one who might bring him any peace. He set out for Faith's tent. He arrived there and met her and Honoree outside.

Honoree stopped and folded her arms. "You," she said, a one-word indictment.

Not mistaking what must be the reason for her harsh tone, he clamped his jaws tight so he wouldn't lash out at her. He would not cause a public scene over his private troubles.

"Colonel," Faith's soft voice interceded, "thee looks hungry. Has thee eaten?"

He shook his head, still regarding Honoree, who stared back at him with galling disdain. "No, I haven't."

"Come with me."

He gladly fell in beside Faith, wanting to escape before his self-control broke and he said something to Honoree he'd regret. He'd only wanted to do what he thought best for his servant.

Faith led him to the hospital cook tent. "Mary Lou!" she called, just outside the opening.

The tall head cook came through the opening and folded her hands over her narrow waistline.

"Does thee have a plate of food thee can spare?"

The woman stared razors at Dev. "This

the colonel Honoree talk about today?"

Dev felt his face and neck flame.

"Yes. And please, I don't want him to have only hardtack tonight," Faith replied.

The woman glared at him a few more moments. "Verra well — just this time, though. I can't be makin' special meals for the whole army."

He held in his hot anger at being judged by this woman. Did everyone with dark skin know that he'd reneged on his promise to free Armstrong?

Soon, outside the nearly deserted mess tent, Dev and Faith sat on camp stools while he ate a plate of beans and rice and drank coffee. He barely tasted the food. He ate to regain strength and to face what lay ahead. He tried to form the phrases to explain himself to this woman.

Faith watched him without speaking. When he was nearly finished, she excused herself and went inside the cook tent. Returning, she handed him a piece of raisin pie and sat down across from him again. "Didn't thee guess that Armstrong would leave today?"

He didn't know why he'd expected sympathy from her. Of course she'd be on Armstrong's side. "No. I didn't expect him to run away."

"He didn't run away. Legally he has been free since January. The two of thee may be *from* a border state, but neither of thee is *in* a border state now."

He clutched his mug of coffee with both hands. "You know he plans to enlist. Do you want what happened to the African Brigade the other day to happen to him?"

"How can thee stop a freeman from doing what he chooses? That is the meaning of *free.*"

"I just want him safe." The words were painful, tortured.

"Doesn't thee think I want that for Honoree? For thee?" She locked gazes with him.

"It's not the same," he declared. "I'm a lifelong officer, expected to fight —"

"It *is* the same," she interrupted. "At the outbreak of war, Honoree and I could have stayed safely at home. Thee could have resigned thy commission and gone to Canada or Europe and left this dreadful civil war behind."

His hands shook, and coffee spilled from his cup. "A man of honor would not, could not do that, and you know it."

"Does a man of honor go back on his word?"

Her question knifed him. Dev set his mug down and bent his head into one hand. "I hate this war," he muttered.

"On that we can agree."

Dev glanced up. "Do you know where he's gone?"

"He went to headquarters to enlist this morning. He has left most of his possessions in Honoree's care."

"It's done, then." *I went back on my word and it accomplished nothing but my disgrace.* He felt sick.

Faith wished she could offer comfort, but there was no balm here.

"I lost Bellamy in the Mexican War, and my father died while I was away," he said simply. "Jack when he betrayed me here. And now Armstrong." He stood.

Here within the cover between the mess tent and the cook tent, Faith rose and moved near him. Concealed within the darkening shadows, she rested a hand on his chest. "I am grieved too, though I don't expect thee to understand. No one ever does. Three days from now will be my twenty-fifth birthday, and the fifth year since I lost my twin. I never heal; the loneliness never goes away. When she died, part of me was amputated."

He didn't say anything, nor had she expected him to. What could anyone say or do?

"So I understand thy loss," she continued. "But I have no comfort to give except to say I am sorry we are in a war, sorry thee didn't keep thy promise, sorry Armstrong has put himself in harm's way."

His hand covered hers and pressed it to himself. Then he leaned forward and rested his cheek against hers as if in defeat.

Faith knew she should gently draw back, but she couldn't. She could feel his heart beating under her palm and the stubble on his cheek against hers. And in this moment she felt comforted. Then he pressed a kiss on the skin right below her ear.

At this intimate touch, she inhaled sharply, swallowing a gasp.

"Good night, Miss Faith. I thank you for the meal." He left her.

For a moment she stood, watching him go, letting the shock waves from his kiss work through her. Then she bent and picked up the tin plates and cup. She turned and found Mary Lou in front of her.

"You in love with that man?" Mary Lou asked.

"No," Faith answered. But then truth prodded her to add, "But I'm in danger of it."

Mary Lou accepted the dishes and made a sound like *humph*. "Best not be courtin' danger."

Very true. "My thanks and good night," Faith said and headed back to her tent, wishing the colonel had walked her home but realizing why he'd had to leave her. He'd disappointed a friend, disappointed himself.

Even if he hadn't, she'd understood what he said about losing family. He hadn't said it but he'd meant he'd lost the one closest to him, and she certainly knew how that felt. She'd lost Patience. And then Shiloh. She knew how bereft she'd feel if she lost Honoree here and now. If only this siege would end. Shiloh might only be miles away, but this siege held them all captive.

After supper Faith headed for her tent in the lull before the evening barrage began. Armstrong had met them after supper. He was now an enlistee and wore a blue uniform. Honoree had gone for her evening stroll with him, respecting Faith's desire to be alone on this day, which would have been Patience's twenty-fifth birthday too.

Faith walked through the clusters of men, feeling the sensation that was never far away — the sensation of missing part of herself. *Am I the only twin to feel this way?* She had no way of knowing. No one talked about what being one of a pair of identical twins felt like. Only those closest to her, like Honoree and her family, had ever tried to understand and comfort her in the face of this special loss. Her twin had always been beside her, day and night since conception. When she'd looked at Patience, she'd seen herself. They had done everything together, shared everything . . . everything but death.

She reached her tent and entered. On the trunk where her brush and comb set was laid out, someone had placed three wilted wildflowers, one a purple coneflower, one a form of sage, and one a type of wild rose. Faith picked them up one by one, sniffing them, and knew who'd left them here for her. Colonel Knight.

She sat down, arranged the wildflowers on her lap, and wept. She would not thank him with words. He had not given them to her directly. He'd left them for her. Just a token that said he knew today was hard for her. Was he missing his longtime companion too?

She whispered, "You would have liked him, Patience."

After all, he had promised to help her go to Annerdale, promised to help her find Shiloh, the one who was lost but who could yet be found.

July 4, 1863

Dev waited near the horse corral preparing to carry Faith to Annerdale Plantation. The unending siege with its daily barrage, shortened rations, and deadly sniper fire had worn everyone down. How long could the Rebs hold out? Were they all intent upon dying of starvation instead of surrendering? Even to the point of sacrificing the lives of their women and children?

Today's trip to Annerdale would get them away from it, though he still expected it to be a fool's errand. But he would do it because he'd promised. He also had another pressing reason to undertake the journey. Ever since Armstrong had left him for the enlisted men's quarters, Dev preferred to be away from his solitary tent and busy as much as possible. Losing Armstrong weighed on him like the interminable siege.

And here came Miss Faith, followed by Honoree. As usual, the latter looked sharp needles if not daggers at him.

He possessed only one lone and flimsy obstacle to Faith's coming with him and his men to Annerdale. "Miss Faith," Dev said, broaching the subject, "I haven't been able to find a lady's sidesaddle for you."

"That won't be a problem, Colonel," Faith said. "I've never ridden sidesaddle. I ride astride."

Her calmly spoken rebuttal shocked him. A lady riding astride? "But modesty —"

She lifted her skirt a few inches to show the bottom hems of a worn pair of trousers above her boots.

He goggled at her.

"An old pair of my brother's pants will answer the concern for my modesty." She grinned at him with an impish gleam in her eyes. "My mother was raised to ride sidesaddle, but we lived far from Cincinnati, so when we rode, we just used this means to remain modest. Where is my horse?"

One of his men, who was evidently trying not to look shocked, led the older horse forward. "This is the mount the colonel chose for you, miss. His name is Horace."

Faith approached the horse's head and spoke to the animal, spending a few moments letting the horse sense her and accept her. "I think we're ready."

Dev kept his mouth tightly closed, not voicing his disapproval of a female riding astride. He moved to stand beside her horse, bent and linked his hands together.

Faith fit her small boot into this cradle and then swung onto the saddle. Dev adjusted the saddle girth for her.

"Now don't worry, Honoree," Faith said, calmly making herself comfortable in the saddle. "The colonel and these men will take good care of me."

"I wish I could go, but I know it's not safe for me," Honoree conceded. "Godspeed."

Once mounted, Dev lifted a hand in farewell, but he could not look at Honoree without thinking of Armstrong. From what Dev had heard, Armstrong was training to be an artilleryman, preparing to kill and be killed.

Dev led a company of his best men through the camp. The artillery barrage for the day blasted to life. He nearly reached for Faith's reins in case the sound spooked Horace. But after the horse shied slightly, he walked on. Even the horses were becoming accustomed to the daily barrage.

Dev tried his best to ignore the curious glances they received. A woman riding astride was not the usual way, but then women nurses in the midst of a war also fell outside the normal social proprieties.

Finally they put the army and the bombardment behind them. The surrounding land showed the marks of war — old cabins and shacks raised up off the ground on wood blocks were abandoned or in ruins. A few were still inhabited, but the residents just stared at them from the windows or open doors. Their looks emanated animosity.

"It's sad, isn't it?" Faith said, riding beside him.

"They chose to secede," Dev replied.

"Yes, but humans often make poor decisions."

He couldn't argue with that. In his opinion this venture was one of them. And his decision not to keep faith with Armstrong had been another.

Faith rode beside Dev through the devastated countryside, Dev following the map he'd sketched from the information Faith had received from runaways in the contraband camp. She tried to keep her anticipation strictly under control, but the hope bobbed up continually that today, after five long years, she might see Shiloh again.

Finally, after several miles, they crossed a low creek, and on a knoll ahead she saw a white-columned house, not very large but imposing. A white sign with the name Annerdale Plantation told them they had reached their destination. She gripped the reins and tried not to let a sudden trembling unsettle her horse.

221

The colonel led her and the men up the curved drive to the house. There, with a command for his men to remain in their saddles, he dismounted and so did she. With a gesture, he forestalled her from going forward.

"Hello the house!" he called, a traditional summons when approaching a stranger's house.

A woman, very thin, wearing a blue print dress that had been washed too many times, appeared in the double doorway, followed by a servant — obviously her butler. "What do you want, Yankees?" Her voice vibrated with disdain as she walked to the edge of the porch. "You've left us nothing else to steal."

Ignoring Dev's admonition to stay put, Faith stepped past him to speak with the woman. "Good day. I have come looking for a friend who might be on this plantation or near here."

"I have no Yankee friends. Get off my land."

Faith chose not to respond to the woman's lack of welcome. "My friend was a free woman of color kidnapped before the war and sold south."

"Your friend?"

"Yes, my friend. Her name is Shiloh. She's

light-skinned and has green eyes just like mine. Does thee know of her or has thee seen her?"

"Your *friend*?" the woman repeated as if not comprehending.

"Yes. Does thee know of a woman fitting that description?"

"No. Now get away from here." The woman glared at them, tight-lipped.

Faith didn't know if she had lied or told the truth.

"Thank you for your trouble, ma'am," the colonel said, hooking Faith's elbow and drawing her back.

Though glancing repeatedly over her shoulder, Faith finally let him help her back onto her horse.

When they were out of earshot of the woman, who remained watchful on her porch, Dev murmured, "I watched the butler's face for a reaction to your question, but he gave nothing away. So we'll ride off, and then I'll double back from the rear and question a servant or two. We've come so far. I want to be sure we have all the information and that it's right."

Faith agreed solemnly as she rode beside the colonel. She tried hard not to let her disappointment and defeat come out in tears. She was a nurse, a steadfast woman;

she could not break down here in front of these men who faced battle and death with a stoicism that regularly broke her heart.

Dev could tell that Faith was struggling to deal with this setback. He wished he could have spared her this disappointment, which he had seen as inevitable. But he must leave no Confederate stone unturned. He would follow this lead to the end so she would accept that Honoree's sister was not to be found here. After their company rode out of sight of the main house, Dev led them in circling around from behind, through a grove of trees, and toward the slave cabins. He left his men in the grove, and only he and Faith approached the humble dwellings, a small garden behind each.

As though she'd heard them coming, a wiry old woman with a cane made her way onto the small porch. "What you come here for?" she challenged them.

Dev couldn't blame the woman for her anger. Both armies regularly commandeered supplies from master and slave.

Faith held up a hand to him. "I will speak to her, Colonel." With that Faith slipped from her saddle. "Good day. I am Faith Cathwell. What is thy name?"

The older woman eyed her with suspicion.

"You a Quaker?"

"Yes, I am, and my family has helped hundreds of slaves to freedom."

The woman nodded slowly. "I'm Clary. And I'm too old for freedom. Too old for anythin' but sittin'."

Faith smiled and approached her. "Hello, Clary." She offered the woman her hand.

Dev slid from his saddle and moved to hold the reins of both horses in the shade of a tupelo tree. Once more he was struck by the Quakeress's easy ways with people.

"Won't thee sit, Clary?" Faith waved toward the lone chair on the porch. "I am young and can stand."

The old woman, who looked to have lost most of her teeth, stumped her way to the chair and sat. "What you come for?"

"Please look at my eyes, Clary."

The old woman did. "You got pretty eyes."

Dev had noticed this himself.

Faith smiled. "I am looking for a freeborn friend who has the same green eyes. She was taken from us, kidnapped and sold south before the war. Her name is Shiloh. One of the women in the contraband camp with Grant's army told me that she'd been here."

The woman studied Faith. "You say she a

friend and she got the same green eyes as you?"

"Yes, she's very light-skinned with golden-brown hair and my green eyes. She's more than a friend, really. We are blood relations."

This last sentence punched Dev. What was she saying?

The old woman held her cane in front of her and leaned her chin on her hands. "I never hear no white person claim a colored as blood before. I never thought I live to hear that."

I didn't either. Dev recalled that Faith's mother had left a plantation in Maryland. Was that the source of the connection? If so, it meant that Honoree was far more than Faith's friend. He drew back from this thought, one he should not even entertain.

Faith rested a hand on the woman's. "Please, has Shiloh been here? Her sister and I have come south to find her."

"I saw her, but she wa'n't here long. Two slavers come through here 'fore the war. They had lef' the river to deliver a runaway slave here and claim the bounty."

Faith nodded encouragingly.

The old woman seemed to be having trouble breathing. She paused to catch her breath, then continued, "The master saw Shiloh with the others and tried to buy her, but he couldn't come up with the high price the slavers wanted. They said they'd get much more down in New Orleans at the slave auction."

Faith gasped and stepped closer to the old woman. "Thee saw her?"

"Just a glimpse, but there was talk about her. She really be a beauty."

Faith nodded, wiping her cheek. She must have been weeping. "Yes, she is."

"That be a curse to a colored woman," Clary commented.

What the woman was referring to was a topic never spoken of, especially not to a lady, and it rankled Dev. But he held his silence.

"I'm sorry for your losin' her," Clary said. "I didn't know she been kidnapped. That's evil, just evil."

"It is. That's why I must take her home."

The old woman gazed up at Faith. "I pray you find her."

"I thank thee, Clary, for telling me of Shiloh and for thy prayers."

"I thank your family for helping our people. I never met a Quaker 'fore, but I hear about what you people do for slaves." Clary grasped Faith's hand tightly. "And now Mr. Lincoln say I free, but it come too late for me." Tears dripped from the old eyes.

Hearing the sudden passion in the woman's words, Dev thought of Armstrong. All those years, had Armstrong longed for his freedom? *Would he have left me if I'd given him the choice? Or stayed?* He'd never thought about it before. *I should have.*

Faith leaned over and kissed the woman's forehead. "Thee will be truly free before I. I will see thee in heaven."

The old woman's tears turned into laughter. "I be there to greet you, Miss Faith. We dance in heaven together."

"Good day, Clary, and again I thank thee." Faith reached in her pocket and gave the woman a cloth packet of what appeared to be sugar, a scarce commodity. Then she descended the one step.

Dev led the horses over to her and helped her mount, and they rode back to his men and away. The old woman's talk and Faith's revelation left him stirred up, disgruntled.

The ride back to camp passed somberly. The question of Faith's family tie to Shiloh begged — no, clamored — to be asked, but he resisted. He would not speak of it.

As his party approached a wide, deep creek lined with spreading oaks, Dev motioned for his men to go ahead and water their horses. Another hot day had left them all depleted. He slid off his own horse and passed the reins to the nearest soldier while trying to come up with any other topic to speak about with Faith but the one uppermost in his mind.

He helped Faith down and handed her reins to another man. He drew her under the shade of one of the nearby oak trees and they drank warm water from their canteens.

Nearby, his men talked and laughed. Some waded in the water or lifted filled hats onto their heads. The large oak with its low green boughs shielded Dev and Faith from the others.

"I thought I'd feel better if I discovered word of Shiloh, but I feel worse somehow." Faith sighed and inched deeper into the shade of the oak tree as if further removing herself from him. "New Orleans may be in Union hands, but until Vicksburg surrenders and then Port Hudson south of here, I can't follow this lead any further. It's disheartening." She leaned back against the gnarled bark of the old tree.

He stepped closer, unable to keep his distance. "I wish I could say something, anything that would make this easier for you."

"I wish for the same to say to thee," she murmured. "Don't I see how losing Armstrong, thy friend, has wounded thee?"

He stiffened. Since Armstrong had left, he'd felt hollowed out inside, but he would not discuss it. "Today isn't about me."

"No, but I can't see thee hurting and not wish I could help." Her gentle tone removed the sting from the words.

Yet he resisted the sympathy she offered. "I can't think about that now."

"I know. We can't let ourselves feel things as we would if we weren't here in this dreadful war."

Dev nearly gave in and folded her into his arms, just to comfort her or take comfort himself. His arms ached with wanting to feel her soft form next to him.

She straightened up from the tree. "I must be strong too. I still have to tell Honoree of Shiloh being taken to the New Orleans slave auction, one of the most notorious. And that we can't continue following this lead yet. We will not stop looking, but this news is a hope and a setback at the same time."

Then Dev couldn't stop himself. Faith's mention of Honoree had broken the dike preventing him from speaking of Armstrong. "Couldn't Honoree have reasoned with

Armstrong? Doesn't his enlisting worry her too?"

She raised her gloved hand as if to stop him from saying more. "We cannot protect the ones we love from harm — none of us can. Does thee think my family wanted me to become a nurse in the midst of a war?"

"No," he said, now also unable to hold back the words he'd thought many times. "I wouldn't think so. Why didn't they forbid you?"

"Because in our family an adult is allowed to make his or her own decisions. I know my parents and family and the Friends at our meeting are all praying for me. And in spite of their faith in the all-sufficiency of God, they do worry about me. But this is the work I felt the Inner Light, the Holy Spirit, leading me to do."

"So they just let a defenseless girl go straight into a war?" He was vexed beyond courtesy.

"Did thy decision to join the military make thy mother spring up and rejoice?" She lifted an eyebrow at him.

"That is completely different."

"Because thee is a man and I am a . . . defenseless girl?"

"Yes." His reply was curt because he didn't want to say more, to be as rude as he felt like being. He still thought her father ought to be horsewhipped for not refusing to let her come here.

"We cannot trap our dearest ones within our love, safe from all harm," she continued. "Not in this world. What if my parents had insisted I stay safe at home but a tornado came? While they watched, I could have died there under their own roof."

He tried to interrupt, but she kept talking. "When my twin sister was sick with that fatal fever, I held her hand, but I could not keep her . . . from leaving me." She bowed her head as if hiding her face.

Then he did fold her into his arms. She was only a few inches shorter than he, so his lips came nearest her forehead. He kissed it and tightened his hold on her.

She accepted his embrace for but a moment before drawing away and moving to their safe, neutral topic of choice. "When thee goes home to Baltimore, does thee know which books thee will be looking for in that favorite bookshop of yours?"

He recognized her intent. Both of them needed to step back from the here and now, the overwhelming and unhappy and unsettling here and now. He tugged his reluctant mouth into a smile. "I thought I might depart from the classics and choose some poetry for a change."

The men were bringing the horses up out of the creek, so he led her from the shady oak to meet them.

"What poet?"

"I was considering Wordsworth."

" 'I wandered lonely as a cloud,' " she quoted, " 'that floats on high o'er vales and hills.' " She looked to him.

He continued the poem. " 'When all at once I saw a crowd, a host, of golden daffodils.' "

"Now that would be lovely, but wait just a moment." She moved away from him and bent and picked some plants growing near the creek. "No daffodils here today. I will have to consult my herbal dictionary, but this looks like a different strain of bee balm."

Her knowledge impressed him once again. She tucked the herbs into her pocket.

His men paused with their horses, and he swung her up onto her saddle and mounted his own horse. They rode toward the Union camp.

As they finally reached the outskirts, Dev halted and rose up in his stirrups. Ahead men were everywhere, talking animatedly in small groups. "Something's happened." He motioned for his company to follow him into camp. As they made their way toward the horse corral, the change in mood became more and more palpable.

"A white flag ahead!" one of their fellow cavalrymen shouted to them. "The generals are conferring over terms! Vicksburg is surrendering!"

CHAPTER 10

Dev noticed that the daily artillery barrage was indeed absent. Surrender had come at last. He felt suddenly as if a great weight were sliding off his shoulders. He sucked in a deep breath and gripped the reins more tightly.

The men around him sent up a cheer, but he remained silent. He looked over and Faith was gazing at him. She did not appear jubilant but rather perplexed. He leaned closer to her. "What's the matter?"

"We've waited for this so long, but . . ." Falling silent, she shook her head and pressed her lips together. "Please help me down. I must find Honoree and tell her the news, the bad news." She closed her eyes for a moment as if controlling herself.

He had a hard time understanding her reaction. "Does this hard-won surrender mean nothing to you?"

She tilted her head to one side. "I am

happy that it means there will be no more killing here. But with Port Hudson between Vicksburg and New Orleans, how can I go to that city to discover whether Shiloh has been sold there at auction? And if she was sold, to whom?"

He understood a little now. One more battle won, but how many more lay ahead of them? And even if they could go to New Orleans, where the girl might have been sold, this lead was so slim as to be barely usable. For all they knew, the catchers could have sold her to someone else before they reached New Orleans and the famous slave auction there. But he held his peace, unwilling to discourage Faith now, when she looked so downhearted.

Then a Scripture passage his mother used to quote came to mind, and he spoke it. " 'Take therefore no thought for the morrow: for the morrow shall take thought for the things of itself. Sufficient unto the day is the evil thereof.' From the book of Matthew."

She smiled, and her shoulders relaxed. "I stand rebuked. I will take joy in this victory. It cost us much." She looked toward Vicksburg. "And cost our enemy even more."

Dev ordered his men to tend to their own horses before they joined in the celebration.

He dismounted and led Faith's horse to the corral. There he helped her down from the saddle. Resisting the urge to prolong his hold around her waist, he released her. "I will have someone see to your horse."

She hesitated and then agreed. She murmured good-bye to Horace, her mount for the day, stroked his head, and hurried away.

Dev couldn't help himself — he watched her walk away till he could no longer see her, swallowed up in the reveling crowd.

The lieutenant beside him, currying his horse, said, "She's quite an unusual lady."

Dev merely nodded his agreement. He listened to the happy voices around him and let the ease of a battle won work its way into his heart. He wouldn't look beyond today. *"Sufficient unto the day is the evil thereof."* Then he wondered what the terms of the surrender would be. But that responsibility lay with Grant, not him.

Heading directly to the hospital tents, where she expected to find Honoree, Faith threaded and pushed her way through the milling men, all shouting or singing. One hatless young soldier grabbed her around the waist and danced her in a circle as if they were at a jollification. She pulled away, smiling but shaking her head at his invitation to celebrate.

Finally, ahead, she glimpsed Honoree outside the hospital mess tent. Faith lifted a hand.

Honoree saw her and hurried forward. "Did you . . . ?" Honoree's voice trailed off.

Faith grasped both Honoree's hands. The artillery barrage might have ended, but the rejoicing all around them created nearly as much noise. Leaning close to Honoree's ear, she said, "We spoke to a slave away from the main house, and Shiloh had been there. But on her way to the auction in New Orleans."

Honoree pressed her hand over her mouth and turned away.

Faith claimed her friend's shoulders and rested her cheek against the bright-blue kerchief tied over Honoree's braids. "Not the best news, but the most we've found to date," she said. "We won't give up."

Reaching back, Honoree put her hand over one of Faith's and nodded. "Port Hudson's still holding out."

"Yes, but how long can they do so now that Vicksburg has fallen?" Faith said, forcing a smile while holding in tears.

Amid the tumult of celebration around them, they stood as an island of sadness.

■ ■ ■ ■

"Is thee certain thee wants to come with us to offer aid to the fallen city?" Faith asked Dev as they walked through camp in the morning. The victory celebration had ebbed into routine. Grant had given his permission, so they were entering the defeated city to aid the civilians there.

The normal day sounds still felt abnormal to Dev's ears. Forty-seven days of almost-constant artillery noise had left him disoriented. Hearing birdsong again was strange.

"I have no pressing duties today," he said, "and I think you will need protection."

"We are bringing food and medical supplies. Why would anyone attack us?"

Dev considered it a foolish question.

"Ella wouldn't come with us today," Honoree murmured to Faith. "She was afraid of entering Vicksburg, said no good would come of it."

Dev didn't know who Ella was, but he agreed with her.

Faith shook her head as if denying Honoree's words. "If that is what thee thinks, perhaps thee should not come either."

This exchange reminded him of their argument over whether or not to nurse Jack.

Personally he thought Honoree should remain in camp. She could be a target of nastiness.

"I'm coming, but I'm not thinking I'll meet any thanks," Honoree said grimly.

Honoree was evidently the realist and Faith the idealist. But he didn't comment, merely walked with Faith, Honoree, and Dr. Bryant beside a wagon packed with food and medical supplies. The colonel had brought a few of his men along for added protection.

The Southern civilians he'd met in similar situations hated the Union with a virulent, sometimes-violent passion. Walking into this defeated city to offer aid would be like trying to help a wounded wild animal. Would they get bitten or savaged for their efforts?

The terms of surrender had been settled. The Confederate soldiers — thirty thousand men — had promised not to fight again and to go home. The day before, Dev had watched them march out of the city, some of them nearly naked in ragged, worn clothing and all looking pitifully starved and defeated.

He'd been proud to see many of his fellow Union soldiers open their haversacks, sharing their hardtack and offering cups of coffee to the defeated Rebels. Some even had given clothing to those who needed it.

But now Dev felt as if he were once more on reconnaissance, exposed to danger and watching for the enemy. He stepped closer to Faith, his every sense alert.

As they entered the city, their party beheld a scene beyond the imagination of most. He'd heard the artillery every day, but now he saw the destruction it had inflicted. Rubble covered the streets, mixed with remnants of exploded shells; destroyed houses leaned against each other. A few gaunt people, sitting on straight-backed chairs in front of a damaged house, turned hollow-eyed stares at them.

Dev couldn't stop himself. He imagined Baltimore, his hometown, devastated like this, and a pressure gripped his heart. Thank God Maryland had not seceded.

"Good day!" Dr. Bryant called to the family in front of the house. "We've brought food and medicine. I'm a doctor, and these women are my nurses. Do you have any sick who need help?"

The people continued to stare in silence.

Dr. Bryant repeated the question louder.

An emaciated woman, her hair unbound, burst out of a nearby home. "You have food? Medicine?"

"For the sick. I'm a doctor. Do you have — ?"

She ran to him and grasped his hand. "My daughter. Come. Please."

Faith and Honoree accompanied the doctor inside. Dev gestured for his men to remain guarding the wagon while he went inside too. On a sofa in the parlor lay a girl of about thirteen, almost a skeleton in a thin nightgown too large for her.

Dr. Bryant touched her forehead and spoke softly to Faith. "High fever." He turned to the woman. "How long has she been ill?"

"Four days. Can you help her, please?" The mother twisted the hem of her threadbare apron in her hands.

"We'll do our best." He knelt by the child and quickly examined her. "It's measles."

That word filled Dev with revulsion. Measles had swept away thousands of soldiers who'd signed up to fight but instead had died in camp.

"We need to bring down her fever and feed her up," Faith said.

"Exactly," Dr. Bryant confirmed. "I will leave her in your capable hands, Nurse Cathwell, while I go on ahead. I'm sure I will be needed elsewhere." He turned to the mother. "Nurse Cathwell has much experi-

242

ence with measles. She will do everything possible for your daughter. Listen to what she tells you."

He turned to go, nodding to Dev as if to say, *Please stay and protect them.*

Dev bowed his head in agreement and tried not to glance at the ill child. Though used to battlefield devastation, he was not prepared for this. A house stripped of all possessions; civilians sick, starving, defeated. He had trouble drawing a full breath.

"I'll do all I can," Faith said, kneeling beside the patient. She looked to the girl's mother. "I am going to add some alcohol to the water thee has been bathing her face with. That will make it more effective. And Honoree will mix some hardtack with sugar and wine for thee to feed thy daughter."

The woman looked surprised at Faith's Quaker plain speech.

Honoree carried a small sack of ingredients to the fireplace mantel and mixed the slurry. She offered the small bowl to the woman. "Here, ma'am. We've found that this is nourishing and helps with fever."

The mother glared at Honoree but accepted the bowl, muttering to herself.

This woman's reaction reminded him of Jack, who'd cursed Faith even as she nursed him. But Honoree had refused to nurse his

243

cousin. Why had she come here today?

When the mother knelt beside her daughter and began to feed her, Faith rose. "We will bring more food before we go back to our camp. Thy daughter most needs nourishment and liquid to help her fight off this fever."

The woman stared at her. "I don't understand."

"Pardon?" Faith halted, gazing at her.

"Why are you helping us?"

Dev could understand why the woman asked the question and why Faith looked confused.

" 'Love your enemies. . . . Do good to them that hate you,' " Faith quoted, and then she and Honoree turned to leave.

The woman glared at them, looking extremely irritated. "Don't preach to me. I'm as Christian as you are."

Faith glanced over her shoulder. "Of course."

The woman continued to scowl at Faith's and Honoree's backs till she looked down at her daughter, and her face softened.

Outside, Dev accompanied the two women as they caught up with Dr. Bryant. He kept close to them. He sensed that Faith, her plain Quaker speech marking her, might act as a lightning rod here. Just as slaves warmed to her when they heard her speak, that same speech today would no doubt attract *unpleasant* reactions.

Out on the main street, more citizens had come out to stare at them.

Then two thin black women in tattered clothing hurried toward their procession. "Kin we come with you to freedom?" one implored, her hands held forward in supplication.

An image of Armstrong hit Dev between the eyes.

"Of course," Honoree said.

A white woman ran after them. "You come back here! You belong to me."

"No, they don't —" Honoree began.

The woman slapped Honoree's face.

Honoree returned the favor.

People from all around surged forward, yelling curses and threats.

"Stop or I'll shoot!" Dev bellowed, raising his carbine. "Back! Get back!" His men drew their weapons too, forming a circle around Faith, Honoree, and the two others, facing the woman who'd slapped Honoree.

Everyone in the area froze.

"If you require food or medical aid," Dev ordered, "you can remain outside. If not, return to your homes. Now!" His heart beat fast. Would he be forced to kill a civilian?

The people around them stared for a moment before beginning to retreat. Finally only the woman who'd slapped Honoree remained, but she looked defeated. "How can you leave me?" she said to the two women who'd run from her. "We've been together all our lives."

Dev repeated her words in his mind. Again memories of Armstrong wrapped around his throat. He lowered his carbine.

"Only because we couldn't leave," the older black woman replied. "We don't wish anythin' bad on you, but we want our freedom."

"I've lost everything and everyone. How can you leave me all alone?" The white woman began to weep.

"We just want our freedom," the black woman repeated.

In Dev's mind, the words echoed, but in Armstrong's voice. *Armstrong, I only wanted your best.*

Her shoulders drooping, the woman shuffled off without a word.

Dev felt her loss as keenly as his own. He stiffened himself, not allowing any of this weakness to show. Besides, their cases weren't identical. He'd always wanted Armstrong to be free eventually, just not in the middle of a war.

Faith and Honoree exchanged glances. "Stay close to the colonel," Honoree urged the newly freed black women, "till we leave."

After a couple of hours, the wagon had been emptied of food and medicine. More freed slaves had joined the first two, and as they walked out of town, the slaves crowded cautiously around the wagon.

Dev fell into step beside Faith. She looked at him. "This must have been difficult for thee today."

He tried to think what she was referring to.

" 'No man can serve two masters: for either he will hate the one, and love the other,' " Faith quoted, " 'or else he will hold to the one, and despise the other.' "

Dev puzzled over the quote. What did that Scripture have to do with him? He didn't often struggle between serving God and serving money — no more than any other man. He covered his confusion with a noncommittal "Oh?"

Just as they left, a rifle shot zipped overhead. Dev drew his carbine, threw one arm over Faith, and ran, bent over, with the others. They hurried out of town. So much for surrender.

With Vicksburg in Union hands, supply

boats had begun docking and delivering food, clothing, medicine, newspapers, and letters and packages from home. While Faith read a letter from her mother, Honoree sat near her, fanning away flies and chatting with Ella, who stood near a bubbling, steaming open kettle. Ella had asked if she could do their personal laundry for extra money, so she'd come today and was boiling their whites over the low fire. Faith and Honoree had taken turns helping to carry water so Ella could work more efficiently. Soon all their underthings and bedding would be fresh and ironed. What a lovely feeling that would be.

The drummers still measured out their days, but everyone looked happier than they had in months. Faith, however, fretted over how they could ever get to New Orleans when Port Hudson, the last outpost of Confederate resistance on the Mississippi, still blocked them — along with other concerns.

In war one did not just set out across military lines. Yet she must somehow get to New Orleans, the only place they might find any information about Shiloh's whereabouts. Faith sighed and continued reading. "Oh!" she exclaimed, holding the letter out

like a snake as she came to the final para-
graph.

"What is it?" Honoree turned to her.

"I'm afraid . . ." Faith swallowed and then
continued. "John has been conscripted, and
thy brother Samuel has enlisted."

Honoree rose and came nearer. "Let me
see."

Faith handed over the letter from her
mother, pointing to the part she'd refer-
enced.

Honoree read the passage and stooped to
be at Faith's level. "I didn't think it would
come to that." Her voice vibrated with concern.

Faith was sick at heart. And now, along
with the colonel and Armstrong, her brother
and Honoree's would be thrown into this
terrible fiery hurricane of war. She linked
hands with Honoree. "God, please protect
our brothers," Faith prayed aloud.

"Your brothers?"

Faith glanced up to see Colonel Knight.
He stood nearby, a full cloth bag in hand.
"Colonel, yes, my brother has been conscripted, and Honoree's has enlisted. We'd
hoped this war would be over before that
happened."

"Your brother will go to war?" the colonel
asked Faith. "I didn't think Quakers served

in the military."

"My mother writes that John found himself caught between opposing violence and desiring to help preserve the Union. He chose the latter."

"And my brother turned twenty-one and made his own decision," Honoree added, picking up their water buckets as if ready to go fetch more.

"Is this John your brother who attended college?" the colonel asked Faith.

Faith nodded. "He began teaching two years ago at a boys' academy."

The colonel shook his head as if in sympathy.

"What can we do for thee, Colonel?" Faith asked, folding the letter and slipping it into her apron pocket. She hoped he'd brought some news about Port Hudson.

"I was going to ask you to recommend a laundress." Dev nodded toward the woman who was tending to theirs. He was a bit surprised to see her helping with the laundry instead of Honoree.

Faith turned to the pretty young woman. "Ella?" The young woman eyed him uncertainly.

"Shall I bring my things here or . . . ?" Dev asked, a bit uncomfortable about the sack in his hand. In the past Armstrong had taken care of his clothing and so much more.

"Is that thy laundry?" Faith asked, eyeing the sack.

"Yes, and I have more — shirts to be washed and ironed too," he admitted, not wanting to meet her gaze.

His reticence about laundry appeared to amuse her. "Colonel, if those are whites in that sack, Ella can add thy laundry to ours today."

"Do my laundry with yours?" Dev was sincerely shocked, his jaw hanging loose.

Faith laughed. "We will avert our eyes so we don't have to watch the *promiscuous* mingling of bachelor and maiden laundry," she teased, snatching the bag from him and tossing it near Ella.

The young woman looked hesitant, but she picked up the sack and emptied it into the large kettle. Honoree grinned in amusement, and Faith shook her head at him, chuckling.

"You are laughing at me," Dev said.

"A bit. It feels good to be able to laugh again."

Dev bowed his head toward her, enjoying her laughter though he didn't say so. Faith moved in his direction. "The colonel will pay the same, Ella."

"No, he won't!"

The four of them turned at the outburst, only to witness a very angry young soldier approaching quickly.

"Landon," Ella said, looking nervous, "I'm just doing our laundry. And I added these good ladies' things to the pot."

"Ella, that's not all you're doin'. And I won't have it. White women don't take in laundry. It's bad enough I can't hire ours out —"

"Ella, won't thee introduce us?" Faith interrupted.

"Miss Faith, this is my husband, Corporal Landon McCullough," Ella said, looking even more nervous.

Faith politely offered her hand. "Corporal McCullough, I'm Faith Cathwell and this is my friend Honoree Langston." Then she nodded toward Dev. "This is Colonel Devlin Knight."

The young man looked uncomfortable but shook Faith's hand as briefly as possible, glanced at Honoree, and saluted the colonel. "Sorry, sir. I was distracted."

"At ease, Corporal." If he'd known this man's wife was from the South, he could have avoided this breach of etiquette. But he'd assumed she was from the North like Faith.

"Corporal," Faith continued, "thy sweet wife is helping us with our laundry, as she said. And white women do take in laundry in the North."

"We're not from the North," the corporal said through gritted teeth.

"That is quite true," Faith allowed, "but while in Rome, one must do as the Romans do."

"What?"

"Corporal, I know in the South a white woman taking in laundry is not the usual," Dev cut in, hoping to avoid trouble for the young wife. "But this is wartime. Nothing here is like it is at home. And I know firsthand that in the Mexican War white women worked as laundresses."

Corporal McCullough chewed on these words and finally nodded grudgingly. "Ella, you can help these ladies. Everybody knows about how much Miss Faith and Honoree do for wounded soldiers. But I won't have you takin' in laundry like a . . ."

"Like a Negress," Honoree finished for him, lacing the word with sarcasm.

The corporal stiffened, flushing red.

"Corporal," Dev said as if he'd not heard Honoree's words, "I just lost my manservant and I'd take it as a personal favor if you would allow your wife to take care of my

253

things this once. I need to go to the contraband camp and find someone to care for my clothing, but I haven't had time."

Landon turned to him. "Well, if you put it that way, I can't very well refuse." He looked to his wife. "Ella, just this time, understand?"

"Yes, Landon." Ella smiled tentatively. "I didn't mean . . . I —"

"Very well," Landon said, drawing closer to her and handing her a knapsack. "You forgot these," he whispered.

With a tremulous smile, Ella accepted the knapsack, and after saluting the colonel, Landon left them.

Dev noticed Faith looking past him, over his shoulder. She smiled and said, "Armstrong, how happy I am to see thee."

Dev stiffened. He turned.

Armstrong stood before him in an artillery uniform with one private's stripe. Dry-mouthed, Dev could only stare at the man.

"Good day, Miss Faith," Armstrong said politely. "Miss Honoree?"

"Armstrong!" Honoree said with obvious pleasure, setting down the buckets she held and coming forward.

Armstrong reached for her hand. "Would you walk with me, Miss Honoree?"

The girl laughed as if he'd told a joke.

"Never," she teased even as she claimed his arm.

Not even glancing toward Dev, Armstrong managed to bow to Faith as Honoree walked away on his arm.

Ignored and miffed, Dev almost asked him to wait. But what could he say? *I'm sorry?* He was sorry, but not at all sorry.

"It is a difficult situation," Faith said with audible sympathy.

He didn't want her sympathy.

"Will thee walk me so I can fetch more water to help Ella?" she asked him, picking up the discarded buckets.

He wanted to deny her, but everything within him strained toward her. Just being near Faith had become his only solace. "As you wish," he said.

She gripped his arm as Honoree had Armstrong's. After a few paces, she asked in a low voice, "What is it about doing laundry that is demeaning to whites? It's honest work."

Dev didn't want to answer her because he wasn't entirely sure how to explain.

She glanced up at him around her bonnet brim. "Colonel?"

"A white woman who's poor can do her own laundry," he replied, "but only black women do laundry for hire."

"Why?"

Dev shrugged, uncomfortable, yet he couldn't understand why.

Faith walked beside him, obviously in thought. They passed other soldiers doing laundry, writing letters, cleaning their rifles.

"That is the worst part of the slave system," she murmured.

"What is?" He couldn't keep his irritation from his tone. Seeing Armstrong and being ignored nettled him, and he hated admitting that even to himself.

"When only black people labor and black people are disrespected, then honest labor loses its respect. Doesn't thee see that?"

"What does it matter?" Why couldn't she leave it be for once?

"It matters because first, it's wrong; and second, slavery is not going to continue. If honest labor isn't respected, who will do the work in the South then?"

"Did you ever think the South might prevail?" he replied, not believing the disgruntled words but not wanting to go along with her line of reasoning.

"No," she said flatly. "The Northern blockade is closing the South's ports along the Atlantic, the Gulf, and now the Mississippi River. Since Lincoln's Emancipation Proclamation made slavery the official issue of this war, Europe is not coming to their aid. And the North is enlisting immigrants as quickly as they come to our shore, a seemingly endless supply of men. An army must have men and supplies. The South has limited numbers of both and is being depleted almost daily."

Everything she said was absolutely accurate, but he didn't reply. He could still hardly believe some of the subjects that came up in this woman's conversation.

"After they lose the war," Faith went on, "the white people of the South will be too poor to hire the freed slaves. Who will rebuild the factories and homes and plant the crops?"

"I don't have an answer for you."

She drew in a deep breath, somehow not finished. "The South's future is not bright. This war is destroying it, and it may not have the will to rebuild since it will lose its free slave labor."

Her words pierced him. He shut his mind to them. He wanted to turn the discussion away from the South's bleak prospects, Maryland's prospects. "I just read a newspaper account of a battle that took place almost concurrently with the surrender here," he said to distract her. "It was in Pennsylvania."

"A battle in Pennsylvania? The Confederate Army penetrated into Union territory?" Faith interrupted.

"Yes. Lee's army."

"What town? My father is from Pittsburgh."

"Gettysburg, a small town in the south."

"Ah, I overheard something about this yesterday, but I haven't had time to read the newspaper I bought from the vendor earlier today. What has happened?"

"While Vicksburg was surrendering, the Union defeated Lee's army at Gettysburg, but at great loss."

Faith tightened her grip on his arm.

"I'm sorry," he said, already regretful he'd brought this up. She was a woman who cared too much. "I shouldn't have told you —"

"Don't be foolish," she said. "I would have found out. I am not some delicate shoot that must be carefully tended in a greenhouse. I'm a nurse in war. I just . . ." She pressed her fist against her lips. Finally she managed to speak again. "Thee knows what I think of this war."

Then the words he'd vowed not to say to her slipped out. "Why did you quote that Scripture to me the other day in Vicksburg?"

She looked into his eyes. "About serving

two masters?"

"Yes." He waited.

"Can't thee guess?"

"No." He couldn't help sounding grumpy.

"Thee does know."

They came upon a pump on the outskirts of Vicksburg near an abandoned house. He walked over and began working the handle for her. The metal's creaking made him grit his teeth. For the moment they were alone.

She held the first bucket under the stream of cool water. "Colonel, thee comes from a slave state but fights to preserve the Union. Thee owned a slave yet didn't want to. Thee planned to free him but didn't."

He didn't respond at first but was unable to keep silent for long. "The passage has nothing to do with that and you know it. It has to do with seeking worldly wealth instead of following God."

She moved the full bucket aside and set the empty one under the water stream. "That is true, but it fits. My family has devoted themselves to following God —"

"Slavery is in the Bible," he retorted. " 'Servants, be obedient to them that are your masters.' "

"At Jubilee, every seven years, slaves were to be freed," Faith replied calmly, evenly. "Nowhere in the Bible does it say one race should enslave another race just because of skin color. And don't insult Armstrong or Honoree by telling me they need us to take care of them. Who took care of thee for the past twenty years?"

He wanted to snap at her, and if her tone had been argumentative, he would have. But she'd said those inflammatory words without emotion, stating them as simple facts. His chest tightened with her rebuke.

"Plantation owners didn't want to pay for the labor because they desired not just to provide for their families but to gain inordinate wealth," Faith said. "That is greed. Thee said thyself that thy mother didn't want to hold slaves and left her family's plantation for that reason. My mother left her family over the same issue. If the South had served God instead of mammon, this war would not have happened."

"It's not as easy as that," Dev muttered, still unwilling to go where she was leading him. "The crops in the South — cotton, tobacco, rice — are different from the crops in the North and need many workers to tend to them. Hence the plantation system." Dev concentrated on pumping.

"Thee is at cross-purposes with thyself," she said, ignoring what he'd said. "A house divided against itself cannot stand. And it sounds to me as if thy family is divided against itself. Thy mother versus thy uncle. Jack versus thee. And thee not keeping thy promise to Armstrong." Not looking at him, she moved the second filled bucket away, then bent and splashed the last of the stream onto her face and neck.

Dev let his pump hand drop. "I don't want to talk about Armstrong." His own rudeness abashed him. "I'm sorry, but —"

She interrupted him. "How long can thee push aside these conflicts? Can't thee see the world is changing around thee? I just posed the problem of the loss of Southern wealth that will come with the war's end."

"I know," he said tersely, again ashamed of himself.

She didn't reply, merely gazed at him.

He picked up the full buckets and led her back through camp, surrounded by snatches of the conversations of the men they passed. He could not bring himself to speak to her. She made it sound so clear and easy to change his outlook, but she was not in it as deeply as he was. Her family wasn't torn in two.

She hummed as if she didn't feel the tension he did. It irritated him.

"I heard from my mother too," he said

finally, trying to regain their usual companionship.

"Some things don't change," she said with a soft smile. "Our mothers' love for us."

Even as everything else changes. He concentrated on the water in the buckets he carried, careful not to spill.

"Is there any news about Port Hudson?" she asked.

He resented the question because he knew why she asked it. How could he persuade her not to go to New Orleans? The times were too uncertain, too volatile for her to travel among people who wished her dead. And then to start asking them for information about a freeborn woman of color kidnapped and sold as a slave! She'd be exposing the ugliest side of slavery.

He must find a way to persuade her to listen to him and drop this quest till after the war.

"Colonel?" she prompted.

"No, no news from Port Hudson." He was forced by honesty to add, "But I doubt they can hold out long now."

"Nothing in this war makes sense to me."

He couldn't disagree. He tried to come up with a topic to turn away from these weighty subjects. But as usual, she was quicker.

"Tell me more about thy library. What book is the most important to thee?" she asked in a much lighter tone.

Inhaling deeply, he replied, "Machiavelli's *The Prince.*" Grateful for the distraction, he vowed that when Port Hudson fell or surrendered, he'd find some way to forestall her. He couldn't understand why she didn't seem to have the sense to fear. But evidently she would not give up on her friend Shiloh . . . or on him.

CHAPTER 11

On yet another sweltering July morning, Faith and Honoree reported to the hospital tent for their morning duties and there met Ella, willing to help as usual. The young wife looked wan, her clothing wrinkled, no doubt just the way they appeared to her. Outside, the drummer finished sounding morning roll call. Gazing around at the sparsely occupied cots, Faith heard herself sighing.

Though she and the colonel had parted without further rancor, she couldn't overcome the prickly part of their conversation. Why was it that an intelligent man, an officer and a graduate of West Point, could not see the contradiction in his own actions and thoughts?

Pushing this question aside, Faith smiled at the first patient she approached. Now that the fighting here was at an end, their tasks had become lighter and lighter as patients recovered and went back to their duties or were sent home, discharged from further service. Even in this quiet period Faith didn't allow herself to think too far ahead. The war had yet to be won. This was merely a lull between campaigns. The Mississippi River had almost been taken by the Union. But that left the rest of the Confederacy to conquer.

And what about Shiloh? Faith sighed again, scolded herself, and began moving from patient to patient, seeing to their needs.

After making the rounds, Faith sat down beside a young soldier whose right sleeve was pinned up over what remained of his arm. He had yet to learn to write with his left hand. She'd brought a small portable writing desk with her for cases like this. "I have time to write letters," she told him gently.

"Thank you, miss."

She began writing down what he dictated, knowing that those receiving the news of his injury and his discharge would be both happy and sad. His wife would say, "At least he's alive," and then she would cry till there were no more tears. Faith fought the temptation to give in to this moroseness. She had work to do.

Dr. Bryant appeared in the opening of the

tent, gesturing to them. "Ladies, please come outside. You too, Mrs. McCullough."

Faith, Honoree, and Ella glanced at each other but obeyed the summons.

"I'll be right back," Faith murmured to the soldier and set her writing desk down on the bedside camp stool.

Outside, Faith saw that one of the photographers who'd recently arrived in camp had now set up his odd-looking equipment here.

"I have decided to have a photograph of our staff taken," Dr. Bryant said. "How do you want us to pose?" he asked the photographer.

Faith's restless mind drew her back to the scene of the colonel pumping water for her and denying the truth that he was as divided as this nation was, warring within himself.

Intruding into her thoughts, the thin photographer in a dusty hat stepped forward and arranged them according to height in front of the tent. He set Dr. Bryant in the center. But he left Honoree out of the arrangement.

Faith cleared her throat and glanced at Dr. Bryant.

"Honoree, please take your place next to Nurse Cathwell," Dr. Bryant said.

"I thought she was a maid," the photographer said, looking puzzled.

"I hear that a lot," Honoree said, inserting herself beside Faith. "But I am a trained nurse."

"Really?" the photographer commented, shaking his head as if he'd heard everything now. He hurried back to his camera and ducked his head under the cloth. "Now hold still. Hold still. Doooon't move."

Faith and everyone around her froze into place. She tried to keep her face pleasant, not liking photographs where people looked as if they were being slowly tortured. The point she'd tried to make with the colonel was that he was torturing himself by his refusal to face reality. Just like Ella's husband, whose ideas of what was proper for a white woman to do would no longer be true after the war. At least, that's how Faith saw it.

Even after her conversation with the colonel had taken a turn for the better — when he'd told her about his most prized book — he'd looked vexed as they parted. That should not matter to her, but it did. *She* would not avoid the truth. But she could not force the colonel to see it. *"There are none so blind as those who will not see."*

Finally the flash of powder and the loud click startled Faith back to the present.

"Done! You can move again!" The photographer came out from his cloth head-tent and removed the glass plate from the bulky camera on stilts. "Shall I take one more in case someone moved?"

Dr. Bryant agreed, and they all went through the process a second time. Faith forced herself to stare at the camera and hold the colonel away from her thoughts.

"I will be taking many photographs around camp," the photographer said. "My tent is to the north side. If you'd like to purchase a photograph, come there before I leave camp. I will be developing film every evening for a while."

Relieved, Faith and Honoree turned to go back inside the hospital tent, Ella in their wake. "Should I purchase a couple," Faith asked Honoree, "to send home?"

"Yes. I don't think it's a case of vanity if that's your concern. Our parents would be happy to see us and the people we work with. And I'd like to give one to Armstrong before he leaves."

Abruptly Faith turned to Honoree. "He's leaving?"

"The fighting here is nearly done. Most of the army will be moving east now, don't you think?"

"I believe thee is right," Faith commented, unhappily picturing the colonel charging into battle again, the thought squeezing her heart.

Ella gasped and swayed, bumping into Faith.

Honoree reached out and steadied the girl. "You look as white as a sheet. We'll get you some coffee."

"Oh no," Ella moaned. "I don't want coffee."

Honoree put an arm around her and propelled her toward the empty hospital mess tent, seating her at a table inside. Honoree headed out through the open back flap to get something for her from the cook.

"What is it?" Faith said, sitting beside Ella and touching her forehead. "Thee doesn't have a fever."

"Miss Faith," Ella whispered close to her ear, "I think I'm in the family way."

Faith stopped, brought up short. She should have expected this, guessed it was coming. She didn't want to say the words that hovered in her throat — *"Not now. Not here."* She bit them back. "That's a blessing."

Ella suppressed a sob and leaned into Faith's shoulder. "I want my mama."

Faith pulled the girl into a sideways hug and patted her back. "Of course thee does."

"But I can't go home," the girl said between muffled sobs. "Ever."

At least Ella was facing reality. "No, not for a long while," Faith agreed.

Honoree came down the aisle with a tin cup. "The cook had some chamomile leaves and brewed tea." She set the cup in front of Ella and sat across from her, half turned. "Sip it. It will help."

Ella gazed blankly at the mug.

"Ella is in the family way," Faith murmured. "And, Ella, Honoree is right. This is good for thee. Chamomile is a calming herb."

"The cook laced it with sugar too," Honoree said, sounding sympathetic.

Ella lifted the mug and sniffed the tea, then sipped it with caution. "Not bad."

"I wish I could send thee to my mother," Faith said. "But it's so far and —"

"I wouldn't want to leave Landon," Ella said, swallowing tears. "He's all I got now." She stared into the mug. "I wish this war had never started."

"We all agree with that," Honoree said with a decided nod. "But who listens to women?"

Ella smiled a bit at this comment and sipped more of the tea. When she had finished, the three of them rose to return to the hospital.

"Thee must not worry, Ella. Honoree and I will make sure thee has enough good food to eat and anything else thee needs," Faith promised. "And this morning, why doesn't thee sit in the shade and roll bandages from the laundry?"

"Thank you, Miss Faith. I think I can do that. I've been a bit wobbly today."

Faith patted her arm and then they entered the hospital, Ella hanging back to collect the bandages near the supply area and Faith and Honoree heading toward the patients they'd left behind.

"I don't know what we're going to do about going to New Orleans." Honoree spoke the words Faith was thinking.

Faith started another long sigh. And then stopped it midway. Trying to go overland through enemy territory — unthinkable, even once Port Hudson fell. *And we'll need a military pass and transportation to get there.*

With these obstacles in mind, she went to the soldier she'd been writing the letter for and picked up her portable writing desk to continue. An errant thought came to her. Would the photographer be taking any pictures of the cavalry? Perhaps of Colonel Knight?

■ ■ ■ ■

July 10, 1863

In the evening Faith and Honoree stepped outside the mess tent. Faith overheard a shout, a "Hurrah!" of many voices nearby.

She turned, waiting to see what had happened. A drummer boy began pounding his drum and a soldier ran by, shouting, "Port Hudson has surrendered!"

Faith halted, and so did Honoree. Suddenly everyone around them was shouting and laughing. The long-fought goal had been achieved. The Confederacy had been cut in two. With the taking of the Mississippi River, no aid from Texas, Arkansas, or Missouri could easily reach the Confederate forces east of the river. And the Confederacy was hemmed in on all sides.

Now they could pursue the lead to Shiloh. But how would they manage it? Faith glanced at Honoree and saw that she too wanted to go where they could talk privately. The two of them headed straight for their tent. The tumult of celebration could not be ignored, but inside the tent they faced each other.

"This means we can go south to New Orleans," Honoree said.

Faith frowned, feeling the weight of their challenge. They were women bucking against men's desire to protect them. "Only if we can persuade them to let us go."

Honoree mirrored her frown, then sighed. "I'm going to find Armstrong if I can."

Faith nodded in understanding. Of course Honoree wanted to share this moment of victory with Armstrong. They stepped outside the tent, Honoree hurrying off. Amid the celebration around her, Faith walked away, thinking of words to persuade the command to let her and Honoree travel to New Orleans.

"Miss Faith." The colonel's voice broke into her abstraction.

She looked up and found herself very near his tent. "Oh." She hadn't intentionally set her course to arrive here.

"I'm on my way to check on my horse. Come with me?"

She fell into step beside him, noting that he was not partaking in the general high spirits either.

He led her through the raucous celebration, such a contrast from their serious mood. After a few paces, he stated, "You want to persuade me that you should be allowed to go to New Orleans now."

"Yes," she admitted. Why try to dissemble?

They passed more rejoicing soldiers, some slapping each other on the back and others singing. "I still don't understand why you can't just wait on this till after the war is over." He sounded irritated.

She pondered how to explain it to him. "If thy cousin Bellamy had not been killed but instead captured by the Mexican army, would thee have tried to free him or would thee just have left him in a Mexican prison until the war ended?"

"I would have obeyed orders." He shielded her as a throng of soldiers passed on both sides of them.

She let out a sound of exasperation. "That does not address my question, and thee knows it."

He drew her away from another group of soldiers who were obviously imbibing. "I am a man. You are a woman. What I can do and should do are different from what you can do and should do."

She stared at him, miffed. She had been raised to think men and women were equal before God, but Devlin Knight, like the majority, no doubt viewed women as inferior. Finally she shook her head at him. "When this war ends, thee is going to have to face the fact that life is about more than following orders and putting everyone into a neat hierarchy."

He picked up the pace, the makeshift paddock just ahead. "Tell me more about your garden."

Recognizing this for the distraction it was, she stifled her aggravation with him, with the military, with men in general. He must still think she could be diverted from her goal. Why had she let herself begin having feelings for this man who could not accept her for what she was: an intelligent, capable woman?

The next day Faith sat in her tent, trying to gather her courage. Honoree was tightening loose buttons on a shirt as Faith sorted herbs in her medicine chest. It was time to seize the moment and try to obtain passage to New Orleans and back again.

After her conversation with the colonel last night, she would not bother to appeal to any other lower-ranking officers. They would no doubt all deny her, belittle her, wasting time and irritating her further. She was left with no other option but going straight to General Grant.

"Miss Faith!" a man called to her from outside the tent.

Faith stepped through the door and recognized one of the orderlies. "Yes?"

275

"Dr. Bryant says come quick, please."

Faith didn't like the urgency in the man's voice. "Of course."

Honoree came out. "Am I wanted?"

"The doctor didn't mention you," the orderly said.

"I'm coming anyway," Honoree insisted.

"Yes." Faith rushed toward the hospital tent. Inside, she paused to look around. And she did not like what she saw. The beds, which had blessedly become nearly empty, were filling up once more. Why? The fighting and shelling had ended for the time being. She stood stock-still for a moment, apprehension gripping her.

"Nurse Cathwell!" Dr. Bryant called to her from near a patient.

She hurried to his side.

He didn't wait for her to speak. "I'm afraid we have yet another measles outbreak."

Fear charged through her. He evidently observed her shocked dismay. "Yes, I know — not at all what we wanted. But it's here and we must face it. Since you and Honoree both survived it in childhood, you are both immune. But I don't want anybody else in here who hasn't contracted it before."

"Yes, Doctor." The calm words masked her inner riot. She wanted to run from the tent, screaming hysterically, *"Measles! Measles!"* Measles had killed her sister and, since the war began, had slaughtered thousands of soldiers, both blue and gray. And now she must face it again, watch others suffer as Patience had — and perhaps die too. A lone tear trailed down her cheek.

Dr. Bryant squeezed her shoulder. "Please begin brewing that willow-bark tea you provided the last time we dealt with this nasty disease."

"Yes, of course," she murmured. "Did we bring this contagion back from our visit to Vicksburg? That girl had it."

The doctor shrugged. "We have no way of knowing. New recruits are arriving by the boatload. Any one of them could have introduced this plague. I'm designating this tent for measles patients only. A quarantine. Go get your herbs, and then we will remain apart and hope we can ride out this onslaught with as few casualties as possible."

"Yes, Doctor," she repeated and hastened to obey. At the tent opening she was shocked to see Landon and Ella coming in. "What is it?"

"Landon has a fever," Ella said. "Dr. Dyson told me to bring him here in case he has measles." Ella's expression pleaded for this not to be true.

Faith leaned forward and touched Landon's forehead with her wrist. "Open thy mouth, please."

"I want the doctor," Landon said.

Faith swallowed her irritation and said, "Whether I'm a doctor or a nurse, I will recognize the signs. Please open thy mouth or I can't let thee go farther. This is a quarantine tent."

"Well, why didn't you say so?" Landon blustered weakly and complied.

Merely glancing into his mouth, Faith caught sight of the telltale spots. She turned. "Dr. Bryant! Here is Ella's husband. I think he has the measles." She looked to Ella. "Thee has been exposed to measles, so thee can stay."

Landon objected weakly, "I don't want her —"

"The doctor will explain." Faith hurried out to fetch her supply of herbs. Would the army never be done with this contagion, too often fatal?

Once again Patience came to mind, the image of her still, white face as she lay within her coffin. Panic nearly brought a cry from deep inside Faith. She wrestled with it. *I will not think of losing her now. I will just obey the doctors. I will not let fear rule me, make me ineffective.*

July 17, 1863

A week of the measles outbreak had passed. The quarantine tent had filled to overflowing with young men too ill to stand. The fevered, sweat-soaked soldiers lay without even a sheet covering them in the stifling heat. Occasionally one moaned in delirium, but otherwise all was quiet. During another long night, Faith lowered herself onto a blanket on the ground at the rear of the quarantine tent, too exhausted to do more. She wondered where Honoree had settled, but in the sparse light she couldn't see her and didn't have the strength to summon her. Faith let her head sink onto her arm.

Patience held out her hand and Faith rose up. She tried to grasp Patience's hand but couldn't. Patience said, "I miss thee."

They were walking behind their home in Sharpesburg, their pet dogs around them, leaping after butterflies. "I'm in love," Faith said. "But there's a war."

Patience smiled over her shoulder and continued to walk just out of reach. Faith hurried forward, but however quickly she moved, she couldn't catch her sister.

"Wake up." A voice summoned Faith and

a hand shook her shoulder. "Wake up."

Faith gasped, her eyes opening.

With a candlestick in hand, Honoree knelt beside her. "You were calling out for Patience."

Faith blinked, nodded, and let her heavy eyelids shut again.

"Who's Patience?"

Faith could hear Ella's voice nearby but didn't have the will to reopen her eyes.

"Faith had a twin sister." Honoree spoke softly in the night. "An identical twin sister. She died from measles just before my sister was kidnapped."

"Oh, how sad . . . for both of you."

Shiloh sat in a chair, bound and gagged. Shiloh! Faith tried to reach her but she couldn't, no matter what she did.

Faith jerked awake and sat up, her heart racing. Had she cried out? On that awful night five years ago, she had been the one bound and gagged, not Shiloh.

The gray of dawn's beginning shone through the flaps at both ends of the tent. She looked around in the scant light, trying to get away from the awful memory of that night, of her helplessness. The two losses, Patience and Shiloh, twined inside her, as piercing as thorns.

She glimpsed Honoree sleeping on another blanket. Ella was not visible. She must be lying next to her husband, whose fever had only recently broken.

The dream of Shiloh had exacerbated her frustration. Measles had kept her here when she wanted to go to New Orleans. It couldn't be helped, but that didn't make it easy to accept. Faith collected herself and rose, aching from too many nights sleeping on the ground.

Walking to the rear, she saw that Dr. Bryant was dozing in a chair by the back opening. Dr. Dyson, fortunately, was occupied elsewhere in the tent. Faith forced herself to pour and sip a cup of cold, bitter coffee left in a kettle on a table there. New measles cases still came in daily. She began praying for the safety of others. So far, thankfully, neither the colonel nor Armstrong had been affected.

Dr. Bryant blinked himself awake. He stared at her for a moment. "I hope you've slept," he said gruffly. "You are trying to kill yourself."

She smirked, pouring him some coffee. "The kettle calls the pot black."

"Humph. We can do so little. If the men with measles are strong, they can fight it off. The rest will go to God."

She nodded solemnly. "Easier said than

accepted."

"Much easier," he agreed, sipping the brew and making a face.

Faith didn't want to admit it, but she missed the colonel. Of course, since she was in the quarantine tent, they hadn't seen each other in days. She must be patient about New Orleans. She tried to recite Scripture to lift her spirits, but all she could come up with was one line from a psalm: *"Be still, and know that I am God."*

"Somebody outside for you," the head cook said to Faith while handing over the large kettle of porridge for the measles patients. One of the orderlies accepted it and carried it away.

Faith peered through the open tent flap. Colonel Knight stood several feet away. She stepped just outside as far as she could go without violating quarantine. "Colonel?"

"Miss Faith, how are you?"

"I am doing as well as I can." She let herself gaze at him. So happy to see a man in good health. So happy to see him. She wanted to ask him further details about his library, but no one else would understand their unusual conversations. "What has thee been doing?"

"Reconnaissance. The usual. Is this onslaught of measles about done?"

"We see signs that the end of this bout is coming."

Then they just stared at each other, forgetting to speak.

"Well, if it isn't love's sweet dream," Dr. Dyson mocked. The man succeeded in breaking their mutual trance.

"I bid you good day then, Miss Faith." The colonel put on his hat, bowing slightly.

"Good day, Colonel Knight." She turned away, making a face at the ill-tempered doctor. But it was just as well. She had a job to do and so did the colonel. And he presented a temptation dangerous to her peace of mind.

August 29, 1863

Over a month and half after the first case of measles, the quarantine tent had nearly emptied of patients. The contagion had once again run its course, though it had gone much longer than Faith had expected. Ella and Landon had returned to their small two-man tent. Today Honoree and Faith had finally been cleared to leave the quarantine tent and now walked through the quiet camp to their larger Sibley tent. Going home after grueling weeks of round-the-clock nursing.

Glancing through the spaces between the tents to the right, Faith noticed the photographer's tent. She'd forgotten all about him. He was still in camp? She led Honoree over. The few men milling around parted, letting her go to the front, where prints were spread out on a portable metal table.

She asked the photographer's assistant whether she might see some of the hospital photographs, and as he dug them out, Faith looked down at the table again, where she spied a photograph of Colonel Knight and his officers. She hesitated, but when Honoree glanced away, she claimed that image too.

When she showed them to the photographer's assistant, he looked a bit surprised at her second choice but said nothing of it, merely charged her. He gave her thin paper sleeves for the photographs and told her to keep them out of the sun.

After Honoree had also paid for hers, they walked away and almost immediately met the colonel. Faith's hand that held the paper bag tingled as if caught in wrongdoing. "Hello, Colonel," she said, feeling strangely guilty and hoping she wasn't blushing. And very aware that she wished she could have donned a clean apron before meeting him.

"Miss Faith," he replied. "So glad to see

you out of quarantine. Where are you headed?"

"Back to our tent."

He tilted his head. "I'm here to purchase a photograph too. I thought my mother would appreciate a current picture of me. So she could see I am not wasting away." With a self-deprecating grin, he bowed and then moved toward the photographer's table.

Not a word about her going to New Orleans. He might have been speaking to a mere acquaintance. Did he think she would forget or had accepted it as impossible? The measles outbreak had dominated her mind, but she was free of it now.

More than ever determined to find a way downriver, Faith walked away with Honoree. She felt the distance the colonel had once more set between them. That shouldn't have bothered her, but it did.

Chapter 12

September 1, 1863

Honoree stood at Faith's elbow outside their tent after supper. "I'll go with you to the general," she offered.

Brushing away an insistent mosquito, Faith glanced at her. "No, I think I had better go alone."

"Why?"

"I can't put it into words. I just think it would be best if I went by myself." She couldn't shake the colonel's disapproval of her going to New Orleans. It had cast a pall over her, made her indecisive, not like herself.

"Well, I'm going with you whether you want me to or not."

"Very well." Faith sighed long and loud and then nearly slapped herself. If she didn't stop, this downhearted sighing could develop into an annoying habit.

With determination, she lifted her plain

white bonnet into place and tied its frayed ribbons; Honoree did the same and they set off.

Over the past weeks, the joy of the ended siege had declined into the boredom of camp life between battles. Men gambled for pennies in small groups in the shade of the few remaining trees. A fiddler nearby was playing a lazy tune for his own entertainment. A few men sat in front of their tents, mending shirts and patching pants.

As Faith overheard snatches of conversation, her agitation stood in stark contrast to the pervasive boredom. She knew that she feared the general would deny her request for a military pass south to New Orleans. If he did, she wasn't sure what other recourse she could take.

And she didn't want to think of how the colonel would react when he found out she'd applied to the general for this favor. She'd allowed Devlin Knight to become important to her. Thinking of him stirred her and stressed her at the same time. But she must let nothing and no one deter her from her goal.

With each step forward, she worked to bring herself into focus, ready to plead her case before the general. "I hate to bother General Grant," Faith murmured to Honoree. "He's got a whole army to think about."

"He won't be rude, if that's what you're worried about. He knows us, owes us after we nursed his son to health."

Yes, but is that enough to lead him to grant us what we want, need? A second time, after Annerdale?

When she and Honoree reached his tent, the general was just coming out. As usual, he was wearing a dusty and wrinkled uniform. Except for the gold braid on the shoulders and hat, no one would know he was the Union commander of the Western Campaign.

"General," Faith said, "may we have a moment with thee?"

He looked surprised, doffing his hat. "Ladies, what can I do to help you?"

General Grant's son Fred, still too thin, had emerged behind his father, and he bowed his head shyly to the women.

Faith tried to think of a way to open the conversation.

"General Grant," Honoree said, "we are coming to ask a favor."

Honoree's forthrightness only heightened Faith's tongue-tied state.

"Fred, bring out some camp stools for the ladies." When this was done, the general waved for them to be seated. "What is it? You know I am in your debt."

Again Honoree took the lead. "Not long ago you let Faith go to that plantation to ask about my sister, who was kidnapped from her employer's home in Cincinnati. Well, she found out . . ." Honoree paused, looking to Faith.

"That Honoree's sister Shiloh had been there," Faith said, able to speak now that the subject had been broached. "At Annerdale, a slave said she'd seen Shiloh and that the slavers who had her in their possession intended to take her to the auction in New Orleans."

Grant had given her his full attention. "Probably traveled down the Ohio to the Mississippi, the quickest way to get far from Cincinnati."

"Yes, General," Faith agreed. "At home, Shiloh's employer had gone away to attend a meeting, so no one realized what had happened until the next morning." Faith didn't mention that she'd been visiting Shiloh to keep her company and take her mind off her own sister's recent death.

"Plenty of time for them to get far away with her," he commented. "And indeed they would take her to New Orleans. The slave auction there was an important one. The slavers could get a better price for her, and so far from your home, no one would identify her as a free woman of color."

Faith drew in a sharp breath. "Admirably summarized, sir."

"So you want to go to New Orleans, but you need a military pass and transportation."

"That's exactly it, General," Faith replied, grateful he'd said it for them.

"I must give this some consideration," General Grant said. "Come back tomorrow. If I'm not here, I will leave word with my secretary."

Faith rose. "We're sorry to bother thee in the midst of all thy duties, but this was only the second lead we've had toward finding her. It's been nearly five years now."

"Do you really think you can find her?" Fred spoke up.

"We will find her," Faith said, "if God wills."

They both curtsied and left the general and his son behind. Honoree claimed Faith's hand, and they clung to each other. As they walked side by side, Faith prayed. Surely God would help them find Shiloh.

After over two months of being in camp since Vicksburg fell, Dev had been glad to mount up with one of his best companies in the very early, cooler morning and head out on patrol. Though Vicksburg had surrendered, the Rebels outside the city had not given up. Union outposts scattered around enemy territory were still being raided. The Union cavalry needed to push back or be overrun by Rebs.

So he was ready to be about his business, yet his conversation with General Grant last evening had left him unsettled, disgruntled, and without a choice.

Miles passed under his horse's hooves as the sun rose higher. The memory of Faith's challenge to him as he'd pumped water for her plagued him even now. Dev tried not to rehearse rebuttals to the Quakeress's Scriptures about two masters and a house divided. He shouldn't care what she thought. He knew his own mind, didn't he? Why did this woman's words vex him so?

Gunfire in the distance. Dev stood tall in his stirrups. "Forward! Engage at will!"

They swooped over a dried-up cotton field toward the gunfire and smoke. A Reb raiding party was attacking an outpost that guarded a supply line along the Yazoo River.

Dev's cavalrymen dashed forward, firing.

Outnumbered, the raiding party turned their horses and raced away north.

"After them!" He spurred his horse and pelted after the retreating Confederates.

One Reb turned in his saddle and fired.

Dev felt the impact in his shoulder but kept his seat and didn't rein in his horse. When another soldier near him fell from his saddle, Dev slowed his mount. "Let them go!" he shouted.

His orders were to harass the raiders but not to bring in any prisoners. The army would be moving soon and couldn't afford to have prisoners slowing them down. They'd routed the raiders, and that was their job today. If they continued the pursuit, this might turn out to be a feint that would lead them into an ambush.

The Rebs disappeared over the horizon. Dev slid from his saddle to see to the injured man who had fallen near him. Kneeling, he bound up the man's arm.

"Who's going to see to your wound?" the man asked, pointing to Dev.

Dev followed the man's gaze and saw blood on his uniform sleeve. He shrugged out of his fatigue jacket and noted that his upper arm had been deeply grazed. "Nothing serious." Now that he was aware of it, the graze began to throb.

"Colonel," one of his men said, drawing near him while still mounted. "One of the

Rebs tossed this over his shoulder."

Dev accepted the folded piece of paper tied to a stone. On the outside, the paper said, *To Col D Knight.*

Dev untied and unfolded it, reading: *Catch me if you can. JC.* He flamed within at the affront, one so reminiscent of their boyhood together. He shoved the paper into his inner pocket. "Just Rebel rudeness. Let's get this man back to camp!"

He helped the wounded man onto his horse, which another soldier had retrieved. The company headed south, back toward Vicksburg. Dev's arm burned from the graze, and his stomach burned with indignation at his cousin.

Leave it to Jack to taunt him. Had he actually been with the raiding party? Dev hadn't seen Jack's cockaded hat. So had Jack given the note to another Confederate to drop near any Union cavalry company?

Back in camp and entering the hospital tent, Dev was grateful to note that Faith and Honoree were not on duty there. He couldn't face another conversation with Faith about this war, Armstrong, and everything else. He especially did not want to see those women after being summoned to the general last night. He might be tempted to argue with them, no doubt fruitlessly.

After a surgeon's cursory examination, he allowed a night nurse to clean and bandage his wound. Then he headed to his own tent. Inside, he sat on his cot and opened the note from the battlefield once more. One would think that a man who'd dishonored his name by breaking his word would not call attention to himself like this.

"Colonel?"

It was Faith's voice. Dev rose and went outside.

"Someone told me that thee had been treated in the hospital."

This was not good news. Though he craved her company, he didn't want people linking him and the Quakeress. "Just a scratch."

"Did thee want me to look at it?"

"No, the nurse on duty took care of me after the surgeon looked at the wound. No stitches needed. I'm fine."

She seemed to struggle with herself. "Very well. Expect to be a bit feverish tonight. Send someone for me if it swells or if thy fever rises to more than moderate."

"Of course." *I won't.* "I'm going to rest now."

"Certainly, but be sure to drink something before thee turns in for the night."

"I will." *Please leave.*

Though she glanced over her shoulder at him a few times, she walked away. He was sorry he couldn't completely hide his irritation at the new orders he'd received last night, but he'd done the best he could.

Dev knew he'd have to face her tomorrow. He hoped she hadn't been the one who'd prompted the general's request that he be the man for this job. Regardless, he'd quell any attempts on her part to draw him into discussions of slavery or the aftermath of this war. That was all too far ahead to contemplate, especially since he probably wouldn't be alive to see it anyway.

The next day, outside the hospital tent, Faith and Honoree were saying farewell to Dr. Bryant as they prepared to leave for the boat they'd received written permission to board for the trip to New Orleans.

"Now you two take care of yourselves," the head surgeon was saying.

Though her stomach churned with uncertainty and excitement, Faith hid a grin. Her father had told her the same thing when she and Honoree left home. "We will, Doctor. And we will return as soon as we are able."

The head cook and the staff whom Faith had hired near Jackson gathered a little ways off, bidding them good-bye too. The head cook had taken responsibility for their tent and other possessions till they returned. Ella stood a bit apart, looking worried.

Then Devlin Knight appeared, also carrying a valise.

Faith looked at him, sudden apprehension flaring to life. "Colonel?"

"Miss Faith," he said, barely pausing, "let us be off to the quay."

"What?" she gasped. "Is thee accompanying us?"

He stared at her. "So you didn't ask the general to order me to accompany you to New Orleans?"

"No." She watched his jaw move as if he were chewing steel.

"Well, those are my orders. I am to accompany you there and back."

Faith absorbed this while Honoree approached them. She glanced at her friend. "Thee heard?"

"We all heard," Honoree said with a touch of irony.

The colonel stiffened. "Shall we be off? The USS *Rattler* is waiting for us to board, I believe."

With a few parting waves and words, Faith and Honoree fell into step with the colonel. The distance to the steamer passed in strained silence. Faith felt the weight of the colonel's displeasure. Of course he didn't want to leave his regiment. Of course he didn't think she and Honoree should go to New Orleans. But they were going, and so was he. For whatever reason, General Grant had seen fit to order this.

At the dock they stared up at the USS *Rattler.* It was easy to see that the *Rattler* had once been a normal steamboat, but now tin panels with gun slots enclosed what must have been the open lower deck before the war. On the upper deck, the bridge and cabins had also been tin-clad, but the area between the cabins and railing remained open.

The colonel asked permission to board, which was granted. They walked up the gangplank. The sailors on the upper deck stared at the two women.

The man who must be their captain — if the profusion of braid on his uniform was any indication — strode forward, meeting them at the top of the gangplank. He was of medium height and weight and looked ready to spit. "I'm Shipmaster Fentress. Follow me." His tone was unwelcoming to say the least.

Faith and Honoree obeyed, trailed reluctantly by the colonel.

"Here is your cabin," Fentress said at the door of a small room near the bridge on the upper deck. He was becoming more irritated by the moment.

"Thank thee."

"Having females aboard a ship is bad luck," the man snapped. "And distracting to my men. You two may walk the deck once in the morning, afternoon, and evening. Otherwise I want you to remain in your quarters. You will eat in your cabin. Is that understood?"

"Thee is the captain," Faith said, not letting the man cow her. "Of course we will accede to thy wishes." She said the last to remind him that they were civilians and therefore free agents.

He glared at them and turned to the colonel. "I hear that you have been ordered to accompany them for their protection in New Orleans. I will expect you to stay with them whenever they are out of their quarters."

The colonel curtly nodded his assent.

The captain marched away, calling, "Cast off!"

Faith looked to the colonel.

"You women best go to your cabin," the colonel said as if they were strangers. "When we are well on our way downriver, I will come and get you for your walk on deck."

Faith bowed her head and led Honoree into the tiny cabin, which had two berths hanging on one wall, leaving just enough floor space for them to stand.

The colonel shut the door behind them.

Hearing his retreating footsteps, Faith resisted the urge to sigh and removed her bonnet. She pushed open the small window and let in a breeze. She sat down on the lower bunk.

Honoree sat beside her. "Well, we're off."

Leaving behind the familiar — the military camp that had been their home for months — hit Faith squarely. She blinked away tears. "Yes, we are."

Honoree drew in a deep breath. "Dear Lord, help us find Shiloh or news of where she is. And keep her safe till we find her."

Faith squeezed Honoree's arm in agreement. "I'm going to lie down." She rose and turned to mount the ladder attached to the bunks.

"No, you don't. I get the fun berth."

Faith chuckled and then shook her head. "We are not children."

"No, but it looks like we're going to be treated like children here, and naughty children at that."

"Yes. The captain was not happy to see us." *Nor the colonel.*

"As long as Shipmaster Fentress gets us to New Orleans, I can put up with that." Honoree rose and looked out the window.

Faith stared at the bunk and realized she felt more like pacing than lying down. But the tiny cabin afforded no room to do so. She joined Honoree at the window and stared out at the lush green scenery as the ship throbbed to life and began moving with the current.

As Faith stood there, New Orleans seemed a very long way to go. How was she going to handle the colonel's reluctant chaperonage? Perhaps she could only endure it. She shouldn't be surprised that they were at odds. She was an abolitionist and Devlin Knight was a man still caught on the horns of slavery. And a war was no time for an ill-fated romance that would not prosper even in peacetime.

Dev waited till most of the morning was past, and then he forced himself to go to the ladies' cabin and call for them. He knocked on the tin-clad door.

Faith opened it.

"I'm here to accompany you on your first turn around the deck." He tried to say the words free of irritation but did not completely succeed.

Faith donned her bonnet and unlatched a parasol. "I'm afraid Honoree is not a good sailor. She is lying down." She shut the door behind her and opened the parasol. "I'm ready to walk."

He did not offer her his arm. They began their circuit of the upper deck.

"This is very different from the riverboats I've been on before," she commented as if the journey were commonplace.

"It is my first time on a gunboat too."

"It's a shame to see it fitted for war. Riverboats can be so lovely. I know thee doesn't want to be here," she continued without missing a beat. "But I said nothing to the general about thee, certainly no request to have thee ordered to accompany me."

"I believe you. You know my opinion that you should wait till the war is over. This is a dangerous venture. And I didn't want to leave my men —"

"Yes, especially since I heard that a Captain Jack Carroll is leading raids against Union outposts."

"You heard that, did you?" He had too. He let loose a sound of disgust and muttered under his breath.

"What's wrong?"

He repeated the sound. "He sent me a note."

"What? How?"

He reached into his inner shirt pocket. The movement caused him a moment of pain. He gasped and bent slightly.

"What is it, Colonel? What's wrong?"

CHAPTER 13

Faith tilted her head to look up into the colonel's flushed face. "Does thee have a fever?" She reached for his forehead.

He shied away like a boy.

But she managed to graze his forehead with her wrist anyway. "Thee is burning up. I thought the perspiration on thy brow was due to the heat today. Come with me." She claimed his arm.

He gasped in obvious pain.

"It is thy arm, then?" She shook her head at him, glaring fiercely. "Thee can die from infection — even from a small wound. Thee knows that," she chided him.

He set his lips in a hard line.

She leaned close to his ear. "Does thee want me to make a scene here in front of these sailors?"

He glared at her. "What do you want me to do?"

"We will go to my cabin. I did not wish to

transport my whole medicine chest, but I did bring some medical supplies with me."

He still didn't appear ready to acquiesce.

"Is this how thee plans to protect Honoree and me?" Her voice rose. "By lying in bed delirious with fever?"

He growled. "Very well." He turned and marched back toward her cabin. She hurried after him.

Leaving the door open for propriety's sake, she showed him inside. "Please sit on the lower berth." She didn't wait to see him obey but bent over her valise and brought out the small bag of her essential herbs and supplies. "Please take off thy jacket and shirt, Colonel."

He grumbled but obeyed her. Still he only revealed one arm and one side of his chest, appearing embarrassed at even this degree of disrobing.

When she saw his upper arm — inflamed, harsh red, swollen with obvious infection — she stifled a gasp. "Why didn't thee tell me?"

"I went to the hospital —"

"Thee would have done better to come straight to me," she reprimanded, removing her bonnet and tossing it aside. "Wherever sick people gather, contagions increase. It's just common sense." She began to swab the area with alcohol-soaked cotton. She heard his quick intake of breath.

Honoree climbed down the ladder from the upper berth, where she had been lying, fighting nausea. "That looks nasty."

"I need hot water, Honoree. Will thee find the captain and ask him for permission to fetch some?"

"Oh, he'll love having me stop in with a request for him," Honoree said, setting her bonnet over her kerchief. "But I'll see to it." She left, muttering about men and foolishness.

After Faith finished cleaning the inflamed area, she glanced at the colonel's face. "I'm sorry that the general's orders upset thy plans and thy sense of duty, but —"

"Here." Sounding disgusted, he handed her the note he'd been reaching for earlier. "This is what's angered me."

She accepted it and stepped to the window to read it. Then she turned to the colonel, frowning. "Thy cousin is an unhappy man."

"That's all you have to say?" the colonel grumbled.

"What else can I say? Thy cousin wants to make thee as miserable as he is. He burns with hatred and resentment. He knows he behaved dishonorably, and he hates thee because thee knows it and can testify to his father against him."

"I would never tell my uncle."

"Then thy cousin knows that too, and it galls him." She handed him back the paper.

"You barely know Jack."

"Some things are as old as time. I mentioned Jacob and Esau once before. Now let's concentrate on dealing with thy infected wound." She knelt on the floor with her mortar and began to grind a mixture with her pestle.

"What is this man doing in your cabin?" the shipmaster demanded from the doorway.

"I would think it is obvious to anyone," Faith replied mildly. She'd expected this foolish question. "The colonel has an infected arm and I'm treating him."

"You're not a doctor," Fentress said.

"Is there one on board?" she asked without looking at him.

"No —"

"I'm a trained nurse, as is Miss Langston." She nodded toward Honoree. "Where is my hot water?"

"I brought it," Honoree said, pushing past the captain into the cabin. "The cook says after you finish with the colonel, will you please come and take a look at his mouth? He appears to have an abscessed tooth."

"Of course." Faith busied herself neatly

sewing a cloth poultice and then soaking it in the hot water. Under the shipmaster's scrutiny, she rose and pressed it to the colonel's arm.

He sucked in air.

"I know it's uncomfortable," she said soothingly, "but I must draw the infection or thee could go into blood poisoning." Then she looked over her shoulder to the captain. "Will thee ask the cook to come to me, or should I go to him?"

"I'll send him up," the captain said, sounding disgusted. He stalked away.

"Men," Honoree said, heaving a loud sigh filled with irritation. "They do go on."

Faith grinned. "We were supposed to stay safely at home while they waged war."

"Exactly," the colonel agreed through teeth gritted against the painful treatment.

Faith faced him. "Should I let thee lose thy arm over a small wound or let thee die of infection? Should I let other men die if I can help them?"

Then, observing his suffering, she repented of her harsh words. "Lie down before thee collapses." She helped him recline on the berth. Then she began to sew very small poultices for the cook.

Soon the cook came, and after examination, she gave him what she'd sewn with instructions.

"You don't think you need to draw the tooth?" the man asked.

"No, I think these will suffice. And will be much less painful."

He left with heartfelt thanks and a promise to send up coffee and broth for the colonel.

Needing space and air, Faith set her bonnet back on and tied its ribbons, then stepped out onto the deck. She rested her forearms on the railing and drew in deep drafts of the hot, humid air. She felt sympathy for Colonel Knight over his cousin's rude, taunting message, but she could not regret treating Jack Carroll.

She'd done what was right before the Lord, and Jack had chosen to betray the trust of his cousin. No good would come of it. She just wished the colonel could forgive himself. Then she thought of Armstrong. Colonel Knight had more than one regret stewing inside him.

And selfishly she hoped the colonel would quickly recover from his infection. He spoke the truth: this was a dangerous venture. How would they fare in New Orleans without his protection?

The day passed with Dev lying on Faith's berth, feverish. He despised this. He hated to feel this weak, hated to have this woman caring for him. But most of all he hated the way his arm throbbed. And how his head spun when he tried to stand. Finally night fell. He brushed away a stray mosquito as it buzzed around his ear.

Faith lit a lantern and knelt beside him.

"I need someone to walk me to my cabin," he insisted, panting in the oppressive humidity.

"We'll see. First I need to determine if it's time to lance the infection."

He closed his eyes. "Do what you must."

And she did, murmuring words about home and poetry and anything that might distract him.

He inhaled sharply when she pierced his skin, and sweat dripped down his face as he held his lower lip with his teeth against crying out.

Finally he smelled the stringent odor of alcohol and felt its cold sting on his arm. The searing burn of iodine followed and then a fresh bandage. He lay breathless.

"We've come to help him to his berth." The cook, flanked by another sailor, spoke from the open door.

Dev worked his way to sitting up and then standing. The room swayed for a moment and then he staggered to the door. The cook and sailor began to help him down the passage to the cabin where he'd sleep.

"Good night, Miss Cathwell," he said formally. Then he forced himself to walk between the two and not to fall on his face. Soon they helped him collapse into the berth in his cabin. His last thought was that he shouldn't have shown Faith the note. *I should have just thrown it away.*

Late in the afternoon two days later, Dev got up and walked outside. His arm still pained him but his fever had lessened. He'd cheated death one more time. But it was only a matter of time before his luck ran out.

He admitted to himself that he'd been foolish not to go to Faith when he had returned to camp after the skirmish. But he knew why he had avoided her. The longing to touch her soft cheek and hold her close rose in him, overwhelming, ill-advised.

"Good afternoon, Colonel."

He turned to see Faith under a pale parasol. He tightened himself against his attraction to her. "I don't know if I'm up to walking with you, miss."

"But thee is standing." The parasol cast a shadow over her face, intriguing him. "Thee can see the shipmaster has relented toward females on board, and I am allowed outside whenever I wish."

Dev didn't try to hide his surprise. Still feeling dry and flat as a falling leaf, he asked, "Is the cook well?"

"Yes, and a happy cook is a better cook," she bantered. "And that makes everyone happy."

He chuckled.

Rapid gunfire.

Faith dropped her parasol.

Dev grabbed her arm, shoved her into his cabin, and shut the door.

"What is it?"

His heart beat fast and he felt the sapping weakness again. "Probably bushwhackers onshore, taking potshots at a Union boat." He drew his carbine.

Outside, the crew returned fire. From the engine below, a grinding and a thrust forward propelled them both backward. Dev tried to grab at the berth railing. But he careened into Faith. They lost their footing and landed on the floor.

He cried out as his arm hit something hard. The pain momentarily froze him. He lay gasping, hating this feebleness.

Faith sat up, and he found his head in her lap.

He tried to move, but the pain and the

weakness defeated him. He cursed under his breath.

"Shush," she crooned. "Thee will regain thy strength." She pressed her wrist against his forehead. "Thee is still running a very low fever. Thy body is fighting off the infection."

He realized he'd lost his hat when he fell. Irrationally he felt stripped of some protection, exposed. "I hate this."

She said nothing but rested her small hands on his shoulders.

He lay still, unwilling to withdraw from her softness. It was all he could do to suppress further reaction to the ache and throbbing in his arm.

They waited, but no more gunfire came from shore. The gunboat sped on and then at last slowed to a normal speed.

"It might even have been a civilian firing on us," Dev said, finally forcing himself to rise.

"Being away from camp and riding this calm river, I sometimes let myself forget that a war is still going on."

Shrugging, he peered through the window. "I think it's safe to go out again."

She picked up her parasol and waited while he stepped out first. After a few moments he waved for her to join him.

In silence they gazed at the thickly green shore sliding past them. "Colonel, I am both apprehensive and eager to reach New Orleans," Faith confessed. "Does that make sense?"

He nodded. "Perfect sense." His lack of energy dogged him. "I can walk you a little way before I must lie down again."

So they walked.

"Before we left camp," Dev said, trying to lift her spirits, or both their spirits, "I received a package from my mother. She sent me a book."

"From thy favorite bookstore on Saratoga Street?" Faith followed his lead, turning away from the war, away from their quest to New Orleans.

"Yes, Robert Burns's *Poems and Songs.*"

"Why that book?"

"I think she thought it would be a change of pace for me, a needed one."

Faith looked up, beaming suddenly. "My mother sent me more stockings."

He laughed out loud. "Mine did too!"

She was glad to hear him laugh. They must not forget how to laugh. The war would end . . . someday. She wondered if he ever thought of Armstrong and then dismissed the question. Of course he did, just as Shiloh was never far from her mind.

313

It wasn't possible to forget. What could she do to help these two men reconcile? Anything? Nothing?

New Orleans, Louisiana
In the sky the smoke from thousands of kitchen chimneys provided the first sign of their nearing New Orleans, a city of over one hundred fifty thousand, rivaling the population of Cincinnati, which Faith knew so well. As the boat sped along, she and Honoree stood on the upper deck, watching the smoke become clearer. The nearer they got, the more impatient she felt to be onshore and going about finding Shiloh.

They turned a bend in the river and caught the first glimpse of the city. Honoree clutched Faith's hand. "I'm not getting my hopes up. She might be anywhere by now."

"Yes. But we know where to ask about her here. I'm sure the auction house kept records of . . . transactions."

Honoree's nails bit into Faith's skin. It was terrible to face that Shiloh had been sold like a head of cattle. A sudden flush of anger filled Faith. She prayed for God's peace, but the anger stung and didn't ebb.

"It won't be long now." The colonel appeared beside them at the rail. Still a bit drawn, he had mostly recovered from his fever and could move his arm normally. But he'd lost weight.

Soon the steamboat joined many other gunboats docked at the quay in the busy harbor of New Orleans.

The shipmaster stopped the three of them as they prepared to walk down the gangplank. "Our stay here will not be more than today and tomorrow," he said more politely than he'd spoken to them when first they boarded. "I am here to pick up supplies, and then I will head upriver again."

Faith curtsied. She understood Grant needed supplies before the army could head east to defeat Lee. Or she thought that was what the general intended to do.

"Please try to take care of your business today," the shipmaster continued. "I want to debark tomorrow unless some hitch comes up."

"Yes, sir," the colonel replied for them. He helped her and then Honoree step onto land. Faith swayed a little and he caught her elbow to steady her.

"I need to get my equilibrium again," she said brightly.

Honoree also accepted his steadying grasp.

They were soon walking up the crowded street, looking for a cab. Before long, they came upon a carriage. "Need a ride, gentleman?" The black driver stood in the shade near his horse.

Faith reluctantly decided her best course of action was to let the colonel — a man and an officer — do the talking for them. She and Honoree traded discreet glances, agreeing to this.

"Yes. We want to go to the auction house where slaves were sold," the colonel said.

The driver halted in midstep. "They not selling any more slaves now that the Union Army come. And Lincoln sent out his proclamation. I'm free."

"We are looking for a kidnapped free woman of color," the colonel continued.

The man looked shocked. "Oh yes, sir, I know right where you want ta go. The St. Louis Hotel, not far from here — corner of St. Louis and Chartres." The driver waved them into his carriage, climbed up on the seat, and slapped the reins.

They bumped over the cobblestone street along the waterfront. Before long, they came to a large, elegant limestone hotel in the classic Federalist style. The colonel helped the two women down. Faith noted that he appeared surprised at the imposing hotel as a venue for slave auctions. "This is where the auctions took place?" he asked.

The carriage driver nodded, his face set in

grim lines. He then asked if they wanted him to wait.

"Yes, please," the colonel replied. He led Faith and Honoree inside the hotel lobby.

The well-dressed clerk, an older man with slicked-back silver curls against his dark skin, greeted them with politeness but regarded them dubiously. "We are full up with Union officers, sir," he explained.

"We don't want a room. We are wanting to see the records of the slave auctions that took place here."

The man looked confused.

"We are seeking my sister," Honoree spoke up.

The clerk's expression became uncomfortable. "I'll have you conducted to the auction office. We are still in the business of selling whenever anybody has anything to sell. Though this isn't an auction day, the auction master is in." The man waved at a young boy who was standing nearby. "Please show these women and this gentleman to Monsieur Dupont in his office."

The young boy with light skin and big brown eyes led them along a hallway and into a spacious, ornately gilded rotunda with a large chandelier. She'd read about this place in Harriet Beecher Stowe's *Uncle Tom's Cabin*. The grand setting jarred Faith.

Why would they build this grand hall for such a sordid purpose?

"This where the auctions take place," the boy said. "I guess slave auctions won't be happenin' anymore." He looked at them hopefully.

"Not as long as the Union controls New Orleans," the colonel replied.

The boy nodded and brought them through the rotunda to a hallway with one small office on each side. "Monsieur Dupont, these people here to see you," he called. The boy waved them inside the office to the right and then departed.

Sickly white and bent, Monsieur Dupont looked older than the clerk at the front desk. He rose with arthritic slowness, eyeing them suspiciously. "How may I be of assistance?"

Faith looked to the colonel. He would no doubt get more information from this man, especially since the colonel spoke with a Maryland accent.

Colonel Knight stepped forward. "We are trying to locate a slave whom we believe was sold at an auction here before the war."

"In mid-1858," Faith murmured.

"Yes," the colonel continued. "She's very beautiful with light skin, golden-brown hair, and large green eyes."

"A quadroon perhaps?"

Though it would doubtless shock the colonel if he realized Faith knew the meaning of the term, Faith was well aware that Creole or French Louisiana society traditionally held "quadroon balls," where mulattas were chosen to be mistresses of wealthy young men. This society even had names for the different shades of color: octaroon (one-eighth black) and quadroon (one-fourth black).

"Perhaps," the colonel said mildly. "We would like to find the record of the transaction of her sale and the name and location of her purchaser."

They needed the man's help, and Faith appreciated Colonel Knight's diplomacy.

"You say mid-1858?" Dupont inquired. "Do you have a name?"

"Shiloh," Faith spoke up. "Her name is Shiloh Langston."

Dupont turned to a bookcase that supported five shelves of black leather-bound volumes. He made a tutting sound as he scanned them. Then he selected one of the tomes and ponderously carried it over to his desk.

Faith and Dev with Honoree just behind them moved closer to the man, who was flipping through the pages, muttering to himself.

Faith felt a bit light-headed trying to control her excitement, vying with uncertainty.

More pages turning, more muttering.

Faith reached back for Honoree's hand.

Dupont's hair fell forward as he leaned farther down. "Ah, here it is. July 22, 1858. Young mulatta named Shiloh. Oh yes, I remember now. She caused quite a stir. The bidding went high, very high. She sold for twenty-six hundred dollars."

Faith swayed a bit, thinking of Shiloh in that elegant room reduced to less than human, less than God made her.

"Who brought her here for sale?" Honoree asked, gripping Faith's arm.

He looked up at them. "Who are you to question me, girl?" Dupont turned to the colonel. "I thought you just wanted to know who bought her."

"That is what I asked," the colonel affirmed, moving forward and casting a scolding glance at Honoree.

After a pause, Dupont replied, "She was bought by William LeFevre, a local planter."

"Where is his plantation located?"

The man suddenly appeared wary. "Why are you seeking this quadroon?"

Faith wished he would stop calling Shiloh that. She was so much more than the color of her skin. "Shiloh was born free but was abducted and brought here."

"That's a serious charge, young woman," Dupont blustered.

"Come now," the colonel said. "You and I both know that this type of thing happened. And you have stated the motive."

"I?" Dupont looked and sounded insulted.

"Yes. She sold for over five times the amount a young woman would normally have garnered," the colonel said. "Now who was the seller?"

Dupont went to shut the book.

Colonel Knight drew his pistol. "Do you want to fall afoul of the Union Army, sir?"

The auction master froze in place.

Faith moved closer to the colonel. "We did not come seeking revenge, Monsieur Dupont. Just information to lead us to Shiloh."

"I was thinking of justice, not revenge," the colonel said evenly. "Now tell me the name of the men who brought Shiloh for sale."

Dupont's face reddened. But he ran his finger down the page. "Claxton. Ned Claxton and his brother, Jay."

"Thank you, monsieur," Colonel Knight said and slipped his pistol back into his jacket pocket.

Dupont stared after them as they left his office.

They retraced their route through the grand rotunda, now empty and silent except for their footsteps echoing on the marble floor.

At the hotel's front desk, Honoree approached the clerk. "Pardon me, but do you know where a planter named LeFevre lives?"

"He's well known, miss. His plantation is Cypress Bank, south of the city on Cypress Road. But he will have gone to war."

"Thank you," Honoree said.

The three of them walked outside into the sunshine.

"What now?" Dev asked, already anticipating the answer he'd get.

"We go to Cypress Bank," Faith responded, as expected.

"We can't leave the city on our own. We will need more soldiers." Dev felt his irritation rising again.

"But New Orleans is under Union control," Honoree objected.

Another carriage passed, hoofbeats on cobblestones.

"But we'll be leaving the city," Dev countered. "The Navy took control of the city, and it is under martial rule. But when we leave the city, we could be in danger. I am only one man. And we could be plagued by bushwhackers. Don't you recall being shot at on the river?"

"He's right, Honoree," Faith admitted. "And thee will have to stay here. I don't want to take a chance thee might be . . . insulted."

Dev deemed taking women into hostile territory unwise at the very least but especially in Honoree's case. He gazed intently at the girl, silently reiterating the wisdom of this caution.

Honoree lifted her shoulder toward them and stood stiffly apart.

Faith touched her arm.

"I know. You're right. I'll stay on the boat." Honoree turned to Dev. "You think you can get some soldiers to go with you?"

"I'll apply to the Union commander here in the city, Major General Banks." Dev waved to the carriage driver, who again had found a shady tree to wait under. "First I'm going to take you ladies back to the ship."

He could see Faith wanted to object, but she merely pursed her lips.

"Our ship will be leaving tomorrow," she began.

"This will take time. I'm a stranger here. But I'll return with soldiers or the promise of them. If the *Rattler* must leave before our business is done, I'm sure we can find another transport north. General Grant's passes of transport will get us places on any northbound gunboat."

Again he saw that this did not sit well with the two women.

Faith leaned closer to him. "Colonel, will thee give me thy word that thee will not go to Cypress Bank without me?"

"It would be better if you left this to me." He stared at her sternly. "But I know you well enough by now not to attempt that. However, we will be entering a threatening region, and you must give me *your* promise to obey me without question or hesitation."

Faith gazed into his eyes. "Very well."

The agreement was settled, yet he sensed the women's frustration. So near and still another obstacle to overcome.

The thought occurred to him for the first time that if they did find Shiloh here, Faith might leave the war and go home. This was exactly what he'd wanted; nonetheless, he found it unpalatable. He sucked in the humid delta air and shut his mind to these feelings.

CHAPTER 14

The rest of the day Dev spent walking from one office to another at the Union head-quarters in Jackson Square, where Andrew Jackson's statue stood proudly. Step by step, Dev obtained permission to leave the city and gained a comfortable number of caval-rymen to join them. General Grant's note, which had accompanied their military passes, asked for all requested assistance and smoothed the way.

Early the next morning, which promised another muggy, uncomfortably hot day, Dev and Faith waved good-bye to Honoree and strode down the gangplank and onto solid ground again, bound for Cypress Bank. Not far from the quay, they met the cavalrymen provided him for the day.

Keyed up, Dev led her to the horses he'd also procured for them and helped her mount. She had borrowed a sailor's extra pair of trousers, which she wore under her dress. He ignored the cavalrymen, who looked shocked at a lady riding astride. These weren't his men, and they didn't know what a special lady Faith was.

At Dev's gesture, the captain in charge of the soldiers rode up beside him. "You know our destination, Captain?" Dev asked.

"Cypress Bank Plantation, sir. I consulted a local map and know how to get there. It's over an hour's ride away."

"Very good, Captain," Dev praised him. "Lead on."

The captain saluted smartly and soon the company was moving through town traffic and then beyond into the thick, lush forest surrounding the city.

"I love the oak trees here," Faith said, gazing around her, "with this gray, feathery moss hanging from them."

An alligator slid out of the bayou along the road, making the horses skittish. Faith eyed it curiously but did not comment.

The sounds of insects and strident bird-calls filled the air. Dev's senses remained alert, seeking the subtle sounds of humans who might be intent on harming them. The tropical forest around them took on a sinister presence. Dev noted that the cavalrymen were on edge. Did they fear bush-whackers here too?

The master of Cypress Bank was said to be off to war. That meant they would meet with the lady of the plantation. He worried about their reception and the touchy nature of the topic of Shiloh, no doubt bought as a mistress.

Finally, after they had passed two other widely spaced plantations, a grand sign near the road read *Cypress Bank.* They turned onto the lane that swept up a rise away from the bayou. At the far edge of the green slope, black willow trees marked the line of what must have been a creek. Ahead sat a traditional one-story French plantation house with a wide veranda on all sides. The house was raised up off the ground with two steps leading onto the porch.

Here and there, slaves stopped what they were doing and walked toward the house, watching silently. A white woman in her thirties, wearing a tattered yellow summer dress, came out of the main door onto the veranda, observing Dev's party intently, arms at her sides, hands in the folds of her skirt.

When they reached the house, Dev leaned over to Faith.

Before he could say anything, she raised her hand to forestall him. "I want to speak to her. You're with the Union Army. One woman might tell another woman more."

Dev sincerely doubted this, but he knew enough about Faith to give in. He'd told her to stay back at Annerdale, and that hadn't worked. And anyway, what could this woman do to her except for perhaps a slap?

He slid from his saddle and helped Faith down. The nearest soldier slipped off his horse to stand and hold their reins.

"Good day," Faith greeted the woman.

The woman, unmoving, just stared at Faith.

As Faith approached the woman, Dev stayed close to her.

"Thy house is lovely," Faith continued conversationally.

"You're not welcome here, Yankees," the woman finally spoke. "Go back to where you came from."

"We were wondering if thee could help us." Faith ignored the hostility and mounted the steps onto the porch. "I'm looking for a friend of mine."

"I said you're not welcome here. Leave."

"Is this the home of William LeFevre?" Dev asked.

The woman stared at him, her eyes dark pools of fury. "Mr. LeFevre isn't at home."

"My friend is named Shiloh," Faith said in a soothing voice. "Mr. LeFevre —"

"How dare you?" The woman's hand whipped up, clutching a knife. She slashed Faith's face.

Faith screamed.

Dev leaped forward. Tried to wrench the knife from the woman's hand. The woman fought him like a wounded, rabid animal, shrieking and clawing, trying to get to Faith.

Dev was finally forced to knock her unconscious and lower her to the porch floor. He then claimed the knife and pocketed it. Several soldiers had surged up around him.

Faith had staggered over and was leaning limply against a porch column. She had her hand pressed against her cheek, blood seeping between her fingers from ear to nose. She stared at him, her jaw loose, eyes wide with shock.

He turned at the sound of running footsteps, drawing his pistol.

"Don't shoot, sir!" an aged butler in faded livery said, holding up a hand. "I brought some clean rags. Your lady's losing blood. You need to bandage that wound quickly."

Dev helped Faith sit down on a wicker chair on the porch and, with the butler's help, folded a thick pad, which he pressed and then bound around Faith's blood-drenched face.

"Thank thee," Faith whispered, her face white.

"Sir, you best leave while the mistress is unconscious," the butler said. "Our master took Shiloh with him —" the man shook his head, looking pained — "as his laundress. That's why Miss Alicia struck out. She hates Shiloh."

Dev didn't need to ask any questions. A man didn't pay over two thousand dollars for a laundress. "Thank you."

"Please," Faith whispered.

Dev leaned close and then relayed her whispered inquiry to the butler. "What is LeFevre's rank, and who is his commanding officer?"

"He's a captain," the butler replied, leaning over his mistress, "and he's with Braxton Bragg."

"Thank thee." Faith looked to the butler. "Does thee want to leave?"

"I can't. I have no family to care for me."

The woman on the porch floor moaned.

"Now go," the butler urged.

Dev swept Faith into his arms and carried her toward their mounts. The captain held Faith while Dev mounted; then the captain lifted her up to Dev, who settled her behind him. She wrapped an arm around his waist, resting her uninjured cheek against his back.

Another soldier led Faith's horse as the column turned and headed away from the plantation house.

"You filthy, vile Yankees!" the hysterical woman screamed behind them. "I hope you all die! And all your children too! I hate you! I hate you!" Then she began shrieking curses.

Dev felt Faith sobbing against his back. He should have seen the attack coming. But he hadn't thought the woman would have a weapon. And she hadn't seemed deranged. He tucked Faith closer and focused on returning to the city.

The ride back to New Orleans went much faster than the one to Cypress Bank. Though still vigilant, the men urged their horses forward at a steady pace. No longer was this a mere ride into the country.

The quay came into view at last. Dev turned to the captain. "Where's the nearest army doctor?"

"No," Faith said with feeling, though muted and faint. "Take me to Honoree. I want no stranger treating me."

"Miss Faith," Dev protested, "you're injured. You need a doctor."

"No, I need careful nursing." Faith was forcing out the words against his shirt. "The only doctor I trust to operate on me is Dr.

Bryant."

"But he's in Vicksburg."

"I know."

Dev turned to the captain. "Please follow me to the gunboat. I'll dismount there and you can return this horse then."

The captain looked pained. "Of course. I'm just sorry this happened. We should have taken better care of the lady."

Yes, they all should have — himself included.

Dockside, one of the sailors on the *Rattler,* exclaiming about Faith, hurried down the gangplank. Faith slipped down to him. After dismounting, Dev claimed Faith again.

"I can walk," she protested.

But he felt her weakness. Her voice quavered.

"Faith!" Honoree shouted and ran toward them.

Forestalling the questions, Dev spoke up urgently. "Her cheek was cut with a knife. I want to take her to the nearest doctor. Honoree, help me persuade her. Quickly."

"Bring her to our cabin and let me see how bad it is." Honoree didn't wait for his reply but ran ahead onto the boat.

He followed, chafed by this delay. But he laid her down on her bunk and watched as

Honoree removed the blood-soaked bandage.

Faith looked up at her friend and behind her, at the colonel. "How bad is it?" She was surprised at how weak her voice sounded. The pain in her face took all her effort to bear. She realized Honoree was tending her as gently as she could, but each touch sent a shard of pain through her. She closed her eyes and clenched her teeth. "Thee knows what to do."

Honoree leaned over and kissed her forehead. "Yes, I do, but it's going to hurt you."

"Hurt me and save me," Faith said, hearing the whimper in her tone.

Faith lay on her side with her wound uppermost, watching dully as Honoree prepared to clean and treat the gash.

"I need to get her to a doctor," the colonel insisted once more.

"No," Honoree said. "The cut didn't sever an artery, so she isn't going to bleed to death. She needs to go to a very good surgeon, and the only one we're sure of is Dr. Bryant."

"But we're in New Orleans!" he nearly shouted.

"I know where we are, Colonel. I also know Faith could die in the wrong hands. Now I'm going to clean the wound and put a clean bandage on. Fentress was just waiting for you two to return, and we'll be on our way back to Vicksburg."

Fentress himself spoke from the doorway. "Miss Cathwell has been wounded?"

"Colonel, why don't you explain everything to the captain as he gets us started on our way north?" Honoree said without looking toward the men.

Thus dismissed, the colonel hesitated, plainly disgruntled, but then moved out onto the deck.

Faith watched him go and braced herself for what Honoree would soon be doing. Faith had done the same so often to others and now she was going to suffer the application of alcohol, followed by iodine. She closed her eyes against the coming ordeal.

"Here, sip this," Honoree said, holding a spoon to Faith's lips.

Faith didn't ask. She knew Honoree was giving her laudanum to help make the pain more bearable. She sipped the nasty liquid. "Dr. Bryant," she whispered. The engines below began quivering to life, even the remote motion hurting her.

"Don't worry. I won't let anybody else touch you," Honoree promised.

Faith sipped all the opium liquid in the spoon and put her arms behind her back, clasping her hands together so she wouldn't fight Honoree. The laudanum was doing its work. She shut her eyes and began praying for herself — for fortitude and healing — and for Shiloh, wherever she was now. When the iodine splashed her cheek, she shrieked.

The shipmaster beside him, Dev stood facing Honoree at the railing outside the women's cabin. Faith's scream just moments ago still echoed in his mind. The ship was moving.

"She fainted," Honoree was saying.

"She should have been taken to a surgeon," Dev insisted, his anger still bubbling.

For the first time, Honoree touched him, resting a hand on his sleeve. "Faith and I have seen many surgeons and witnessed what harm they can do. Faith has studied and read much and knows that if she falls into the wrong hands, she could die of infection and complications."

"She could die." The words caused Dev to stop breathing. *This is my fault. I should have protected her.*

"This isn't your fault," Honoree said as if reading his mind. "She knew she was taking a chance. But she won't rest till my sister is found. Neither of us will. What did you find out? Anything?"

He'd almost forgotten. He inhaled and gazed out at the lush green riverside passing by. "Shiloh had been there. When Faith asked about her, the lady of the house slashed her with a knife. She'd held her hands down by her sides within the folds of her skirt. The worst I thought she might do was slap or hit Faith. I was ready for that."

"My sister wasn't there?"

"No, he . . . LeFevre took her with him to war. As his laundress."

Honoree let loose a sound as if someone had jabbed her hard. She covered her mouth with a hand.

The shipmaster cleared his throat. "I'm sorry this has happened. But we are making the best time we can against the current. And I'm afraid we may be in for questionable weather."

"Questionable weather?" Dev repeated.

"Did you see the bright, rosy dawn this morning? 'Red sky in morning, sailor, take warning,' they say. This is September. Storms and hurricanes can come on fast." The man looked up at the sky. "Those high, dark clouds mean stormy weather. We'll try to outrun it." The captain bowed his head to them and headed for the bridge.

"You said LeFevre took my sister with him?" Honoree pressed.

"Yes," Dev said, unable to keep the disgust out of his tone.

Honoree sent him a pained look. "I have to go back to Faith." She turned away.

The tin-clad riverboat chugged upstream, the vibration from the engine throbbing two decks below his feet. Dev stared out at the passing scene: the cypress trees with their knobby knees in the water and the other riverside trees and plants. He'd let Faith and Honoree have their way about Faith's injury, but what if they were wrong? What could happen to Faith in delaying surgery for three days at the least? *God, help me make this work.*

Then a drop of rain plopped on his hat. He looked up, and another drop trickled down his cheek. The sky had changed in moments. Sheets of gray clouds were scudding overhead. And a massive thundercloud was building over the trees behind. *"Red sky in morning, sailor, take warning."*

The wind buffeted the ship. Thunder clapped ominously ahead and to the west. The steamboat was racing northward. Did the captain still plan to outrun the storm? Or was he heading toward a safe harbor to wait it out? The west wind hit the side of the boat like a great fist. Dev grabbed for the railing to keep upright.

Ahead, Dev glimpsed a small bay. The steamboat appeared to be tracking there, toward the tiny river town onshore. Western waves threatened to wash over the tin cladding surrounding the lower deck. When the boat turned toward the relative protection of the bay, Dev breathed a sigh of relief.

Gunfire cracked from shore. Ducking, Dev glimpsed telltale gunsmoke among the foliage.

"Man your stations!" the shipmaster bellowed over the plopping of rain upon the river surface.

He wasn't going to return fire, was he?

"Prepare foremost gun!" The captain's voice lifted above the storm.

Dev clung to the railing, aghast.

"Fire!" Fentress roared.

One cannon blasted a ball over the houses on stilts along the shore, ripping through the high trees. Dev could only hope that it missed every living soul.

The steamboat finally slipped forward, within the protection of the bay. "Lower anchor —"

The words were cut off by pounding thunder. Hail pelted down. Dev yelped and rushed inside Faith and Honoree's cabin, slamming the door behind him.

Hail hit the tin and clattered as if they

were being stoned.

Faith shrieked, setting his teeth on edge. She began thrashing on the bunk. Honoree grabbed both Faith's hands to keep her from tearing at the bandages wound around her head and face.

Dev grabbed Faith's waist with his two hands.

Intense hail continued to hammer the tin cladding, deafening them. Faith babbled, moaning, twisting, and shrieking.

"It's the opium," Honoree called into his ear. "She's having a nightmare and thinks it's real."

"Josh!" Faith screamed. "Josh! Don't go near the river!" she screamed.

The sound tore at Dev. "Faith, you're all right!" he shouted against the din. "Nobody's going into the river." He hoped he was right. Could a storm like this cause their boat to founder?

Faith did not stop thrashing, but she began to moan instead of screaming.

He still kept Faith pinned to the bunk, gripping her waist. "Who's Josh?" he asked and then regretted it.

Honoree struggled to grip Faith's hands, restraining her. "She was engaged to him before the war."

Unpleasant surprise shot through Dev.

Faith had been engaged?

Faith continued writhing, trying to break free. Between that and the hail and thunder, communication was impossible. Finally Faith went still.

Honoree let go of her. "She's passed out."

Dev released her too. He staggered back to sit on a three-legged stool, and Honoree sank onto the end of the lower berth at Faith's feet. The storm moved eastward. The hail ebbed and the rain slowed to a shower.

"I hope you won't regret not taking her to a doctor sooner," he said, exhausted by the day's events.

Honoree ignored his scold and merely stared at him. Then she leaned over Faith and touched her forehead. "Fever's started," she murmured. "You said that Shiloh's 'master' took my sister with him. What officer does he serve under?"

Dev searched his mind but could not bring up the information. He grimaced. "I know I heard it, but I can't call it to mind now. It will come back to me."

Honoree shook her head but didn't chastise him. No doubt taking pity on him.

Dev leaned back against the wall, shutting his eyes, drained. Of everyone in this war, he'd wanted to protect Faith most of all. He'd failed. He couldn't change what had

340

happened or control what might happen. He was a feather on the wind. And he hated that.

Dev woke with a jerk. Where was he? Scant moonlight flowed in through the window, enough light that he realized he'd fallen asleep on the stool in Faith's cabin. Why hadn't Honoree woken him and sent him to his own room?

The moonlight cast a shaft over Faith's hand, making it glow white in the dim light. He had touched that hand, had felt it clasp his arm when she walked with him. A tenderness filled him. Faith. The only bright spot in the war — and he might lose her.

He moved silently and knelt beside her. Would she wake if he lifted that hand? He imagined himself pressing its softness to his cheek and burying his face in her palm. Women were soft and life was hard.

The ship moved and the angle of the moonlight exposed her bandaged face. Sickened, he withdrew from her. He walked to the door and let himself out to feel his way to his cabin. The moist, cloying night air drenched his face.

He still accepted the fact that he wouldn't survive this war, but he had expected this good woman to make it through. Fear clutched him. *Don't die, Faith. Live. Go home to your garden.*

Faith woke and saw that daylight had come again. Her cheek hurt with an intensity she'd never experienced before. The pain controlled her. Barely moving her head, she glanced around the tiny cabin. She swallowed and tried to speak. "Honoree," she whispered through dry lips.

Honoree turned from the window and hurried to her, immediately feeling Faith's forehead.

Faith then became aware of her fever. Her face radiated heat. "Close to Vicksburg?" Each word cost her pain and energy.

"Closer," Honoree replied. She walked to the three-legged stool, lifted a teakettle, and poured out a cup. She carried it over. Sitting beside the lower berth, she spooned the tepid sweet tea into Faith's mouth.

The perspiration-soaked bandages over her face felt odd, but Faith resisted the urge to touch her face, disturb them. She recalled an illustration in a newspaper of Egyptian mummies and how they were wrapped in strips of cloth. That must be what she looked like, wrapped like a mummy.

"Infection?" Faith asked, speaking with care and barely moving her lips.

"You know there will be some, but I'm doing what I can to keep it at bay. How bad is the pain?"

"I can . . . bear it."

Honoree frowned. "Laudanum?"

"Only when I can't," Faith whispered.

Praying softly, Honoree continued to spoon tea to Faith's lips.

Speaking those few words and sipping tea exhausted Faith. As she swallowed, she also prayed for healing and strength. She was no use to anyone like this, not even to herself. The thought of the coming surgery tried to bring up fear. She fought it. *"Fear thou not; for I am with thee: be not dismayed; for I am thy God."*

Vicksburg, Mississippi

Dev glimpsed Vicksburg high over the river. Relief drenched him. The captain wasted no time docking in port, and soon Dev was carrying Faith down the gangplank. Honoree followed him, toting her valise. A sailor trailed her, carrying Dev's valise as well as Faith's.

Dev paid little attention to the town as he led the other two toward the camp. Faith was conscious but said nothing. He went straight to the hospital tent area. Once there, he glanced around for Dr. Bryant.

"I'll get him." Honoree set her valise at Dev's feet and headed into the tent. "Take Faith to our tent. She won't want to be operated on in the hospital tent."

Before Dev could argue this point, Dr. Dyson appeared.

"What's happened?" the doctor snapped.

"Miss Cathwell has been wounded," Dev said.

"Dr. Dyson, where's Dr. Bryant?" Honoree asked, turning.

Dyson ignored her. "Wounded? You mean the woman finally met someone who wouldn't put up with her impertinence?"

Dev surged toward the man. "Where's Dr. Bryant?"

"I'm the surgeon on duty. I'll perform the surgery. Bring her into the tent, Colonel."

"No!" Honoree exclaimed.

"No," Dev echoed. "Miss Faith insists on Dr. Bryant. Where is he?"

"It's not up to her to decide who will operate. But it's just like her managing ways." Dyson motioned to two orderlies. "Take this woman to the operating table."

Neither man moved.

"You'll be fired if you don't do as you're told," Dyson blustered.

"Miss Faith the one who hired us," one of the black men said. "We not doin' anything she don't want."

"You're fired!"

"Dr. Bryant will perform her surgery," Dev said, leaning forward, nearly nose-to-nose with the surgeon. Dev turned to the two orderlies. "Please find Dr. Bryant and tell him to come to Miss Faith's tent."

The two hustled off.

With Faith tucked close to him, Dev and Honoree headed toward the tent the two nurses shared. The sailor followed them there, deposited the baggage, saluted Dev, and left for his ship.

Dev laid Faith on her cot and stared down at her.

She gazed up at him, only her eyes, nose, and mouth visible between the bandages.

The sight wrenched him and he blurted out, "If only you'd stayed safely on the boat in New Orleans and let me take care of this, you wouldn't have been wounded."

She closed her eyes.

"I'm sorry," he apologized, ashamed of scolding her.

She barely nodded.

Dev heard Honoree's voice. He turned and saw Dr. Bryant coming inside.

Dr. Bryant stepped near Faith and studied her. "I hear you've been wounded. And don't want me to operate in the hospital tent?"

"Yes," Faith whispered.

The surgeon shook his head at her. "Still believe in microscopic disease carriers?"

Dev didn't know what Bryant was talking about, but he realized the doctor was trying to lighten the mood.

"Exactly," Faith whispered.

"Very well. I'll clean my hands, and Honoree is —" he turned toward the opening — "soaking my instruments in alcohol as I speak. And we'll move you into the sun so I can see better what I'm doing. Two orderlies are bringing an operating table. But first I think you need a stiff dose of morphine." The doctor opened his bag and soon was helping Faith to sip the dark, nasty-smelling liquid.

Once Faith fell asleep, Dev and the doctor carried the cot out into the sun. Dr. Bryant donned a clean surgical apron, and scrubbed his hands in a basin.

Honoree stood beside him with his surgical tools.

The sun beating down on his shoulders, Dev stood nearby while still giving the doctor and Honoree room to work. He watched the surgeon as he carefully unbandaged and then slowly stitched up Faith's cheek. Dev felt the needle each time it pierced Faith. Finally the ordeal ended.

"That does it," Dr. Bryant said. "Honoree, you did an admirable job of nursing. And I'm glad you let me perform the surgery. I've done my best, but I'm afraid your friend will bear the scar of this attack for the rest of her life. It's a pity for such a beautiful young woman."

"Thank you, Doctor," Honoree said. "Faith trusted you to do the best surgery she could hope for."

"That is high praise from a lady I respect. Honoree, the army is going to be marching again soon. I am going to recommend that you be allowed to travel home by riverboat. Nurse Cathwell will need careful tending and complete rest. She'll do better at home."

"Well, I'll try to persuade her, but I doubt she'll go," Honoree replied. "And even by riverboat, Cincinnati is a far way from here. If you can let her travel lying in one of the hospital wagons, she would do just as well as getting shuttled from one riverboat to another."

Dr. Bryant shed his surgical apron and put on his frock coat. "I take your meaning. And I assume you're still looking for your sister."

"We are." Honoree had washed the man's

tools in the basin and was drying each and returning it to the leather holder near his bag.

"Did you find out anything in New Orleans?" The doctor was shooting his cuffs and straightening his collar.

"Yes." Honoree proceeded to tell what had happened. She turned to Dev. "Have you remembered the man's commander?"

Dev felt himself flush. "It will come to me." He and the doctor carried Faith back inside the tent.

"Sometimes a crisis causes a memory to elude us." Dr. Bryant accepted his medical bag from Honoree. "I know I don't need to tell you what to do, Honoree. But call me if she takes a turn for the worse. Watch for blood poisoning."

"I will, Doctor, and thank you again."

"When the army moves, I'll make sure there's room for Nurse Cathwell on one of the wagons." The man nodded in acknowledgment and departed.

This news finally hit Dev. The army would be moving east. "I'll check back later," he told Honoree. "I have to report to my immediate superior." He hurried away, unhappy that Honoree wasn't even going to try to persuade Faith to go home, where she belonged.

Chapter 15

Faith woke and gasped, the searing and throbbing pain in her cheek overwhelming everything else.

"Faith," Honoree said, "I'm here." She gripped Faith's hand. "Is it very painful?"

Faith started to nod and halted. Any movement sent shocks of agony through her very teeth. "Surgery?" she asked in a dry whisper.

"Dr. Bryant did just as you wanted. Everything clean. And he did his very best stitching."

"Thank . . . him?"

"I did. I'm so sorry, Faith. I didn't imagine anyone would attack you like this," Honoree lamented once again.

"Didn't either. Colonel?"

"He'll come back. Faith, the colonel told me you found where Shiloh had been. And that her master took her with him to the army." Honoree began to weep. "I'm sorry."

She wiped her wet cheeks with the back of one hand. "I'm glad to know she's alive, but when I think of how she's been treated, I want to . . . hurt someone." Honoree's hand fisted around Faith's.

"Understand." Faith panted with the exertion of speaking.

Honoree's voice became quicker, stronger. "The army's moving soon. Dr. Bryant wanted me to take you home via steamboat."

"No."

"Don't worry. I said no. You shouldn't be traveling at all, but the army — or part of it — will be on the move again eastward any day now." Honoree visibly struggled with herself. "Perhaps we should stay here. There will be a few troops left to guard Vicksburg."

Faith read the concern for her in Honoree's expression. "No. Shiloh . . . east. We . . . must go. Otherwise . . ."

Honoree gripped her hand again. "I know. If we don't stay with the army, it will be just like trying to get permission to go to New Orleans all over again. And we want to go east. That's where the bulk of the Confederate Army is."

"Yes." They had no choice. Faith felt as flat and flimsy as a sheet of foolscap.

"I think I better foment your wound. I

need to keep it from infection." Honoree
patted her shoulder.

Even her friend's touch was anguish to
Faith. Too exhausted by this conversation,
Faith merely blinked in reply.

Honoree left the tent and returned with a
small kettle of water. Soon she was spoon-
ing a scant dose of laudanum to Faith. Then
Honoree prepared a poultice and set it on
Faith's cheek.

Faith let out a muffled shriek. And lay
panting. The pain . . . the pain . . .

Honoree murmured comforting apologies
and Scripture verses and then began singing, " 'Hold on. Keep your hand on the
plow; just hold on.' "

Faith felt herself drifting away.

Duties delayed Dev and it was nearly night-
fall before he was able to go see how Faith
was faring. He found the young wife from
Tennessee sitting with Faith, who lay on a
pallet just outside her tent.

"I'm Ella, sir," the girl reminded him
when he asked.

"Miss Ella." He acknowledged her, removing his hat. "Miss Faith." Faith's large green
eyes were pools of anguish. He wished he
could do something for her.

"Honoree is helping Dr. Bryant now," Ella

351

explained, "so I'm watching Miss Faith. I was thinking, sir. She needs to be sat up for a while. She must be aching from lying so long."

Dev moved closer to the pallet. "Miss Faith, would you like me to lift you and prop you up for a bit?"

"Please." Faith's voice was a thin thread.

Ella rose. "Maybe you could let her lean against you?"

Not looking directly at Faith's bandaged face, Dev lifted and moved Faith gently to a camp stool. He sat down beside Faith, allowing her to lean on him, under his arm. "Is this all right, Miss Faith?"

"Better," she whispered.

Again he wished Honoree were here so he could ask her how Faith was doing. She seemed so weak.

Ella supplied information without his needing to inquire. "Honoree says her infection is steady, not gettin' worse. Will you stay with her now, sir, till Honoree comes back? I need to go to my husband."

"Of course."

The young woman moved away quickly, wishing them good night.

Dev looked to Faith. "I suppose you are still refusing to go home by riverboat?" he asked.

"Yes. Remember?"

He knew what she was referring to. "No, I can't recall LeFevre's commanding officer's name. It's still just out of my reach."

Maybe he truly didn't want to remember, to lead her further on this quest that had proved to be so dangerous. If he hadn't helped her go to Annerdale, they would never have ended up in New Orleans. . . . He stopped that line of thought. What was, was.

"I can't . . . remember either."

The anguish in those few words tightened around his throat. He couldn't think of anything to say. Finally he told her the latest information going through the camp. "General Grant has been promoted to the rank of major general of the regular Union Army, not just of the volunteers. Sherman was also promoted to brigadier general of the regular army."

"Good."

In light of his guilt, he tried to rein in the pleasure of sitting so close and feeling her next to him. He failed. He supported her, reveling in her nearness.

"Need to lie down."

He quickly laid her back down onto the pallet.

"I'm glad you've come, Colonel," Honoree

said, approaching the tent. "I need help moving the cot back inside the tent for the night."

"Of course." Dev helped Honoree make this adjustment.

"Night." Faith closed her eyes.

And he watched her fall asleep. "How is she?" he asked Honoree in a low voice.

"She's holding her own. She won't let this beat her. But it's going to take a while for her to come back to herself."

He nodded, bade Honoree a polite good night, and left. As he walked through the deepening twilight, he couldn't stop himself from thinking of what lay under Faith's bandages. The thought of it twisted inside him like a red-hot wire. To him, she remained as beautiful as ever, even more so. Nevertheless, how would such a lovely woman deal with a scarred face?

September 16, 1863
The order to move out came sooner than expected. Two mornings later, Honoree, with Ella's help, fashioned a pallet for Faith on top of boxes of medical supplies in the rear of a Sanitary Commission wagon. Two of the orderlies climbed up and lifted Faith through the rear circular opening in the wagon's cloth covering, and the wagon

jerked forward over a rut.

Faith's whole body ached with fever, and her cheek flamed and throbbed with each beat of her heart. Every move was agony. She kept her lower lip tucked under her front teeth as the wagon bounced beneath her.

Ella, weeping, and Honoree, frowning, walked behind the wagon, watching her through the opening. As the miles passed, often Honoree recited Scripture to her.

" 'God is our refuge and strength, a very present help in trouble.'

" 'The Lord is my rock, and my fortress, and my deliverer; my God, my strength.'

" 'The Lord is my strength and song, and he is become my salvation: he is my God.'

" 'The Lord is my light and my salvation; whom shall I fear? the Lord is the strength of my life; of whom shall I be afraid?' "

Faith listened, jolted, wrenched, falling in and out of consciousness. When would this torturous day end?

The order to halt for the day finally came, long after Dev began wishing for it. Being in the saddle again felt good, but his worries over the effects of this troop movement on Faith's health left him uncertain, ill at ease. He wanted to seek her out immediately, but he had duties to attend to. And he needed to eat his evening meal — he had to stay strong.

Under the darkening sky, a molten-red sun on the horizon, he finally heated a can of beans over the fire outside his tent. And thought of Armstrong. It was lonely eating by oneself. He and Armstrong had always satisfied the prohibition against whites and blacks eating together by having Armstrong eat half-turned away from the fire.

Now that Dev recalled it, the practice seemed foolish, just plain foolish. He remembered Faith's pointing out his inconsistencies in regard to slavery, but he brushed them aside for the time being. He didn't need any more to deal with. He was already weighed down with worry and guilt over her. She could die. He blanched, iced with that fear.

After breaking up some hardtack — remnants of what he'd gnawed on for lunch — he shoveled the mixture of hardtack and beans into his mouth just to fill his empty stomach. Even if good food had been offered him, he would have had no appetite. Then he drank some badly brewed coffee, wishing Armstrong had taught him how to brew something worth drinking before he'd left.

Dev had thought of trying to hire another valet but had not wanted a stranger around him. And manservants did not appear in contraband camps very often. So many of them had been taken to the war with their masters.

Generally dismal, Dev chugged two more mugs of the dreadful coffee. Then he rose and headed for the hospital wagon area to find Faith and Honoree. They might need something, and he had to face once more what his negligence had allowed.

He threaded his way through circles of men around campfires, all eating their meals from cans and brewing coffee. He envied their camaraderie. But he was an officer and had to hold himself apart. Armstrong's voice spoke in his mind, snippets of conversations they'd had. Nothing special, just words with someone he'd known all his life. He finally saw Honoree standing beside a wagon.

The back of the cloth wagon cover had been loosed, and as he neared, he heard Honoree speaking to someone in the wagon bed.

"Honoree," Dev said, "how is she doing?"

"Colonel," Faith quavered.

"I'm here." He hurried forward.

Faith was lying on a pallet inside the

hospital wagon. She offered him her hand.

He took it gently. He almost asked how she felt but quelled the urge. "You're awake," he said a bit lamely. He turned to Honoree. "Have you eaten? I can stay with her —"

"I've brought their meals from the hospital cook," Armstrong said from behind Dev.

Dev stiffened. He hadn't expected to meet Armstrong here, but he probably should have. The connection between Armstrong and Honoree had become more than apparent.

Accepting one plate from Armstrong, Honoree turned to the wagon, to Faith. The meal prepared by the hospital cook, whatever it was, smelled a lot better than what Dev had eaten tonight. Honoree began to feed Faith.

Dev didn't speak at first, only listening to Armstrong and Honoree speak in undertones. But then he realized Honoree was letting her food go cold in order to feed Faith first. "Sit down and eat your food, Honoree," Dev offered. "I can help her eat."

Honoree stared at him, then handed him the plate of food. She sat on a camp stool near Armstrong, who, averting his gaze from Dev, sat on the one beside it. The separation between Dev and Armstrong felt like a physical wall. Of ice.

Dev hoisted himself up onto the back of the wagon beside Faith. "Miss Faith," he said gently, "allow me to help you eat." Faith's bandaged face filled him with sharp regret. He pushed this down. "Can you sit up?"

"No. Weak."

Fear roiled in his stomach. He ignored it and propped her up slightly with sacks of what felt like cotton or bandages. Realizing she couldn't chew very much, he slowly spooned bits of food into her mouth and watched her gingerly chew and swallow. He wanted to ask Honoree again about Faith's condition, but perhaps Honoree would hesitate to be frank in Faith's hearing.

"No more," Faith whispered, panting as if exhausted.

He looked down at the plate. She'd eaten barely a fourth of a normal meal. He turned to Honoree to ask if he should insist she eat more.

"You eat the rest, Colonel," Honoree said, "while I finish my meal. She ate more than I expected."

His pride prompted him to refuse, but his stomach insisted he accept the food. "Thank you." He began eating the well-seasoned beans and rice. His stomach sighed with pleasure.

Sitting so near, he caught snatches of Armstrong and Honoree's conversation. Armstrong sounded happy, innocent somehow of what lay ahead of him as a soldier. Dev felt a hundred years older than his former servant. Too soon the man would discover that freedom could turn and savage him. He looked to Faith. She was watching him with solemn eyes.

Honoree rose, holding out a cup in one hand and, with the other, asking for his now-empty plate. "Could you help her sip some coffee?"

Dev assented and traded his plate for the cup.

"I put a lot of sugar in the coffee to give her nourishment," Honoree said.

Dev also smelled a hint of whiskey. He recalled that Faith had used this on his cousin, his faithless cousin, to help break the fever and ease his pain. The memory was a needle in the heart.

Faith let Dev lift her shoulders onto his arm and sipped from the tin mug. She gasped with the effort, and as if her neck had no strength, her head lolled on his sleeve.

From behind him, Honoree sighed. "I'm already exhausted from today, and how many more days will we be marching north?"

"I've heard," Armstrong said, "that we're on our way to tangle with Lee if we can."

Dev noted the eagerness in the man's voice. Dev thought with thick irony that it was very clear Armstrong had never faced battle. Only the unseasoned soldier looked forward to engaging Lee, a general who outfoxed all the others.

Still helping Faith drink the coffee, Dev added, "We're heading north to Memphis so we can move eastward through southern Tennessee. I will resume reconnaissance tomorrow. We'll be moving in and out of enemy-held territory. Honoree, be sure to stay close to the shelter of the wagons. Bushwhackers will pick off anyone they can."

"I will," Honoree agreed for once without arguing with him — or at least that's what it felt like to him. He and Honoree often seemed at odds. He finished assisting Faith with the whiskey-laced coffee.

Honoree rose and came to him. "Have you recalled the name of the officer my sister's despoiler is with?" Her voice challenged him as if he were purposefully withholding the truth.

"I've tried all day to bring up the name,"

he said, keeping his voice mild, "but it's like it's just beyond my grasp."

Armstrong let out a sound of disbelief.

It stung Dev. He wanted to snap at Armstrong that he was trying, honestly trying to remember. "I will recall it in time. We can't do anything more now than we are in any event. LeFevre wouldn't be serving west of the Mississippi River, so we must be going toward him."

"That's true," Honoree said. "Very well. I believe you truly can't remember — Faith can't either. But one of you will soon."

"Thank you, and again, I'm sorry that this happened while Faith was under my protection."

"You're only human," Honoree said. "This is an evil world with plenty of evil people."

"The mistress was probably jealous of your sister," Armstrong said to her.

Dev agreed but said nothing, now averting his own gaze so their eyes wouldn't meet.

"I'm going to foment Faith's wound again and then get her ready for sleep." Honoree moved to the wagon and opened the wooden chest Dev recognized.

Dev glanced into Faith's eyes, hoping for an invitation there to stay. But she was too ill, obviously too deeply wrapped up in pain to do more than whimper at him.

He wanted to ask Honoree, *"Will she be all right?"* But he realized that would only make everyone uncomfortable, and how could Honoree know that for sure?

"Do you need me?" Dev asked.

"No, I can manage," Honoree said with a glance over her shoulder toward Armstrong.

Dev felt dismissed and decided to accept it. He bowed his head and walked away, still not looking at Armstrong. He hoped Faith would recover and not have her health broken by this fever, but that was out of his control. Like everything else in this accursed war.

Faith awoke in the night. She tried to think, but her mind was stuffed with cotton. The agony in her cheek had not relented, but gnawed at her, voracious and cruel. Even drawing a breath ripped her facial nerves, and she whimpered at the pain.

Why had this happened? Her mind supplied a familiar verse of Scripture: *"In the world ye shall have tribulation."* But it didn't help. How long had it been since they left Vicksburg? She wanted to wake Honoree, who lay beside her on the tailgate of the wagon, and ask her friend to lift her, move her, help . . .

Faith's very bones ached from lying in one position for so long. *Oh, Father, save me from this wound. I haven't found Shiloh yet.* That she might die of this infection was very real. Her limbs felt like rags, and her whole body burned with fever.

Colonel Knight came to mind. He'd come to her and helped feed her. She remembered that. But she couldn't recall the attack that left her in this state. She could see the plantation — Cypress Bank — the company of soldiers riding up to the house, the Spanish moss moving in the breeze, the woman in the worn dress on the porch . . . and then nothing.

Honoree had asked for the information that would lead them to Shiloh. The thought that beautiful Shiloh had been reduced to the status of camp follower still broke Faith's heart. She wept without tears. The fever had burned them up. *God, help me. Take down this fever and let me live. I must find Shiloh. I must.*

Then Patience sat down next to her. *"Don't worry, Sis. Thee will get better."*

Faith stretched out an arm to touch her, hold her. But she couldn't reach. "Don't leave me, Sister. Don't leave me. Patience, Patience."

"You're having a dream, Faith," Honoree said from beside her. Honoree lifted Faith's head, righted her pillow, and propped up one side of her body with discarded flour sacks.

The slight shift in position felt amazingly good.

"You're bed-sore. That's all."

"That's all," Faith parroted, trying to reassure herself. But of course it was not all. *Father, please don't let me die yet. I have so much left undone.*

October 1, 1863

The days of moving north following the Mississippi River merged into monotonous misery. Once again, Dev and a company of his men were on reconnaissance. At present, as afternoon rain poured down on them, they huddled together under oilskin capes draped over their hats and backs. Nearby, after hours of carrying the men, their horses steamed in the warm rain. Confederate raiders had been active in this area. Dev wanted to track them down but so far had not come near enough.

Dev gnawed hardtack and sipped tepid water from his canteen, as did most of the others. Visions of the delicious meals he'd eaten at his mother's table taunted him.

365

Mashed potatoes rich with thick cream. Warm biscuits dripping with sweet butter and honey. Ham so tender it almost melted in his mouth. His nearly empty stomach ached for a good meal. The hardtack had the consistency of sawdust and was just as tasty.

"I hear there's a new bunch like Quantrill raiding ahead of us," one of his men commented between attempts to consume his hardtack.

Quantrill — that notorious Confederate guerrilla operating in Missouri. He and his men ambushed Union patrols like this one, as well as supply trains.

"This bunch has burned a few homes of Union sympathizers in Tennessee," another soldier added.

Dev held out his hardtack to let the rain soften it. "How did you hear of this bunch?"

"Word of mouth," the first man said, following Dev's example and moistening his hardtack in the rain. "They call themselves Carroll's Rangers."

Dev dropped his hardtack and then retrieved it from the muddy grass. He wiped it on his sleeve and bit into it — hard. Just because his cousin was capable of this didn't mean that he was the Carroll of these raiders. The taunting note still hid in one of

Dev's inner pockets.

Then he thought of Faith, who'd been delirious with fever when he last visited her. Neither of them had yet recalled the information that could lead them to the girl Shiloh. Could nothing go right? Was he incapable of righting his wrongs before it was too late?

Days later, further into October, Faith stared up at the sunlight coming through the cloth roof of the supply wagon. Like sunshine after the rain, her mind had cleared.

"I've brought breakfast," Honoree said from outside the rear of the wagon.

Faith watched her friend set a tray down carefully on the open tailgate. She wanted to speak, but her mouth was so dry she didn't think she could. She made a sound.

Interpreting it correctly, Honoree lifted her head and helped her sip tepid coffee from one of the mugs.

"I remember," Faith whispered. "I remember."

Honoree froze. "You remember LeFevre's commanding officer?"

"Braxton . . . Bragg."

The cup in Honoree's hand trembled. She closed her eyes, then opened them and helped Faith drink more.

"We still have a war between us and Shiloh," Faith said.

"Yes. I know." Honoree gripped Faith's hand. "We won't give up hope. Or just plain give up."

Faith tried to smile, but it tugged her taut, raw-feeling skin.

Honoree pressed a hand to the part of Faith's forehead that wasn't bandaged. "Your fever is going down. I think we're winning against the infection."

"Thanks to thee and Dr. Bryant," Faith whispered.

"He's a rare gentleman," Honoree agreed and began propping Faith up to help her eat breakfast.

"I can feed myself," Faith said, reaching for the spoon. She managed to eat several spoonfuls of porridge before the weakness claimed her again.

Honoree fed her the rest. "You are getting better. It just takes time."

Faith saw tears dripping down Honoree's face. Faith patted her friend's forearm as Honoree continued to spoon the porridge. "Way will open," she whispered.

Honoree nodded and went on feeding her. "We need to ask the colonel to find out where Bragg is."

"Yes." Colonel Knight came every evening to see her, help Honoree with her care. But they'd not talked privately for so long. She missed him. She shouldn't, but she did.

As soon as the name was out of Faith's mouth, Dev knew it was right. "Yes, that's it. Braxton Bragg. I don't know why I couldn't bring it to mind before."

"You don't want us to go on with this," Honoree said.

"That may be true, but I didn't withhold the information for that reason — for any reason," Dev said, his voice rising.

"Peace," Faith said, her hand outstretched in entreaty. "What happened was a shock. To both of us."

Dev could see that speaking was still taking its toll on Faith. He claimed her outstretched hand. And then, though he wanted to keep hold of it, he set it down gently in her lap. He looked to Honoree, silently asking after Faith.

"Her fever is going down, and the wound is healing. I think we got most of the infection out. She's on the mend."

Warm relief washed over him in waves. But he still worried about the lasting effects of this trauma on Faith's health. "I'm glad to hear it." Unable to stop himself, he laid his hand over Faith's. "I'm so glad."

Faith gazed at him, her eyes smiling around the bandages that crisscrossed her face.

He withdrew his hand, feeling guilty. "I'll go to my immediate superior and see if I can find out anything about this Confederate. We'll need to know where Bragg is now." Then he kicked himself for saying *we*. If any action was taken, he needed to be the one taking it.

"Thank thee," Faith whispered.

"We were going to ask you to find out where Bragg is. We know we can't just walk up to him and ask for Shiloh," Honoree said sarcastically. "But we figure he's east of here, and after a battle when things are stirred up, we might be able to find Shiloh."

The girl's words chilled him. He did not want either of these women where things were "stirred up." Didn't the two of them have any sense of danger? "Did you ever think that she might have run away from LeFevre? I mean, slaves are running to the Union Army lines every day."

Honoree frowned. "My sister knows her worth. And her danger." She wouldn't meet his gaze. "Shiloh wouldn't leave relative safety for sure peril." Then she looked him in the face. "Unless her situation was dire."

"I'm sure after the price he paid for your sister, LeFevre would guard her and prize her," Dev said, trying to reassure the two of them but also knowing that each word would wound them.

"As his possession," Honoree said bitterly.

Faith moved her hand toward Honoree.

The situation sickened him too. But he decided to try to reason with them again. "Miss Faith, since you're somewhat better, can't I persuade you two to go home? I can look for Shiloh. You should be recuperating at home, not . . ." His voice trailed off.

The two women now shared the same stubborn expression.

He gritted his teeth. "Very well. Don't listen to reason. I'll go to Osterhaus and see what he knows of Bragg." Dev turned away.

"Thank you, Colonel," Honoree said.

He marched off, trying to distance himself again from these vexatious women. He repeatedly erected a wall, but somehow Faith always tore it down, leaving him exposed to feelings he didn't want to have, shouldn't have.

Not far from the wagon, the young Ella McCullough stepped out and stopped him. "I heard you try to persuade them to go home. I'm worried. Will Miss Faith recover?"

"She's receiving the best of care," Dev said, trying to sound reassuring, though the very thing the young woman feared was exactly what he dreaded.

Ella smiled. "Thank you." She walked toward the wagon Faith was resting in.

This awful war. The girl belonged in her father's house, filling her hope chest and going to church socials, not marching east with the army.

He hurried off directly to Osterhaus. Each morning after roll call he reported there anyway. Today he'd arrive early and see what, if anything, was known about Bragg and his location.

At Osterhaus's tent, Dev saluted and was acknowledged.

"You're early today," Osterhaus commented.

"I wanted to ask for information about a Confederate officer."

Osterhaus eyed him. "Carroll's Rangers, by chance?"

Dev repressed his marked reaction. "I've heard of them. We'll get them soon."

Osterhaus nodded. "I hope so. What Reb officer are you looking for?"

"Bragg, Braxton Bragg."

"According to what I've read in Southern newspapers, he's bounced around plenty, starting in Texas. Now he's ahead of us — Army of Tennessee, I think."

"Is that where we're headed?"

"In a word, yes." Osterhaus looked over Dev's shoulder. "Here come the rest of the officers."

Dev stepped back and turned to greet his fellow officers for their morning briefing. No doubt he'd be out again today, searching for Rebel raiding parties and perhaps finding unexpected Confederate troops. The two armies played cat and mouse, taking turns in each role.

Faith's bandaged face glimmered in his mind. He was convinced his guilt over that would end only when he no longer breathed. Who knew how long that would be? But he hoped he would have long enough to bring Jack Carroll to book. Betrayal burned in his stomach.

Chapter 16

October 20, 1863

In the last of the summerlike heat, Dev and his regiment had skirmished their way east from Memphis, pushing back Confederate raiders who were harassing Brigadier General Sherman's advance eastward toward Chattanooga.

After the Union defeat at the Battle of Chickamauga, Grant and Major General Rosecrans were holed up in the southeastern Tennessee mountains near Chattanooga, facing the Confederates Hood and Bragg. Chattanooga now was the prize each army wanted. It was a major railroad hub and the gateway through the mountains into Georgia. Railroads conveyed the lifeblood of any army — supplies — and whoever controlled one controlled the other.

Today, under a cloudless blue sky, Dev and his cavalry regiment rode along both sides of the railroad tracks running north to south. The noise of the chugging steam engine they shadowed made it impossible to hear anything else. Alert, Dev scanned the tree line along the tracks that ran amid horse pastures and the occasional farm field.

Here and there, fall red edged a high maple leaf. Outriders patrolled farther afield on each side. Dev would not let this train of desperately needed supplies fall into Rebel hands.

They hugged the cover of the tree line wherever they could, wary of bushwhackers. As he rode, his senses on guard, his mind worked on the problem that had perplexed him for weeks. How could he get Faith to go home? She'd suffered a serious wound and he wanted her safe, away from the war, even more than he had before. So far, however, his entreaties had fallen on deaf ears.

But now that this railroad line lay in Union hands, why couldn't she just ride north by rail and then board an Ohio River steamboat and travel east to her home near Cincinnati? Willful stubbornness was the only rationale he could come up with.

Ahead, he saw they'd nearly completed their day's mission. Sherman's Army of the Tennessee was encamped on the horizon, awaiting the supplies on this train. Mentally he sighed with relief. No Reb in his right mind, not even Jack, would attack the train with the whole army nearby. The train whistle sounded, and the long train of cars began to slow. He led his regiment to the rail depot, where they would guard the supplies as they were off-loaded.

Hours later — nearly evening, just as he was about to dismiss his men from the depot area — Dev overheard a woman saying, "Yes, I am looking for the hospital wagons. Can thee help me?"

Thee? He rode closer and glimpsed a woman near his mother's age wearing distinctly Quaker garb, so like Faith's. She glanced his way, and the family resemblance to Faith struck him between the eyes. He dismounted, led his horse through the men still helping to unload the train, and went straight to the woman. He doffed his hat. "Pardon me, ma'am?"

She regarded him. "Yes?"

"Allow me to introduce myself — Colonel Devlin Knight." He inclined his head. "You wouldn't be from Ohio, would you?"

"Yes, we're from Ohio." She raised an eyebrow.

"You look so much like one of our nurses who's also a Quaker —"

"Thee knows Faith Cathwell?" the woman asked, her eyes lighting with excitement.

"Yes, ma'am."

"She is our daughter." The woman nearly danced on her toes as she formed signs with her hand toward the large gray-haired man beside her. "I am Honor Cathwell, and this is my husband, Samuel."

Dev recalled Faith's telling him that her father was deaf and her family communicated with him through finger signing. He watched, fascinated.

"Where is our daughter?" Honor asked.

"I can take you to her," Dev said.

Honor hesitated. "We have brought supplies for the army — we collected them from the members of our meeting in Cincinnati. Medicine, clothing, and food. But we also have a few boxes of personal items for our daughter and Honoree. Thee knows Honoree too?"

"Yes." He motioned for two of his own men. "Mrs. Cathwell, tell this man which boxes are for your daughter. They'll be marked as hers, and my men will make sure they're delivered to her tent." He glanced at the men, a silent order that they were to guard the boxes meant for Faith and Honoree. Though he hated to admit it, some soldiers thieved when they could.

His men nodded their promise to bring the women their supplies.

Honor directed the men to the boxes, which were then chalked, *Cathwell.* Finally she faced him. "Could thee take us to Faith? We are so anxious to see her again."

"Of course. Follow me." He gave his men parting orders and turned, taking his mount away.

Then another concern hit Dev. Did they know about the attack? "Have you heard from your daughter recently?"

"The last letter we received was in late August," Honor said, while simultaneously communicating with her hand to her husband.

Dev observed this with interest as they strode through the crowded camp.

"Since Faith told us her hospital unit was with his troops," Honor continued, "we've been following newspaper accounts of the movement of the troops with General Grant."

So they hadn't heard anything for almost two months. Dev debated with himself. Surely he must prepare these parents for Faith's changed appearance. But how much did they know?

"Our daughter was wanting to go to New

Orleans," Honor said. "Did she get permission?"

Well, that led into what he needed to say. "Yes. Though I advised her to stay safely in Vicksburg and let me go and make inquiries into Honoree's sister's whereabouts, she insisted on traveling to New Orleans." They passed a man selling newspapers.

"Thy face is downcast. What happened in New Orleans?" Honor's steps slowed. "Do not hold back. Please."

He felt the unwelcome sting of tears and shook it off. He continued to direct them but more slowly, between men headed the other way. "I traveled with your daughter and her friend to New Orleans in mid-September. We visited the slave auction house where . . . Honoree's sister was sold. Then we went out to the plantation she'd been taken to." He fell silent.

Faith's parents walked beside him, their expressions sinking from mere worry to fear.

"Was Shiloh dead?" Honor asked, watching his face.

"No! I'm sorry," he blurted. "The fact is, the lady of the house attacked your daughter . . . with a knife."

Honor smothered a tiny shriek, pressing a hand to her mouth. "How badly?"

"Your daughter's made an almost-full

recovery, but —" he tightened his grip on his emotions — "her cheek was scarred. She was weak and ill for several weeks."

Honor clutched his sleeve, halting him. "But she is well now."

"The wound is healed, but I think she's still weakened. She tires more easily than she used to." He faced her but gestured for them to proceed through the narrow lane clogged with soldiers. "I shouldn't have let her go to the plantation. But I swear I never once thought she'd be attacked."

"I doubt thee could have stopped Faith from going. Was Honoree hurt?" Honor began walking again.

"We'd asked her to remain safely on the gunboat that brought us south. Leaving the Union-controlled city would have been even more dangerous for her."

"I see," Honor said solemnly. "I take it thee didn't find Shiloh there?"

"No." He couldn't bring himself to tell this Quaker lady the truth about Shiloh's whereabouts.

They walked on in somber silence, surrounded by the bustle and noise of the military camp.

"Thee mustn't blame thyself," Honor said. *Easier said than done.* "Yes, ma'am." Then hope glimmered. Perhaps these two could persuade their daughter to go home. Surely they would do so without prompting from him.

He took them through the maze of tents, finally arriving at Faith's. He noted that her mother was holding a handkerchief to her nose. He sympathized. Army camps had their own distinctive stench.

"Mother! Father!" Faith ran to them, her arms outstretched.

Dev stepped back and allowed himself the pleasure of observing a family reunited.

Then, with only a wave, he quietly walked away, returning his horse to the corral. He'd prepared her parents, and now Faith needed time alone with them. He thought of his own mother. Perhaps he'd be granted a Christmas furlough this year and would see her again. And then he considered Jack. Carroll's Rangers were busy in eastern Tennessee. He grimly longed for another family reunion, but a very different one from Faith's.

Seeing her parents so unexpectedly released the dam that held back Faith's tears of joy and sorrow. She had hoped the war would be over the next time she hugged her mother. But that didn't lessen her joy, couldn't. Her father opened his strong arms, and for a moment she reverted to a little girl, wrapped safely within her father's embrace.

Then she remembered her scarred cheek, and before she could stop herself, her hand flew upward to cover it. Though remaining tender, her wound had healed. Faith tried not to think of it. Still, she had yet to look into a mirror at that side of her face.

Her mother closed her hand over Faith's and drew it down. "The colonel told us thee was attacked." Honor leaned over and kissed the deep welt.

Faith felt tears stream down her face. "Mama," she said like a child and leaned into her mother's shoulder. Then both her mother and father enfolded her as she wept.

Finally they drew apart and Faith conveyed them to her tent, where she sat on her cot and they lowered themselves onto the two camp stools. "I didn't know thee was coming."

"We collected a train-car load of food, clothing, and medical supplies. We gained permission to deliver them through Tippy's father. You remember Tippy — Blessing's friend?"

"Yes. Tippy's father was a state legislator?"

Honor nodded. "He still has connections

and was able to get our supplies included in the ones coming down the Ohio to the railroad line southward through Nashville, and he obtained a pass for us to come too." Her mother glanced around her. "Thee is living very simply, Daughter."

Faith chuckled at this. "Yes, we are. Any simpler and we'd be sleeping under the stars on the grass."

Trying to smile but failing, Honor gazed at her. "I am grieved thee has suffered such pain."

"I am too," Faith agreed and conquered the urge to press her hand over the scar again.

"Thee is recovered then?"

"Yes. Dr. Bryant and Honoree took good care of me." She wasn't ready to admit that she tired more easily and lacked stamina. Surely that would rebound with time. "I'm fine," she reassured them.

"Miss Cathwell?" a voice outside summoned her.

She ducked out the open flap. Outside, two cavalrymen were setting down several boxes in front of her tent. "Yes?"

Honor peered out. "Those are for thee and Honoree."

"Oh." Faith thanked the soldiers, who politely tugged the brims of their caps and

383

then headed away with their mounts.

Faith could hardly believe the largesse. "Mother, what is in these boxes?"

"Winter clothing for thee and Honoree. More herbs from thy garden, food, and anything else anyone could think to send."

Faith sat down on one box, weak with sudden relief. "Thee doesn't know how much we need the smallest thing." She drew in a deep breath, suppressing the urge to open every box immediately.

"Where is my namesake?" Honor asked, looking around at the tents. The drummer sounded supper call nearby.

"Honoree will be back soon, I'm sure." Faith guessed that Honoree had taken advantage of the low patient numbers in the hospital tent to seek out Armstrong. They were spending more and more time together.

Faith glanced up to find her mother staring at her, worry in the lines of her face. Faith hoped her mother would not join Colonel Knight in urging her to go home and leave her duties and the search for Shiloh behind. The knife attack had only highlighted why she must find and free Shiloh.

Drawn against his will, Dev sought out

Faith's tent late the next evening. He'd been out on patrol all day. Carroll's Rangers were harassing the railroad, and Dev's job was to stop him. He only wished he had succeeded.

Dev had one goal this evening. If they hadn't tried yet, he would attempt to persuade Faith's parents to take her and Honoree home with them. When he reached their tent, he found Dr. Bryant had also come to meet the Cathwells. The group, including Faith, sat in front of her tent on camp stools and wooden boxes.

In greeting, Dr. Bryant saluted Dev, and he returned the salute. Dev bowed to Faith's parents, pulling the brim of his hat in their direction.

"Your daughter is such an asset to our patients," Dr. Bryant was saying.

Dev noticed that Faith had positioned herself so that the side of her face bearing the scar was pointed away from the rest of the group.

"We are grateful she is of help," Faith's mother said, still spelling the words with her fingers. "She and her late sister always had the gift of healing. Even as children they brought home injured birds and pets of other children."

"I did the same as a child," Dr. Bryant said. "If your daughter had been born a

385

man, she would have made a good doctor."

"I agree."

"Well, I must go back to the hospital." Dr. Bryant stood.

Dev began to marshal his arguments to persuade Faith's parents to do for her what he wished.

After shaking hands with the Cathwells, Dr. Bryant turned.

Just then, Landon McCullough rushed forward, his wife, Ella, in his arms. "Dr. Bryant!" he called. The corporal halted, panting. "My wife's —" He swallowed.

Faith leaped to her feet, instantly looking worried. "Bring her into our tent." She waved the young man through the open flap.

Dev moved forward in case he was needed but stopped outside the entrance.

Faith pointed to her cot, and Landon laid his wife down. Dr. Bryant came in after them, followed by Honor Cathwell.

"I didn't know what to do," Landon said, backing away to let the doctor draw near to his wife. "She just said she was feelin' poorly and then she started bleedin'. . . . Is she losin' the babe?"

Honor moved to stand near Landon while Faith and Dr. Bryant attended to the young woman.

Just outside the opening, Dev tightened

his jaw. No one had told him Ella was expecting.

"Are you having any abdominal pain?" Dr. Bryant asked the girl.

"Yes, cramping," Ella whimpered.

Faith claimed Ella's hand and began murmuring softly to her. She looked to her mother. "Why doesn't thee take Corporal McCullough outside? It's crowded in here."

Honor touched the corporal's shoulder. "Will thee come with me? We'll just sit outside while the good doctor examines thy wife. All right?"

Dev moved away from the entrance to let them pass.

"Yes, ma'am." Landon followed her outside and sat where she indicated on one of the boxes.

"Corporal McCullough," Dev said, "these are Miss Faith's parents. Mr. and Mrs. Cathwell came down from Cincinnati with supplies."

The young man managed to nod to them and doff his hat belatedly.

Honor poured him a cup of coffee from the kettle sitting on the fire nearby. "Would thee tell us about thy family?" She asked the question no doubt to give the young man something good to think about, not knowing the truth about his situation.

387

"Got no family, no home." He looked near tears as he accepted the cup. "All I got left is the army and Ella." He looked toward the closed tent flap.

"The war forced thee from thy home?" Honor went on, standing so she blocked the entrance to the tent.

Still trying to distract the young man, Dev thought.

"Yes, ma'am. Americans should stick together, not secede. But we had to leave home over secession and now Ella's in the family way and we're in the midst of the war."

"Well, Faith's father and I will be going home tomorrow on the northbound train," Honor said. "Would thee like to send Ella home with us? If she's able to travel?"

The young corporal upset his cup, spilling some coffee. "You mean it?"

"Of course." Honor signed to her husband, who nodded firmly and gestured. "My husband says she is welcome, most welcome."

"I wouldn't send my wife with just anybody," Landon said earnestly, "but Miss Faith is known for her kindness and honesty."

"We are glad to hear it, though not surprised," Honor said.

"I was hoping," Dev began, sensing the time had come to broach his purpose for coming tonight, "that you'd take Miss Faith home with you too. She's not in the same health as before her wounding, and we'll be in winter before you know it."

He looked to them pleadingly, trying to convey to them how bad wintering with an army could be. "Winter camp conditions are harsh and could break her health for the rest of her life." *Or kill her.*

"Colonel Knight," Honor said, "we would love to take Faith and Honoree home tomorrow. But they are adults and must make their own decisions. I will try to persuade her, but . . ." She raised and dropped her shoulders in a gesture of helplessness.

Then she watched her husband's hands and chuckled. "My husband says Faith takes after me. Stubborn." She took a seat beside him.

Dev wanted to rail at them. But they were civilians; they had no idea what their daughter faced in the coming winter.

"I think you should try to convince her," Landon said. "I been prayin' for a way to get Ella somewhere safe."

"Some way," Honor repeated. "Quakers say, 'Way will open.' That means we should pray, and God will open a way, some way."

Landon drew in a long breath. "I believe that now. You are a godsend, ma'am."

"What's happening?" Honoree approached through the surrounding tents with Armstrong at her side.

Dev rose, as did Faith's father, who greeted Honoree with hand signs. She signed back to him and said aloud, "This is Armstrong."

"Thy young man?" Honor moved forward, her hand outstretched.

"Ma'am, sir." Armstrong removed his hat and shook their hands. "A pleasure."

During this exchange, Landon slipped nearer the tent.

Honor explained Ella's condition to Honoree.

"I'm sorry she's having difficulties," Honoree said.

"If she's not able to travel tomorrow," Honor said, "we'll remain a few days longer."

"I'm afraid, ma'am," Dev spoke up, "the army has unloaded all the supplies and we move on the morrow. Please consider what I said about taking Miss Faith and Honoree home with you. I don't want them to suffer the rigors of winter camp."

"Faith and I won't go home till we find

Shiloh," Honoree said flatly.

The doctor came out and went directly to Landon. "I think your young lady is going to be fine. Nothing serious. But she must not be moved tonight. Nurse Cathwell invited her to stay here."

"Can I see her now?" Landon asked.

"Go right in," Faith said, emerging. The young man slipped inside and she let the flap drop, giving him and his wife some privacy.

Dev couldn't help himself. He stared at Faith. The desire to take her hand, pull her close, and kiss her . . . He stopped his mind there.

"Faith, we'll be taking Ella home tomorrow," Honor said and signed. "Colonel Knight tells us the army is moving forward in the morning."

Faith merely nodded.

"The colonel has also tried to persuade us that thee should leave with us." Honor gazed intently at her daughter.

"Mother," Faith said, "I will be honest. I know I am better, but not completely well —"

"Exactly," Dr. Bryant interrupted. "I think you should go home, Nurse Cathwell. We all need a furlough from time to time."

"I just can't," Faith said, sitting on the

nearest box. "I must stay the course."

Dev wanted to break the ensuing silence but didn't. He had no responsibility for Faith. Or the right to order her to do anything. He'd been certain her parents would insist she come home with them. And now, with her own admission of weakness . . .

"Thee is thy own woman, Faith," Honor said with obvious reluctance. "But I am older than thee and must say that if thee doesn't take care of thyself, going on like this could do lasting harm to thy health. Thy youthful vigor will wane soon enough."

"That is the truth," Dr. Bryant agreed. "But they are young and don't realize how quickly it can go, never to return."

Dev thought of his own vitality in his first war. But he still could push himself when he must, and he definitely didn't have to worry about the future. A minié ball or a sniper bullet would get him one of these skirmishes.

"I am listening to this advice," Faith said, "but while I am yet able, I will stay. A soldier —" she looked straight into Dev's eyes — "would not be discharged over this slight wound." She touched her cheek.

But you're a woman, a lady. Dev held in a burst of angry words. He couldn't take this.

"Then I will bid you all good night." He turned and walked swiftly away.

Faith watched Colonel Knight stride off. He was angry with her. Like most men, he thought her weak. Well, she was in some ways, but not in all ways. Just because she couldn't swing an ax with as much force as he did not make her weak.

Dr. Bryant bade everyone good night and left too. Landon came out and excused himself, said he would go to his tent and pack up Ella's valise. That left Faith, her parents, Honoree, and Armstrong by the fire.

"Now that almost everyone has gone, please sit and tell us about thyself, Armstrong." Honor motioned toward the boxes.

Honoree and Armstrong sat down side by side. Faith left them and went in to Ella.

The sad-eyed girl rolled onto her side and looked pitifully toward Faith.

She hurried forward and, perching on the wooden frame of the cot, claimed Ella's small, cold hand. "Thee is going to be all right. Dr. Bryant said the bleeding was minor, and all was well."

"Landon said . . ." The girl swallowed tears. ". . . said I'm going home with your parents."

"Yes, and, Ella, I believe this is best. My parents are good and kind people, and they will take the very best care of thee."

"I know." The girl swiped away tears with the back of her hand. "I just don't want to leave Landon. He's all I got."

"That isn't true. Thee has the child thee is carrying."

Ella fought tears. "Landon said he wanted me away from this camp and . . ."

"It's for the best," Faith said, stroking a stray hair away from Ella's face. "Landon loves thee and wants thee safe and cared for."

"That's real love," Ella said, "isn't it?"

Faith recalled the colonel trying to persuade her parents to take her home and saw it in a new light. She and the colonel would not talk of love, not here and not now. Maybe never. But she realized now that prejudice against her as a woman had not prompted his words to her parents. It was how he'd shown that he cared about her.

Faith patted Ella's shoulder and continued stroking her hair into place. She softly prayed for the baby and for Ella. And silently for Devlin Knight.

Tomorrow she would trek onward with the hospital wagons, and he would no doubt go out on patrol, and either one of them could be picked off by a bushwhacker. She hurried that thought away and let Ella cling to her hand and weep. A war was no time or place to fall in love.

The next morning, heavy gray clouds covering the sky promised rain. Faith and Honoree walked the last few paces to the train depot. Faith had slipped her hand into the crook of her father's arm, and Honoree walked beside Honor, who had put an arm around her waist. Behind them, Ella and Landon brought up the rear. Ella leaned on her husband and wept silently.

At the train, puffing white billows and ready to leave, Faith stood on tiptoe and threw her arms around her father's broad shoulders, burying her face in his soft flannel shirt. Everything within her wanted to leave with him.

A train whistle made her step back. He leaned down, kissed her, and signed, "I love thee, my dear daughter. Stay safe. And may God bless thee."

Faith's fingers signed nearly the same words back at him. Then her mother claimed her farewell hug, and Faith forced down tears.

"Now if thee changes thy mind for any reason, both of thee must promise to come home," Honor said to Faith and Honoree, just as she prepared to let Samuel help her onto the train. "No one will think the less of thee."

"Yes, Mother," Faith said, and Honoree nodded in agreement.

"Come, Ella," Honor said. "Let thy good husband help thee up the steps. Landon McCullough, we will take the best care possible of thy dear wife and baby. We will write as soon as we are safely in Sharpesburg."

"Ma'am," Landon said, "I can't thank you enough. Godspeed." He kissed Ella once more and then handed her up the steps onto the train. Ella, weeping still, allowed Faith's parents to lead her into the nearest car, reserved for the few passengers. Faith glimpsed them as they sat down by a window and waved to her. She and Honoree drew close together and held hands.

Faith could not make herself move till the train chugged out of sight. Then the tears came. Honoree settled her arm around Faith's waist, and Faith did the same to Honoree. They turned to head back to the Sanitary Commission wagon, about to go on the move again. Landon mumbled his thanks and assured them if they needed help, they only had to ask. Then he hurried off.

Faith thought of Colonel Knight. He was no doubt out making their way safe. Divided within itself between Unionists and Rebs, Tennessee was rife with Confederate raiders. She thought of Jack Carroll.

If she hadn't nursed him, he would probably have died or lost both arms. She still didn't regret nursing him. He had been given a second chance at life and had decided to use it to take lives. He was in God's hands.

And so was Devlin Knight. Again she thought of his persistence in trying to persuade her to leave. This war had brought them together and probably would tear them apart.

"You're thinking deep thoughts," Honoree commented.

Faith tightened her arm around Honoree's waist. "How are things between you and Armstrong?"

"We're still hoping to marry."

In the middle of a war? Faith swallowed these words with difficulty. Her mother had let her stay, saying she was a woman who knew her own mind. She would not presume to lecture Honoree. Even if she wanted to.

CHAPTER 17

November 1, 1863

Dev and his men once again ranged over the rolling Tennessee countryside, nominally under the control of the Confederates. The Union cavalry continued protecting the railroad supply line that stretched from Nashville southward, while "Billy" Sherman's army marched southeast toward Chattanooga.

So here he was again, looking for Rebs — especially one Reb. Jack Carroll's name had become more and more notorious in Tennessee.

"Sir!" One of Dev's outriders sped toward him. "A raiding party just ahead, lying in wait for a supply train, no doubt."

His group of around thirty men gathered close to hear the details. Dev sized up the situation and gave his orders. They would attack from the south and drive the raiders away from the coming train. As quietly as thirty men on horseback could, they pelted northward following the rails, hedged on both sides with thick forest.

Two sounds alerted them: gunfire and an advancing steam engine. They galloped full-out. Dev loosened his saber and drew his carbine. They turned a bend and dove straight into the raiders. Amid the gun smoke, Dev thought he glimpsed Jack's cockaded hat.

Then staying alive dominated everything else. Surrounded, he fired, slashed, fell back and reloaded, surged forward, fired. His ears rang with gunfire. His arm ached from slashing, and he choked on gunpowder. A Reb crowded close, trying to unseat him. His pistol empty, he clubbed the man with it and pulled away. And suddenly the Rebs were racing away north as the train they'd wanted to ambush whistled triumphantly, chugging southward.

"Pursue them! Engage at will!" Dev shouted, following his own orders, reloading his carbine.

Then, starting to follow them, he'd barely gone twenty yards when he looked downward and saw Jack himself, lying near the railroad track. Dev slowed and slid from his saddle. Shock stunned him.

He dropped to his knees beside Jack and

felt for a pulse. Jack's eyelids fluttered. For a second Dev thought he still lived. But the eyes went blank, staring. Dev put his fingers to Jack's neck again. Again. But Jack's heart no longer beat.

"Jack," he whispered. "Jack."

He sat down with a bump and gathered Jack's head and shoulders onto his lap. Feelings roiled up inside him. Tears clogged his throat. He grabbed Jack's hat, crushing it in his fingers.

A shot sounded. Dev felt the impact. He clutched his shoulder, falling backward for cover. Shoving the hat inside his jacket, he rolled over, dragged out his carbine, and crawled toward his horse. He held the reins and gazed around, trying to see any movement, see where the bushwhacker hid. Finally he pulled himself up into the saddle with his good arm.

Another shot, another. Dev felt the impacts of two more bullets. He leaned forward and wrapped the reins around the pommel with one hand, blood flowing down his other arm. Then, pointing his horse homeward, he pressed in his heels and raced away. He hoped he'd make it back to camp. Or would he fall from his horse and lie lifeless beside this rail line? Like Jack?

■ ■ ■ ■

Faith sat on the back of the Sanitary Commission wagon, jolting and rocking across Tennessee. She supposed the colonel was just ahead of them, patrolling the railroad line to keep supplies going south to Chattanooga. He wouldn't leave her mind no matter how hard she tried to push him away. Her conversation with Honoree as they walked away from the train that morning still played through her mind in snatches.

"Marrying Armstrong in the middle of a war?"

But that objection had come out of Honoree's mouth, not hers.

"Yes," Honoree had continued. "I know that's what you're thinking. But we both know Armstrong might not survive this war. And I could die of dysentery or something else any day of the week."

Faith had not voiced any objections. Honoree and Armstrong did not face the barriers she and Devlin Knight did. The colonel refused to address his inner conflicts, and they all had to do in some way with his and his family's turmoil over slavery — an institution she could not tolerate. She recalled what he'd told her of his family — his mother, who'd left the plantation to get away from slaveholding. An uncle with two feuding sons like Jacob and Esau. And Devlin pulled in both directions.

She gave up. The lives and fortunes of those she cared about were not her responsibility. *I'm not God.* But she might be forced to deal with losing the colonel. This remained the worry that would not leave her.

"Your colonel's luck ran out," Dr. Dyson sneered at Faith when the march ended for the day.

"What?" She stopped where she stood overseeing the orderlies raising her tent. Horror rippled through her. Was he . . . ?

"He's in surgery now. It doesn't look good."

Faith ignored the man's cruel tone and turned, running toward the hospital wagon that held the "at-the-ready" surgical supplies and table. She reached it, gasping. "Dr. Bryant!"

"Do not come in," he called from inside the wagon. "I'm operating on the colonel. Don't worry — I cleaned my instruments and my hands."

"How bad is he?" she managed to ask.

"Bad."

She stumbled around to the shadow of the covered wagon and dropped to her knees. Her heart seemed to have fallen within her. She closed her eyes against the tears seeping from them. Pressing a fist to her lips, she prayed. *Father, please guide Dr. Bryant's hands. Hold back the infection. Stop the bleeding. I love him so.*

At the end of the surgery, as Dr. Bryant climbed down the last step of the wagon, Faith met him.

The surgeon clasped her, a hand on each shoulder. "He came through surgery. But it's still bad."

Prayer had helped settle her mind. She faced him levelly. "How bad?"

"He was wounded in the shoulder, but not a lot of damage there." He inhaled. "Then there's his hip. I don't really know how he managed to stay in the saddle. His right hip was shattered. There was little I could do but reconnect what was left of the sinews and vessels and sew everything up." He paused, looking her straight in the eye.

She prayed for more strength.

"The worst was a gunshot very near the heart. I frankly am not sure how it missed both his heart and lung, but I dug out the ball and sewed him up. Nurse Cathwell . . . Faith, it will be a miracle if he survives."

She absorbed the blow, merely tucking her

lower lip under her teeth to hold back vain denial. "May I see him?"

"More than that. I'm putting him exclusively in your care. Call me if anything tears loose, starts bleeding. Do whatever you can for him."

Unspoken was *Nothing you do can hurt him. I think he's going to die.*

"Thank thee, Doctor." Her voice wobbled. "I'll go to him and then fetch my herbs."

The doctor leaned over and kissed her forehead. "Do that. And God bless." He walked away, heading toward the area their cook had set up.

Faith climbed the narrow steps into the wagon. Looking away from the gore-stained operating table secured with latches in the center of the wagon, she went to one of the berths attached to the inside of the wagon and supported by folding struts. There the colonel lay, very pale, nearly bloodless, covered in a stained wool blanket. He'd been deeply drugged. She laid her hand on his forehead and prayed for healing.

A cacophony of sorrow tried to freeze her into place. She broke free and turned to go for her medicine chest. And Honoree. They had a battle ahead of them, fighting the inevitable infection that could kill Colonel Knight — Devlin. Kill her heart.

Dev blinked. Sunlight above but through cloth. *Where am I?* His mind felt clogged like an uncleaned gun barrel. Someone was speaking.

" 'Yea, though I walk through the valley of the shadow of death, I will fear no evil: for thou art with me; thy rod and thy staff they comfort me.' " Faith was reciting the Twenty-third Psalm.

"Faith," he whispered . . . or thought he did. Was she here praying over him? Or was his mind playing tricks?

He felt the fever then. He was burning with it. Pain attacked. He couldn't stop the moan, long and low, that forced its way through his dry lips.

Faith's face appeared above his. She lifted his head enough to dribble something into his mouth. He tasted it. Salty . . . Broth? He swallowed and swallowed, so thirsty. Then the taste changed to sweet coffee and whiskey. "Faith," he whispered.

"I'm here, Colonel. I won't leave thee."

"Jack. Dead."

"I saw his hat."

Her soft hand bathed his face with a damp, sweet-scented cloth. He tried to understand the pain. Where had he been hit? But his whole body ached and burned. Pain forced its way through the fog of his mind.

A spoon nudged at his lips. He obeyed and swallowed some medicine. "Ask Armstrong," he whispered. "Mother's address. Write her. Jack's dead."

"I will. Now rest. Thee is weak."

He almost retorted, *I know that.* But he didn't have the strength it would demand. He felt himself drifting away. Perhaps he would not wake again. He tried to clear the fog to see Faith once more. . . .

November 5, 1863
Faith rose from kneeling beside the colonel's berth.

"Miss Faith, here's the hot water you need," Armstrong said as he climbed into the surgical wagon. Four days after the colonel had been wounded, Armstrong had come to the wagon to see Honoree and had immediately offered his help.

"Thank thee, Armstrong. I need to foment his wounds."

Leaving Armstrong to help Faith, Honoree had gone to fetch supper from the hospital cook.

"Is there hope?" Armstrong asked from

the rear of the wagon.

Faith heard the concern and sorrow in Armstrong's voice.

"There is always hope. He's a strong man, and I am doing all I can to draw out the infection. He will live if it's God's will." She went about selecting the herbs for yet another poultice.

"Three wounds. He should have bled to death before he got back here. And Jack's dead." Armstrong sounded tired, sorrowful. "Miss Faith, I want you to take Honoree and go home."

She had begun sewing herbs into another cloth pouch, but now her chin snapped up. "Thee too? Everyone wants us to go home. They have since we arrived." She couldn't help the bit of sarcasm that invaded her tone. "Perhaps thee should commiserate with Dr. Dyson over our lack of cooperation."

Armstrong ignored this. "We're going into winter soon. I know what that means, being encamped in the winter. This war is not ending anytime soon."

Faith nodded in politeness but didn't waste energy speaking. She was soaking the poultice in a basin of hot water.

"I plan to marry Honoree and send her home where she can be safe. Then, if anything happens to me, I will leave her my savings and war pension for widows."

She held the poultice over the basin, letting the excess water drip. "That is between thee and Honoree." She applied the first poultice to the colonel's chest wound, the most troubling of the three.

"I would carry on looking for Shiloh. You can trust me to."

"I'm sure thee would." She pressed down on the poultice, the hot water stinging her palms.

"If I was looking for Shiloh, you two could go home."

Though drugged, the colonel moved against her hand as if trying to get away from the treatment. But he was too weak to do more than squirm.

"I will not convince Honoree to do anything," Faith said. "Stay or leave — it's up to her."

After a sound of frustration, Armstrong just watched her. "The colonel will never serve again."

"Yes, the war is over for him." *Please, God, just his soldiering, not his life.*

"Then why don't you take him home to recuperate?"

Faith looked up this time. "He is too sick to travel right now."

"Really?" Now sarcasm infused Armstrong's tone. "Pray tell — what exactly is it we are doing every day?"

Faith sat back on her heels, shaken. Armstrong had spoken the facts. The wagons rolled daily. Other patients had been left at Union hospitals in houses or churches along the way. But Dr. Bryant was allowing her to keep the colonel with her, letting her ride with him. Was it because he hoped she could save the colonel or because he thought the colonel would die?

Honoree appeared outside, behind the wagon. Armstrong climbed down from the wagon first and then turned to help Faith negotiate the narrow steps. She left the poultice on the wound to do its work of drawing out the infection so she could lance it, drain it — ugly work.

The three sat around the fire at first, eating in silence. Though the beans and rice with salt pork were monotonous, they were prepared well and filling, thanks to the cook's skills.

"I suppose Armstrong has been trying to persuade you to persuade me to go home along with you?" Honoree said conversationally.

"Yes," Faith said, listening for any sound that meant the colonel needed her.

"Armstrong," Honoree said in a gritty tone, "just because you love me doesn't mean I am going to become one of those helpless women —"

"I don't want that," Armstrong responded with heat.

"Good," Honoree replied with a tart smile. "I am not leaving my nursing, but I will marry you."

"I don't want you to have to winter —" Armstrong began.

"I believe, my dear, that you have expressed that thought previously," Honoree reproved with a teasing smile.

Reluctantly Armstrong chuckled. "I can see that being married to you, I'm going to lead a dog's life."

"Yes, a pampered and petted dog," Honoree promised, pressing her lips together to keep from laughing.

Armstrong laughed out loud.

Faith blinked back tears. They were so happy, and she was happy they were, but what of the colonel? And her? Fear as cold as January snow fell upon her heart.

Honoree turned to Faith. "Now we have to discuss what you are going to be doing."

The statement was so unexpected that Faith paused, openmouthed.

"The colonel isn't going to survive without

warmth, good nursing, good food," Honoree said. "It will take a long time, and you need to do it."

"I will."

"I talked to Dr. Bryant today, and he told me that we will come upon a railroad spur tomorrow, a small depot. We are going to have the colonel and you ready to travel. And you will take him north by rail." Honoree held up a hand to stop Faith from responding.

But Faith sat still, unable to speak.

"I went to the colonel's commander, Osterhaus, on my way to the mess tent tonight, and he's written you a military pass that will get both of you free passage and preference on any carrier in Tennessee and Kentucky."

"But —" Faith couldn't speak further, words jammed in her throat.

Honoree plowed on. "I will be safe now because I will be a soldier's wife." She gripped one of Armstrong's hands. "His whole regiment will protect me. I'm young and strong and can stand the rigors of wintering with the army. And at the same time, I can stay on the lookout for Shiloh."

Faith suppressed a sob.

Honoree let go of Armstrong's hand and claimed Faith's. "And you are going to marry the colonel."

"What!" Faith jerked backward.

"Yes. I discussed it with Dr. Bryant and Brigadier General Osterhaus. It isn't appropriate for a maiden lady to travel alone with a man, but a *wife* traveling with her *husband* is quite appropriate."

"A good idea," Armstrong commented, nodding.

Faith stared at them. "But the colonel — we — he doesn't want to marry me. We aren't a couple."

Armstrong snorted. "You may think you aren't, but everybody knows you are."

Faith stood. "I . . . I . . ."

Honoree rose too, still gripping Faith's hand. "You must do this, Faith. There isn't a good Union hospital near here, and even if we left you at one to care for the colonel, you might run into the same problem, a maiden lady nursing a man not her husband. And what's best for the colonel?"

"But —"

Honoree held up her free hand again, forestalling Faith's interruption. "Here the doctors know you and your skills. Somewhere else, you might even be prevented from nursing him at all. And who knows what kind of insulting, incompetent country doctors you might run into. The medical community is filled with Dr. Dysons."

"But —" Faith stammered again.

Honoree raised an eyebrow, again shushing Faith. "You need to do what I say and not hesitate. The weather is fine now, but what if we run into thunderstorms and the weather cools down sooner than expected? And I expect we're heading straight into more fighting. How could you ignore a hospital of dying men and just treat the colonel?"

Withdrawing her hand from Honoree's, Faith clasped and unclasped her own. "I can't marry a man just to satisfy convention. The colonel and I have never . . ." She couldn't go on. Putting their difficult relationship into words would be impossible.

"You've never come to an agreement about being a couple," Honoree supplied.

"But this isn't a plan that includes that," Armstrong said in a soothing tone. "The colonel needs you, and he needs to go someplace where you can care for him. Your parents' home is the right place, the best place."

Faith sat down. All her strength seemed to have leaked out in these few minutes of discussion. "I don't know what to do."

"When the colonel is awake, I'll explain matters to him," Armstrong said. "I'll make sure he agrees. When we get to the town with the depot ahead, we'll find a preacher to marry us — both couples — and you'll go on north."

Armstrong looked to Honoree. "I want my wife to go with you, but if she won't, she can come with me. She's right. My regiment will protect her."

He left unsaid, ". . . *if anything happens to me.*"

Faith looked from Honoree's face to Armstrong's, still unable to respond. Her mind rebelled even as her heart drew her toward the man lying in the berth nearby. *Father, what should I do?*

Dev woke. The pain slammed him as before, and he panted with the effort not to cry out.

"Here." Armstrong's voice summoned him.

He looked up and blinked, thinking he was hallucinating.

Armstrong lifted Dev's head and helped him drink what tasted like herbal tea. "Miss Faith is resting. We — you and I — haven't talked . . . since the day before my birthday, but now I've got something to say."

"What?" Dev mumbled, still parched.

Armstrong lifted his head and helped him drink more.

The effort caused Dev to lay gasping. He didn't have enough strength to lift a hand.

"I'm marrying Honoree when we reach the next town. And you —" Armstrong pinned him with a stare — "will propose to and marry Miss Faith."

"What?" Dev croaked.

"Don't bother arguing. We both know you could very well die of your injuries."

Dev reeled but knew it to be true.

"I'm marrying Honoree now and not waiting. In case anything happens to me, my savings will go to her along with my war pension. We talked Miss Faith into taking you home with her to try to save you. But you've got to marry her first."

Dev could hardly believe what he was hearing. He must be dreaming again.

Armstrong pursed his lips for a moment. "As a maiden lady, Miss Faith can't travel alone with you — wouldn't be right. You need to marry her to save her reputation and keep people from getting the wrong idea." Armstrong stared at him.

Dev scrambled to come up with an answer. "She agreed?"

"If it's what you want, she'll go along. So?"

Dev merely nodded, too weak to do anything but obey. And no doubt Faith would be a widow before long. At least he'd be buried in a private grave at her home in Ohio, a place his mother could visit. He'd not be buried in haste in an unmarked grave here in Tennessee.

Armstrong helped him drink more tea and then left without saying more.

Dev stared up at the cloth overhead. Pain and fever consumed him. He forced himself to keep listening, keep awake. He finally heard footsteps.

Faith leaned over him.

The nasty red welt across her pale cheek caused guilt to flood him. He nerved himself, and the words came out in a rush. "Miss Faith, will you do me the honor of being my wife?"

"Does thee think I should?"

"Yes. You can annul . . . if you want. Later." He was unable to say more.

She gazed at him with an expression he couldn't read. "Then I will not give thee laudanum until we are on the train. We are just approaching the town. One of thy men is going to find a preacher to marry us, and the train will arrive soon to switch tracks and head back north."

"Good," he whispered, spent.

An hour or more passed — Dev couldn't keep track of time. He forced himself not to moan with the pain and to stay awake, not pass out. The groom must at least be awake for his wedding.

The wagon lumbered to a rocky stop, and Armstrong and two of Dev's cavalrymen carried him out on a stretcher and onto the broad, shallow steps of a modest white church, where they laid his stretcher down. Many of his men stood around the church, somber, their hats in their hands as if at a funeral.

A stranger in a black suit stood before the church door with a Bible open in his hand. "I've never performed a ceremony like this. One colored couple. And one groom flat on his back."

"Well, today is the day you do," one of Dev's men said, touching his sidearm.

The pastor swallowed. "Very well. Will the first bride come forward?"

Faith stepped to Dev's side, knelt down, and gripped his hand. "Please proceed, Pastor. We must be ready to leave as soon as the train arrives." She plainly didn't like this at all, but it must be done. A rushed marriage of convenience and then a long trip home with a critically ill husband. No wonder this felt more like a funeral than a wedding, Dev thought.

The pastor hurried through the marriage vows and then produced a marriage certificate, which two of the cavalrymen signed as witnesses, followed by Faith. Finally she held the Bible with the certificate on it, and Dev managed to scribble something that might resemble his name. He did not meet her eyes. She couldn't look into his eyes either, apparently. They had never spoken of anything but books and herbs, never love or marriage.

The pastor then performed the same ceremony for Honoree and Armstrong, followed by the signing of an identical certificate. Armstrong handed the man a five-dollar bill. "Thank you, sir."

The man pocketed the money and hurried inside the church, firmly shutting the door behind him.

A whistle alerted them all to the approaching train. Her new husband's stretcher was carried away and once more laid on the Sanitary Commission wagon tailgate while Faith climbed up onto the wagon bench in front. They arrived at the tiny station moments before the steam engine chugged into view and changed to the northbound track.

Faith watched as Armstrong, along with a handful of cavalrymen, went to the train and arranged matters. Very soon they returned, and a few of the cavalrymen carried first the colonel and then both Faith and

Devlin's baggage onto the train.

The cavalrymen had somehow secured him a berth in the lone Pullman car, a type of car Faith had never seen. The rest of the Pullman was empty. Had they moved everyone out? Or were there merely no other passengers able to afford the cost of a berth in the sleeping car? She didn't have the energy to think or ask. She was simply grateful and hoped their isolation would last. She couldn't face strangers and their prying questions. The two cavalrymen who'd acted as their witnesses, along with Honoree and Armstrong, had boarded the car with them.

Devlin was obviously in pain. But he addressed the two cavalrymen. "My thanks. Tell all my men farewell."

Both leaned forward and saluted him where he lay; then they left together. The train whistle blew, and Faith could feel the engines building steam.

The moment of parting had come. Faith threw her arms around Honoree, who did the same in return. They clung to each other, weeping.

Then Armstrong drew Honoree away. He looked down into Dev's face. "Be a good patient. Get better. Farewell."

"Farewell," Dev muttered, sounding exhausted.

Armstrong urged Honoree out of the car and down the steps. Faith followed to the doorway and watched them step onto the station platform. They turned and, along with the cavalrymen, raised their hands in farewell.

Faith also lifted hers, her heart squeezed tightly at the parting. The train jerked to a noisy start and began rolling forward. Soon she'd left behind everyone who'd come to bid them farewell. The train picked up momentum, heading north. When it rounded a bend, she could no longer see Honoree, so she turned back to the colonel — her husband. She felt like she was walking in a dream.

Then he moaned, bringing her back to reality.

She knelt by Dev's berth and helped him sip some wine she'd brought with her, following it with laudanum syrup. He looked exhausted and tormented with pain.

She hadn't wanted to leave Honoree, leave the search for Shiloh. She hadn't wanted to marry the colonel — well, certainly not like this. But this was war, and nothing in war went as planned. At least that was how she saw it.

Dev's eyes drifted shut and she sighed with relief. At least she had something to give him for the pain. But what would ease the pain in her heart if she became his widow?

CHAPTER 18

November 13, 1863

Well over a week later, in the early twilight of winter and in a pouring rain, Faith superintended Devlin's stretcher as he was carried off the steamboat onto the wharf in Cincinnati. Since he was a wounded soldier, they were ushered off the boat first.

They were almost home. Thunder rumbled in the distance, and chill November rain pelted her bonnet, washed her face, and trickled down the back of her neck. Somehow she'd reached this city and her husband still breathed. Would they come all this way only to lose him here?

She lifted a hand, beckoning a carriage. One drove up to her. "Please. I need help." She tried to keep the tremor from her voice. "My husband is recovering —" she hoped so, anyway — "from his wounds. I need to get him out of the rain."

"A soldier? Yes, ma'am." The driver hustled down and helped a boatman lift the stretcher into the carriage, propping each end on one of the seats. Then he helped Faith in and handed her the wooden chest she'd carried. "Don't worry, ma'am. I'll see to your luggage." He loaded in the rest of their cases, thumping them into the rear. "Where to, ma'am?"

She was still getting used to being a *ma'am,* not a *miss.* "The Brightman-Ramsay house. Do you know it?"

"Certainly I do." The driver shut the door, and soon the carriage began to move over the rain-slick streets up the bluff, from the Ohio River into the city proper.

Faith clung to the leather strap dangling from the ceiling as she swayed with the carriage, and though the flashes of fading light through the moving window revealed little, she watched Devlin. She'd begun to call him that at his insistence — sometimes even Dev. They must, if nothing else, at least sound like husband and wife.

Within minutes she leaned out the window and glimpsed her sister's familiar street. She was so close to her final destination. Her heart quickened. *Almost home.*

The driver got down and splashed through the rain to the door. Faith heard the pounding of the brass knocker, followed by voices.

She leaned against the inside of the carriage — after days and nights spent nursing Devlin, on little sleep, she was too tired to move.

"Hello!" The carriage door opened.

Faith recognized her sister's voice. "Blessing?"

"Faith?"

"Yes."

"Oh, my!" Blessing reached for her hand. "Thee came home!"

Arriving at last to safety and family, Faith began to weep. She could let her guard down now.

"Who is this?" Light fell onto Blessing's upturned face.

Faith found she couldn't tell the truth. A sob forced its way up her throat. She began to weep harder as the rain fell with greater intensity.

Then, since Blessing's character matched her name, a flurry of activity — not another round of questions — ensued. Blessing and her husband, Gerard, along with several of their staff, swarmed around, and soon Devlin, shielded by umbrellas, was carried into the house and upstairs.

Faith wearily dragged herself up each stair behind his stretcher. When she saw Devlin safely into a luxurious bedroom, she felt herself sinking and heard Blessing cry,

"Catch her!"

Faith woke to the stringent odor of smelling salts. For a moment, as she stared up at the ornately plastered ceiling, she couldn't think where she was.

Then her sister's voice called her back to her senses. "Faith?"

"Blessing?"

"There thee is again. Sit up. I have broth for thee, and bread," Blessing said, setting a small tray on the bedside table.

As she sat up in the bed, Faith heard the sound of water pouring into metal.

"Now eat, and by the time that's done, we'll have thy bath ready by the fire," Blessing said in a soothing tone.

Food, a soft bed, and a bath — heaven. Faith accepted the tray on her lap, sipped the salty broth, and dipped the crusty, buttered bread into it.

"Who is the man traveling with thee?" Blessing asked, sitting in the chair beside the bed.

"Colonel Devlin Knight of Maryland. My husband," Faith replied, looking down into the bowl of broth and hearing Blessing's sharp intake of breath.

"That's what he told Gerard, but I could hardly believe it."

"It was sudden." *A necessity.* Faith still refused to meet her sister's gaze.

"Well, that's one way to put it. Is thee taking him home to recover?"

"Yes."

"I'm sorry to see thy injured cheek," Blessing said gently.

Faith had dreaded the rest of her family seeing her scar. She finally looked to Blessing's kind face. "I'm too tired to explain."

"No need. Mother told us everything. Eat up and we'll get thee clean and warm and into bed. Time enough in the morning to talk."

"The colonel?"

"Thy husband?" Blessing reminded, her head tilted in question.

"Yes. Who is taking care of him?"

"*My* good husband, his valet, and our butler are seeing to his supper and bath."

"He should not be allowed to soak in water for long."

Blessing rose. "I will go tell Gerard. Should a doctor be summoned?"

"No. All that a doctor can do has been done." *Only God can save him, save us.*

Blessing paused to search Faith's eyes, her expression. "I will be right back."

Faith finished her supper and let her sister and her maid help her bathe and, afterward, tuck her into bed in a pale-blue flannel nightgown, fresh and soft. Faith let her eyes shut, and sleep came almost immediately. She didn't have to worry about her husband here. Blessing and Gerard could be trusted.

Cincinnati, Ohio

Days later, Dev looked at the bit of blue-gray sky visible to him through the carriage window across from where he lay on the softly cushioned seat and wondered why he still lived. First he'd been sure he would die on the train, and then he'd been sure he'd die on the steamboat. He'd never expected to make it this far.

Beside Faith sat her fashionable sister and her sister's well-dressed husband. The four of them were on their way to the Cathwells' home. He had been surprised by the quality of the mansion Faith's sister lived in and by the number of servants employed there. He hadn't thought Quakers owned luxurious mansions. A mystery there.

This road was becoming bumpy. The skin covering his wounds had closed, but the pain had become a deep, relentless, teeth-clenching ache. He refused opium now, fearful of becoming addicted. Yesterday his wife had painstakingly removed his stitches. She'd told him around two weeks had passed since he was wounded, since he'd seen Jack dead.

He still felt mostly dead himself. He'd looked at his arms and legs during his bath that first night in Ohio. Just skin over bone, almost no flesh. The fever still burned low and constant in him, sapping his strength, and he hated it. The deep infection within would kill him. He'd seen it before. It was just a matter of time until he would fall asleep and not wake. A sad way for a cavalryman to die.

On the other hand, Jack had fallen while fighting.

He turned his attention to Faith — his wife — who gazed back at him, serious, pale, drawn. The trip had taken its toll on her, too. If nothing else, however, marrying him and taking him home had pulled her away from the war. For that, he could be grateful. Her parents should be grateful. Yet the red scar on her cheek still cut him like a whiplash.

The constant fatigue claimed him then, and his eyelids refused to stay up. He didn't fall asleep, but he did relax and let his body roll with the carriage as it worked its way over the uneven road.

He'd soon see the place he'd die and be buried. Would he be able to describe the location in Tennessee where his cousin had fallen so his uncle would not be left wondering?

I must stay alive long enough to write or dictate a letter to my mother. Then she can write my uncle. Two wars, and now none of them — neither Bellamy nor Jack nor he — would live to start a new generation. Their line would end with his death.

"Write my mother," Dev had said to Faith before he'd fallen asleep last night.

Instead, this morning Faith had avoided this duty and had left her husband in her mother's care. She'd wanted to get outside, breathe fresh November air, try to clear her mind. She'd wrapped up in a shawl and walked around the property and the cluster of homes that made up her hometown.

Somehow she needed to face the turn her life had taken. She'd been on a quest to find Shiloh and help the Union cause, but she'd been cut off, diverted from both of these goals, and separated from Honoree. Why hadn't God let her stay the course? Find Shiloh?

Now she'd married a man who had proposed out of necessity. She knew the story of her parents' marriage, which had taken place when they'd known each other barely even a week. But that hadn't been during a war, and Devlin might still die. Nothing made sense.

After exhausting the places she could visit in her small hometown, finally she made her way to her dried-up herb garden. She'd known how it would look. And in a way she felt like her stricken plants. Images from the war crowded her mind no matter how hard she tried to expunge them. How were Honoree and Armstrong? Where were they at this moment? Would they find Shiloh?

She heard someone coming and turned. Her father was walking toward her from the glassworks behind the Cathwells' large cabin and the other cabins where Honoree's parents and the other glassworkers and staff lived. Her father came to her and set his arm around her shoulders, pulling her close against him. He didn't need to say anything. His concern came through his touch.

She tucked herself into his thick wool shirt under his embrace and wept a few tears.

He touched the back of her head and she watched him sign, "Why is thee crying?"

She tried to come up with a single reason, but so much was tangled together. She shook her head in despair.

"Thee went to find Shiloh. Is thee sad that thee wasn't successful?" he signed.

A harsh sob forced its way up her throat and she wept harder.

Her father stroked her back with his strong yet gentle hand. Then he lifted her chin with his index finger. "I never told thee, but I never expected thee to find her. Some tasks are too big for us."

She stared at him, her tears drying up. Her father's simple words clarified so much. She nodded yes.

"We couldn't save Patience from the fever that took her, and only God can bring Shiloh home."

She began crying again, remembering that night five years ago when kidnappers had drugged and bound her and stolen Shiloh from them.

Her father held her close and continued rubbing her back as if she were a child again. She allowed the healing in his touch to begin its work. Finally she straightened, pulled herself together. *I release Shiloh to thee, Lord. We are in thy loving hands.*

Hearing the dinner bell, she signed, "Time for lunch."

He nodded. "Good. I'm hungry."

She realized she was too — ravenous, in fact. The two of them walked arm in arm to the house. Her tears had washed away her guilt over failing to find Shiloh. God would

431

have to bring Shiloh home.

Still, Faith could hardly believe she herself had arrived safely at her own home again. How could life *here* go on as always when, south of here, men were shooting at each other, killing each other? One existence must be a dream or nightmare, not real.

But both, she knew, were all too real.

Inside, Faith helped her mother set the table — just three places, for Faith and her parents. None of Faith's siblings remained at home, though Ella was living here at present. This morning, however, she had gone to help a neighbor with her canning.

The long time away at war had caused Faith to see her parents with fresh eyes. She noted that her father's hair was salt-and-pepper and Honor's blonde hair was threaded with abundant silver.

Both her parents were letting the younger generation take over Cathwell Glassworks. Though Samuel and Honoree's father, Judah, still occasionally crafted some special-order glass, neither worked the long hours they once had. Faith's adopted cousin, Caleb, supervised the glassworks. Caleb and his wife and children lived in a cabin behind the glassworks. Two young men from Judah's church had served as apprentices and now manufactured the regular glass orders.

The cook, Annie — one of the glassworkers' wives — knocked at the door. Honor opened the door and the plump woman hurried inside with a tray.

"I hope it's not gone cold," Annie said. "How is the soldier?"

"I'm still here," Devlin muttered from his makeshift bed by the fire.

"Well," Annie said, "I hope you're hungry. I made cream of celery soup and biscuits."

"I'll do my best. Thank you," Dev said.

Annie spoke a few more encouraging words before returning to the detached kitchen near her cabin.

Honor said grace and served the lunch. Faith moved to feed Devlin.

"You eat first," her husband said. "I don't have much appetite."

The lunch conversation was stilted. Faith could see from her parents' concerned expressions that there was much they wanted to ask about her and Devlin and their sudden marriage. But they did not choose to do so — yet.

After lunch, Honor left, carrying the tray of used tableware to the kitchen for washing, and Samuel headed toward the glassworks. Faith went to her husband, propped him up, and set a tray on his lap. Then she

433

sat down beside him. He'd decreed he'd feed himself or go hungry.

She gazed at him. He had survived this far. God had obviously decided the time had come for both of them to retreat. She sighed suddenly. "Nothing has gone as we wanted, has it?"

Dev glanced at her sharply. "That just occurred to you?"

She ignored the edge to his voice. "It has been hard for me to face that I've returned home without Shiloh."

He patted her hand awkwardly.

"Thee can say it." She sent him a lopsided smile. "The undertaking was too large for two women in the midst of the war."

"I believe I did mention that," he said more gently.

"My father just reminded me that some tasks are too big for us. I must leave Shiloh in God's hands."

Dev felt miserable and couldn't hide it. He picked up his spoon. "Even if it means you'll never see her again." His harsh words struck her, and he regretted them.

"I will see her again regardless," Faith murmured.

He wanted to say he was sorry, but instead he dipped his spoon in the creamy soup.

"Please, I want you to write my mother today."

Faith nodded, conceding. "I will. And I need to write to Honoree and Armstrong and let them know we arrived safely. Does Armstrong have family?"

"Yes. I'm sure my mother will tell his family the news." Feeding himself took as much effort as he could muster. He tasted the salty, buttery soup and nearly sighed aloud. After months of camp food, this was ambrosia.

"Thee is recovering, but it will take a long time before thee feels like thyself again." Faith rested her hand on his arm.

He tried not to react to her touch. Impossible. Still feverish and weak, Dev wondered at her false hope. But he said nothing as he sipped the creamy soup. Delicious just like the food at home. He let himself gaze at Faith. She was so beautiful, even with the scar that marred her cheek. "I'm so sorry I didn't protect you better." He brushed her cheek with the back of his hand.

He expected her to bow her head and turn away as she had done every time before. Instead she pressed her hand over his, keeping it in place.

"Thee must not blame thyself. How could we know that woman would attack me with

435

a knife?" She glanced downward and then at him again. "I will grow accustomed, and it won't bother me. I never thought myself vain, but this has made me more . . . conscious of myself." She drew in breath and lifted her chin.

Then she did something else he didn't expect. She turned her face into his palm and kissed it.

The breath caught in his throat and emotion rushed through him, sensations he didn't want to experience. *I'm dying. I'm going to leave her.* He knew he should say words to put her away from him, but he found he could not speak them. He could only sit, letting himself feel what he truly felt. He had no energy to deceive himself. Or her.

Finally she withdrew her face, breaking their contact. "Now eat thy soup. I will get my portable writing desk."

He forced himself to eat, spoonful by spoonful, though the effort cost him. He watched her move about this log-cabin room. What a contrast. Her sister lived in a mansion, and her parents lived in a frontier cabin.

For the first time he really looked around the comfortably furnished space, which combined the dining and sitting rooms. He took in the tall bookcase filled with leather volumes of different shades. If only he could walk to the books, pull each one out, and feel and smell the leather and the smooth pages.

Faith sat down beside him again. "Shall we begin?"

Dev nodded, dry-mouthed, and began to dictate the letter. He could not stop gazing at her. He had long ago adjusted to being a bachelor, but now he had a lovely and wonderful woman as his wife. And he was going to die without ever holding her in his arms. The bitter thought soured within.

Faith looked to Devlin, who had finished dictating the letter. His eyelids were drooping. "I will send this off today," she said. "Our neighbor is going to Cincinnati, and he will leave it at the post office there. That will get it on its way to Baltimore more quickly."

He barely nodded.

She rose and carried the portable desk to the nearby sofa. Then she lifted the lunch tray from Devlin's lap and took it to the table. When she returned to him, he'd already fallen asleep.

The door opened and her mother entered, letting in cool wind. Honor immediately looked to Dev. "He's asleep again?"

"Yes."

"It must take the body an amazing amount of effort to heal." Honor walked over to Faith. "Now, how is *thee* healing?"

Faith rested her head on her mother's shoulder. "I cannot tell thee how horrible being in a war was. All of it. I feel like I've awakened from a bad dream. And I still feel guilty about leaving Honoree behind in the nightmare." *And Shiloh.*

Honor tucked her close and kissed Faith's scarred cheek as if unaware of its ugliness. "I was never in a war, but the little I saw when we visited thee gave some taste of what thee faced daily. And now thee comes home married, and to a man who has been deeply wounded." Honor released Faith and went to sit on the sofa, took out her knitting, and began working on something that looked like a baby sweater in white yarn.

"We only married to meet propriety." Faith looked to Devlin. "We had never talked of love or marriage."

"But that didn't mean thee didn't love him."

Faith could never hide much from her mother. Her heart sped up. "I do love him."

"And he loves thee?"

"I know he has feelings for me. But we're

so different, Mother." She recounted briefly the colonel's refusal to free Armstrong, breaking his long-standing promise.

"A house divided against itself?" Honor asked wisely, her fingers moving in and out of the yarn with the wooden knitting needles.

"Yes." Faith was grateful for her mother's quick comprehension. She inhaled fully. "He can't make up his mind. He's at war with himself just like the Union and the Confederacy."

Honor looked to Dev. "He must come to his own resolution. Though he's put off coming to a decision, I think it's because he doesn't believe he's going to live."

"Yes. But I think he is going to. He is a strong man, and Dr. Bryant is a gifted surgeon."

"And thee is an excellent nurse," Honor commented. "Then he will be forced to face the truth and work out his salvation."

Faith knew what her mother meant with those words. Her husband would have to look the truth in the eye and figure out how to accept God's will.

At that moment, Ella opened the door, returning from helping the neighbor. "How is the colonel?" Ella was already wearing a loose dress to accommodate her pregnancy.

439

She came over to see Honor's progress in knitting a garment for her coming baby.

Faith smiled, thinking of the little one to come by spring — something good, something hopeful in this war-scarred and weary world.

After Ella and Honor left to visit a neighborhood mother with a newborn, Faith reread the letter her husband had dictated. And then realized that he'd left out so much, no doubt because as far as his injuries were concerned, he was still not out of the woods — particularly in his own estimation. But more needed to be added. She must tell his mother everything, not leave her in ignorance. So she added a postscript of her own.

Thy son married me, Faith Cathwell, the daughter of the house where he is staying.

How could she explain that? Several possibilities came to mind, but she decided none would sound right on paper. She did her best, regardless:

I was a nurse with the Union Army. My mother, Honor Cathwell, invites thee to come and stay with us. If thee comes to

Cincinnati, ask to be taken to the Brightman-Ramsay house. My sister Blessing Ramsay lives there with her husband, and she will bring you to us in Sharpesburg. Please come.

She reread the letter, dwelling momentarily on the news that Devlin's cousin Jack had died. Dev had not given her or his mother any but the bare facts, though surely he was still affected by the experience.

Faith dusted the sheet of stationery with sand and then folded and addressed it, sealing it with wax. She donned her shawl and hurried down the road to Thad Hastings's house. He was leaving soon for Cincinnati.

Faith hoped Devlin's mother would come here to visit. She didn't believe her husband was going to die, but that didn't mean it was impossible. The thought sliced her composure and exposed her fear.

That night, Faith rose to go to the low fire to prepare her husband a cup of willow-bark tea laced with whiskey to help him sleep.

In her robe and slippers, Ella came out of her bedroom and shooed Faith away from the kettle that hung on a hook over the fire. "I'll brew the tea. You go sit with your man."

Still exhausted from the trip and from

worry, Faith nodded and returned to the bedroom to prop her husband up in bed so he could drink the tea.

Soon Ella entered, carrying a cup.

Devlin let her hold the cup while he drank it down. Before the tea was drained, his eyelids had begun drooping. He finished the tea, and she helped him lie back down. She read suffering in his expression. And it cut to her heart.

She carried the cup back into the main room and set it atop the tray resting on the table. Ella was sitting by the fire, staring into the flames. "Is anything wrong, Ella?" she murmured.

"I don't understand. I mean, I know the colonel and you liked each other, and I know you couldn't travel with the colonel unless you was his wife, but you two don't act married-like." Ella looked to Faith in the low light from the fire and the candle on the mantel.

Faith sank into the rocking chair across from Ella. Here in the dark with Ella — who wasn't family and who had been in the war too — Faith found she could open up, speak her confusion. "We didn't plan to marry. We never talked of love . . ."

"But anyone who saw you two together knew that you cared for each other. It was plain as day."

"Just because two people care for one another doesn't mean that they will marry."

"Why not?"

Faith thought a moment. How to explain this to Ella, who saw life so much more simply? "What if thee hadn't agreed with Landon that the Union must be preserved? Or what if he'd enlisted in the Confederate militia and you thought the Union must be preserved?"

Ella very obviously considered this, rocking and staring into the fire. "I see. But you and the colonel both agree about being against slavery and for the Union."

"Not exactly."

"What does that mean? I don't want to be nosy, and I won't repeat anything you tell me, but I want to understand."

"I wish it were easy to explain." Faith burned with sudden irritation. "The colonel is caught in between. He owned a slave but was antislavery."

"You mean Armstrong?"

"Yes. The colonel must settle the conflict in his own mind before the conflict between us can be resolved. He must take action."

"Like you did?"

"Yes."

"And you can't love him like a wife till he does?"

"No, I could love him." *I do love him.* "That's not it." Faith sighed. "It's tangled. He can't really love with a whole heart till his heart knows what it wants."

"I don't understand."

"I don't either, completely. I just feel the truth of it."

"I kind of see what you mean. Landon was really sure about not seceding. But he believed black people needed us to boss them. Now I don't know. I see the men who work glass here. They're black and they don't need to be told what to do. And Honoree was as good a nurse as you. Will Landon and I quarrel if after the war I think black people should be free and he still doesn't?"

"I don't know if thee will quarrel. But thee will both be different. People don't go through a war and come out just the same."

"But you're the same."

"On the outside I am, and my thoughts on slavery are the same, but I've had to give up seeking Honoree's sister. That has changed."

Ella nodded. "Why can't life be easier?"

"Because men sin, disobey God."

"I just wish I could see Landon and hug him."

Knowing what this felt like, Faith stared into the fire before rising. "We need our sleep." She offered Ella her hand.

Ella rose and lifted the candle while Faith banked the fire low again. Ella accompanied her to her bedroom and then, after Faith kissed her good night on the cheek, she departed for her own room.

Faith slipped into bed beside Devlin, wondering when he would make up his mind and settle matters within himself and with her. *Open his eyes and let him see, Lord.*

December 7, 1863
December had come, and Dev had a hard time believing he was still alive. Alone in the house for once, he sat with his feet propped up on a stool by the fire, looking at the newspaper Samuel Cathwell had handed him on his way out the door earlier. The headline read, "Union Victory at Missionary Ridge." He had not gotten farther than the name General William Sherman before his mind took him back to the days before he was wounded. His men had been in this battle, he was sure. Who had taken his place?

Thinking of the war carried his thoughts to his wife, Faith. He still had some trouble believing they were married. As he grew stronger, being near her but not reaching for her as his wife had become more and more of a struggle. Did she want to be married to him in every sense, not just in name?

His mind brought up her challenge to him about serving two masters. The whole question felt moot now. Armstrong was a freeman. Slavery would only survive if the North lost the war. The South was hanging on, but not for long. His uncle's family in Maryland was losing its wealth and had already lost its sons.

Dev had not yet regained his health. He ran a low fever every afternoon and evening. Everything around him had changed, but whenever he and Faith were alone, he still felt her leveling that challenge at him. What did it matter, really? He'd made the wrong choice when he hadn't freed Armstrong, but —

The sound of a carriage outside distracted him.

He set the newspaper on his lap, hoping someone outdoors would see to the visitor. He couldn't rise to answer.

Blessing Ramsay, Faith's eldest sister, came in without knocking. "Brother-in-law, someone is here to see thee." She stepped aside.

And his mother entered. "Son."

He gasped and could not speak. The paper slid to the floor. He tried to rise but could lift himself only inches, his hip shouting with pain.

His mother hurried to him and bent to wrap her arms around his neck. "My son."

He felt her tears against his cheek. "Mother." *I didn't think I'd live to see you again.*

"Honor Penworthy!" Dorothea exclaimed when later introduced to Faith's mother, disbelief in her tone.

From his place near the fire, Dev watched Faith's mother move forward, a question in her expression.

"Thee looks familiar, but . . . ," Honor began.

"I was Dorothea Carroll of Carroll Plantation. I was a debutante in Baltimore in 1814 with your cousin. I can't remember her name, but she married Alec Martin. And she . . ."

"She left him," Honor said, gazing at Dorothea. "Now I remember thy family." She offered Dorothea her hand, her expression inscrutable. "Welcome to my home."

Dev looked to Faith, who had entered with her mother. "Did you know my mother was coming?"

"No, but I did invite her to come. With railroads and steamboats, travel is not as difficult as it once was," Faith said blandly.

She was fencing with him. She had added to the letter he'd dictated nearly a month ago without a word to him. He hid his irritation. What right did he have to complain?

By evening all the introductions had been exhausted. Dev's mother, now sitting across from him in a rocking chair by the fire, had unpacked her valises in the room she'd share with Ella. Faith was clearing the supper table, and Honor had gone out.

Dev had watched Faith leave with the tray. His mother had risen to shut the door behind her. Alone at last — what he'd feared.

"Where is Armstrong?" Dorothea asked, gently rocking her chair back and forth.

"He enlisted." Then Dev stared into the flames in the hearth.

"I was afraid he might do that when his birthday arrived and you freed him."

The words nearly stuck in his throat, but he forced them out. "I refused to give him the manumission papers."

His mother stopped her chair. "You what?"

"I knew he planned to enlist, so . . ."

"So he did anyway." She shook her head at him. "I blame my brother for this. If he hadn't given Armstrong to you, you would never have been in that situation in the first place. It was underhanded of him since he knew why I'd left our home."

She gripped the carved wooden arms of her chair. "And that explains why I remembered Faith's mother. She had the nerve to stand up to her family about slaveholding, on her own. She lost everything, but she took a stand. I merely found a man who agreed with me, married him, and left home and the problem behind me. Or tried to."

Dev processed this brand-new information. "Uncle Kane gave Armstrong to me to get back at you?"

"To snare you." Her lips twisted with disapproval. "If Bellamy died in a war, he wanted you to take over the plantation. He never trusted Jack. He was too much like Bellamy's namesake, our father — wild and willful."

His mother's sharp and unblushing assessment of his grandfather's character startled Dev. She never said things like this.

"Why didn't you free Armstrong years ago?" Dorothea pressed him, leaning forward.

Dev's rationale seemed insufficient even to himself, so he said nothing.

"Well, you need to sort that out." She sat back. "This war is the end of slavery. You had best plan what your future will be."

What she said was true. But why did he need to sort matters out? Everything was changing around him. Did what he believed or thought matter anymore? The familiar discomfort at talk about the future tightened Dev's nerves, made him jumpy.

Faith reentered. "It's beginning to rain." She shook out her shawl before hanging it on one of the many pegs on the wall.

"I notice my son is just sitting around," Dorothea said. "I think tomorrow we'd best get him up walking."

"Yes, it's time," Faith agreed firmly. "I'd requested Blessing bring crutches on her next visit, so we are ready to begin."

Dev looked from one woman to the other, and it finally dawned on him. His fever had lifted a few days ago and now he was weak not from the fever, but from almost two months of inactivity. By this point his wounds had healed as much as they ever would. *I'm not going to die . . . not now.*

His mother had said, *"You had best plan what your future will be."* He hadn't expected to see the future. But the future had come.

450

And he knew that before he could handle the future, there were two matters he must deal with: Armstrong, the friend he'd disappointed; and Faith, his own unexpected wife. He could evade them no longer. But how to make things right?

On Christmas Eve, Faith's and Honoree's families gathered in the Cathwell cabin. They were dressing warmly to visit the family burial plot, as was their custom. Tonight they remembered the loved ones lost: Faith's twin, Patience; her brother and sisters who'd died even younger; and the runaway slaves who had perished while hiding in the secret room at Cathwell Glassworks. Devlin appeared bemused by this unusual family tradition but was coming along.

The sound of a wagon driving up turned them all toward the door.

"I wonder who is coming," Honor said and moved forward.

Faith had been hoping that Honoree and Armstrong would get a Christmas furlough and come home. Had they? She followed her mother.

Honor opened the door before anyone knocked. "Hello?"

Over her mother's shoulder, Faith recognized the snow-white hair of Honoree's

grandfather Brother Ezekiel. He was helping a woman down from his wagon. The
moonlight illuminated the woman's face.

"Shiloh!" Faith gasped, wondering if her
eyes were playing her false.

Shiloh ran toward them. "It's me! I'm
home!"

Pandemonium broke out.

Royale, Shiloh's mother, pushed past
Faith and Honor and wrapped her arms
around her daughter, her long-lost child.
Faith stood back, watching and weeping.
She'd searched and searched, and here was
Shiloh. Relief drenched her. She wanted to
ask a hundred questions, but amid the
homecoming chaos, she couldn't.

Then Faith noticed a stranger standing by
the wagon, a tall black man dressed in army
fatigues with a sling holding up one arm.
He leaned back as if tired.

She hurried forward through the two
families milling around Shiloh. "Come in. I
think thee should sit down."

The man followed her to the nearest chair
at the table. "Thank you, ma'am."

Shiloh broke free of her family and moved
to stand beside the stranger. "This is Jim
Sanford. He served with Armstrong and was
wounded at Missionary Ridge."

The soldier was welcomed warmly.

Faith swallowed all her questions once again. How had this happened? How had Shiloh finally come home to them?

"Let's go to the family plot," Shiloh said. "And when we come home, I'll tell you everything. But I hoped to arrive in time to take part in this remembrance."

Quiet approval greeted these words.

"I'll stay here with Mr. Sanford," Dev offered.

Faith nodded her agreement and then, leaving the two soldiers behind in the warm cabin, they all set out for the family plot in the woods behind the glassworks.

Shiloh's parents linked arms with their daughter, and the three walked in step.

The group observed the simple ceremony, where each name was solemnly read aloud. At the end, Brother Ezekiel led them all in a prayer that concentrated on gratitude for Shiloh's safe return and concern for the Union soldiers.

Back inside the warm house, everyone gathered around. Faith sat beside Devlin at the table. The younger members of the family lounged against the walls or sat on the floor. The tension in the room was palpable. No one wanted to miss Shiloh's story.

"I was able to escape during the battle that Jim was wounded in," Shiloh began, gazing toward the fire. "I reached the Union line without getting killed by a stray bullet." Her tone was matter-of-fact. "When things calmed down, I went to the hospital to offer my help, and . . ." Her voice faltered. "I found my sister."

Faith's throat was knotted with emotion.

"I worked with her until all the wounded had finally been treated."

Faith knew that meant days, not hours.

"I met her husband, Armstrong, and finally, after five years of bondage, I was able to breathe free once more."

No one spoke. A log on the fire disintegrated and gave way.

"I'd nearly lost my arm," Jim spoke up, "but Miss Honoree told the head surgeon she could save it with a little work, and he let her treat me." He grinned. "I still have my arm, and I was able to get a furlough to go home. Only I don't have a home. I'd run away in Mississippi during the Siege of Vicksburg." He turned to Faith. "I recognized you from camp there."

Faith managed to nod.

Shiloh smiled at the soldier. "So Honoree decided that Jim could safely escort me to our home. He can rest up before he has to go back."

"You are very welcome here, Jim," Shiloh's

father, Judah, said. "Now I think we should take Jim to our cabin and get him settled. He looks exhausted."

Faith held up a hand. "Before thee leaves. Shiloh, this is my husband, Colonel Devlin Knight."

Dev rose and bowed over Shiloh's hand. Shiloh sent Faith a questioning look over his head, but they couldn't speak with everyone here watching.

Shiloh and her family left with farewells, and Faith's family sat around the table, too stirred to seek their own beds.

"I'm so happy," Faith said, trying to put into words her relief and the backlash of some emotion. "But it doesn't feel real somehow."

Her mother reached over and took Faith's hand. "Thee focused on finding Shiloh for so long, and then God restored her to us by his good will and in his time."

"Shouldn't I have gone looking for her?" Faith asked, trying to put it together.

"Of course thee should have, as thee did. I never discouraged thee. And think of all the men thee helped as a nurse. Would thee have been half so insistent on going if not for thy search for Shiloh? Half as determined not to be dissuaded or turned back by those who opposed thee?"

Faith considered this. "True, I was able to help soldiers, but there were so many I couldn't help."

Her father cleared his throat and said in sign, "We can only do what we can. Nothing more."

Faith gazed at her father and mother and thought of Patience. Shiloh had returned to them, but her twin sister never would. She recalled what King David had said when he'd discovered that his child with Bathsheba had died. He'd said something like, *"I shall go to him, but he shall not return to me."* And it was true, for now. But she would see her dear sister someday, and that was certain.

Now, when she thought of how she and Honoree had believed they could locate one woman in the whole of the South in the midst of a war, she could only wonder at their presumption. Only God was capable of returning Shiloh to them. And he had.

A few days later, Dev and Faith were alone in the cabin. Faith sat by the fire, mending. The rest of the family, including his mother, Shiloh, and Jim, had gone to Cincinnati for Sunday meeting. This was among the first times he and his wife had been alone since his health had taken a turn for the better.

He was both glad and nervous. The time had come to face the truth, the future.

Trying to think of a way to say what he wanted to her, Dev walked on his crutches to one wall, turned, and walked back to the opposite wall. He was alive. He was walking with pain but he was upright again. He couldn't quite believe it.

After days of practicing little by little, today he would exercise till he became too weak to go on. Then he would sit for an hour and get up to do it again. He lacked stamina, and there was only one way to regain that. He must push himself to his limit again and again.

"Faith," he said, pausing by the large round table on one side of the room, "I'm going to write a letter." He edged himself onto one of the chairs at the table. She offered to fetch what he needed, and he heard her moving around the house.

Soon she stood beside him and set down ink, pen and paper, sand, seal, and wax.

"Thank you."

She smiled, went back to the fire, and sat down to her mending.

Dev stared at the paper for a moment; then, with determination, he picked up the nib pen, dipped it in the black ink, and began writing.

December 28, 1863

Dear Armstrong,

I write to you from Faith's family home in Ohio. After many weeks of recovery, I am able to take pen in hand and write.

I have had no direct information from anyone in my old regiment but know that Sherman has taken Chattanooga and will head to Atlanta. No doubt you've seen action by this point.

Now I am walking with crutches and Mother has come for an extended stay. Your mother is at her home, seeing to the household while my mother is away. Before leaving Maryland, Mother visited my uncle and told him the news of Jack's death. I don't know if I shared this with you, but I saw my cousin fall in the skirmish where I was wounded. He was dead, or nearly so, when I was finally able to dismount and reach him.

I thought I too was going to die of the wounds I received that day, but here I am, alive. And now I must face a very different life.

I don't only mean the fact that my damaged hip will never let me walk without a cane (or at least I hope I will graduate from my present crutches to a cane in the future).

I am referring to the much different country we will face after this war.

He began a second sheet.

Once and for all, I ask your forgiveness for breaking faith with you. You above all others have always been honest and stood as my true friend. I should have kept my word. I have no excuse. My motive of wanting to keep you from facing battle does not absolve me.

I know that I also feared losing you and, in that, losing the way things had always been. But it makes little sense now. Who can hold back the tide of history?

I never wanted to hold you in bondage — even as I did.

Faith confronted me with Matthew 6:24, how no man can serve two masters. And she was right, as she so often is. Even as I fought for the Union, I was trying to keep from choosing sides; thereby I branded myself foolish and I own it as true.

Faith is not going to return to the battlefield since I cannot. She plans to busy herself here, gathering supplies to send to Dr. Bryant and trying to help those in the contraband camps.

I hope this letter finds you and your wife safe and well. We rejoiced to see Shiloh home at last. Let us know if you need anything in particular and we will try to send it to you.

Again, please forgive me, Armstrong, for betraying your trust and treating you as if you needed me to decide what was best for you. I hope when we meet that you will shake my hand as you once hoped and forgive me for my double-mindedness.

Ever your obedient servant
and, I hope, friend,
Devlin Knight, Colonel, retired

"Faith, I'd like you to read this letter."

Faith had been curious about whom he was writing. She laid her sewing in the mending basket and joined him. Standing at his shoulder, she read the letter silently.

Warmth flooded her heart. "Devlin, I'm so glad." She gripped his still painfully thin shoulder, wishing she had the nerve to lean over and kiss him. Would he never speak to her about them, about their marriage?

He looked up into her face then. "Please sit beside me." He took her hand and nudged her.

She did so, giving him all her attention, hoping the moment had come. "What is it?"

He cleared his throat, suddenly thick with the importance of what he had prepared to say. "Faith, you married me out of necessity. I never said to you the words I should have said."

"Thee was ill," she replied gently, trying to help him say what she so longed to hear.

"But I have not been deathly ill for weeks now — though for some reason that didn't dawn on me till my mother arrived." He paused, gathering his courage. *Now or never.* "I was ill but still not ready to admit I was wrong. I love you, Faith. I have for a long time, but I refused to admit it even to myself because of our situation."

"I understand. We faced death every day."

"Yes, imminent danger, but also I was a man who was refusing to face reality."

"Has thee faced it now?" she asked, though she'd read it in his letter to Armstrong.

"Yes. I admit that I was a double-minded man, thinking one way and behaving in another. Living at cross-purposes. You said it all to me, challenged me. I hope that

461

Armstrong can forgive me." He claimed her hand. "And I must ask. Do you want to be my wife?"

"Thee means do I want to be thy wife in more than words?"

"Yes. You are aware of my physical limitations, but I don't think that —"

"— matters to me," she finished for him.

"In the letter, I have asked Armstrong to forgive me, and now I ask God to forgive me and you to forgive me as well."

"Of course I forgive thee for thy confusion. Thee was torn between thy mother's ways and thy uncle's ways. Ideas sound easy, but people can make matters hard to see." She smiled and chuckled at him, drawing closer. "And I love thee, silly man."

"I have been more than silly. I've been foolish." He nudged the letter. "I said so here."

She did not look at the pages but met his gaze. "Armstrong will forgive thee."

He believed her. *If only Armstrong survives.* "I hope we get to meet again after the war."

"That is in the Lord's hands." *Is thee going to kiss me, Devlin Knight?*

Her nearness prompted him. He brought her hand to his lips and kissed it. "My sweet, my wife." He leaned forward boldly and kissed her lips. They were as sweet as he'd imagined.

She returned his kiss.

Her wholehearted response flooded him with an energy he'd not felt for a very long time. "Tonight," he promised.

She chuckled at him again, stood, and went to shoot the bolt on the door. "We will be alone for hours." She offered him her hand, her everything.

Almost not believing her, he rose and slipped his crutches under his arms. "Lead the way, wife."

So she did, shutting the door to their bedroom and kissing him with all she felt for him, all the love, all the passion.

He returned her kisses and held her close, as he had long desired. They would become one at last.

EPILOGUE

April 30, 1865

Faith and Dev waited, listening, beside the railroad track west of Columbus to watch President Abraham Lincoln's funeral train pass by. They had decided not to join her sister Blessing and her family the previous day to pay their respects to their fallen president in crowded Columbus, Ohio's state capital. The funeral train had stopped there for one of the many memorial services on its way from Washington, DC, to Springfield, Illinois, where the president would be interred.

America was in mourning. Even here, far from any city or town, the railroad tracks on both sides were lined with people dressed in black, some holding flags, many women weeping.

Faith's heart was also heavy. How soon the joy over Lee's surrender at Appomattox had turned to sorrow when Lincoln had been murdered in cold blood.

Dev moved, obviously shifting his weight from his damaged hip. He still leaned heavily on a cane beside her.

She wanted to tell him they could return to their gig. But she was always careful not to mention his daily pain nor point out his physical limitation. Her husband liked her to ignore it.

Then the chugging of the steam engine came to her ears. Every head turned toward the sound. Silence fell. A baby cried and the mother crooned softly, soothingly.

The funeral train appeared around the bend. Men removed their hats. Faith felt tears streaming down her face. She thought of the president's family, their sorrow and suffering through the long, terrible war — and then to lose their husband and father so horribly. She pressed a handkerchief to her lips, holding in the sobs that wanted to burst forth.

The slow train passed, draped in black crepe. No one spoke; no one looked away. Even when they could no longer see it, merely hear the sound in the distance, they still stood. Finally Dev shifted and turned to her. "Let us go," he murmured in the continued hush.

Grieving, Faith made a sound of agreement, still unable to speak words. People nodded to them as they wended their way to their gig. He propped himself against the side of the vehicle and helped her up into the seat. Then he walked around and climbed in beside her. They would spend the night at an inn and drive the rest of the way home tomorrow. It would be good to be home with their family. Again Faith said a prayer for Mr. Lincoln's family to be comforted. What would have happened to their nation if a lesser man had led them through this dreadful war?

When Faith glimpsed her family's home, she felt instant relief. Ella came out to welcome them, still dressed in mourning for her husband, who had fallen at Atlanta. "You'll never guess!" she called. "You'll never guess who's here!"

Dev drove up to the Cathwell door, and Faith climbed down, hoping she was guessing right.

Honoree ran from one of the nearby cabins. "Faith!"

Faith flew to Honoree and they wrapped their arms around each other. Faith couldn't speak, but her tears flowed. Finally the two of them parted, still holding hands.

"I'm so glad to see you home at last —"

"Where's Armstrong?" Dev interrupted.

"He's here. He's been mustered out. Right now he's over yonder watching them make glass," Honoree replied. "We stopped in Maryland and found his mother had gone to Baltimore. She is with your mother, Colonel, and intends to move here with her."

That was the plan. Dev had decided not to return to Maryland, and that suited Faith. She never wanted to leave her family again. Dev had recently taken over keeping the books for the Cathwell family business.

He and Faith would build their own home in Sharpesburg with quarters for his mother. Ella and her little daughter would also live with them. Though not for long, perhaps — one of Thad Hastings's grandsons, newly home from the war, was already courting her.

Faith couldn't stop staring at Honoree. The war had dragged on and on, taking more and more lives. Peace felt strange. Unfortunately Jim Sanford, who had accompanied Shiloh home in '63, had fallen in battle as well. So many lost. So much sorrow. But both Shiloh and Honoree had been spared.

Shiloh appeared, carrying a cake. Behind her trailed her daughter and son, five and four years old respectively. Their father — LeFevre, the man who had bought Shiloh — had shown enough sense to leave them in the care of a free woman of color in New Orleans when he took Shiloh off to war. Honor and Samuel had traveled with Shiloh by river to New Orleans and brought them home in '64.

"Come in," Shiloh said. "It's nearly time for luncheon. The men will finish and be in soon."

Faith, Dev, and Honoree went inside. Faith shed her bonnet and gloves and helped set the table, unable to stop looking at Honoree. They were all home safe now. And that made her think of the president's family again. The war was over, but there had been no happy ending for them.

Samuel, Honoree's father, and Armstrong entered. Armstrong had gained some gray hair and lost weight. He looked older yet stronger somehow. Faith looked over her shoulder at her husband, wondering how he would react to seeing his former slave.

The moment Dev had waited for had come at last. Would Armstrong forgive him? He walked over to Armstrong and offered him his hand. Silence fell over the room.

Dev kept his hand out, hoping Armstrong would take it, not rebuff him as he deserved.

Armstrong accepted Dev's hand.

Dev's heart beat faster with relief. He shook Armstrong's hand, knowing that he'd been forgiven, though he didn't deserve it.

"Well, we both survived," Armstrong said. He released Dev's hand and clapped him on the back.

Dev nodded, holding up his cane. "Just a little worse for wear."

"And we gained good wives in the bargain."

"Truer words were never spoken." Dev waved Armstrong farther inside and walked over to sit back down.

Faith felt tears sting her eyes again.

A baby's cry sent her to her feet. She hurried into the room she shared with Dev and brought out their nearly year-old son — Samuel, after his grandfather. His grandparents had kept him safe at home while she and Devlin observed the funeral train. She carried him into the large room.

When he saw his father, the boy stopped crying. He reached out both arms to Dev, who claimed him. He stood the child on his lap. "Well, Son, did you miss your parents?"

Little Samuel giggled and danced up and down with Dev's hands, one under each arm, holding him up.

Honor stood from her place at the table.

"After forty-five years of working to end it, I can hardly believe that slavery has finally been outlawed." She wiped tears from her eyes.

Royale rose and stood beside her. "It was a long time coming, all right. But we are free at last, truly free."

Faith could hardly bear it. So much happiness. No more slavery. No more war. Those battles were done. And the battle for a better nation had begun. The assassination of the president had sparked a wave of anger, a thirst for revenge, in the North.

But now, setting aside the nation in turmoil outside the door, Faith gazed around. She was home. Honoree and Shiloh were home. Dev and Armstrong had survived the war. She would be grateful to the Lord for peace, no more killing, wounding, or dying. *Praise God from whom all blessings flow.*

HISTORICAL NOTE

So we come to the end of this series of three Quaker brides: *Honor, Blessing,* and *Faith.* Each has her own story and her own struggles and her own love. It was a privilege to be able to write their stories.

Faith's story was especially challenging because the amount of historical research I had to do was many times more than the research for both *Honor* and *Blessing* combined.

First, I had to choose a part of the war to use as my setting. I finally selected the crucial Western Theater, where the Union forces fought under the command of Ulysses Grant. Most people don't think about this theater of the war, but it was critical for success and made Grant into the commander who finally achieved the victory.

If you've read the previous books in this series, you know that while many Northerners disapproved of slavery, most would not raise a hand to oppose it. Then in 1852 came the bestselling novel *Uncle Tom's Cabin* by Harriet Beecher Stowe. Though the novel fell into disrepute in the twentieth century, it brought the evils of slavery fully alive — for the first time — in the minds and imaginations of many Northerners.

Today we wonder why we had to fight a war to end slavery. And such a terrible war that devoured over six hundred thousand lives.

To prepare for writing *Faith,* I read five published memoirs or diaries of Civil War nurses. The most memorable was *Civil War Hospital Sketches* by Louisa May Alcott, the author of *Little Women,* who was also a nurse in the war.

Almost as unbelievable as slavery is the way women nurses were disrespected at this time. Englishwoman Florence Nightingale had begun the movement of modern nursing in the Crimean War in the decade before the American Civil War. When she returned to England, she tried to institute the training of nurses and to elevate the status of female nurses, but she met with stiff opposition.

Now we think of male nurses as out of the ordinary. How times change. We hope for the better — for a world without discrimination.

And as Dev's mother reveals when she recognizes Honor, Dev's and Honor's families have a history with each other in Maryland. In my novella *Where Honor Began,* I reveal the event that set this series in motion and that comes full circle with the marriage of Dev and Faith and the end of slavery.

Again, I've enjoyed the challenge and opportunity to tell the story of those who worked for freedom against all odds. To me, it demonstrates how a minority can end up changing the mind of the majority, kind of like the first-century Christians, who prevailed in spreading the gospel against all odds.

DISCUSSION QUESTIONS

1. During the Civil War era, many churches and Christians endorsed slavery. What was their rationale for doing so? How can we avoid supporting an injustice just because the culture around us justifies it?

2. Faith lost her twin, Patience, at a critical time in her life. How does this tragedy affect her throughout the story?

3. Dr. Dyson is regularly abrasive and disrespectful toward Faith and Honoree. Why does he act this way, and how do these women respond? How would you advise someone in a similar situation?

4. Though Armstrong has been free since the Emancipation Proclamation, he decides to stay with Devlin until Dev gives him manumission papers. Why does he choose to remain Devlin's manservant

when he's no longer enslaved? Why is it so damaging to the men's relationship when Devlin breaks his promise?

5. When Devlin goes back on his word to Armstrong, Faith accuses him of being a "double-minded man." Have you ever found yourself caught between two principles as Devlin is? What choice did you end up making?

6. Faith and her family regularly help escaped slaves hide on their property. Is it ever right for a Christian to break a law as a matter of principle? If so, under what circumstances?

7. At the beginning of the story, Faith is determined to find Shiloh under her own power and determination. But eventually she realizes she's incapable of finding Shiloh on her own — that she must rely on God to bring her friend home. What makes her change her mind? What does it look like to trust God in our circumstances while also taking an active role?

8. For most of the book, Devlin is certain he is going to die during the war. Why is he so convinced of that? When he realizes

he's going to live, how does his outlook on life change?

9. In the epilogue, Faith reflects, "So much happiness. No more slavery. No more war. Those battles were done. And the battle for a better nation had begun." What makes her hopeful for the future in spite of Lincoln's recent death and the widespread tragedy of the Civil War? What do you see ahead for Faith, Devlin, Honoree, and their families?

10. What do you view as the legacy of the Civil War in our modern times?

ABOUT THE AUTHOR

Lyn Cote, known for her "Strong Women, Brave Stories," is the award-winning, critically acclaimed author of more than thirty-five novels. Her books have been RITA Award finalists and Holt Medallion and Carol Award winners. Lyn received her bachelor's degree in education and her master's degree in American history from Western Illinois University. She and her husband have two grown children and live on a small but beautiful lake in northern Wisconsin. Visit her online at www.LynCote .com.

The employees of Thorndike Press hope you have enjoyed this Large Print book. All our Thorndike, Wheeler, and Kennebec Large Print titles are designed for easy reading, and all our books are made to last. Other Thorndike Press Large Print books are available at your library, through selected bookstores, or directly from us.

For information about titles, please call:
(800) 223-1244

or visit our Web site at:
http://gale.cengage.com/thorndike

To share your comments, please write:
Publisher
Thorndike Press
10 Water St., Suite 310
Waterville, ME 04901